# THE
# ESCAPE
# ARTIST

THE

# ESCAPE
# ARTIST

DIANE CHAMBERLAIN

 HarperCollins*Publishers*

HarperCollins books may be purchased for educational, business, or sales promotional use. For information please write: Special Markets Department, HarperCollins Publishers, Inc., 10 East 53rd Street, New York, NY 10022.

FIRST EDITION

*Designed by Ruth Lee*

Library of Congress Cataloging-in-Publication Data

Chamberlain, Diane, 1950–
    The escape artist / Diane Chamberlain.
        p.   cm.
    ISBN 0-06-017651-2
    I. Title.
    PS3553.H2485S6   1997
    831'.54—dc20                                                    96-30228

97 98 99 00 01 ❖/RRD 10 9 8 7 6 5 4 3 2 1

To the Mount Vernon Writer's Group: Ann Allman, Barbara Bradford, Jane Drewry, Linda Rainwater, Jeanne Van Dusen-Smith, Joan Winslow, and those other special writers who have slipped in and out of our writing haven over the past twelve years.

Special thanks to Kathy Hansen and her toddling son, Patrick, as well as to all the other mothers who gave me insight into how they'd react in Susanna's situation. I'm also grateful to D'Ann Taflin, Pat Bernhardt, Brittany Walls, and Gary Fuller for sharing their expertise in various fields, and to my husband, David, for his insightful reading and never-flagging confidence in me.

*T*he cloud was back.

Not in the sky. The evening sky over Boulder was a vivid violet-blue, broken only by a jagged line of gold as the sun fell behind the Rockies. Yet, as Susanna made her way through the cemetery, Tyler in her arms, she felt the cloud over her shoulder, keeping pace with her.

She had endured the cloud's dark shadow once before, eleven months earlier, when Tyler was born with a damaged heart. It had pained her own heart, seeing her son suffer, knowing she might lose him. She'd suffered along with him, spending day after day in the intensive care nursery, touching his tiny hands through the restricting holes in the side of his plastic bassinet. Talking to him. Singing to him. He was stoic, her little baby. She saw the determination in his face, the fight. He was not a quitter. He had not inherited her propensity for giving up. She hoped she'd learned a thing or two from his bravery.

Tyler's heart was healthy now. "Nearly good as new," the surgeon had said. It was the best heart she could imagine. Her son had a gentle, affectionate nature and a laugh that, until recently, had brought tears to her eyes each time she heard it. With all he'd been through, the fact that he could laugh with such abandon renewed her faith.

And Tyler had learned patience. Even while being carried around the cemetery for the past hour, he had not once protested

1

the seemingly fruitless journey. He hung onto her with one arm around her neck, clutching his stuffed monkey, his eyes looking ahead as Susanna moved among the headstones, stopping to read each one. Not names; she didn't care about names. But she read every date, particularly those on the smaller headstones. It was those small stones that merited her scrutiny. The sort of stone the parents of an infant might select.

Tyler's downy blond hair brushed lightly against her chin. Soon, he'd be able to walk. She wanted to savor this last month or so, when he still could not explore the world without her.

Tyler finally made a sound of impatience, a whimper, a "Mom, aren't we through here *yet?*" sort of sound. With a sigh, she leaned over to set him down in the grass, and he crawled to the nearest headstone and hoisted himself up by it, dancing up and down as if he heard a tune inside his head.

She stood up and stretched, her hands pressed against the small of her back, and the warm breeze wrapped her long skirt around her legs. For the first time since arriving at the cemetery, she let herself look toward the foothills above Chatauqua Park and realized she could see Linc's house from here. It was nearly in the shadow of the mountains now. A faint wash of fading sunlight lit up one side of the house and gilded the huge satellite dish in his yard, and she felt tears fill her eyes. She wished she could tell Linc her plan. But that wouldn't be fair to him. Not that the plan itself was fair. She was going to keep her child, but in the process she would lose the man who had been her strength and support for the past two years. For far, far longer than that, if she were honest with herself. How she would get by without him, she didn't know. This was the first major decision she'd made in years without consulting him. She was not the sort of person who did things entirely on her own, without the advice of friends. She'd never possessed that sort of courage. But she would have to find it now. If she did indeed lose custody of Tyler to Jim and Peggy, she would have to put her plan in action and, in so doing, never see Linc Sebastian again.

It was so dark by the time she found the small, cold marker that she could barely read the words carved into the stone. *August 16, 1968–September 14, 1968.* Perfect. She read the name. *Kimberly Stratton.*

Susanna sank to her knees near the marker and pulled a small notepad from her purse. She copied the information onto the pad and started to get to her feet again, but something held her down.

Why did this baby die? Less than a month old. She thought of Tyler as a newborn, wounded and fighting. How had that mother felt, losing her baby before she'd even gotten a chance to know her? And who was Susanna to take this baby's name? This baby's life? She felt suddenly weighed down with responsibility. She leaned forward, resting her hand on the cool grass above the grave. "I'll try to do right by you," she said. "I'll try to be worthy of having your name."

She thought she felt something, a current of warmth spreading up her arm, into her chest, but Tyler crashed into her from behind, shaking her from her imagined communion with the child whose name she was stealing.

She gathered Tyler and his monkey into her arms and stood up slowly. The cloud settled around her shoulders again, but she dismissed it with a shake of her head. She had escaped from that cloud once before. She would escape from it again.

*A*ll rise."

Susanna got to her feet as Judge Browning entered the court-room and took his seat behind the bench. When she sat down again, she was barely breathing. The judge looked like Santa Claus, his full beard snowy beneath his ruddy cheeks, but he had shown no inclination toward jolliness these past few days. He was not, in any way, a benevolent presence.

He shuffled the papers on his desk, seemingly unaware of the tension in the room as everyone awaited the decision he'd promised to deliver that afternoon. When he glanced up, Susanna could suddenly see the courtroom through his eyes, and if she hadn't already guessed his decision, she did then. For a week now, he'd looked out from his bench at the cast of characters in front of him. At the table on his left sat a small, wiry-haired female attorney, Ann Prescott, and Susanna, the anxious, pale, overworked, poorly paid, divorced woman who was her client. The client who had spent the month after the breakup of her marriage in a psychiatric ward, threatening to kill herself—and her unborn baby. Ann had brought in the psychiatrist from the hospital to testify that Susanna was well now, that she was a good mother. But that ploy had backfired, only serving to remind everyone of Susanna's stint as a psychiatric patient.

At the table on Judge Browning's right sat a dapper, silver-haired attorney and his client, James Miller, an attorney himself

4

and Susanna's ex-husband. Handsome, sharply dressed without overdoing it, sincerity in his blue eyes. When he answered questions on the witness stand, he would turn and look at the judge, something Ann had encouraged Susanna to do herself. She hadn't been able to, though. She'd felt frozen on the witness stand, unable to take her eyes off her interrogator for even a second.

Seated directly behind Jim was his wife. Not any wife, but Peggy Myerson, yet another attorney. She was also beautifully dressed. Her smooth dark hair swept her shoulders. It was obvious that she was in love with her husband. She'd lean forward to touch his shoulder, to whisper to him. Right now she was smiling confidently at him as though they both knew these five days had been only a formality. They'd known they would win from the start.

Susanna could not look at Peggy for long. She always felt small and simple around her. Peggy was a woman with whom she could never hope to compete.

And what else did the judge see in this courtroom? Susanna closed her eyes against the images forming in her head. Behind Jim and his lawyer and Peggy, Judge Browning would see Peggy's older brother Ron, the surgeon who had saved Tyler's life, and Peggy's parents, who had been there during every single moment of the hearing. And behind them sat Jim's sister and mother, women who had once been Susanna's friends and confidantes. All of them were perched on the edges of their seats, waiting anxiously to hear the fate of the little boy they already thought of as theirs.

Seated several rows behind Susanna, the judge would see only one person, Linc Sebastian, a man known to the community as a convicted murderer turned disc jockey. Linc was the host of a weekly, nationally syndicated radio program, and he was something of a cult figure. One of Boulder's folk heroes. He'd taken out his earring for this week in court, even though Susanna had told him not to bother. Who was he trying to kid? His blond hair still brushed his collar, and one look at him told you he had chosen a lifestyle somewhere outside the norm. "A man with a questionable past," Jim's lawyer had said in describing him, and no one could honestly argue with that assessment.

Judge Browning cleared his throat, and Susanna wrapped her

arms across her chest to wait out the inevitable. Her stomach ached, and she was glad she had not tried to eat lunch.

The judge lifted a single sheet of paper from his desk as though he might read from it, but instead, his Santa Claus eyes moved from person to person in the courtroom as he began to speak.

"This court awards custody of Tyler James Miller to his father, James Miller," he said simply.

Susanna heard Peggy's squeal of joy and Jim's laughter. She tightened her grip on her arms until her fingers turned white. She heard someone on the other side of the room whisper the word "congratulations" to Jim.

"Susanna Miller will be allowed visitation every other weekend and one night each week," the judge continued. "And she is forbidden to have any member of the opposite sex spend the night during those times she has visitation with her son."

Her cheeks burned as if the judge had slapped her. He stood up and left the courtroom, and Susanna became vaguely aware of Ann Prescott's hand on her arm.

"They simply had too much in their favor, Susanna," Ann said. "I'm sorry."

Susanna pulled her arm away. In those horrible moments when she'd imagined this scene, she'd sobbed. But there were no tears now, only a numbness, a disbelief. They were going to take her baby away from her.

"Let me go see what the plans are," Ann said, and Susanna could not even acknowledge her as she left the table.

"Sue?"

She turned to find Linc standing next to her. She stood up and barely noticed the red in his eyes before he drew her into an embrace. It was a quick hug, nothing more than that, as if he did not want to make a public display of the fact that he was that close to her. "I'm so sorry, Susie," he said.

She opened her mouth, but no words came out and she sank into her seat again. Linc sat down next to her, holding her icy hand in his warm one. She knew he thought of himself as a major factor in her losing custody of Tyler, but she doubted her relationship with him had made that much difference. As Ann said, Jim and Peggy had too much in their favor.

They had the combined income of two attorneys, which was far more than she could ever hope to achieve as a secretary in a bank. They lived in a big, elegant house in a beautiful neighborhood. Wonderland, the area was called. How could the judge deprive a child of living in a neighborhood called Wonderland? Never mind that Susanna had selected that house. Never mind that the week after she and Jim had moved into it, she'd come home early from a conference to find Jim sharing their bed with Peggy. So Susanna was in the little rental apartment, while Jim and Peggy sprawled out in "their" five bedroom house and erected an elaborate swing set in the back yard for "their" son.

It had been her word against Jim's regarding the abortion, and Jim had scoffed at her accusation from his seat on the witness stand. "I'm pro-life," Jim had said, his blue eyes flashing in a self-righteous fervor. "I would never suggest that *any* woman have an abortion, let alone a woman carrying my own child."

She'd been too ashamed to admit to any of her friends, other than Linc, that Jim had wanted her to get an abortion when she'd told him she was pregnant with Tyler. Linc, who knew the truth, did not testify. Ann thought it would "invite too many questions we don't want to deal with" if he did, and so Jim's only challenger was Susanna herself. And no one seemed to pay much attention to anything she had to say. But she would be damned if she'd turn her son over to a man who had wanted him aborted and a woman immoral enough to sleep with another woman's husband.

Ann returned and stood on the opposite side of the table from Linc and Susanna. "They said you can keep him tonight," she said. "They'll be by to pick him up tomorrow around two. Is that okay?"

Susanna looked helplessly at her attorney. "What choice do I have?" she asked.

Ann shook her head. "None, Susanna. I'm sorry."

"Come on," Linc tugged at her shoulder. "Let's get Tyler and enjoy tonight with him," he said.

She was dimly aware of the festive atmosphere on the other side of the courtroom as she left with Linc, and she turned her head away from the celebration. She didn't want to see their joy.

Linc held her hand in the car, letting go of her only when he shifted gears or needed two hands to turn the steering wheel. She sensed him looking at her from time to time, but kept her own eyes on the road. The silence between them felt alien.

Linc turned off the main road onto Susanna's street with its row of apartment buildings, and parked in front of the building housing Tyler's day-care center.

"Would you mind very much getting him?" she asked. She couldn't bear Margaret Draper's questions today. Margaret would be outraged to hear Susanna was losing Tyler, and Susanna had enough rage of her own to deal with.

"Sure." Linc got out of the car, and she watched him walk up the sidewalk to the building. He had on gray pants, a pinstriped shirt. He'd worn a tie today, too. Every day this week. He'd tried hard, but he only looked as if he'd accidentally put on another man's clothes in the morning. His effort touched her, though. It made her love him more than she already did, and that only made what she had to do harder.

She saw Margaret open the door to the center and step back to let Linc inside. He would be telling Margaret now, Susanna thought, and she hoped he could keep Margaret from coming out to the car to offer her sympathy. She didn't want to talk. She only wanted to get home with her son.

After a minute, Linc emerged from the apartment, Tyler in his arms, and the legs of the little boy's stuffed monkey flopped up and down in rhythm with Linc's stride. Susanna got out of the car and met them on the sidewalk, hungry to get her son into her own arms. Tyler was puffy-eyed and a little grumpy.

She knew that look, that mood. "He was in the middle of his nap, huh?" she asked.

"Right." Linc opened the back door of his car to put Tyler into the car seat, but she hugged the little boy tighter.

"It's only a block," she said. "I'll hold him."

Linc opened her door, and she settled into the passenger seat with Tyler and his monkey on her lap. Tyler curled against her contentedly, and the warmth of him against her body thawed the tears that had been frozen inside of her. They spilled over her cheeks.

Linc got in behind the steering wheel and saw that she was crying.

"Oh, Sue." He leaned over to hold her. Tyler, oblivious to his fate, was cradled between their bodies. "It's not fair," Linc whispered.

She couldn't speak. If she spoke she knew she would say too much.

Linc pulled back from her and brushed his hand over her wet cheek.

"I want to stay over tonight," he said, "but I guess that's against the rules."

She tried to pull herself together again, wiping her eyes with the back of her fingers. The judge had unwittingly made this easier for her. She hadn't been sure how she would keep Linc away tonight. "I know," she said. "I wish you could stay."

"I'll stay till you go to bed."

"Actually," she bit her lip, "I think I need to be alone with Tyler tonight."

Linc looked at her in surprise. It was not like her to cut him out. She usually despised being alone, but that was going to have to change. It was true that Susanna Miller would never cut herself off from the company of others, but tonight Susanna Miller would die.

"Susanna," Linc said, "I *love* Tyler. I'd like the chance to be with him tonight. With both of you."

He'd been there from the moment Tyler drew his first, labored breath. He'd been with her through the entire pregnancy. She'd leaned on him for everything, probably more than she should have. That she would cut him out of her grieving tonight would make no sense to him.

"I'm sorry," she said. "I'm not feeling well, and—"

"Then let me take care of you."

"Linc—I can't explain it." She thought of letting him come over for a few hours, but that would be impossible. She had too much to do tonight. "I'm going to give Tyler his dinner, tuck him in, tell him a story. Maybe sing him a song. And then crawl into bed. "

"I could—"

"Please, Linc," she said. "You're making this harder on me."

He sat back, defeated. "All right." He started the car and neither of them spoke as they drove the block to her apartment. She knew he was hurt, but she would have to hurt him now to spare him later.

Linc parked in the small lot by the entrance to her apartment building and walked ahead of her to the front door. He unlocked the security door with his own key and she followed him up the steps and into her apartment. Quietly, they moved around the rooms, Linc changing Tyler's diaper, Susanna checking her answering machine. There were a few messages from her coworkers at the bank, anxious to know the judge's decision. She would not be returning those calls, and she erased every one of them.

When she came into the living room, Linc was setting Tyler down on the floor next to the old salad bowl filled with plastic blocks.

"I could make dinner for you," Linc suggested, "or would you rather I just—" He gestured toward the door.

She nodded. "I'll need more from you tomorrow night," she said, looking down at her son. "That will be my first night without him."

Linc shoved his hands in his pockets, then knelt down to kiss the top of Tyler's head. "Bye, Ty," he said.

She walked with him to the front door, where he stopped and rested his hand on her shoulder. "Are you regretting—I mean, maybe we shouldn't have continued seeing each other when the whole custody thing came up."

"I couldn't have gotten through this without you," she said. "I don't regret us being together at all."

He leaned over to kiss her goodbye, lightly, as if he wasn't certain how she was feeling about him at that moment, and the reality of what she was about to do washed over her. She closed her arms around him, holding onto him, fighting hard against her tears. This was the last time she would see him.

"You've been my best friend for so long," she whispered.

"And I always will be."

"No matter what?"

"No matter what."

She was as close as she'd come to telling him about her decision. She had to get him out the door before the words spilled from her mouth.

"You've got to go," she said. "I love you."

He looked suddenly alarmed. "You don't sound like yourself, Susanna."

She read his thoughts, saw the worry in his eyes. He thought she might do something really crazy. Kill both herself and Tyler. She nearly smiled at his misperception. She was over that now. That sort of depression could not get its grip on her again.

"I'm all right," she said.

"Do you want me to be with you when Jim and Peggy come for Tyler tomorrow?"

She shook her head. "Tomorrow's Wednesday. You have to tape your show."

"The music's already picked out. It doesn't matter what time I get around to it."

"I think I'd better do it alone," she said.

"Well, if you change your mind, please—"

"I know. Thanks." She leaned forward to kiss him. "I love you, Linc," she said.

"I love you, too. And I'm going to call you later tonight to check on you, all right?"

"All right." She wished he wouldn't, but she couldn't possibly tell him not to.

She shut the door quickly behind him and immediately went into action. She fed Tyler and got him into bed, read him a story. Then she positioned herself in front of the bathroom mirror, scissors in hand.

She had worn her blond hair long all her life. Very long. She probably could have selected a more flattering style, but she'd loved the way people stared at her hair, the way they wanted to touch it. She knew it made her look far younger than twenty-nine.

Her hand shook as she raised the scissors, and it shook as she placed them down on the sink again. Not yet. She'd do everything else she had to do first. But she got the bottle of dye she'd been saving for weeks from her bathroom cabinet. Copper Glow, the color was called. It was an auburn shade, and the woman on the package smiled coyly from beneath her deep, coppery bangs. Susanna read and reread the directions. She'd never dyed her hair before. She was a true blond. A pale blond. Her features belonged with blond hair. Nearly invisible eyebrows and eyelashes. Delicate white skin. Pale blue eyes that Tyler had inherited. She looked in the mirror and tried to imagine her face with darker hair. It wasn't going to work. Her disappearing eyebrows would be a giveaway. No one with auburn hair would have such pale eyebrows. It said right on the package not to use the dye on eyebrows, but she was already breaking more laws than she could count. She would break that one as well.

She walked into her bedroom and reached between the mattress and box spring of her bed, pulling out a large, thick envelope. It held the copy of Kimberly Stratton's birth certificate she'd sent for, using the information from the headstone in the cemetery. The envelope also held nearly eight thousand dollars she'd withdrawn from her savings account, as well as the copies of Tyler's medical records she'd requested. The money was in hundreds and twenties, and she divided it up, slipping some of the bills into her purse, some into her duffel bag, and some into Tyler's diaper bag. She left a thousand on her dresser to put in her pocket the following morning.

She made several peanut butter and jelly sandwiches for herself and put them in a bag, along with some bananas, baby oatmeal, formula, crackers, and juice boxes. Then she carefully packed a few sets of clothing for Tyler and her in the duffel bag. She did not let herself think about all the things she was leaving behind. It would do no good to dwell on losses. She would have her son. Her priorities were very clear.

She had done everything but cut and dye her hair by the time Linc called at eleven-thirty. She sat on the edge of her bed feeling wired and restless, but she tried instead to sound tired on the phone, yawning loudly, muffling her voice. She hated this dishonesty with the person who knew her better than anyone else.

"Are you getting depressed again?" Linc asked. There was anxiety behind the question.

"No, really, I'm fine. Just wiped out from this whole fiasco." She looked at herself in her dresser mirror and pulled her hair away from her face, trying to imagine how she would look with her new identity. She would be a different person in the morning. A stronger person. More independent. Gutsy and self-reliant. She would have to be.

Linc was talking quietly, completely unsuspecting, probably

picturing his sweet, blond girlfriend on the other end of the phone line, and suddenly, she could stand it no longer.

"Linc?"

"Yes?"

"Is it too late for me to request a certain song for your show Sunday night?"

"No. What would you like to hear?"

"'Suzanne.'" It was one of her favorite songs, and Linc often sang it to her, along with a dozen other songs that incorporated some variation of her name.

"I should have guessed," Linc said. "Whose version?"

"The original." She didn't really care what version he played, but she knew that was Linc's favorite.

"Leonard Cohen," he said. "Okay."

"Please make a note to do it."

"I won't forget."

"I'm serious, Linc. I want you to write it down. Do you have a pen?"

"Uh—hang on. Yeah, I've got one."

"Write down, 'Susanna wants to hear me play "Suzanne" for her on Sunday night.'"

"How about we spend Sunday night listening to it together?"

"Please just write it down. Word for word."

She heard him sigh.

"Okay," he said. "I never knew you were so demanding."

"Now tape it to your bathroom mirror.

Linc laughed. "What's with you, Suze?"

"Nothing's with me. Just promise me you'll tape it to the mirror in your bathroom before you go to bed tonight, okay?"

"If you say so."

She drew the conversation to a quick close, afraid she might be tempted to give him even grander hints. Then she returned to her own bathroom. She read the directions on the dye through once more. This was it.

She focused on her image in the mirror as she raised the scissors to her hair, and with the first cut, high and deep, she knew there was no turning back. She was going to kill Susanna Miller. She was bringing Kimberly Stratton back to life.

$\mathcal{L}$inc didn't bother going to bed. He made himself a cup of coffee and sat in front of the wall of windows in his living room, looking out at the lights spread over Boulder like a blanket of glitter. He would have given anything for a cigarette. He hadn't lit up in a year and a half, not since Susanna told him she was pregnant. He'd wanted to be able to help her out, and he hadn't wanted that unborn baby breathing second- or third-hand smoke, so he'd taken the opportunity to quit. He must not have had a physical addiction to nicotine because quitting had not been that hard. Or maybe, as Grace had suggested slyly, he'd found something that met his needs better than smoking. But if there had been a Marlboro in the house tonight, he'd be a fallen man.

There'd been a message from Grace on his voice mail when he got home after dropping Susanna and Tyler off at the apartment. "I heard the verdict," Grace said. "I hope you and Susanna are okay. I assume you're over there tonight, so give me a call tomorrow. Love you."

Linc shook his head at the memory of that message. He took a swallow of coffee and stared out at the lights. He could see nearly all the way to Susanna's apartment complex on the eastern side of town from here. Was she asleep yet? And why didn't she want him around tonight? It seemed crazy. She hated being alone. Okay, so tonight was different from any other night. Tonight was her last night as custodial parent of her son. But until now, she'd always included him in Tyler's life. He'd gone through the childbirth classes with her. He'd been there for Tyler's birth and held her hand during those first uncertain, unnerving days of Tyler's life. Susanna had treated him as though he were Tyler's father, and he'd slipped happily into that role. When it came right down to it, though, she apparently did not think of him that way at all. Maybe she blamed him for the custody verdict after all.

He'd talked with her lawyer about it at length. How much did his involvement with Susanna figure into whether or not she retained custody? Not much, Ann had assured him. "It just doesn't help her case any." That struck him as an understatement. Having a relationship with a man who'd served four years in prison for murder hardly made a woman an attractive choice for custody. Early on, he'd asked Ann if he should end his relationship with Susanna. It was too late, Ann had said. Everyone already knew about it, and it would only seem like a calculated move to the judge. Then Linc suggested that he and Susanna get married. He fully intended that to happen one of these days, anyway. And he had money. Jim and Peggy would no longer have the battle won on financial resources. But Ann thought that was a terrible idea.

Linc got up, stepping over Sam, who was asleep at his feet, and walked into the kitchen. He pulled out a few of the drawers, hoping one of them might yield an old pack of cigarettes. He remembered cleaning the kitchen well when he quit, but still he couldn't resist the temptation to see if maybe one lone, stale cigarette existed in an overlooked corner of a drawer. Nothing. He poured himself a second cup of coffee and carried it to his studio, where he pulled out the Leonard Cohen CD with "Suzanne" on it to add to the stack of CDs he'd be using to record his show the following day.

He was opening the jewel box to check the disc when his eyes fell on the framed photograph standing on the table next to the mixing board. It had been a gift from Susanna for his last birthday, an enlargement of a picture she'd had for years: the two of them as children on a swing in his back yard. Susanna was sitting on the swing and Linc was standing behind her, his feet on either side of her. She was just six years old in the picture, a slender child with long white braids. Linc, at twelve, had been wiry and tall, but equally as blond, and in this picture he looked like he might be the older brother of the little girl. Her protector. He had fancied himself that back then, although he had never quite known how to go about protecting her. He only knew that she needed it.

He and his mother had moved next door to the Wood family a few months before that picture had been taken, shortly after his father's sudden death from a stroke.

His mother had tried to manage the family butcher shop in Philadelphia alone, but her heart had never been in it, and when her sister in Boulder pleaded with her to move to Colorado, she and Linc were easily swayed.

Linc suffered culture shock when he arrived in Boulder. "Fifteen square miles surrounded by reality," people said of the town. It was filled with natural food stores, head shops, vegetarian restaurants, and counterculture politicians. But Linc quickly found friends who shared his love of music, and his mother found work in her sister's small coffee shop, which catered to students at the university, and Boulder soon began to feel like home.

The day after they'd moved into their small house near the center of town, Linc's mother was stacking dishes in the kitchen cabinets when he caught her staring out the window. He followed her gaze to the small, blond waif playing hopscotch by herself in the driveway next door.

"That little one looks like she'll break in two if you breathe on her," his mother said, and for weeks Linc couldn't look at Susanna without picturing the seedball of a dandelion, delicate and fragile.

Sometimes, if Susanna's parents were going to be out at night, they'd ask Linc to baby-sit for her. That was how he came to know what life was like in the Wood household. Susanna's father was mean. Downright cruel. Linc didn't see it at first, because it was so unimaginable to him that a father could be that way. His own father had been soft-spoken and gentle. Linc had friends whose parents yelled at them or put them down, but this was different. There was always a threat in Paul Wood's yelling.

"You behave while we're out or else," he'd say to Susanna as he and his wife walked out the door, or "you get those toys picked up or you know what will happen, don't you?" Susanna would nod, and her father would come back with, "*Say it*. Say it out loud.

What will happen if you don't pick up your toys?" And he'd grip Susanna by the arm until she answered him in a voice as pale as her hair. "I'll get the belt." You couldn't blame someone for having an aversion to conflict when every altercation in her growing up years had led to that sort of pain.

It wasn't only Susanna who suffered her father's abuse. Linc saw him kick a neighbor's dog one day, and Susanna once told him she'd seen her father kill a squirrel. Then there was the incident with the kittens. But that was later, and Linc had worked hard to block it from his mind.

Susanna had liked Linc to read to her when he baby-sat, although she had very few books of her own. She liked to draw as well, and he thought she was pretty creative for such a little kid. Once she drew a picture of a lion, and he suggested they hang it on her refrigerator, but she said they couldn't. Her parents wouldn't allow it.

When Linc realized how bad Susanna's situation was, he told his mother he didn't think he could baby-sit for her anymore. Being in the Woods' house made him feel sick, he said. His mother listened to him carefully and then said he needed to go over there more often, not less, even when he wasn't being paid to baby-sit. "And we need to have her over here, too," she'd added. "I'm afraid her parents have a serious drinking problem. She desperately needs good people in her life."

He'd never really known anyone with a drinking problem, and so he'd never thought to notice it next door, but after his mother mentioned it, the smell of booze in the Woods' house became inescapable. He understood then the reason that Susanna's father could be almost docile one minute and brutish the next. And he knew why her mother couldn't hold a job, why she was so often "sick."

He never actually saw Susanna's father hit her, but he'd seen the bruises on her legs. He'd seen them on her mother's face and arms as well. And sometimes in the summer, when everyone had their windows open, he and his mother could hear the battle being waged in the Wood household. His mother called the police a few times, but Susanna's father always managed to get out of whatever charge was levied against him, and her mother would never stick up for her. That tore Linc's mother apart, and she'd once again talk about how much Susanna needed their help, their love. She started inviting Susanna to their house after school or for dinner. She'd buy the little girl books and let her hang her pictures all over their kitchen walls. Susanna was a different child, a happy, relaxed child, at his house. He liked thinking that his home had become her haven. So he grew up with a special feeling for his younger neighbor, a bit fatherly, a bit brotherly. At least he'd felt that way for a while.

When he formed his band during his second year of high school, Susanna would sit on the mildewy sofa in his garage and listen to them practice. That went on for years. She might do her homework or, when she got a little older, sketch one of the guys or the instruments or whatever caught her eye that day. She grew into an excellent artist. Whenever her school needed a poster designed for the hallway or for one of the offices, it was Susanna they called on. She won a couple of contests, and she was planning to enter a huge, statewide competition when her father was killed. She dropped out of school then, and her interest in art died when her father did.

Linc had had a string of girlfriends, all of whom were ridiculously jealous of his young next-door neighbor. He'd thought they were crazy at the time, but later he wondered if they'd known more of what was in his heart than he did. Back then, though, the age difference had been so great that it never would have occurred to him to think of Susanna as a potential girlfriend. He hadn't even realized how startlingly beautiful she was until a new guy joined the band and was unable to take his eyes off the leggy, long-haired blond idly sketching in the corner of the garage. Linc began thinking about her differently after that, but his fantasies about her had a forbidden quality to them after having treated her like a sister for so long. He wondered if things might be different between them after she graduated from high school, when the difference in their ages would not seem so great.

But then prison happened to him. And Jim happened to her.

*That little one looks like she'll break in two if you breathe on her.* Linc still thought that was an accurate description of Susanna. Maybe that wasn't fair of him. It was true that she would go out of her way to avoid conflict or dissension; she was quick to put her own needs aside if it meant avoiding a fight. Yet, she'd been strong enough to say no to Jim when he wanted her to have an abortion. Strong enough to give birth and to stay by Tyler's side while he suffered through those horrific medical treatments. Yet he worried about how easily Susanna could be broken in two.

Sam suddenly appeared in the studio. He walked over to the chair and rested his head on Linc's knee, and with a resigned sigh, Linc stood up. "You're right, fella," he said. "It's time for bed."

He walked toward his bedroom, wishing he could shake the bitterness that threatened to overwhelm him. It wasn't fair. Susanna had been so determined to give Tyler the sort of safe, secure, and happy home she herself had never enjoyed. She was a good mother. The best. The first thing she'd felt truly confident about in a long time. Now she'd been told she wasn't good enough.

In his bedroom, he reached for the phone, cradling the receiver in his hand for a moment. He wanted to call her again, but he feared disturbing her if she'd somehow managed to fall asleep.

On his night table, he saw the note she'd had him write earlier that evening. He saw no point in taping it to his bathroom mirror now that he'd already added the record to his list for the following day, but she had been so insistent about it. So he hung up the phone, read the note through once again, then walked into his bathroom to tape her words to the mirror.

*I*t was still dark when Susanna got Tyler dressed in the morning. The little boy babbled for a few minutes when she first lifted him out of the crib, then seemed to decide she'd made a mistake about the time and went back to sleep as she changed him from his pajamas to his overalls and tied his blue tennis shoes onto his feet.

The first bus didn't leave for Denver until 5:50. She hadn't slept all night, but she'd forced herself to lie still in bed anyway, planning her morning over and over in her head. Now, as she dressed Tyler and poured juice into his bottle and slipped the thousand dollars into the pocket of her jeans, she knew the routine as if she'd done it ten times already.

She slowed down only long enough to groan at her image in the mirror. She looked like an auburn-haired, pale-eyed scarecrow, and she quickly pulled brown mascara from her medicine cabinet and applied it to her eyelashes.

She'd cut her hair to chin length and given herself bangs. She would never find a job as a hair stylist, that much was certain. She'd put the lopped off hair and the empty dye bottle and its package into a garbage bag she planned to take with her. She didn't want to leave any clues behind.

She glanced at Tyler's crib as she finished dressing. It would have to be replaced, along with the high chair and—what else? The car seat and—*don't think about it.* She couldn't afford to get overwhelmed right now.

She gathered the duffel bag, the diaper bag, her purse, her son, and their lightweight jackets and, without a backward glance, left the apartment. In the foyer downstairs, she set up the stroller and lowered her sleeping son into it. Poor Ty. Just as well he was asleep, though.

She took a minute to put his jacket on him, then slipped into her own. It would be easier to wear them than to carry them. She shoved the diaper bag under the seat of the stroller and opened the foyer door.

It was cooler outside than she'd expected, and she was glad she'd brought their jackets as she walked the four blocks to the nearest bus stop. There were five other people there, four men and a woman, all of them dressed for work. She should have thought of that. She stood out in her jeans and denim jacket, pushing a baby. People smiled at the two of them, and she smiled back and looked away, wishing she were invisible. The first leg of her trip would be entirely too traceable. But what choice did she have?

The bus arrived and she lifted Tyler into her arms, collapsing the stroller with one practiced movement. She was glad she had vetoed any thought of bringing more with her than she already had. Between the stroller, her two bulky bags, and the baby, she had more than enough to manage.

She was last to board, and the driver, a small, gray-haired man who looked too frail to be driving something as big as a bus, did a double take as she climbed up the steps with her cargo.

"Going to Denver?" he asked, as though she'd made an error.

"That's right." She smiled at him with such confidence that she was surprised to see her hand shake when she handed him the fare.

She walked toward the rear of the bus. The fewer boarding passengers who walked past her, the better. With the duffel bag and diaper bag, she and Tyler were packed tightly into their seats, but the trip to Denver would only be an hour, and she was grateful that the baby seemed content to sleep in her arms.

She wished she could sleep as well, but she was as alert as she'd ever been in her life. Her fellow travelers seemed uninterested in her, and for that she was grateful. Some of them read, others appeared to be trying to work. A few nodded off, their heads bobbing against the windowpanes.

She was doing the right thing. From the moment she'd thought of leaving Boulder with Tyler, she hadn't wavered in her decision. The next few days would be rough, filled with the unknown and uncertainty, but she would get through them and then she and Tyler would be together and they'd be okay. She wouldn't let herself think about the possibility of being caught, and the only other thing that could derail her determination would be thoughts of Linc, and so she made a conscious effort to keep them at bay as well. She closed her eyes as the bus turned briefly toward the foothills, in case she might be able to see Linc's house in the distance.

She didn't get off the bus until it reached its last stop—the bus terminal in Denver. Her plan was to take one of the first buses heading out of town, no matter where it was going, as long as it was far away. She wanted to go someplace where she knew no one and no one would think of looking for her. She would let fate make the major decisions for her.

There was an 8:10 bus headed for St. Louis, Missouri. Missouri might have been on another planet for all she knew. She wasn't certain she could even find St. Louis on a map, and that made it very appealing.

She bought a ticket for ninety-eight dollars, glad to see that Tyler could ride for free, but a little shocked to hear that the bus would arrive in St. Louis at 4:50 the following morning. It was going to be a long trip, and she and Tyler would be dumped out into a strange city practically in the middle of the night.

She used the terminal bathroom, carting all her paraphernalia with her, then settled onto one of the plastic seats to wait for her bus.

The garbage bag was stuffed in her duffel bag and she pulled it out. She sorted through her wallet, removing anything with the name "Susanna Miller" on it. Her driver's license, her checks, her check cashing card from the grocery store, her credit card with its small, never-to-be-paid-off balance. *Everything* had her name on it. She threw them all into the garbage bag, along with a picture of Linc that she didn't allow herself to look at before dropping it in. She carried the garbage bag over to the nearest trash can, pushed it through the swinging door in the lid, then returned to her seat.

The people waiting in the bus terminal looked tired. They read newspapers and sipped coffee from cardboard cups. Some of them stared at her, smiles flitting briefly across their sleepy faces as they noticed the baby. It was hard to be inconspicuous when you were carrying around the world's most adorable kid. She practiced looking unworried, yawning as though she were thoroughly relaxed.

There was a candy machine across the aisle from her, and she caught a glimpse of her reflection in its shiny plastic window. She looked away quickly. Her stupid hair. She should have waited to dye it. If they traced her to the bus, they would know that she had dyed and cut her hair. She should have bought a wig for that leg of the trip.

A woman sat a few seats away from her, knitting, a small gray square of yarn taking shape between her hands. She caught Susanna's eye and smiled.

"He's precious," she said, nodding at Tyler. "What's his name?"

"Cody," she answered quickly. That had been Linc's suggestion for the baby's name. She'd selected Tyler in the eleventh hour.

The bus to St. Louis was finally ready for boarding, and Susanna was relieved to see that she and Tyler would, at least initially, have two seats to themselves. She wanted space around her. She closed her eyes, but as she started to doze off, she was jerked awake by a half-dream. She'd pictured the bus making a stop in a town she didn't recognize. Two policemen got on board and stomped down the length of the bus to her seat. One of them grabbed her roughly by the shoulder while the other wrested her son from her arms.

Susanna shook her head to wake herself completely and hugged Tyler tight enough to make him whimper. No one was even looking for her, she told herself. At least not yet.

She was afraid to close her eyes again for fear of falling asleep. If the police did try to board the bus, she needed to be ready for them. Although, what exactly could she do? What could she say?

*I'm Kimberly Stratton*, she practiced. *This is my little boy, Cody. He's eleven months old.* Hard to fudge on that one. Anyone who knew kids would be able to guess Tyler's age.

*I was born on August 16. My father is a—famous artist and my mother's a professional dancer.* She nearly laughed. Why not? They could be anything she liked. But no. She should make them unremarkable. *My father is an orthodontist and my mother works in his office.* Or maybe it should be the other way around. *My mother is an orthodontist and my father helps out in her office.* She laughed out loud, then immediately sobered, and pressed her lips to the top of her baby's head.

"Tyler," she whispered, "what are we doing?"

When Tyler finally woke up for real, he was filled with his usual morning energy and she wondered how she would ever be able to contain him on this long trip. She gave him his bottle, which he looked at in annoyance as if wondering how she could have forgotten he'd graduated to his tippy cup weeks ago. But the bottle had seemed easier for her to manage on a trip, and after a moment's hesitation, Tyler took to it hungrily. Then Susanna broke a banana into chunks and watched her son gum them to a pulp, his four little front teeth flashing as he chewed.

When he'd had his fill, he climbed to his feet and held onto the back of the seat to peer at the woman sitting behind them. Susanna thought of pulling him down, but it was apparent that the woman didn't mind.

"You little show-off," the woman cooed. Susanna couldn't see her but she could hear her making kissy noises that put Tyler in one of his giggling moods. The woman played peek-a-boo with him while Susanna held onto his legs so he didn't tumble backward.

"You are the cutest little thing," the woman said. "I'm going to take you home with me, what do you think of that?"

After another minute or two, Susanna made Tyler sit down again. She used to enjoy the attention strangers paid to her son, but now it felt intrusive and oddly threatening.

Tyler was not happy about being banished to his seat. "Mamamama," he said.

She reached into the diaper bag for his monkey, smiling to herself. Would Jim know the difference between the "mamamama" that meant "mama" and the "mamamama" that meant "monkey?" Would Peggy? She doubted it. Peggy would probably think he was calling her mama. *Sorry, Peg. He's mine, not yours.* She smoothed her hand over his blond hair. He settled against her, his monkey curled in one of his arms, his thumb locked into his mouth. Susanna closed her eyes and breathed in his warm scent. She couldn't get enough of it.

Grace and Valerie had given the monkey to Tyler the day after he was born. Tyler had been too sick to leave the nursery, but Susanna told the staff that Grace and Valerie were his godparents, and the nurses let the two women join her and Linc as they sat next to the incubator watching Tyler in that early fight for life. She remembered Grace propping the monkey on the top of the incubator. The nurses were good about keeping Tyler and the monkey together, as best they could, no matter where Tyler was in the nursery.

Grace and Valerie would take care of Linc for her. How would Linc tell them about her disappearance? Before she could stop herself, she pictured Linc waking up that morning. By now, he'd probably tried to call her. What would he think when he got no answer? Would he go over to her apartment? Would he panic, thinking she was lying there, dead from an overdose or—*cut the drama*.

"The escape artist," he'd called her, because she always tried to escape from any difficult situation instead of facing it head-on. Well, she'd outdone herself this time.

Tyler whimpered at her side. She felt the wiriness in his body and knew he was yearning to get up and climb all over her, all over the seats of the bus.

"I'm sorry, Ty—Cody." She winced. She was a bad mother, confusing him. She hugged him close. "We'll have a few rough days here, honey," she whispered. "Then we can settle down in our new life."

That new life had to start now, she thought. She was Kim Stratton. And she would never call her son Tyler again.

$P$eggy in Wonderland!"

Peggy stood back from the door to let Nancy Curry into the house. "That's me," she said. She did feel a little as though she lived in a fairy tale these days.

"What a great house!" Nancy gave her a hug, then leaned back to study her. "You look terrific," she said.

"And you look like California agreed with you." She hadn't seen Nancy in a couple of years, but her old friend looked the same. Overweight by twenty pounds or so, short brown curly hair, and huge green eyes. She and Nancy had been best friends at one time, but Nancy had moved to Santa Barbara right before Peggy started seeing Jim. Peggy had been thrilled to hear that her old friend was returning to Boulder. Nancy and her husband would both be teaching at one of the middle schools.

"This is for you and Jim and the baby." Nancy handed a wrapped gift to Peggy.

"Thanks." Peggy took the package and ushered Nancy into the living room. The phone and doorbell had been ringing nonstop since she and Jim arrived home the evening before. People had heard about the court decision through the grapevine, and they'd been calling with congratulations and dropping gifts by. Tyler's crib was filled with so many stuffed animals that there was little room for the baby himself.

"Wow, what a view!" Nancy said. She walked over to the windows and looked out at the mountains. Then she turned around to face Peggy, warmth in her eyes. "Oh, Peg," she said, "you deserve this."

"Thanks," she said again. "Somebody's definitely been smiling down on me these last few years, that's for sure." She looked at her watch. It was only 12:30. Another couple of hours until Tyler arrived, and her stomach was tied in knots. "Do you have time for a cup of coffee?"

"Sure, but do *you*? What time do you get the baby?"

"Jim's working this morning and then picking him up at two."

She and Jim had talked for a long time the night before, trying to agree on who should pick up Tyler. Jim thought it should be both of them, but Peggy was adamant that Jim go alone. It wasn't going to be easy for Susanna to give Tyler up to Jim; it would be even harder for her to hand him over to Peggy. Susanna despised her, and Peggy couldn't really blame her. She hoped that someday Susanna would be able to see that the court had made the best decision for her son.

"I've done everything I can to get ready," she said. "Now I just have to sit around here and be nervous. It would help if you'd sit with me."

She showed Nancy the nursery while the coffee was brewing. She'd painted the room a pale yellow and added a wallpaper border of sunflowers. It cheered her every time she walked into the room.

"This is gorgeous," Nancy said. She stroked her hand over the white crib.

"We already had the crib and high chair and playpen and some toys, since we've had Tyler here every once in a while. He's really a good baby." Peggy felt herself tearing up. "He's been through so much and he's—a little trooper, you know? He endures whatever he has to and comes out smiling." She picked up the picture of Tyler from the white enameled dresser and handed it to Nancy. "He's about eight months there," she said.

"Oh, he's adorable." Nancy grinned at the picture, then reached into the crib and pulled out a teddy bear. "This is one lucky little kid."

Peggy stroked her hand over the stuffed bear. She hoped she

would be able to wean Tyler from the monkey he carried with him everywhere. That monkey had been washed so many times it was more of a rag than a stuffed animal.

Nancy looked at the picture again. "I heard he was sick when he was born," she said.

"Yes. He was in terrible shape. Part of his aorta—the part closest to the heart—was too narrow." She had not seen Tyler then, but she'd heard about his condition from her brother. "His arms and legs were blue. He could hardly breathe, and for a while they didn't think he'd make it. He needed to have the narrow section of his aorta removed and a synthetic graft inserted. My brother—remember Ron?—did the surgery and now Tyler's fine." That her brother had saved Tyler's life seemed like a good omen to her. Her family could offer Tyler built-in medical care.

"Does he need any more treatment?"

"Just checkups. Yearly echocardiograms to make sure everything's working all right. But he should be fine. Jim's made sure that Susanna's gotten him all the medical follow-up he's needed so far."

"Oh, I'm so glad they're giving the baby to you."

"Me too, although I do feel badly for Jim's ex-wife." She did not like to think about how Susanna must be feeling this morning.

They walked back to the kitchen and Peggy poured each of them a cup of coffee. Sitting at the table, she opened the package Nancy had brought and uncovered a small, silver-topped photograph album.

"Perfect!" she said, leaning over to give Nancy a kiss on the cheek. "Come back in a week and it will be full."

"I plan to come back." Nancy blew on her coffee. "I want to meet this husband of yours. I've heard he's handsome as sin."

Peggy laughed. "I'd have to agree. He's good-looking, intelligent, and a great lawyer," she said as she rested the photograph album on the table.

Peggy was her husband's biggest admirer. Jim had grown up in a family of six children raised on a factory worker's salary, and he'd had to struggle for everything he had. He'd been student body president of his high school and won scholarships to any number of schools. He was one hundred percent self-made and proud of it.

"Jim was at the top of our law school class," Peggy said, then added with a smile, "or maybe second to the top. We were always in competition with each other. I'm not sure which of us actually ended up in first place."

"What does your family think of him? Are your parents still living in San Francisco?"

"Yes, they're still there, and they're in love with him," she said. "They were here during the hearing, and they'll come back in a few weeks to spend some time with their new grandson." She wished she could add that her brother liked Jim as much as her parents did, but Ron had not yet warmed up to her new husband. She wasn't sure what the problem was, and she worried that Ron might think Jim's less than affluent background had attracted him to a woman who'd never wanted for anything. There'd been wealth in her family for generations, although her immediate family had certainly never lived ostentatiously. Her parents were philanthropists, firm believers in sharing what they had with those who had less, and that's the way she'd been raised. That's why she'd elected to work for Legal Aid instead of some posh law firm. And that's why Ron occasionally treated babies whose families could not ordinarily afford the best. But why there was this subtle, unspoken animosity between her brother and her husband, she didn't know.

She suddenly broke into a grin. "Can you believe I'm going to get to be a mother after all?"

"I'm so glad for you." Nancy had been Peggy's confidante three years earlier, when Phil Rudy broke off his engagement to her after she had the hysterectomy. Phil had wanted children, and he was going to find a woman who could give him some. Jim, on the other hand, didn't seem to care. He never made her feel as if she were less of a woman for having had a hysterectomy at the age of thirty.

"Why did Jim's ex-wife lose custody, Peg?" Nancy asked the question gingerly. "I thought it was pretty much a given that a mother would get custody—unless she was totally unfit."

"Well, fortunately this particular judge was level-headed and kept Tyler's best interests in mind. And I would never say Susanna was unfit, exactly, but there are definite problems. I mean, it's not as though she's on drugs or abusive, at least as far as I know. But she's single, with zero family support. She works in a bank, so he's in day care all day."

"What bank?" Nancy asked.

"Rocky Mountain National."

"Really? My sister, Julie, is a teller in the North Street branch."

"She must know Susanna, then, because that's where she works." Peggy studied the reflection of the overhead light in her coffee. "Susanna's made some poor choices in her life, and I feel sorry for her. But that's not a good enough reason to allow her to keep Tyler when we can give him so much more."

"You don't make much money in a bank," Nancy agreed.

"Money's only a small part of it, though," Peggy said quickly. She would never fight a woman for her child based on finances alone. Besides, Susanna was not in such bad shape financially. Jim was generous with child support, and he was buying her out of the house. It would take him a few years, but eventually Susanna would have her share. "Susanna's not terribly stable," Peggy said. "After she and Jim split up, she spent a month in a psychiatric ward because she threatened to kill herself. She'd stockpiled whatever pills she could find in her boyfriend's house. And it's the boyfriend that worries me the most. He's Linc Sebastian. Do you know who he is?"

Nancy frowned. "His name's familiar. Is he on the radio or something?"

Peggy nodded. "He has a syndicated show called *Songs for the Asking*. Old folk-rock sort of music. But he's an ex-con."

"You're kidding? What was he in for?"

Peggy leaned forward. She couldn't help herself. The story was so remarkably lurid that it never failed to get a rise out of an audience. "Murder," she said. "And guess who he murdered?"

Nancy shook her head.

"Susanna's father."

"What? Jim's father-in-law?"

"Well, he would have been, but Linc killed him before Jim was ever in the picture. It happened when Susanna was sixteen and Linc was twenty-two. He lived next door to Susanna's family, and he was over there one day and her parents were apparently inebriated, which I gather was typical, and a fight broke out. Linc claimed that the father started knocking the mother and Susanna around, and that the mother was actually knocked unconscious, and Linc got the father's gun and killed him to stop him from beating them up. The mother, on the other hand, denied that's what happened. She said that the father never hit either one of them—and there were no bruises on either Susanna or the mother, except for a cut on the mother's cheek, which she said happened when she fell. She did admit to passing out, but said it was because she was drunk." Peggy shook her head. She worried that Tyler might have a genetic predisposition toward alcoholism. "The mother said that what really happened was that Susanna's father was incensed because he suspected Linc of having a sexual relationship with his daughter, and so he started berating him, telling him to get out of the house, et cetera. That's when Linc got the gun and shot him."

"Holy shit, Peg. Which story did the jury believe?"

"Hard to say. They found him guilty. He admitted killing him, after all. But he denied anything more than a friendship with Susanna. The jury was never sure whether Linc killed the father in self-defense or if he was protecting Susanna and the mother or what. That's why he got such a light sentence. Jim knows the whole situation best, of course, and he feels pretty certain that Susanna and Linc were involved with each other back then. Actually," she said, "he thinks they've been lovers all along. Even while he and Susanna were married."

"Oh no."

Peggy shuddered. The whole situation made her skin crawl.

"Did Jim know at the time that she was having an affair?" Nancy asked.

"He could never prove it, and she denied it vehemently. But as soon as she and Jim split up, she was with Linc. She moved right into his house. You don't have to work very hard to put two and two together." Peggy looked at the clock above the stove. Twenty-five minutes to two, and her stomach was not pleased about the coffee.

She remembered well the hurt look in Jim's eyes when he first told her about his marriage. He'd made a mistake in marrying Susanna, he'd said. He'd gotten himself trapped. He was a bright, ambitious man married to a woman with few aspirations.

"The main reason they broke up was simply that Jim outgrew her," Peggy said.

"That happens all the time." Nancy drained the last of her coffee. "I'm so glad Gary and I are in the same profession. We really understand each other."

"That's critical," Peggy agreed. "Jim was spending his days with all these bright law students and going home to Susanna at night. He and I became good friends, going out to lunch and studying together, and he'd confide in me about how unhappy he was. After school, we went our separate ways. He went to Black and Courrier, and I—"

"Wow." Nancy's green eyes grew even larger. "I didn't know he was working *there*."

"Uh huh. And I went to Legal Aid. And then one day we bumped into each other. We went to lunch. He told me his marriage was worse than ever. He told me about Linc, that he'd asked Susanna not to see him anymore, but she said she had to, he was an important friend. This guy who killed her father, right?"

Nancy made a sound of disgust.

"I'm sure she and Linc were having an affair and Jim simply could never admit it to himself. Then she got pregnant. Jim was really upset. He told me he couldn't bear the thought of her being the mother of his children."

"I don't blame him," Nancy said. Then she added quietly, "Are you sure Jim's the father?"

Peggy drew in a long breath. This was something she'd wondered about herself. "Not one hundred percent," she said. "But we've decided it doesn't matter one way or another. Tyler's still ours."

She was skipping something in the telling. She always skipped it, and even with this old friend, she couldn't bring herself to tell the truth, because it was the one thing she'd done in her life that shamed her. She'd started sleeping with Jim when he was still married. If she lived to be one hundred, she would never forget the look on Susanna's face when she walked into the bedroom and found them together. She'd often wanted to talk to Susanna about that horrible night. She wanted to apologize, but how could she ever broach the subject? *Look, Susanna, I'm very sorry about the time you found me making love to your husband.* That night had been the first time she'd gotten a good look at Susanna. She'd heard so many negative things about her that she had not been prepared for her to look so vulnerable, so hurt. She'd been trying to rid her mind of that image of Susanna ever since.

The phone rang and she jumped to her feet to answer it.

"I'm just about ready to leave," Jim said.

"I'll be waiting." She got off the phone with a smile. "Jim's on his way to get Tyler."

Nancy stood up. "Well, I'm not going to stay any longer. Don't want to intrude on your family reunion here."

Peggy was suddenly ashamed of herself. "Oh, Nance," she said. "I've spent the last hour yakking about me, myself, and I, and I haven't asked you a thing about you or Gary or the kids."

Nancy kissed her on the cheek. "We're all doing great. And how many times have you listened to me go on and on about my kids? It's your turn now, and I love hearing about Tyler. Give me a call when you're ready to show off your son, okay?"

*Your son.* Peggy loved the sound of those words. "I will," she said. "And thanks again for the album."

She watched Nancy drive off, then sat in a chair in the living room and, although she'd read it four times already, opened the book on one year olds her mother had given her. Her eyes darted between the book to her watch, to the window, to her watch again. At three o'clock, she had the ominous feeling that something was wrong. Jim should have been home half an hour ago.

The phone rang and she walked into the kitchen to answer it.

"I'm on the car phone," Jim said.

"Is everything all right? Do you have Tyler?"

"I did tell her attorney two o'clock, didn't I?"

"What do you mean? Yes you did. I heard you. What's wrong?"

"Well, nothing, I hope. It's just that Susanna's not here. Or else she's not answering her door. Maybe Ann Prescott told her the wrong time."

"Is her car there?"

"Yes, it's here. So I figured maybe she took Tyler out for a walk.

I've been waiting on the steps leading up to her apartment, but she's not back yet."

Peggy's heart was pounding. "What are you going to do?"

"I thought I'd wait here another half hour or so."

"She wouldn't do anything stupid, would she? Like—she wouldn't kill herself, and—?" *and Tyler,* she thought, but she couldn't say those words out loud.

"She's probably out for a walk or something." Jim avoided her question. "I'm going to start looking around. If she's not back soon, I'll try to talk to some of the neighbors."

"All right."

She got off the phone and paced around the house, hugging her arms to her chest. She called Ron at his office, not certain what she wanted from her older brother, but she had always turned to him when she was anxious about something. Ron's calm approach to life could usually soothe her.

"I'm sure everything's all right," Ron said patiently. "And look, Peg. I'm going to be disappointed in you if you turn into an anxious, overprotective mother."

"I won't," she said, although she knew she was three-quarters of the way there.

"It's true that Tyler's had some special medical problems," Ron admitted, "but he's fine now. He needs to be treated like any other little kid."

"I know," she said. "All right. Thanks." She got off the phone feeling a little disappointed in her brother. Ron had two healthy kids of his own. He couldn't possibly understand how she was feeling.

At four o'clock, Jim pulled into the driveway. From the living room window, she watched him get out of the car and walk toward the house, his arms empty. She rushed outside and met him in the driveway.

"What happened?" she asked.

"I don't know." Jim looked tired and perplexed. He ran his hands through his dark hair, then put his arm around her and turned her in the direction of the house. "I've been trying to call Linc Sebastian to see if he knows anything," he said as they walked toward the house. "But I got his voice mail. I think he tapes his shows on Wednesday, so he's probably there but not picking up his phone. Not that he'd be too quick to help me figure out what's going on anyway."

He pushed open the front door and headed for the kitchen.

Peggy followed him. "I think we should call the police," she said.

"Let me try her attorney first." Jim pulled the phone book out of one of the kitchen drawers. "Maybe she misunderstood me. Maybe she thought I said *Thursday* at two. Or maybe Thursday at ten. Or—"

"You said tomorrow at two. I was standing right there. She heard you."

Jim rested the phone book on the counter and dialed Ann Prescott's office number. Peggy listened while he asked for the attorney. She was not in, and Jim left a message for her to call him as soon as possible.

"Try Linc again," she said as soon as he'd hung up the phone.

Jim nodded and dialed the number from memory. Peggy sat on one of the barstools, leaning across the counter, holding her breath as they waited for Linc to answer.

"What if he's taken off, too?" she asked. "What if—"

"Sh." Jim held up his hand. "Linc? This is Jim Miller. Do you know where Susanna is?"

Peggy wished she could hear Linc's answer.

"No, she's not," Jim said. "I went over to pick Tyler up at two and she wasn't there. Her car was, though."

"Ask him if she knew it was today at—"

Jim hushed her again with his hand. "I thought of that," he said into the phone, "but I waited over an hour and she didn't show up. Could she have the time wrong or something?"

"What is he saying?" Peggy couldn't stand it any longer.

Jim cupped his hand over the receiver. "He says she knew I was going to pick him up today. She was dreading it and—" He removed his hand from the receiver. "What, Linc? All right, good. I'll be there in twenty minutes."

Jim hung up the phone. His face was pinched and white. "Linc sounds worried himself."

"Oh, God," Peggy said. "If she did anything to Tyler, I'll—"

"Hold on, Peg. No point in borrowing trouble."

"You're going over there?"

"Yes." Jim reached for his car keys on the counter. "He has a key to her apartment, so he'll meet me over there in twenty minutes and we can make sure there's—you know, nothing wrong."

"I'm coming too."

"No."

"Yes, Jim, I am." She grabbed her sweater, and he didn't object as she followed him out to the car.

Neither of them spoke on the ride to Susanna's apartment complex on the other side of town. Peggy was afraid to give words to her fears. They reached the apartment a little after six and parked on the street.

Linc pulled up in his van as they were getting out of the car. He looked more like himself now than he had in court. The small loop earring was back in his ear again, and he was dressed in jeans and a long-sleeved, dark green jersey. Well, his conservative get-up in court hadn't helped him much.

"Did you ring the bell?" Linc asked.

"We just got here," Jim said.

They followed Linc to the front security door of the complex and watched as he rang the buzzer for Susanna's apartment.

"Someone let me in earlier," Jim said. "I went up and knocked on her door, but there was no answer."

When it became apparent that no one was going to respond to the buzzer, Linc slipped his key into the lock. They followed him up the stairs to a long hallway where he knocked on the first door to his right. Peggy had never been here before. The hallway was dark and smelled of mildew.

She realized she was holding her breath as she watched Linc unlock the door. He poked his head inside. "Susanna?"

She and Jim followed him into the apartment. The living room was small, but neat and uncluttered, and Peggy felt relief. She realized she'd been expecting to find Susanna and Tyler lying in a pool of blood.

"You two stay here," Linc said.

Jim started to protest, but Peggy took her husband's arm and nodded toward the sofa. Linc scared her a little, and she thought they should go along with whatever he said. She sat down on the sofa as he walked into the kitchen, but Jim paced back and forth between the window and the entrance to the hallway.

"There's got to be a simple explanation for this," he said, peering down the hall. "I can't believe that Susanna would have the brains or the gumption to defy a court order."

Peggy pressed her hands together in her lap and bit her lip to keep from speaking. For the first time, she was wondering if Jim had ever really known his ex-wife.

There was nothing out of order in the kitchen, but Linc did not have a good feeling about this situation. He had to force himself to walk into the master bedroom. The curtains were open and there was still a splash of sunlight on Susanna's neatly made bed. No sign of anything out of place. The bathroom looked clean and orderly, and he felt a relief he did not want to give a name to. He hadn't really expected her to harm herself, though. She was not the same person she'd been when Jim left her, and he couldn't imagine her trying to take her own life at this point. But where was she, then? What the hell was going on?

Tyler's room was on the other side of the hall and the first thing that greeted Linc was the mural she'd painted on the wall across from the crib—a large, colorful rendition of Noah's Ark. She'd painted it a few months earlier, terrified that her landlord would have a fit when he discovered it. He stood in the middle of the small room and turned slowly in a circle. Nothing missing or out of the ordinary, as far as he could tell. Except . . . He frowned at the changing table. She usually put Tyler's diaper bag there, but the changing table was bare. That didn't mean much, he told himself. He checked the crib. Tyler's monkey was gone, but that made sense. Wherever Tyler was, he'd have his monkey with him. It would have been more ominous to find the monkey alone in the crib.

Back in Susanna's bedroom, he checked her closet where she kept her old duffel bag. It was not there.

*Susanna*, he thought, incredulous. *You didn't.*

"Linc?" Peggy called from the living room. "Have you found anything?"

"No," he called back. He knew he'd have to let them see for themselves. He was walking past the bathroom again when he noticed a small, reddish brown smear on the countertop. He froze. Blood? He stared at it for a minute. Hair dye. He knew that's what it was. Knew it beyond any shadow of a doubt, and he took a few sheets of toilet paper, wet them, wiped the stain away, and slipped the damp paper into his jeans pocket. Starting right then, he began looking not so much for clues to her disappearance as for clues she might have left behind that someone else might find. There was a pain in his heart, but it was born of understanding. He went back to the living room, forcing himself to keep his face expressionless.

Jim, arms folded, was leaning against the wall by the window. Peggy stood up from the sofa, the look on her face so frightened and worried that he could not help but feel an instant of sympathy for her.

"There's no sign of her," he said. "The apartment looks perfectly normal. I don't see Tyler's diaper bag or his monkey, but otherwise, everything seems to be in place."

"I told you we should have gotten him last night," Jim said to his wife.

"You were right," Peggy said. "I just thought she should have one last night with him. I never thought she'd—"

"Is she at your place?" Jim looked at Linc with what had to be hatred.

"Sure," he said. "She's at my place and I'm snooping around here for my health."

Jim scowled at him. "I want to look around myself, and then I'm getting the police on the phone," he said. He walked into the kitchen, calling back over his shoulder. "And you don't go any-where."

Linc could barely tolerate Jim's pomposity. The man was a walking ego. But he managed to swallowed his annoyance as he sat down next to Peggy to wait for Jim's return.

"When did you talk to her last?" Peggy asked. "Did you see her this morning?"

"I spoke to her last night." He had tried to call her several times today. He hadn't really been worried, though. She was often out, walking Tyler or running errands. He was still stunned by the real-ization that she'd taken off without telling him. He hadn't thought she was that gutsy.

"When was the last time you talked to her?" Jim asked as he walked back into the room.

"Last night," Peggy answered for him. "What did the police say?"

"They're sending someone over here." He turned to Linc again. "Did she say anything about going away?"

"Not a word."

Jim raised his eyebrows as if he didn't believe him, and Linc could easily picture him in a courtroom, grilling a witness.

"No hint?" Jim asked. "Nothing? What sort of mood was she in?"

"Oh, she was in a great mood. She couldn't wait to give her baby away."

"Cut the sarcasm, all right?" Jim said. "You'd better get used to answering questions because I have the feeling you're going to be getting plenty of them."

"She was down," Linc said. "Quiet. Exactly what you'd expect from a mother who'd been told she has to give up the child she loves."

"Linc," Peggy pleaded. "The judge made the right decision. I'm sorry you don't see it that way but it was the only sane decision anyone could possibly make."

"Spare me." Linc stood up and walked to the window. As soon as he was out of here, he was buying a pack of cigarettes.

He saw the police car pull up outside and let out a long sigh. Jim was probably right; he was going to have to face a torrent of questions. He was suddenly glad that Susanna had left him none of the answers.

There was just one officer, which seemed to distress Peggy and Jim no end. He was middle-aged, gray-haired, well-seasoned, and unexcitable, and he doubted that Susanna was really missing.

"In cases like this," he said, standing in the middle of Susanna's living room, "where someone's been gone just a few hours, they usually turn up visiting their sister down the street."

"She has no sister down the street," Jim said in annoyance. "She has no family, period."

Linc tried to play along with the officer's casual demeanor. "Sure, Susanna probably bumped into a friend at the grocery store and they got to talking and she forgot she was supposed to give her baby away today." But he knew better. Susanna had a long history of running away. Even as a child, she'd escape to the little room above his family's garage. He knew that was her hiding place and he'd find her there, give her a little lecture about not running away from her problems, and take her home. This time was different, though. She was no longer a child, and his family no longer owned that garage. He didn't have a clue where to look for her, and he knew she'd planned it that way.

The police officer told them to contact him again when—and if—Susanna remained missing for twenty-four hours. Linc let Jim and Peggy out of the apartment the same time the policeman left, but he remained behind. He looked through the rooms one last time, deciding to take Susanna's photograph albums home with him. If Susanna did indeed remain missing, he didn't want all those pictures of Tyler to end up with Jim.

It wasn't until he was driving home that the hurt and betrayal overwhelmed him.

*Why didn't you tell me, Suze?* He pounded the steering wheel with his fist. *How could you just walk out like that?* Where did she go? Would he ever see her again?

He felt numb that night as he walked Sam down the winding street in his neighborhood, numb as he smoked a Marlboro and stared out at Boulder from the glass wall of his living room. But when he went into the bathroom to brush his teeth and get ready for bed, he saw the scrap of paper he'd taped to his mirror.

*Susanna wants to hear me play "Suzanne" for her Sunday night.*

Suddenly, he understood her words. His show was nationally syndicated. It reached listeners across the United States every Sunday night. No matter where Susanna was, she would be able to hear him.

He read the words again and shook his head, not certain if he should laugh or cry.

The bus smelled like the inside of a locker room by the time it reached St. Louis. People were sleeping in their cramped seats, some of them snoring, but Kim Stratton was wide awake. She had dozed off only once or twice during the night, and Cody had slept fitfully, sometimes on the seat next to her, sometimes in her lap. He was awake now, but understandably cranky, confused by the upset in his routine and the strangeness of the hour. It was not quite five in the morning.

Her peanut butter and jelly sandwiches had grown mushy and inedible sometime the evening before, the white bread purple where the jelly had seeped through. Her stomach was growling, and poor Cody was entirely off his schedule despite her attempts to keep him on track. Yet she was not anxious to leave the safety of the bus. She perched on the edge of her seat, looking out the window, hunting in the darkness for a police officer who might be awaiting her arrival. There were a couple of men in uniform out there, but she thought they were bus drivers. From where she sat, it was difficult to separate one uniform from another.

For the past hour, Cody had been making his screaming, yelping sounds of annoyance, those sounds he made when he wanted her to get him out of his crib and get him started on the day. Plus, he was in dire need of a change. She turned around to look apologetically at the couple riding behind them.

"Sorry he's been so noisy this morning," she said.

The woman smiled at her. "Too long a trip for a baby," she said.

Kim knew the woman meant the comment sympathetically, yet she heard criticism in the words.

Her body was stiff as she worked her way down the tight aisle of the bus carrying Cody and the diaper bag. The rest of her belongings were in the belly of the bus, and once on the sidewalk, she looked anxiously over her shoulder as she waited for them to be unloaded. When she had everything she owned with her, she moved into the terminal. The lights seemed far too bright inside and her eyes hurt for a second as they adjusted. Cody, back in his stroller once again, began to howl.

"I know, baby," she said to him. Looking around the nearly empty terminal, she spotted the ladies' room a few yards to her right. A police officer stood in front of a takeout vendor near the room's entrance, and Kim hesitated, but the cop seemed oblivious to her. He was laughing with the woman pouring him coffee, and Kim walked past him without incident.

She changed Cody in the not-too-clean rest room, then washed her face and brushed her teeth, staring in amazement at the copper-haired stranger in the mirror.

It was not even five-thirty—still dark enough to put the next part of her plan into action. She left the rest room and shoved her bags in one of the terminal's lockers, then pushed Cody outside. The street was well-lit, but there was one dark patch near the rear of the terminal, and she headed toward the cars parked at its core. She selected one at random, pulled a small wrench from her pocket, and knelt down by the car's front bumper to remove its license plate. Her hands trembled. She could not quite shake her guilt over what she was doing.

When she had removed both plates and slipped them behind the seat of Cody's stroller, she walked back into the terminal. The police officer had disappeared, so she bought a cup of coffee and a stale doughnut for herself and mixed some formula for Cody. Then she bought a newspaper and sat down in the corner, relieved to see that more people were filling the terminal. She and Cody would not stand out quite so much.

Cody drank a little of the formula, but he seemed more interested in sleep now that he was back in the familiar confines of his stroller. Kim opened the paper to the used car ads. She was allot-ting fifteen hundred dollars to a car, and she'd decided it was safest to buy from an individual to avoid having to fill out a lot of paperwork. There were several cars that fell into that price range, and she circled two of them. An '85 Toyota Corolla. "Runs great," the ad read. It was exactly fifteen hundred. The second, an '85 Toyota Celica was sixteen-fifty "firm," but she liked its description: "very well-kept; a gem to drive." Plus, it had a sunroof.

She worked the crossword puzzle and read about most of the news in St. Louis to try to keep herself awake until eight o'clock, when she thought it would be late enough to call on the cars. She would get as much information as she could over the phone, because she wanted to be sure the car would do before she went to look at it. She would have to take a taxi to the car, and she didn't want to have to call another taxi to cart her away again.

She fed Cody some oatmeal and a banana, then made her calls from a pay phone in the terminal at exactly eight o'clock. The Corolla sounded good, but it was red. A red car would stand out too much. She told the owner she would call back if she were still interested.

The Celica's owner was a woman with a deep, rich voice. "It is a *stupendous* car," she reassured Kim. "Only has seventy-five thou-sand miles on it. You're going to love it."

"What color is it?" Kim asked.

"Dark blue. Really pretty."

"Do you think I could make a long trip in it?"

"Oh, sure. You've got to try it out. Come over and you'll see what I mean."

"All right." Kim wrote down the woman's address on the edge of the newspaper. She collected her bags from the locker, then walked outside and approached a waiting taxi. The driver was a burly black man who didn't bother to hide his scowl when he saw the mishmash of baggage she was lugging around with her. He helped her load the stroller and duffel bag into the trunk before she settled into the back seat with Cody. No car seat, of course. That made her nervous.

The driver had to look up the address on a map. It was ten miles away, he told her.

"Would you mind taking back streets?" she said. "So you could go slowly? There's no car seat for my baby, and—"

"Geesh!" The driver turned away from her with a shake of his head and she slunk down into the seat, Cody in her arms.

The taxi snaked through residential streets, and Cody whined and rocked against Kim like someone who'd been trapped inside too long and was about to give up hope of ever being free again. She held him tightly, pressing her lips to the soft hair on his head.

The cab finally pulled into the driveway of a small brick house on a quiet street. The driver helped her unload her belongings, piling them on the sidewalk, and Kim paid him before settling Cody in the stroller. Her duffel bag slung over her shoulder, she pushed the stroller up to the front door of the house.

She rang the bell, hoping she didn't look as desperate as she felt. How could she appear to be anything else? She obviously had no car to take her away from this house. Either she had to buy the car, or start walking.

A woman about her own age opened the door and smiled.

"Are you one of the people who called about the car?" she asked.

*One* of the people? It suddenly occurred to her that the car might already be sold and the thought made her tighten her grip on the stroller. "Yes," she said. "Do you still have it?"

"Uh huh." The woman reached behind her to pick up the keys from a table, then walked out the door and led Kim around the side of the house. "You're the first one to come look at it," she said.

The car sat at the end of the driveway, next to a garage, and Kim understood what the woman had meant by the words "very well-kept." At least on the outside, the car was in great shape. No dents. The finish on the dark blue paint still had a little shine to it. Through the windows, she could see that the upholstery was torn in a couple of places, but who cared? She could make covers for the seats.

"I've kept it in the garage," the woman said. "It was my first car, and I was determined to do everything right with it. Want to take it for a drive?"

"Yes, I'd like that." She wondered if she should open the hood and act as though she knew what she was looking at, but she opted for driving it instead.

"I'll come with you," the woman said. "You can leave the stroller and your bags here." She opened the side door of the garage, and Kim wheeled the stroller inside. She lifted Cody into her arms and carried him back to the car.

She hated driving without a car seat for Cody. That would have to be her first purchase.

"How would you feel about holding my son on your lap?" she asked the woman. "I don't have a car seat with me."

"Love to." The woman smiled as she took Cody on her lap, and for once Kim was grateful her child was so easygoing with strangers.

"Where's your car?" the woman asked as Kim carefully backed out of the driveway.

"My cousin dropped me off," Kim said. "She's running some errands and then—" Then what? "I'll call her if I decide not to take the car, and she'll come get me. I've got the plates from my old car, though, in case I decide to buy this one."

This seemed to satisfy the woman. She pointed out a route for Kim to take around the neighborhood. The car drove well, at least as well as her car back in Boulder. She knew she should see how it handled on the highway, but she didn't want to go that fast with Cody sitting untethered on the woman's lap.

"I'd like to buy it," she said, as she pulled back into the driveway.

"Great! It's sixteen-fifty, firm."

"That's fine." Kim didn't want to haggle with her. She stepped out of the car, then got her wallet from her duffel bag and counted out sixteen hundred-dollar bills and a fifty. Her hands were shaking, not because she was handing over so much of her precious money, but because she knew she must seem like a suspicious sort of character to the car's owner. Here she'd shown up early in the morning, alone, with luggage and a baby in tow. What if her face and Cody's had been splashed across the country on TV? Maybe on one of those "most wanted"-type shows. Would a mother taking her own child merit that sort of attention?

But the woman seemed concerned only with selling her car. She pulled the certificate of title from the glove compartment, took a pen from her shirt pocket, and asked Kim for her address.

Kim had thought this through, but for a moment her mind

went blank. She rattled off a fictitious St. Louis address, and was relieved when the woman offered the first three numbers of the zip code. Kim picked a couple of random numbers to finish the code, and the woman jotted them down on the form without batting an eye. Then she helped Kim replace the license plates on the Celica with the stolen ones.

When they had finished, Kim stood up from the bumper, her knees creaking. "Where's the nearest store where I could buy a car seat?" Kim asked, then added, "Not expensive."

"There's a K-Mart close by. Just turn here, then go about a mile. It's on your left."

She thanked the woman, then got back into the car—*her* car—and pulled out of the driveway.

At the K-Mart and the grocery store next to it, she bought more formula, juice, bananas, baby food, animal crackers, and a car seat. Before even setting up the car seat, though, she gave Cody his bottle. She sat with him in the back seat of the car, rocking him and talking to him, apologizing for uprooting him. He seemed soothed by the food and her words, and was soon sound asleep. She buckled him into the car seat, then looked up at the sky. The sun was to her left, so that had to be east. Pulling out of the parking lot, she headed in that direction.

She stopped four times that first day on the road. She was not in a rush. There was nowhere she had to be. She and Cody enjoyed a long, welcome nap, parked in the shade in a church parking lot. They stopped to eat at a picnic table and to play in a playground. And each time she got back in the car, she headed east. She didn't need a map. Every intersection she came to, she took the road heading away from Colorado. She would go as far from Boulder as the highway could take her.

At six o'clock, she decided to stop for the night. They were outside of Henderson, Kentucky, and she found a motel along the road. There was a restaurant next door, and after she'd registered and dumped her things in the room, she walked over to the restaurant with Cody in his stroller.

The hostess sat them next to a window and brought over a high chair. "What's his name?" she asked, as Kim lowered Cody into the chair.

"Cody," she said, and then added, "and I'm Kim." She wanted to get used to saying both their names out loud.

"He's adorable." The hostess handed Kim a menu and told her a waitress would be right over.

The waitress, a young blond woman with short curly hair, arrived at the table a few minutes later. She all but ignored Kim as she talked to Cody. "Hi, there, punkin'," she said. "What can I get for you tonight?"

Kim ordered pasta to share with Cody and was pulling a bib from her purse when two policemen walked past her table. Her hand froze in mid-air. The two men sat down in a booth directly across the aisle from her. The youngest of the two was facing her, and he caught her eye. She quickly looked away. She could barely get the bib tied around Cody's neck, her hands were shaking so hard.

There was a little container of crayons on the table and the placemat was a line drawing of a clown. She put the placemat on the table in front of Cody and filled in the drawing, while he tried to stick the crayons in his mouth. She kept her concentration on her son, but she was keenly aware of the two men across the aisle.

The waitress delivered her spaghetti, with an extra plate for Cody, and Kim began cutting his portion into short pieces.

"So where are you two from?" the waitress asked.

Kim wondered if the policemen had heard the question. The young officer caught her eye again, and she looked up at the waitress.

"Oh, we've been visiting my mother in Owensboro." She remembered seeing a sign for Owensboro on the highway. "But we want to get home to Daddy in St. Louis by tomorrow because it's his birthday. We still have to get him a present, right Cody?" She was glad that most of what she said to her son went right over his head. She could not imagine living this dishonest sort of life with an older child who would have to be party to the deception.

"What are you getting him?" the waitress asked.

It took Kim a minute to understand the question. "Oh! For my husband, you mean?"

The waitress nodded with a smile.

"I still don't have any idea, would you believe?" Kim said.

"Well, what does he like?" The waitress seemed to think that helping her pick a gift was part of her job description. "Is he into sports?"

"Oh." She thought of Jim. Watching back to back football games was his idea of heaven. On the other hand, Linc thought dog-walking was a sport. "No, he's not really a sports fan. I thought we'd get him some CDs. He loves music."

"Good idea. There's a great record store in Henderson. Doesn't open till ten tomorrow, though. You'll probably be on your way by then, huh?"

"Right," Kim said. "We'll find something, thanks."

"No problem."

She watched the waitress walk away. If the cops asked her about the lady and the baby, the waitress would tell them she was on her way home to St. Louis to celebrate her husband's birthday, and the cops would think to themselves, well she only looks a little like that woman and baby everyone's looking for.

*Paranoid,* she told herself. *People are not hanging on your every word.*

Back in the hotel room, she got her first good look at herself since leaving Boulder. No one would recognize her. She barely recognized herself. Except for the road-weary eyes and the unkempt hair, she looked good. Copper glow was a pretty shade. Too pretty, perhaps. She should have picked a mousier color that would let her fade into the woodwork. No wonder that young cop had been looking at her. She did not look half bad.

The room had a king-sized bed, and she lay down next to her exhausted son.

She wished she'd thought to pack a few of his favorite books. She sang him a couple of songs instead, "Froggie Went a-Courtin'" and "The Old Woman Who Swallowed a Fly," songs Linc liked to sing to him. Then she sang "The Name Game," using Cody as the name. "Cody, Cody, Fo Fody . . . " until the little boy could barely stop giggling. She wanted him to get used to his new name. She needed to get used to it herself.

Toward the end of her pregnancy, she and Linc had often sat up late into the night with the baby name book. They'd usually be at his house, with its spacious rooms and its unobstructed view of

Boulder. She'd been feeling stronger about herself then, able to talk about Jim with anger rather than self-recrimination. She'd felt buoyed up by Linc's strength and caring, two things she had known nearly all her life. They hadn't started sleeping together yet; that didn't begin until Cody was a few months old, even though once they started it seemed as if they had always been lovers. But their friendship had been deep and abiding, nonetheless.

Linc had loved the name Cody. He'd leave little slips of paper around his house and hers, "Cody Miller" written on them so she could see how good it looked. But she hadn't been able to get the name Tyler out of her head. Her son was nearly six months old when she finally realized why she'd given him that name: Jim had once said he liked it. If they ever had a male child, he'd said, he would like to name him Tyler.

"Still trying to please Jim," Linc admonished her.

Kim stared at the ceiling above her hotel room bed. She did not want to think about Linc. Imagining how he'd felt when he discovered her disappearance this morning was the only thing that could destroy her resolve right now. She could not allow that to happen.

Cody was sound asleep, his beloved monkey tight in his arms, and Kim turned on the television, keeping the volume low. David Letterman was on, and his guest was a musician who looked undeniably like Linc. Kim held the remote in the air between herself and the TV, trying to cover part of the man's face to see which features most resembled Linc's. The blue eyes, definitely. Not the eyebrows, though. The hair, of course, was totally wrong.

This was torture. Why was she doing this to herself? She turned off the TV and closed her eyes.

She would never be able to touch him again. Never make love to him, or hold him all night long. Never pick up the phone to hear his voice on the other end, joking with her, making her laugh. Telling her he loved her.

She would be able to listen to him, though. Sunday night. On the radio. At least she could still have that much of him.

or two more days, Kim drove east. The pace she set was slow and easy, with plenty of rest stops for herself and Cody. It was impossible to rush when you had no idea where you were going. On Thursday, she bought herself an inexpensive bathing suit, and both Thursday and Friday checked into motels early so that she and Cody could play in the swimming pools. It wasn't until late Friday night when she was lying alone in bed that she began to feel the inescapable awareness of her homelessness. She could head east only a little longer. Sometime tomorrow, she was going to run out of country. Maybe that was fine. She'd keep going until she ran out of road, and then she'd plant herself wherever she'd landed.

Then how was she going to support herself? She couldn't get a job in a bank; that would be the first place anyone would look for her. She should never even tell anyone she'd worked in a bank. Maybe she could get a different sort of secretarial position, but she'd be able to offer no references. And then she'd need day care, and she was nowhere near ready to let Cody out of her sight. Maybe she could take in word processing jobs. She was a great typist. Hated it, but did it well. She could work out of her home— wherever, whatever "home" turned out to be. She hoped it would not be the back seat of the Toyota. If things were ever that bad for her, she would take Cody back. She had no right to him if she couldn't provide for him any better than that.

From behind the steering wheel of the car Saturday morning, she knew she was hitting civilization in a major way. The traffic was wild, and before she knew it, she'd been dumped onto the Capital Beltway—the wide, fast, frightening highway that looped around Washington, D.C. She'd heard somewhere that if you were trying to hide, a big city would be your best bet, but the thought chilled her. If she got sucked into the mass of buildings and cars inside the beltway, it would be like being in prison. So she continued circling Washington, taking the first exit east she could find, Route 50.

It was nearly time for lunch, and Cody was assertive in letting her know it. He kicked his legs out from the car seat as though trying to escape. She couldn't blame him. Poor baby, trapped on the road for—she'd lost track—five days? He was entitled to kick. She sang "The Name Game" again, for what seemed like the zillionth time in the past few days, but he was having none of it. It was food or nothing.

She pulled off the road at Annapolis. Annapolis was the capital of Maryland, she was quite certain, and she expected a large city to greet her, but instead found herself driving through a quaint little town. The streets were narrow, and she felt as if she'd stepped back in time. A tall gray and white dome rose high above the city from a large brick building, and the rest of the town seemed to fall away from that dome in all directions. She drove around, enchanted, until she came to water, a river or a bay perhaps, and it seemed that she had stumbled upon the heart of the city. She was in a large square surrounding an enormous dock filled with boats and activity. People dotted the square, walking, taking pictures, eating at sidewalk cafes, or simply sitting on benches overlooking the water.

There was a parking lot, and she managed to pull into a space as someone was leaving. The sun was warm and bright as she lowered Cody into the stroller. She was smiling to herself, but Cody whimpered with hunger. Her first stop had to be to get something to eat. One of the buildings edging the square was filled with a variety of take-out restaurants. The smell of fish was strong inside and not at all unpleasant, and she bought fish and chips for herself and a container of strawberry yogurt for Cody.

As she walked toward one of the benches overlooking the dock, she passed the side of a restaurant and was immediately captivated by a mural painted on the windowless brick. She stepped back to look at it.

The painting was of a tall ship, white sails billowing, set against a midnight blue sky dotted with white stars and a full moon. The artist's name, Adam Soria, was painted in the lower right-hand side, below the white-capped sea. There was something surrealistic about the painting, and until Cody started his I-am-terminally-hungry wailing, she could not tear herself away.

She pushed the stroller to a vacant bench by the water and began feeding her hungry son. A sense of calm surrounded her as she sat there. This beautiful little town was a capital city? There were plenty of people around, to be sure, but no one seemed rushed or harried. Seagulls swooped through the air over the water and pecked at crumbs on the wharf. The air was filled with the sound of lapping water and the scent of brine. She had lived in landlocked Boulder all her life. She'd had no idea what she was missing.

She poured juice into Cody's bottle and handed it to him. An older couple walked by and smiled at the two of them. She smiled back.

"Oh, Cody," she said. "Does this feel like the end of the road to you?" Her excitement was edged with trepidation. Once she actually stopped traveling, she would have plenty of time to think about what she'd done—and what she'd lost in the process.

She lifted Cody out of the stroller when he finished eating and let him toddle around, holding on to the bench or her knees. He was fascinated by the seagulls, jumping up and down as though he wanted to be up in the air with them, flying.

Kim spotted a newspaper vending machine a few feet away, dug a quarter from her purse, and bought a paper. She kept one eye on Cody as she turned to the classified ads. There were only a few rooms for rent in Annapolis proper and several apartments. One of the apartments, though, claimed to have a view of the Naval Academy and the Severn River, and that was enough to intrigue her. It was partly furnished, and rented for four hundred and fifty dollars a month.

A man dressed in a gray suit walked past the bench, and she asked him if he knew where Maryland Avenue was.

"You go up Randall Street and make a left on Prince George," he said, and when he saw her look of confusion, added, "You can get a map from the visitor center over there." He pointed to the opposite side of the parking lot.

"Thanks." She put Cody back in the stroller and began walking toward the visitor center, where she got a map. She opened it on the hood of her car. Spread out in front of her, the town looked as small and manageable as she'd guessed it would be. She found Maryland Street. It looked like an easy walk, and she turned the stroller in that direction.

The houses were small and packed tightly against one another. Some were brick, some wood, and all of them were very, very old. Older than anything she'd ever seen in Colorado.

Maryland Street, though, was lined with tiny shops. Antique shops, gift shops, book stores. Peering ahead, she could see nothing that resembled an apartment building. She checked the address, wondering if the apartment might be above one of the shops. She continued walking, and the shops gave way to small homes and a church. Soon, she spotted a large house standing alone on what was, comparatively speaking, a huge lot graced by a lone towering maple tree. Where the other houses hugged the brick sidewalks, this house was set back from the street a good thirty feet or so. It was obviously quite old, but its yellow siding and white shutters looked freshly painted. Jutting from the front lawn, an Apartment For Rent sign beckoned. She checked the address. Apparently, the apartment was in the house. She hadn't expected that, but she liked the idea. It would be like having a real home of her own, rather than a little cell in a huge apartment complex like she'd had in Boulder.

A wide front porch was graced by four rocking chairs and a glider. "Hey, Cody," she said as she pushed the stroller up the walk. "I think this is it."

She left the stroller on the sidewalk and carried Cody onto the porch with her. The window on her left was open, and music— well, sounds, really—trickled from the house inside. It sounded like a waterfall or maybe the ocean. She could hear the cawing of seagulls in the background.

She knocked on the door, and after a moment, a woman opened it.

"Hi." The woman smiled. She was partly in shadow, but she looked young, maybe in her thirties, and she glanced at her watch. "Are you here for an appointment?"

Maybe she should have called first. "No, I'm sorry," she said. "I guess I should have called. But I'm very interested in seeing the apartment you have for rent."

"Oh!" The woman laughed and stepped out onto the porch, and the fine lines around her eyes and mouth came into view. She was older than she had first appeared. Her long brown hair was subtly streaked with gray. "Forgive me," she said. "I thought you were a new client of mine. I'm a massage therapist and I—" She shook her head. "Sorry. So you're here about the apartments?"

Kim nodded.

The woman looked hesitantly at Cody. "I'm not sure about a baby," she said, but she reached out and stroked the back of her fingers down Cody's cheek and the little boy smiled. Kim had the feeling the battle was over before it had even begun.

"He's good-natured," Kim said. "Quiet."

"It's just the two of you?"

"Yes. My husband and I are getting a divorce and he got the house."

She knew immediately that she'd spoken the magic words.

"Oh, I know what *that's* like," the woman said. "Come in."

Kim stepped into a foyer. On her right was a table with a huge vase of daisies, and ahead of her, a long flight of stairs leading to the second story. To her left, a door stood ajar, and she could see inside to a cramped, but comfortable-looking, living room. A sweet, subtly floral scent emanated from the room.

"It smells good in here," she said, shifting Cody to her other hip.

"I use aromatherapy with my clients," the woman said by way of explanation.

Kim nodded as though aromatherapy were an ordinary part of her life as well.

"My name is Ellen King," the woman said. "I live on the ground floor, and I just turned the upstairs into two apartments. Neither is rented out yet. This was the house my husband and I lived in until *our* divorce."

"Oh," Kim said. "My name's Kim Stratton, and this is Cody. That's great you could keep the house."

"Well, it's pretty tight. But I think with the rent from the upstairs, I'll make it." She started up the stairs with Kim and Cody close behind her.

"Do you work at home?" Kim asked. She wasn't crazy about the idea of Ellen's clients coming and going. The fewer people around her the better.

"Uh huh."

There were two doors at the top of the stairs, one on either side of the small landing. Ellen unlocked the door on the left.

As soon as Kim stepped inside, she knew she wanted the apartment. The rooms had all the charm of an older home, with high ceilings and walls set at odd angles to one another. Yet despite their obvious age, the rooms were clean and fresh and sunny. The living room was spacious and was furnished with a couch and two chairs and even a small television set on a table in the corner. At the opposite end of the room stood an old oak table and four chairs. The kitchen was tiny, but usable, and the bedroom held a full-sized bed, a dresser, and just enough extra space for a crib.

She felt Ellen's eyes on her as she explored the apartment. From the two windows in the living room, and one of the windows in the bedroom, she could see the river in the distance.

"I would really love to live here," she said finally.

Ellen nodded. "Great!" she said. "Come downstairs and I'll get the paperwork. And I'll need to get some credit references from you."

"Oh," Kim said, flustered. She should have expected as much. She was tempted to tell Ellen she'd had a sudden change of heart about the apartment, but realized she would encounter the problem of a credit check no matter where she went. Ellen might be her only chance.

"I'm just starting to build up my own credit," she said. "Everything was in my husband's name."

Ellen wrinkled her nose. "Oh, nothing like adding insult to injury," she said. "I learned my lesson there. If I ever get married again, I'm keeping everything in my own name." Ellen looked thoughtfully out the window. "Well, let's approach this from a different angle, then. Where do you work?"

"I'm not working at the moment." She laughed nervously. "I must sound really pathetic! I was working in a bank, but I plan to take in word processing jobs." She couldn't believe she'd told the first person she met that she'd worked in a bank. "I want to work at home so I can be with Cody."

Ellen looked disappointed. "I really can't rent to you if you have no income."

"Well, I get child support," she lied. "And I'm very ambitious. I expect I'll have a good income very soon. Plus, I can give you two months rent, right now. If I'm not making enough money to handle the rent by the end of next month, you can kick me out." She felt her cheeks flaming with lies and embarrassment.

"All right," Ellen said. "I'll write up a lease for just the two months, and we'll try it out."

"Thank you so much, Ellen. I can understand your reluctance, but it'll work out. Honest."

She followed her new landlady out the apartment door to the landing.

"Where did you and your husband live?" Ellen asked as they walked down the stairs.

"New Jersey." She hoped Ellen didn't need any more specific information than that. What was the capital of New Jersey? "Near Trenton," she added. She thought about the Missouri plates on her car, and hoped they had gone unnoticed.

"What brought you down here?"

"Oh, I have some family in Maryland. But I really don't want to lean on them. I want to make it on my own."

"I know the feeling well." Making a right at the bottom of the stairs, Ellen led her into her own living room. She walked over to a roll top desk in the corner and took a few sheets of paper from a folder in one of its drawers. "Have a seat." She pointed to the sofa and Kim sat down. Cody squirmed to get out of her lap, but she kept a firm grip on him. The floral scent was strong in there, and the ocean music began to calm her nerves. She could see past the open door to the next room, where a massage table was draped in white sheets.

"All right," Ellen said as she wrote something on the lease. "I've changed it to two months." She handed the papers to Kim, who dared to put Cody on the sofa long enough for her to read the lease, sign it, and count out nine hundred dollars. She handed the money to Ellen.

"Thanks, Ellen. Can I move in right away?"

"Sure." Ellen looked surprised, but not displeased. "The sooner the better. Do you have someone to help you move?"

"No, but I don't need any help. I just have a few things, really. I want to start fresh."

"Sounds rough." Ellen handed her a set of keys. "This one's for the front door, and this one's for your apartment," she said.

She stood up, lifting Cody into her arms, and walked with Ellen out to the porch. "Can you suggest where I can go to buy a few things?" she asked. "A crib and linens and such?"

"Don't you even have a crib?"

"No. He's keeping it for when Cody visits." She was getting in deeper by the minute. "He gave me money to buy a new one, but I'd like to keep the cost low."

"Your best bet is the mall on Route Fifty." Ellen gave her directions, and Kim thanked her and walked down the steps to put Cody back in his stroller.

Once she was back on the street, she let it all sink in. She was going to live in Annapolis. Someone else's life in someone else's town. She'd made her decision in a split second based on the quaintness of the streets and the smell of the air. She hoped there would be enough word processing work to let her pay the rent when the two months were up.

She looked up at the house again, at the windows of her apartment, then shifted her eyes to the windows on the right side of the second story. She hoped it was a while before Ellen was able to rent out that other apartment. She didn't want to have to answer another person's questions, at least not yet. She'd already gotten herself far too tangled up in lies.

She did not even need the map to help her find her way back to the dock and her car. She took herself on a cautious shopping spree, buying only what she needed, and buying cheap. She bought a crib and a small, portable playpen, sheets and towels, pots and pans and dishes, and loads of child-proof locks for the cabinets. A couple of books for Cody. He needed some toys, too, but she'd noticed a few garage sales listed in the paper. Most of them were only being held that day, Saturday, but there were two listed for Sunday, and one of them promised toys. She'd wait until then. She had to be careful with her money. She would need to buy a fairly good computer and printer if she wanted to earn a living doing word processing. Her final purchase was a radio, and this she splurged on. When she heard Linc's voice the following night, she wanted to hear it clearly.

She picked up a few groceries on the way back to her apartment. She would save the big shopping for the following day. There was no sign of Ellen, which was just as well. She didn't want her landlady to feel as though she had to help her cart things up to her apartment, and she didn't want to answer any more questions.

She carried the playpen up the stairs first so she had a safe place for Cody while she worked. Then she hauled the rest of her purchases and belongings up the stairs, and by the time she'd gotten everything, including the still-boxed crib, into the apartment, she was exhausted.

She fed Cody, then laid him down on her own freshly made bed while she worked on the crib. She had it up but still unmade when she fell into bed herself, and she didn't open her eyes again until morning.

Sunday was filled with grocery shopping, as well as a toy, book, and clothes buying spree at one of the garage sales. In the afternoon, she and Cody discovered a nearby park and its colorful plastic playground, and they relaxed there for over an hour. But Kim knew all her activity was a preamble to that evening, when she would be able to hear Linc's show. She'd had a moment's panic when she'd first seen the radio schedule in that morning's paper. Linc's show was syndicated, but she knew there were a few parts of the country it didn't reach. It hadn't occurred to her that she might have settled in an area where she wouldn't be able to hear it. But then she found it on the public broadcasting station, playing as it did everywhere else in the country, from eight to ten on Sunday nights. The thought of hearing his voice again after these few lonely days was overwhelming. It pervaded her thinking in the park, and at the garage sale, and during every other waking moment of that day. It intruded on her newfound sense of peace as she settled Cody and his monkey into his crib, and later, as she sat on the comfortable old sofa in her new living room, looking out at the river, waiting for eight o'clock to roll around.

At eight o'clock, the strains of Paul Simon's "Song for the Asking" filled the room. Linc always opened his show with that song, and the pain of hearing the familiar, simple, haunting music was more than she had expected. She lay down on the sofa and stared at the cracked ceiling, not bothering to fight the tears that had been close to the surface all day long. He had undoubtedly taped this show on Wednesday, as he always did. She doubted that anyone had realized she was missing by then. They wouldn't have figured it out until Jim came to pick up Cody that afternoon. Then would Jim have called Linc? Or would Linc have already tried to call her and become concerned when he couldn't reach her? What on earth did he think when he realized she was gone? *Don't be angry with me, Linc.*

She remembered when they were kids, and she'd run away. Linc always knew he could find her in that little room above his garage. He would talk her into going home, even though that was not always wise. Linc finally discovered that after the last time, but he figured it out a little too late.

"Good evening," Linc said from the radio, once the song had ended. Even though he taped his show in the middle of the day, in the middle of the week, he always sounded as if he were right there with you on Sunday night.

"Tonight we're going to focus on Joni Mitchell," he continued. He went on to give a little history about Joni Mitchell, and Kim was completely certain that he had known nothing about her disappearance at the time he taped the show. He was his usual soft-spoken, untroubled self, completely ignorant of what she'd done.

He played music by Joni Mitchell, interspersed with a few other songs, including "Suzanne." She nearly laughed out loud when she heard the first line: "Suzanne takes you down to her place near the river." Prophetic, she thought. She'd had no idea when she'd requested the song that she would be living in just such a place by the time she heard it.

The smile faded from her face, though, as Linc's show continued, and reality sank in.

*Forever. You've left him forever.*

*You are completely alone with a baby to raise and not a soul who
knows you, and you'll never meet another person in your entire life
with whom you can be completely honest about who you are. You've
never made it on your own before. What makes you think you can
do it now?*

Jim had destroyed whatever faith she'd had in herself. She
could hear him telling her, in a kind, almost fatherly voice, that
going back to school as an art major made no sense. "How do you
know you even have any talent?" he asked her.

"I used to," she'd said, although she had no proof of that. All
her artwork had been destroyed.

"I've never seen you draw a single thing."

He was right. After her father died, she seemed to have lost all
motivation. But the interest was still there.

"And besides, it makes a hell of a lot more sense financially for
me to go to law school before you go back to school yourself," he
said. Jim viewed studying art as a waste of time. "And even if you
could get a job as an artist, there's no money in it." He told her to
stick with banking. She'd have a chance for growth in banking, he
said. For promotions.

Linc was talking about Joni Mitchell's anger toward men in her
early work. "She could be kind of cruel with her words," Linc said,
"but you had to listen hard to hear it." He began to play "I Had a
King," and Kim stood up. There was a half-hour left of his show,
but she turned the radio off. She'd thought it would comfort her to
be able to hear him. But this had been torture, not comfort.

*What have I done?* The tiniest seed of regret edged its way into
her mind. But she walked into her bedroom and leaned over
Cody's crib. He was lying on his side, his monkey nestled under his
arm. He'd been so good on the long trip across the country, and
now she was looking down at the face of an angel. The regret
melted instantly away. She had her child with her. He was very
young; he would never remember the confusion and heartache of
the past few days. He would only remember the life she made for
him from this day forward. She would make it a good life.

8

$\mathcal{P}$eggy grabbed Jim's arm as soon as he came in the door Monday evening.

"I've been trying to reach you all day," she said. "I got loads of information this morning."

"I'm sorry." He kissed her. "I was in court all morning and in meetings all afternoon. Let me change out of my suit and you can tell me what you found out."

She watched him climb the stairs to their bedroom, then walked into the kitchen to gather the brochures and booklets and notes from the table. She carried them into the living room and sat down on the sofa to wait for him.

It had been a painful few days. She didn't dare screen her phone calls in case someone was calling with news about Susanna or Tyler, but that meant she was taking dozens of cheerful calls from well-meaning friends, all of whom wanted to know how she was doing as a new mother. She told each of them what had happened, quickly and without embellishment, and let them know she didn't have time to talk just then. Trying to find Tyler had become her full-time job. She'd provided identifying information about Susanna and Tyler to the missing children's hotline and she'd pushed the police to obtain search warrants for Susanna's bank records. She'd collected photos and made posters. As long as she kept busy, she was okay.

Jim finally came downstairs and sat next to her on the sofa.

"First of all," Peggy said, "I spoke with Bill Anderson—you know, the private investigator Detective Rausch suggested?"

Jim frowned. "I thought we were going to let the police see what they could come up with first."

"I know, but I just wanted to talk with this guy. See what he had to say about the situation, in case we need him later. I wanted to lay the groundwork." What she really wanted was to hire him right that minute, but she knew Jim didn't think it would be necessary.

"So what did he say?"

"He says we should have a press conference immediately. Get the word out about the kidnapping."

Jim nodded. "I agree."

"We should try to get as much media attention as we possibly can. And we should offer a cash reward to anyone with information leading to Tyler's safe recovery."

"Hmm." Jim looked up at the ceiling. "Did he suggest an amount?"

"Not really, except that it should be substantial. I was thinking twenty thousand."

Jim's eyes widened. "I was thinking more like ten."

She'd guessed as much. She and Jim rarely saw eye to eye on money. "Someone might be more willing to take a risk for twenty than they would for ten," she said.

"Well, we can decide on an amount later," Jim said. "What else did you find out?"

She pulled a thick booklet from the pile in her lap. "The National Center for Missing and Exploited Children sent this to me. It describes what we need to do, step by step."

Jim smiled at her and took her hand. "I think we're already doing everything we possibly can, hon."

"There's a lot more we can do," she said. "To begin with, we need to badger people. The police, this national center." She held up the booklet. "I spoke with a case manager there. He's ours. He'll stick with us until Tyler's found. He said that they send out these little postcards with the pictures of children and their abductors on them to thousands of households. They get a really good response from them."

"And can they do that for Tyler?"

"In the future, maybe," she said. "They have a big back-up, and of course the kids who have been taken by nonfamily members get priority. But we can be a little pushier than we have been. I'm going to call this guy every day until we get Tyler back."

"Don't become a thorn in his side, though."

"I won't." She set the booklet aside and looked at the notes she'd taken while talking on the phone that morning. They covered two sheets of legal paper. "I spoke with Detective Rausch," she said. "Susanna is now classified as a felon. They have a warrant for her arrest."

Jim let go of her hand to comb his fingers through his hair. "This is getting ugly," he said.

"Yes, it's ugly. But what she did is serious. The police aren't going to bother with her if we act as though it's no big deal."

"You're probably right."

"Bill—the PI—suggested we alert doctors and hospitals, since Tyler is very recognizable by his surgical scar and the fact that he has a medical problem. But it's expensive to send out those sorts of announcements."

"Well, do they work?"

"I talked to Ron. He said it will work if it hits the right doctor at the right moment." Actually, her brother had said that most doctors would end up filing the flyer away or throwing it in the trash. But she didn't want to paint such a negative picture for Jim. They needed to do all they could to maximize their chances of having Tyler found.

"I called that TV show, *Missing Persons*."

Jim laughed.

"Don't laugh. This is the sort of thing they handle. It's just that you have to call them when they're planning a show about parental kidnappings, which won't be for a while. But I left them my name and number." Although she prayed they would never need it. Surely this would all be resolved soon.

"I really like Detective Rausch," she continued. "He understands that a custody violation is every bit as serious as a kidnapping."

"Is the FBI going to get involved?"

"Not unless there's evidence that Susanna crossed state lines. And even then, Detective Rausch said they're not thrilled with the prospect of putting time into a parental kidnapping case. But now that Susanna's a felon, if they *do* figure out that she crossed state lines, the FBI will go after her for unlawful flight to avoid prosecution." Peggy had become an instant expert in parental kidnapping.

"I think it's Sebastian they should be going after," Jim said. "They need to rake him over the coals. I'm sure he knows more than he's saying."

"Rausch talked to him today. He made Linc go into the station for the interview, thinking it would be better if he were not on his home turf, but he said he didn't get anywhere with him."

"I would guess that Linc's an old pro at being interviewed by the police," Jim scoffed. "What about tapping his phone?"

"Rausch said it's too expensive and the taps have to be manned twenty-four hours a day. But they *are* getting a search warrant so they can look at his phone records to see who he's called and who he's received calls from. That'll cover his faxes, too. And they can check his bank records to see if he took out a lot of money to help her get away or if he's taking out money to send to her. Also, the police have checked Susanna's bank records."

Jim raised his eyebrows. "And?"

"And she withdrew eight thousand dollars over the last few weeks, bit by bit."

"Phew. Still, that won't get her too far for too long."

Peggy laughed. "Susanna's more frugal than you are," she said. Actually, Susanna could probably last a lot longer on eight thousand dollars than either she or Jim could.

She'd reached the end of her stack of information. With a sigh, she leaned her head against Jim's shoulder and rested her hand on his chest. "Does it surprise you that she did this?" she asked. "I mean, you always said Susanna lacked ambition. Get up and go. This took quite a bit of get up and go, I'd say."

"Well, I don't know about that," Jim said. "If you ask me, this fiasco is simply the work of an unstable mind, and that she definitely has. I have to admit, though, that I never thought of her as much of a fighter. Mostly, I *am* surprised that she hasn't screwed up and gotten caught yet." He let out a long sigh. "I should have listened to my father."

Peggy understood what he was talking about. Long ago, Jim's father had tried to dissuade him from marrying Susanna. "She'll hold you back," he'd warned him. Jim's family may have had little money, but they had plenty of pride, and ambition to spare. They didn't want someone like Susanna to pull them down.

Jim moved forward on the sofa, turning to look at her, and she saw love in his eyes. "I'm sorry this happened, Peg," he said. "It seemed for a while as though everything was going to work out just the way we wanted."

"I know."

He touched her cheek. "You're so beautiful," he said. "I hate seeing that sad look on your face."

"I'm okay." She smiled at him.

Jim leaned away from her and stretched. "Why don't we have some dinner?" he suggested. "We can talk more about this later. Maybe in bed?" He looked hopeful, and she felt torn between guilt and annoyance. Her libido had disappeared. Nothing like losing your baby to kill desire. Jim had wanted to make love this past weekend, too, and she'd put him off. She didn't know how he could even think about sex with everything else going on.

She looked down at the pile of information on her lap. "Jim, I feel like I'm doing this all on my own."

"Doing what?" he asked. "You mean, getting the information on finding Tyler?"

She nodded.

"Oh, I'm sorry, Peg." He put his arm around her and pulled her against him again. "It's just that you've got this time off, and I'm working like a dog. I do appreciate all you're doing, though. You let me know how I can help, okay?"

Now that he'd offered, she wasn't sure what she could suggest. He was right. She had the time to do this. He didn't. She simply didn't like the sense of being alone in the battle. She'd talked to Nancy Curry about the situation the other night.

"Men just have different ways of handling disappointment," Nancy had reassured her. "They can't deal with it directly, so they have to block it out with work or sex or whatever they can find to keep their minds off it." That fit Jim, all right.

"What I would really like," Peggy said, "is your permission to hire the PI."

Jim sighed. "If you honestly think it would help, go ahead."

She smiled. "Thank you." She leaned forward to kiss him, and he didn't let her go. She tried to let her lips linger on his, but all she could think about was making the call to Bill Anderson.

Jim shook his head, pulling away from her with a smile. "You've got one thing on your mind, don't you, and it's not going to bed with your husband."

He was right. She kissed him again, told him she loved him, then went into the kitchen to make the call.

ill Anderson leaned forward on the sofa, notepad on his knee, and Linc noticed that the private investigator was keeping one wary eye on Sam. The dog, who was now lying at Linc's feet, had let out a wise and knowing growl when Anderson walked in the door, and Linc had had a hard time keeping a straight face.

"So," Anderson said, "when was the last time you saw her?"

Everyone's favorite question. "I've already answered—"

"I know. For the police. But not for me. So bear with me, all right?"

Linc sighed and gave in. Bill Anderson was small and a little too slick in his three-piece suit, and he was suffering from an upper respiratory infection, sniffing grotesquely every few seconds or so.

"I last saw her in my car after the judge's decision," he said. "We picked up Tyler from day care and I drove them home."

"And what did you talk about?"

"I don't remember," he answered honestly. "We were both pretty depressed."

"Did you go into the house with her?"

"No. I went home. We spoke again on the phone that night. She sounded all right. She certainly didn't say anything about leaving." He didn't mention how odd it was that she hadn't wanted him around that evening.

"Had she ever mentioned to you places she might like to visit?" Bill asked.

Linc hardly heard the question. His mind was on his knapsack, where a fresh pack of Marlboros was waiting for him. Grace and Valerie were in the house, though. He didn't dare light up with the two of them there. He tried to bring his focus back to the investigator's question.

"Sorry," he said. "What did you say?"

Anderson repeated his question.

"Contrary to what her ex-husband might have told you," Linc answered, "Susanna is not stupid. She wouldn't try to hide out someplace she'd told people she wanted to go."

"Well, tell me anyway." Bill Anderson wore a patronizing smirk.

"She hadn't traveled much," Linc said. "I think the only place she'd ever been outside of Colorado was California. She said she'd like to go to Hawaii one day. And Europe. She was intrigued by Italy, because she wanted to see all the old artwork." He hoped that would be enough to keep the little guy happy.

From behind the closed kitchen doors, he could smell the aroma of the chicken soup Grace and Valerie were making. He'd found the women waiting on his doorstep when he got home from teaching his class at the university that afternoon. They were going to nurse him "back to mental health," they insisted. As soon as Bill Anderson's car pulled up, though, Linc had shoved his friends into the kitchen and told them to stay there. He didn't want Anderson badgering them, too.

"Any family you know of in other parts of the country? Hers, or possibly yours?" Bill Anderson sniffed again, and Linc considered getting the box of tissues from the bathroom and shoving it in his lap.

"I have a few cousins in Colorado Springs," he said, "but Susanna really doesn't know them, and she has no family herself. Besides, she wouldn't go someplace where people knew her."

Bill jotted something down on his notepad. Sam rose to a seated position, resting his big black head on Linc's knee and riveting his dark eyes on the PI, who recoiled slightly under his gaze.

"What about her mother?" Bill asked. "Do you know where she is?"

"She hasn't seen her mother since she was a teenager." Linc scratched the dog behind his ears. "And I'm certain Susanna has no idea where she lives. Even if she knew, she would never turn to her for help." His own mother would have been a more likely choice, but she had died two years ago.

"Any other name she might go by?"

He shook his head. He had thought about that himself. What name would she use if she decided to change hers?

"How about her maiden name?"

"No. She hated the name Miller, but she hated Wood even worse."

"What was her understanding of Tyler's medical condition?" Bill asked.

"She understood it completely."

"Do you think Tyler's in danger?"

"Not in the least." Maybe he could sneak a cigarette after the PI left and before Grace and Valerie realized he was alone. He needed to check the faxes in his studio. He could lock the door, and—

"What special skills did she have?"

"Special skills?" Linc was unable to stop his quick smile, and he could have kicked himself when Bill Anderson gave him a knowing grin in return. He was disgusted with himself for allowing this man a personal glimpse into his relationship with Susanna.

"Besides *those* skills," Anderson said.

Linc ignored him. "She's great with children," he said. "She's a terrific mother."

"Yeah, yeah." Bill waved a bored hand through the air. "Tell it to the judge."

"She's nurturing and compassionate and very sensitive to other people."

"Uh huh."

"She's artistic."

Bill's dark eyes narrowed to slits. "Artistic? Her husband didn't say anything about that."

"That's because her husband didn't care. He wanted her to waste her talent working in a bank so he could go to law school and find himself a lawyer to marry."

"Well, aren't we bitter?" Bill smirked again. "What else can you tell me that I haven't already heard from her husband?"

"She's smart. I'm sure you didn't hear that."

"Do you think her taking off like this was smart?"

"Do you want me to help locate her, or do you want me to get into a philosophical and moral discussion about the wisdom of her leaving?" he asked. "Because I have plenty to say on that topic."

"Forget I asked."

"She can type like a bat outta hell. She's good with numbers, with money."

"Yeah. I spoke to her supervisor at the bank," Bill said.

Sam stood up and walked over to the PI, tail wagging slowly, waiting for a pat. Bill raised his hands into the air. "You wanna call your dog off?" he asked.

Linc had to laugh. "Come here, Sam." He reached out his hand, and Sam returned to lay at his feet once again, while Bill slowly lowered his hands to his lap.

"Besides you and her coworkers at the bank, did she have any other good friends around here?"

"Just Grace Talbot and Valerie Diehl."

"Oh, yeah. The lesbos."

Linc rolled his eyes.

Bill flipped through his notes. "Let's see. Talbot works in the library at the university, and Diehl teaches psychology. She's a shrink, right?"

"That's right." *And they're also in my kitchen right this minute, but I'll be damned if I'm letting you talk to them.*

"Any chance Miller could have taken off with another woman?" Bill asked.

That did it. "I think you've worn out your welcome, friend," Linc said, standing up. "I don't know what more I can tell you."

Bill Anderson stood up himself. "If you *honestly* don't know where she is and whether she's safe or whatever, I would think you'd want her found," he said.

"Look," Linc said, "I'm not hiding anything from you. Susanna was smart enough to leave me in the dark too." And he had not yet forgiven her for it.

He and Sam walked Bill Anderson to the door and watched as the investigator negotiated the long, winding driveway in his aging Mercedes. Back in the living room, Linc looked down the hall toward his studio. Not enough time for a cigarette. He walked instead into the kitchen, where Grace was stirring the soup and Valerie was pulling dinner rolls from the oven.

"God, what a jerk," Linc said.

Grace shoved a shock of short, prematurely white-gray hair behind her ear as she looked up from the stove. "Put him out of your mind," she said. "Just sit down and let us lesbos take care of you."

He groaned. "You could hear him?"

"He sounds like an asshole." Valerie set a basket of the rolls on the table along with a plastic tub of margarine. She took Linc's arm and sat him down at the head of the big oak table.

"You guys are going to join me, I hope," Linc asked.

"Absolutely." Grace carried two bowls of soup to the table, and sat down next to him. Valerie joined them a moment later with her own steaming bowl.

"Smells great," Linc said, dipping his spoon into the soup. It was very thick, more of a stew, and he suddenly realized he was hungry. "He might want to talk with you two," he said after he'd eaten a bit. "I told him you were friends of hers."

"Let him," Grace said. "I doubt we'd be able to help him much." Grace was the head of the American Studies section of the university library. Linc had met her when he'd donated part of his American music collection to the library, and their friendship had been quick to develop. She was outspoken, loud-voiced. It was hard to believe she was a librarian.

Valerie, on the other hand, was quiet and analytical. The two women were the same height and build, and they wore the same hairstyle, but Valerie's hair was as black as Grace's was white. Linc thought they looked terrific together. Salt and pepper shakers.

Grace leaned over and sniffed the shoulder of his shirt. "You're smoking again!" she accused.

He sniffed his shirt himself, taking a deep breath of stale tobacco smell. "I was in a smoky restaurant for lunch," he lied.

"Oh, Linc," Grace said. "You're going down the tubes."

"Give him a break," Valerie said. "He's endured a terrible blow. Let him regress a little."

"Yeah, let me regress." He offered Grace a smile, but she turned away in what he hoped was mock disgust.

"I think you should go out with Val and me tonight," she said. "We can do a movie. Okay?"

He shook his head. "No, I have to tape the show tomorrow morning, and I haven't put it together yet. I haven't even checked my faxes yet." Most of the musical requests for his show came in by fax these days.

"Do you think Susanna can hear the show?" Valerie asked.

"Yeah, actually I do." He swallowed a spoonful of soup. "Before she left, she asked me if I'd play 'Suzanne' for her, so she must have been thinking she would hear it, wherever she was. I've been trying to come up with some way to get a message to her through the show. I'd just like to say hello somehow, but I'm afraid the cops, and this PI, and who knows who else, are going to be listening pretty carefully. They seem certain I'm in on her escape somehow. They even have a search warrant to check on who I make phone calls to and who I get them from. And they can get a list of the return addresses on my mail from the post office."

"Big Brother," Valerie said. "Why don't you play 'Suzanne' for her every week, then? She'll know it's your way of keeping in touch with her."

"Every week." He groaned. "I don't want to think about her being gone that long."

"So, you're hoping they find her, huh?" Grace asked.

He rested his spoon in his empty bowl. "I want her back," he said, "but not if she doesn't want to be here." It still hurt to think that she could leave him with such ease.

He helped the women clean up after dinner, then disappeared into his studio to read his faxes—and smoke a cigarette—while they watched TV in his family room. He felt like he was being baby-sat, but it didn't bother him. It was after ten when Grace knocked on his studio door.

"Come into the family room," she said. "Hurry!"

He walked into the family room to see Peggy and Jim on the television.

"It's a press conference," Grace said.

Linc picked up the remote from the coffee table to turn up the sound. "What have they said so far?" He sat down on the floor next to Grace.

"Nothing. The announcer's been—"

"Sh!" Linc interrupted her as Jim opened his mouth to speak.

"We have reason to believe that Susanna Miller has kidnapped our son, Tyler," Jim said.

Linc let out his breath from between clenched teeth. Until now, no one had introduced the concept of Susanna having kidnapped Tyler. All he'd heard in the news reports was that she and the boy were missing.

Jim and Peggy looked ashen-faced in the flashing lights of the cameras.

"Tyler has a very serious heart condition," Jim continued, "and we are extremely concerned that he be returned home to get the medical care he needs. Susanna Miller has a history of mental illness—"

Linc pounded his hand on his knee. "What crap," he said. He missed whatever Jim said next.

"Please," Jim continued. "We are offering a twenty thousand dollar reward to anyone who can give us information leading to the safe return of Susanna and Tyler Miller."

A photograph of Susanna and Tyler appeared on the screen, along with an 800-number. The picture was one Linc had taken of the two of them at the park, Susanna holding Tyler on her lap at the top of a sliding board. The photograph had been framed and sitting on top of the television in her apartment. The police must have taken it, and he was glad he'd thought to rescue her photograph albums.

He muted the sound on the TV when the newscaster moved on to his next story.

"Mental illness," he said. His face felt hot and he knew that telltale patches of red were standing out on his cheeks, as they always did when he was angry or upset. "She was depressed, you bastard," he said to the TV. "She never would have been in that hospital if it hadn't been for you."

"Down, boy," Grace put her hand on his arm.

"Let him get it out," Valerie argued. She was always one for encouraging people to express their emotions.

"I'm sure *he'd* be the picture of mental health if he walked in on pretty Peggy-O screwing another guy," Linc said.

"You tell him!" Valerie said.

"He makes her sound deranged. I just hope Susanna's far enough away that she can't see Peggy and Jim begging for the safe return of 'their' baby on TV. Christ."

"I don't get Peggy." Grace leaned back on her elbows. "I mean, she could write her own ticket as far as a job goes, and she's married to one of those lean, mean money-hungry lawyers, but she works at Legal Aid. Does that make sense?"

He shrugged, not wanting to talk about Peggy. It bothered him to think she might have one or two noble bones in her body. He had no room to feel sympathy for her when his mind was fixed on Susanna.

"Peggy's not worth the energy it would take to figure her out. It's Susanna I'm concerned about." He shook his head. "I'm really mad at her right now."

"Of course you are," Valerie agreed.

"She shouldn't have run away," he said. "She did it so much as a kid that it's her natural response to a problem. I'd always find her and drag her home. And then you know what would happen?"

"What?" Grace asked.

"She'd get beaten up. I'd take her home and the bastard—her father—would beat the shit out of her." Until the last time he brought her home, at least, when Linc put a permanent end to the beatings. But he didn't want to get into that now. Grace and Valerie knew he'd killed Susanna's father. Everyone knew it, but no one, not even these two close friends, ever dared to question him about it.

"Men are scum," Valerie said.

"Thanks," he said sarcastically. "That helps."

"You are the rare exception to the rule." Grace got to her feet. "Are you all right to be left alone?" she asked him.

"Hallelujah." He looked up at her from his seat on the floor. "You two are leaving and I can finally light up."

"Like you haven't been smoking in your studio all night," Valerie said. "Call us if you hear anything, okay?"

He didn't bother walking them to the door. Nor did he really feel like smoking. Instead, he lay down on the floor, his head on a throw pillow, and watched the muted TV until he fell asleep.

# 10

Ellen and one of her massage clients were talking on the front porch, and Kim was trapped in her apartment. She sat on the sofa, staring out the front window at the branches of the maple tree. She was gutless. Why didn't she simply walk past the two women, nod hello, get in her car and drive to the computer store as she'd been planning to do this morning? It wasn't Ellen she feared. It was the stranger with her. She trusted no one. The fewer people she had to meet, the better off she would be.

Everyone looked suspicious to her lately. She'd taken at least one long walk every day since her arrival on Sunday, pushing Cody in his stroller over the brick sidewalks and trying not to look as uneasy in public as she felt. All eyes in town seemed to be trained on her and her son, and she worked at being inconspicuous. It was a lonely existence she was carving out for herself. She had not thought about how unbearable self-imposed isolation could be.

Cody looked up at her from his seat on the floor, annoyance in his face. She didn't blame him. She'd put his sweater on him in preparation for going outside, and then made him sit in it for ten minutes in the too-warm apartment.

"We'll give them five more minutes, Cody," she said, glancing toward her door. She'd left it open so she would know when Ellen and her client finally decided to come into the house. "If they haven't left the porch by then, we'll do it anyhow. What's the worst that could happen?"

The worst that could happen was entirely too easy for her to imagine. Maybe Ellen's client down there on the porch was not a bona-fide client at all. Maybe she had called Ellen to make an appointment for a massage, hiding the fact that she was, in reality, a private investigator hired by Jim. What better way to worm her way into Kim's new home than through Ellen? Jim had no doubt hired someone to help him locate her. It would be clever of him to hire a woman.

She'd kept busy the past few days, afraid to allow herself too much idle time for thinking. The day before, she'd gotten a phone number and car insurance in her new name, along with a new driver's license, new plates for her car, and a checking account. Kim Stratton existed now. Once you existed on paper, you were real. She practiced her new signature, giving all the letters a backward slant, hoping that even an expert would not be able to equate Kim Stratton's signature to that of Susanna Miller. She stared at the driver's license for hours, studying the picture of the fair-skinned, copper-haired stranger next to the stranger's name. She thought again of the baby in the grave back in Boulder. She'd stolen that baby's life, and she felt a keen responsibility to make it a life worth living.

She'd found the library the day before, a short drive from the center of town. She'd walked inside, pushing Cody in the stroller. He was quiet for as long as it took her to study the map of New Jersey and pick out a little suburb of Trenton as the place she would have lived with her mythical husband, in case anyone ever asked her to get more specific. Then she turned to the Maryland map. Where would her imaginary family, the people she'd moved to Annapolis to be near, live? She selected Bowie, not too close, yet not too far. She began thinking about that family. There was warmth and love between its members. She had sisters, she decided, several of them. And brothers who had teased her and protected her as she was growing up. The fabricated family became so vivid and real in her mind that she scared herself. This was the happy, normal family she'd always wanted, the family she'd thought she could create with Jim.

Her attention was drawn back to the maple tree outside her apartment window as a squirrel suddenly hopped onto a branch, only a couple of feet from where Kim was sitting.

"Cody," she whispered, leaning toward her son.

He crawled to her and she lifted him onto her lap and pointed at the squirrel. He started to let out one of his squeals of delight.

"Sh," she whispered. "Don't scare him away."

The squirrel was nibbling on something, its jaw working furiously and its tail jerking back and forth, and Kim was jarred by a sudden memory. She'd been seven or eight years old, peeking into her parents' bedroom from behind their slightly open door. Her father was in the room, standing by the window, and he was dressed handsomely, although his tie was partly undone and a strand of blond hair fell over his forehead. A cigarette dangled from his lips and, as usual, an open bottle of whiskey rested on his night table.

Slowly, very slowly, he moved his hands toward the bottom of the window. Susanna watched in curiosity as he carefully removed the screen. Only then did she see what her father had been looking at through the open window. A few yards away, a fat gray squirrel sat on one of the branches of a tree. Her father never took his eyes off it as he quietly opened his night table drawer. He reached inside and pulled out a gun.

At first she thought it was a toy. Her eyes widened and she had to bite her lip to hold in her surprise. She had never seen a gun in their house before, had never even known her father possessed one. She watched as he raised the gun in front of his face and pointed it at the squirrel.

*It's a toy*, she told herself. *It has to be.*

She closed her eyes as he pulled the trigger and the sudden explosion made her yelp, but her father didn't seem to hear her. When she opened her eyes, the squirrel had disappeared, as had any remaining shred of trust in her father.

That was the first time she ran away. She'd thought of simply going next door, where Linc's mother, Geri, would hug her and rock her and reassure her that the squirrel had probably hopped to another branch at the last minute. But she knew that Geri would eventually make her go home, and so she ended up hiding in the little room above Linc and Geri's garage instead. Her parents never even realized she was gone. Could you call it running away if your parents didn't miss you?

She'd returned home after spending one night above the garage, but for weeks afterward, she avoided the part of the yard where the squirrel would have fallen. That way, she could continue to pretend it had found its way to safety.

A sudden burst of laughter slipped through her open apartment door, and she knew that Ellen and her client were finally inside the house. Ellen's door closed with a click, and Kim stood up, Cody still in her arms.

"We're on our way, Cody-boy," she said.

Downstairs, she pulled the stroller from the closet where Ellen was letting her store it and carried it onto the porch and down the front steps. She put it in the trunk of her car, then strapped Cody into his car seat before checking the directions Ellen had given her. Computer Wizard, the store was called. "Best prices on computers," Ellen had said, although she admitted she didn't own one herself. But she knew about the store through the grapevine. Ellen had her fingers on the pulse of Annapolis. She seemed to be the hub of a network that was both impressive and unnerving. It would be hard to hide much from Ellen King.

Kim drove out of town by a new route, stopping for a red light at a busy intersection. Cody pointed to the side of the bank building on the corner, and it was a minute before Kim understood what had caught his attention. There was another of the murals, only this one was unfinished, a work in progress. The painting was of a whimsical village, snow-covered, but only half there, and she wondered if one day she would stop at this corner to find the artist lost in his work.

Besides the painting of the tall ship with the billowing white sails, she had noticed several other murals during her walks through town. All of them had been painted by the same artist, Adam Soria, and all were identifiable by their clear, intense colors. She spotted them on the sides of buildings, some almost hidden from view, others out in the open, and she found herself walking longer and farther in an effort to discover more of them. Her favorite was a jungle scene with a circle of white birds in flight against a deep green backdrop of trees. In the lower right-hand corner, Adam Soria's name stood out in gold.

She'd studied the murals with fascination, admiring the artist's skill, and thinking about how rewarding it would be to have such a huge and public canvas on which to paint. She thought back to the smaller mural she'd painted on Cody's wall at home. What would her old landlord think when he discovered Noah's Ark in the baby's room? She used to worry that she'd never get her security deposit back on that apartment because of the painting. That worry seemed pretty laughable at this point.

What would Ellen say if Kim asked permission to paint on one of the walls of her new apartment? She'd better not ask until she could offer Ellen something more than two months rent.

She'd sat up late the night before, counting her money. She had forty-eight hundred left, and she knew the computer and printer were going to take an enormous bite out of that. There would probably be about eighteen hundred left after her purchases today. That would be all that stood between her and starvation. She would have to find work quickly.

Computer Wizard was an enormous building standing alone in an expansive parking lot. She knew very little about computers. She could operate the word processing program she'd learned at the bank and that was about it.

She put Cody in the stroller and walked resolutely across the parking lot. The salesman who greeted her at the door was no older than twenty. He reminded her of Jim when he was younger— perfectly groomed, a little too bright-eyed, and ready to set the world on fire.

"I'd like to buy a personal computer," she said. "I'll be using it primarily for word processing."

It was as if she'd pushed a button. He was instantly off and running, talking about megabytes and memory and serial ports and CD-ROMs, and she wished she were back in Boulder. There were loads of people in Boulder she could turn to for guidance in buying a computer, Linc being the obvious first choice.

When he paused for breath, she threw herself on his mercy. "I don't know about any of that stuff," she said. "You'll have to tell me what I need," she said.

"Well, why don't you take a look at what we've got?" he suggested. He began showing her computer after computer, until the machines turned into one massive pile of plastic in her mind. She had to admit, though, that these computers were a lot more fun than the one she'd used at work. The salesman let her play with a graphics program, and as she twisted shapes and curved lines and changed fonts, she got an idea for a brochure she could use to advertise her word processing business. This was going to be fun.

She finally settled on one of the computers. It came with everything she could ever imagine wanting, and then some. She forced the salesman to slow down his spiel and tell her in detail about the features. She made him tell her enough so that she no longer felt anxious when she touched the keys. Then it was only the price tag that gave her fear. If she bought this particular computer, she'd have very little left. What if Cody suddenly needed medical care and she had no money?

"I love it," she said, reluctantly taking her hands from the keys. "But I really can't afford it."

"Hmm," the salesman said. "Well, I think you're in luck."

She looked at him with hope. He was so slick that she doubted the veracity of anything he told her, but she badly wanted to be in luck.

"Look over here." He walked toward the register.

She followed him, pushing Cody, who was now asleep in the stroller. On the counter next to the register stood a computer very much like the one she'd been using, but this one had a large red label stuck on the monitor, and the price on the label was hundreds lower than any other price she'd seen.

"Is this the same model?" she asked.

"The very same," he said, his hand resting on the top of the monitor.

"Then why is it marked down?"

"Because it's an open box."

"What's that?"

"Someone bought it and then decided they didn't want it, for one reason or another. So they returned it, but we can't sell it as new, even though, in reality it *is* new." He winked at her as though that was their little secret. "But since we can't sell it as new, it becomes a real bargain. Plus, the guy that had it left a ton of software on it, so whoever buys it gets a bonus."

"Can I see what's on it?"

"Sure."

He turned it on, and she began perusing the various programs. There was the word processing program she was accustomed to using, as well as a financial program—it would be a while before she'd need *that*—and some games and a screen saver. Very tempting, but the "open box" concept worried her.

"It's nice," she said, "but why would the person bring it back? Something must be wrong with it."

"Oh, there could be a zillion reasons why someone would bring a computer back, none of them having to do with the quality of the product. As a matter of fact, I'm pretty sure this particular computer was just a loaner."

She eyed him suspiciously. He looked as though he was thinking fast.

"Yeah, that's it," he said. "I remember now. One of our customers brought in their own computer for repairs, but they needed one to use while theirs was being fixed. So we loaned him this one."

She didn't believe a word out of his mouth. It didn't matter, though. She wanted this computer. "Can I bring it back if I decide I don't like it?"

"Of course."

What was there to lose? "Okay then," she said. "I'll need a printer, too."

The salesman helped her pick out a printer, along with a simple graphics program, some paper, and few other supplies.

It wasn't until all her purchases had been loaded into her car that she noticed the large art supply store across the street. She stared at it for a moment, wondering if she were being given some sort of sign. First there were the murals, now a huge art store had suddenly popped up in front of her. Maybe it was time for her to start drawing again.

It was a challenge getting across the highway with the stroller, but she finally made it. She spent nearly an hour walking the aisles of the store, immersing herself in the scents and sensations that had meant so much to her as a teenager, and when she finally walked out the front door, she was carrying a sketch pad and a pencil set, the first she'd owned since she was sixteen years old.

She waited until Cody was in bed that evening before setting up the computer on the oak table in the dining area of her living room. She had never gotten a computer up and running on her own before, and she approached the task slowly and methodically. Everything worked as it was supposed to, and she was proud of herself for putting it all together without help from anyone. Still, she was worried. Why had the previous owner returned the computer? Would she learn what was wrong with it at the worst possible moment? She could see herself with a hard-won word processing job, a tight deadline, and a broken computer.

Not only had the previous owner of the computer loaded some of his own software on it, but he'd left a file on it as well, and she hoped he'd made a copy of it before turning the computer in. She opened the file, wondering if perhaps he had left his name on the document. Maybe she could call him to ask the real reason behind his returning the computer.

The document was a two-page list of names and addresses, tagged with curious information.

*Katherine Nabors, 448 Labrador Lane, Annapolis, 47, 2 children, 2 adults. September 27, 8:30 A.M., home.*

*Sellers, Sellers, and Wittaker, 5588 Duke of Gloucester Street, Annapolis, every damn day of the year: Use October 17, 2 P.M. (so all will be there).*

*Ryan Geary, 770 Pioneer Way, Annapolis, 51, elderly couple, November 13, 9 P.M.*

There was another page and a half of similar cryptic listings of individuals and a couple of businesses. Kim wanted to clear them off her computer, but she couldn't bring herself to delete them when they might still be needed by their creator.

Reluctantly, she called the store, but the salesman who had worked with her had already left for the night.

"Well, maybe you can help me," she said to the woman who answered the phone. "I bought an open box computer there this afternoon, and there's a file on it that obviously belonged to the person who had the computer before I did."

"Well, I'm sure if it was important they would have made a copy of it before they brought it in." The saleswoman sounded as if she didn't want to be bothered.

Kim wasn't so sure the woman was right. If the person had thought to copy the file, wouldn't they also have thought to erase it from the hard drive?

"Well, I was wondering if you might want to call that person to tell them that—"

"No, it's not necessary," the woman said. "It's your computer now. Go ahead and erase it."

Kim hung up the phone with a grimace. The store had made its sale. What did they care if some poor soul woke up tomorrow morning desperately needing this list of names? She copied the names to a floppy disk before erasing them from the hard drive, then she slipped the disk into her top dresser drawer so it wouldn't get mixed up with her own work. She couldn't remember if she'd given the woman at the store her phone number, but she wasn't about to call back. She couldn't afford to be that memorable in anyone's eyes.

It was midnight by the time she got to bed, and she lay there feeling the pain of her isolation. She wished she could call Linc to tell him she'd put together a computer entirely by herself, just as she'd wished she could tell him about every other new adventure she'd experienced this past week. But she couldn't. Couldn't tell a soul. And she rolled over and pulled the blanket over her head to block out the loneliness.

Over the next couple of days, she taught herself the graphics program for her computer. She designed and printed business cards for herself, then created matching brochures, hoping that the colorful, eye-catching composition would make up for her slim credentials. She got a directory of businesses from the Chamber of Commerce and stuffed envelopes labeled with the addresses of one hundred businesses in the town. She bought stamps, and on Sunday, dropped the stack of envelopes filled with her brochures and business cards into the mailbox outside the post office. She stared at the mailbox for a moment after she heard the stack fall to its metal floor with a thud. She'd done her best. Now she'd just have to wait.

She was still by the mailbox, her hands on the bar of the stroller, when she spotted a young couple standing in front of the post office building. They were in their twenties, she guessed, and they were oblivious to the world. The man was leaning against the building, the woman pulled tightly against him in an embrace, and he was kissing her. The woman's head was tipped back and her blond hair hung in waves over her shoulders. The kiss was no simple peck on the cheek, but deep and passionate, yet careful and tender all the same. Kim stayed frozen, facing the mailbox as though fascinated by it as she watched the couple from the corner of her eye. Her lips tingled. She wanted to be that woman, being gently ravished that way. And she wanted the man to be Linc.

The man slowly raised his hand up the woman's side until he reached her breast. With her eyes closed, the woman tipped her head back even further, away from his mouth, as though she needed space to catch her breath.

Kim forced herself to turn away. She began pushing the stroller in the opposite direction from the couple, her thoughts torn between astonishment over their brazen, public display, and pure, unadorned jealousy. She knew it would be a while before she would get the image of them out of her mind.

She walked farther from her apartment than she had at any time since her arrival in Annapolis, and she knew it was a form of sublimation. Her brain was clogged with prurient thoughts and impossible yearnings, and she planned to walk until her mind was clear again.

She was in an unfamiliar neighborhood when she came to a house entirely surrounded by yellow police tape. The house was small and square, with gray siding and black shutters, and it sat close to the sidewalk. A carefully tended flower garden filled the space between the sidewalk and the narrow front porch of the house.

Apparently, there'd been a fire in the house. The porch was blackened, and the ragged looking opening where the front door had been was covered by plastic sheeting. Above the porch, the roof appeared to be on the verge of collapse.

Two women stood in the street in front of the house, pointing and talking. Curiosity got the better of her, and Kim pushed the stroller slowly toward them.

"What happened here?" she asked when she'd gotten close enough for them to hear her.

"An explosion," the older woman said.

"They think it was a bomb," the second woman added. She was dark-haired and quite a bit overweight. "The gal who lives here opened an express mail package that someone left on her porch, and it blew up in her face."

"How horrible," Kim said. "Is she—did she survive?"

Both women shook their heads.

"We didn't know her," the older woman said. "We're just out for our daily walk and we'd heard about it and decided to come see." She looked at the house and shuddered. "Terrible sight," she said.

Kim's already shaky sense of security grew instantly more precarious. "Annapolis seemed so safe to me," she said.

"Oh, it's a perfectly safe town," the older woman reassured her. "This sort of thing never happens here."

"No place is safe," the other woman said. "You just can't get away from crime and violence."

Maybe not, Kim thought, but she could get away from this neighborhood. She said good-bye to the women and began walking in the direction of home.

After dinner that night, she moved the radio to the shelf behind her bed and tuned in to the station that carried Linc's show, even though he wouldn't be on the air for another hour. It had been a week and a half since she'd seen him. He would have taped tonight's show this past Wednesday, when he most definitely would have known what she'd done.

She sat on the bed with her sketch pad and pencils while she waited, listening to the classical music from the public broadcasting station, drawing anything that caught her eye in the bedroom: the crib, the window, the closet door. The pleasure of drawing, if not the skill, quickly returned to her, and she filled the entire hour—and several pages of the sketchbook—with drawings of the objects that made up her new life.

She put the sketchbook on the floor when Simon and Garfunkel began singing "Song for the Asking," and she got beneath the covers to wait for Linc to speak. He'd be featuring the Byrds that night, he told his audience when the song was over, and as he talked about the history of that group, Kim listened for any trace of emotion in his voice. She was certain that she heard it. The police had probably put him through the wringer. He was not a favorite of the Boulder police department to begin with. There were still some cops in Boulder who had been around when her father was killed. A few of them had actually been at the scene. They undoubtedly remembered finding her father in a pool of blood on her bedroom floor, her mother lying unconscious beside him. They'd remember Susanna sitting numbly at her desk, while Linc sat stoically on the edge of her bed, the gun resting in his hands. Some of the police felt that Linc got off way too easy, and it irked them that a man who'd served time for murder could end up a popular public figure. She hoped they would be able to put their negative feelings about him aside and believe him when he said he'd known nothing of her plans.

Did he know she was listening? There was no way to tell. At least not until the very end of his show, when he once again played "Suzanne."

*Oh, Linc.*

She listened to the song, her mind suddenly drifting back to the couple by the post office. She raised her own hand slowly up her side, wanting to know exactly how that woman had felt, but as she neared her breast, she dropped her hand to the bed. What was the point? It would be better not to know.

Other than the receptionist, there was only one woman in the small, square waiting room at Legal Aid, and Peggy glanced at the next name on her list.

"Bonnie Higgins?" she asked from the doorway.

The woman looked up from the stack of papers in her lap. She had the swollen features and red eyes of someone who'd been crying a great deal, and she gave a slight nod at the mention of her name.

"Please come in," Peggy said. She led the woman down the hallway to her office, and once there, took a seat behind her desk. "I'm Peggy Miller," she said.

The woman did not speak, although she did try to smile, and Peggy wondered if either of them had the energy for this appointment. It was her first day at work since Tyler's disappearance. If things had gone according to plan, she would have been off for another two months. But there seemed little point in sitting at home. She could at least work part time to keep herself busy.

Her concentration, though, was worse than she'd expected. Finding Tyler had become her consuming passion, and it was difficult to put that search out of her mind even when she had a client sitting in front of her. Between appointments, she found herself staring at his picture, framed in silver on her desk. He was only eight months old in that photograph, and she tried to remember how he had changed betwen the taking of the picture and his disappearance. Already, she had forgotten his smell and the feel of him in her arms. She could not quite hear the sound of his laughter, although she did remember how easy it was to elicit his mirth.

The receptionist had given Bonnie the lengthy Legal Aid questionnaire to fill out. Peggy took it from her and began leafing through the pages.

"You're interested in a divorce?" She glanced at her client.

"Well, no, not really." Bonnie's eyes quickly filled with tears. "But my husband is."

"Does he say why?"

"Just that he's not happy anymore." Bonnie looked helpless, and Peggy felt sorry for her. "He says he feels trapped and wants to be free."

Peggy figured there was a whole lot more to the story, but for now she kept her mouth shut and continued reading the questionnaire. Some attorneys were quick to make the opposing spouse into an ugly, manipulative adversary. She tried to avoid doing so, even when the truth begged for that sort of assessment. Divorce was hard enough without turning two people into enemies for life, especially when there were children involved. As there were in Bonnie Higgins's case.

"Your children are four and five," she said, reading from the form. "Has your husband said anything about custody?"

"He hasn't said a word about the kids," Bonnie said, then added bitterly, "He wants to be free, remember?"

"Do you think he's seeing someone else?"

Bonnie looked out the window, the tears thick above her lower lashes. "He says no. I can't imagine it. I don't want to imagine it." She shuddered. "I don't know when he'd have time. He's pretty much always working."

Peggy looked over the rest of the form and began questioning Bonnie about the family's financial situation. She spent the next half hour talking about what Bonnie needed to do to protect her assets. She would help her fight for fifty percent of everything, she promised.

"But he says I don't deserve half of everything because he's the one who's been bringing home the money all these years."

"While you've been raising the children and managing the household, right?"

Bonnie nodded, a small, hopeful smile on her lips. "Right."

Peggy was a firm believer in a fifty-fifty split. She'd even managed to talk Jim into making that sort of settlement with Susanna. He'd been resistant at first, but she'd helped him see that if it had not been for Susanna's working, he would not have been able to attend school and get his law degree. It was true that Jim got the house, but Susanna would eventually receive half its value. Jim had already given her a fair amount of cash. Susanna had left a big chunk of that money in the bank, though, obviously fearful that withdrawing too much at one time would attract unwanted attention to her account. She'd acted very foolishly, Peggy thought. Not only had she left that cash behind, but she'd cut herself off from the money Jim was paying her for the house each month, as well as from child support and health insurance and an eventual share of his retirement.

She walked Bonnie to the door at the interview's end. "Call me if anything comes up before our next meeting," she said, shaking the woman's hand.

She saw two more clients that morning, her concentration worsening with each interview, and at noon she left the office. She was anxious to get home. She planned to call the Center for Missing Children again. Prod them a little.

When she turned onto her street in Wonderland, she saw several cars in front of her house. Ron's car was there, and she thought the blue one belonged to Bill Anderson. Jim's car was in the driveway.

She was filled with cautious optimism as she pulled her own car behind Jim's and rushed into the house.

The three men were sitting at the kitchen table, laughing, drinking beer. It was odd to see her brother drinking in the middle of a workday. Then she remembered that Mondays were his day off.

"Is this a celebration?" she asked. "Did something happen?"

Jim looked immediately contrite. He stood up and walked over to her, kissing her cheek. "No, hon," he said. "At least, not what you're hoping for. But Bill does have some news."

The private investigator leaned back in his chair. "I wanted to meet with all of you so we could talk about what I've found out," he said, "but I didn't realize you'd gone back to work, Peggy. So I hope you don't mind that I've already told your—"

"What?" Peggy pulled away from Jim and sat down next to Ron, across from the PI. "What did you find out?"

Bill ran a hand over his small, smooth chin. "Well, to begin with, I'm certain Susanna Miller was on a bus to St. Louis, Missouri, the morning of the day she disappeared."

Peggy leaned toward the man. "Tell me everything. How do you know that? Tyler was with her, wasn't he?"

"I've been talking to the ticket people and to some of the drivers at the bus terminal in Denver, as well as to the drivers who serve the routes nearest Susanna's apartment. I told them there's a good chance she altered her looks. A wig, maybe. Or dyed hair. The bus driver for one of the routes near her house recognized her and the baby from a picture. He said the woman looked very different, but they stood out anyhow. Usually he just picks up the same people on that route, day after day. People commuting to Denver for work. He picked her up around five-thirty in the morning and let her off at the terminal in Denver at six-thirty."

"Oh, my God." Peggy squeezed her brother's hand, and Ron gave her a smile in return. "Then what?"

Bill shifted in his seat and took a swallow of beer. It was obvious that he enjoyed giving her the information bit by bit, keeping her in suspense. He liked the power, and in any other setting Peggy might have called him on it. Right now, though, she didn't want to do anything that would alienate him.

"The driver wasn't the greatest at descriptions," he said, "but he did say that her hair was a lot darker and a lot shorter. He didn't think it was a wig, but some of those wigs can look pretty natural, so who knows? Anyhow," he reached into the folder on the table in front of him, "I had a computer-generated picture made up of what she might look like now."

He pulled the picture from the folder and turned it around so Peggy could see it.

"Oh, no," she said, dismayed. She doubted she would ever recognize the woman in the picture as Susanna. The short dark hair changed her features dramatically. "No wonder we haven't gotten any calls from the photographs we've been showing on TV," she said. "She looks like a totally different person."

"Bill said we can get this altered picture on the news, though." Jim stood behind her, rubbing her shoulders. "And we can show it in St. Louis, too."

"What were you saying about St. Louis?" she looked at Bill.

"Right," Bill said. "Quite a few people at the bus terminal remembered this woman and her baby. She was not too smart, picking that time of day, when she and Tyler were the only mother and child out there with all the commuters. But anyhow, the ticket agent was one of the people who saw her. He couldn't remember specifically where she was going. So I got a schedule of the buses leaving the station that morning. Then I spoke with those drivers. One of them said she and the baby had definitely been on his bus. They rode all the way to St. Louis. Said the baby was really good. Hardly cried at all."

"Maybe he was sick," Peggy said.

"He's not fragile, Peggy," Ron said. "He's not going to break."

"But she's carting him all over the country," she said. "Who knows what she's doing with him?"

"Look, Peg." Ron sounded impatient. "He's fixed, all right? He needs good follow-up. Just checkups. Maybe an echo every now and again, just to know everything's working as it should be. That's all. You won't be doing him any good if you get to be his mother and you coddle him like he's some delicate little flower."

Peggy didn't respond. She felt betrayed by her brother's attitude. "And then what happened?" she asked Bill. "Is she still in St. Louis?"

"That I don't know. None of the ticket agents there recognized her, but that's a much bigger and busier bus terminal. I'm working on it, though. And I'll want to get this doctored-up photograph spread around St. Louis."

"Does she know anyone in St. Louis?" Peggy leaned back to look up at Jim, who shrugged. "What about Linc?" she asked. "Maybe he'd know—"

"Bill doesn't think it's a good idea to involve Linc in this just yet," Jim said.

"That's right." Bill wore a serious expression. "I'm not so sure he's not in on it. We don't want him to be able to give her a heads up on what we've found out."

Peggy supposed that made sense. She'd listened to Linc's show the night before, wondering if he might use his program as a vehicle to send Susanna a message of some sort. She'd only heard his show once or twice before, and last night's program had sounded the same to her, full of old and sometimes obscure folk-rock music. If he were sending a message to Susanna, he was being very subtle about it.

"So, this means the FBI can get involved now, doesn't it?" she asked.

"That's right," Bill said. "She's a felon. They can get her for unlawful flight to avoid prosecution."

Ron made a sound of disapproval. "Sounds like overkill to me," he said, almost under his breath.

"Now," Bill sat back in his chair, "do you have any videos of Tyler?"

Peggy and Jim nodded in unison.

"Send them to me, along with whatever other pictures you have lying around that you haven't already given me. I'm going to get them to *Missing Persons*, you know, that TV show?"

"I already called them myself," Peggy said. "They told me it would be months before they'd be doing another show on parental kidnappings."

"That's true, but when they start planning that show and it comes down to them covering our case or someone else's, they'll choose the case they have the most readily available material for."

"But *months*." Peggy looked helplessly at Jim. "It seems silly to . . . this just can't go on for months."

"We certainly hope it won't," Bill said, "but we need to be ready in case it does, all right?"

She nodded, but without conviction. "All right," she said. "I'll make copies of the videos and get them to you in a few days."

"Good." Bill flipped through his notepad. "We're keeping tabs on the health insurance company, too," Bill said. "If Susanna tries to use her insurance, either for Tyler or herself, then we should be able to track her down. The insurance company flagged her file.

They know to notify us if they get a claim from her or a change of address or anything."

"That's good." Peggy said. "He's due for his inoculations soon." She had marked the date on her calendar so she'd be sure to make the appointment for him.

"Isn't it likely, though, that she'd assume we've alerted the insurance carrier?" Jim asked.

"Yes, but maybe she'll get desperate."

"Or, God forbid, she might skip his inoculations," Peggy said. "Or maybe she won't even remember when it's time for him to get them."

Ron made that disapproving sound in his throat again. "There's one other thing you should know, Peg," he said. "I got a call from Della in my office this morning. Bill had asked her to pull Tyler's medical records, and she found a note in his file. Apparently Susanna had requested—and received—a copy of all of Tyler's records a couple of weeks before she took off."

"She'd been planning it that long?"

"Uh huh." Ron nodded. "And I have to hand it to her. I'm not sure I would have had the presence of mind to remember those records before I split."

"*Ron,*" she said. "Whose side are you on?"

"Tyler's," Ron answered quickly, and Peggy knew he'd given this whole matter a good deal of thought.

"If you're on Tyler's side, then you'd want him here," she said. "You'd want him safe with Jim and me."

"Whatever you say, Peg." Ron drained his beer and stood up. "I've got to pick up the kids from day care."

She stood up, too. She walked her brother to the door in silence, then turned to him. "You know, Ron, I don't think you can relate to what's going on with Tyler and Susanna and Jim and me. You have two beautiful healthy children at home. You know they're safe. I have a stepson out there somewhere, and I have no idea what's happening to him. I have no idea if I'll ever get to see him again." She didn't want to cry. Much as she adored Ron, he'd always had a way of provoking her tears.

He reached out and pulled her into a hug. "I feel one hundred percent certain that Tyler is safe," he said quietly. "I don't think you want to hear that, though. I don't think you want to hear me say that I think Susanna is a perfectly fine mother. She never missed an appointment with me. She did everything she was told to do to take care of Tyler."

She nodded woodenly as she let go of him. They said good-bye, and she turned to walk slowly back to the kitchen. She knew she should be heartened by his assessment of Susanna's ability to care well for Tyler, but he was right. She didn't want to hear it.

It was not the first time Kim and Cody had visited the park a few blocks from their apartment, but it was the first time they were not alone at the playground. A young woman about Kim's age was pushing a toddler on the swing, while an older child, a boy, played in the collection of huge plastic tubes. Kim had intended to push Cody on the swing as well, but seeing the woman there changed her mind. She lifted him out of the stroller and began walking toward the slide instead, but Cody reached toward the swing set, trying to twist out of the confines of her arms.

"Deh, deh!" he said, his word for "swing," a word only a mother could understand.

"All right." She gave in and carried him over to the swings, slipping him into a molded plastic seat, one swing over from the woman and the toddler.

"Hi." The woman smiled at her. She had short dark hair and looked a little like Valerie. "I haven't seen you here before."

"No. We're new in town."

"I'm Roxanne," the woman said. "This is Brandon. And that's Jack over there." She pointed toward the little boy in the plastic tubes. He was talking loudly to himself, yelling with bravado.

"I'm Kim, and this is Cody." She looked at the baby in the swing. "How old is Brandon?" she asked.

"A year yesterday."

Kim leaned closer to the little boy. He had curly dark hair and enormous brown eyes. "Happy birthday, Brandon," she said.

She pushed Cody in the swing, but her son's attention was on Roxanne. He twisted in the seat to see her, reaching toward her with his arm.

"Bawrie, Bawrie!" He opened and closed his fist as though he wanted to grab hold of the stranger.

Kim smiled. "No, honey, that's not Valerie." She was surprised that he too saw the resemblance. They were both only seeing what they wanted to see. "You remind him of a friend of ours," she said.

"Ah," said Roxanne. She was keeping one eye on her older son as he shot through one of the tubes head-first, and she shook her head. "I can't let Jack out of my sight for an instant. He's a hellion."

"How old is he?"

"Four, going on fourteen."

Even at this distance, Kim could tell that Jack was one of those wired little boys—far too loud and far too active. He was the type of child she'd prayed Cody would not turn out to be.

"Cody's about eleven months, right?" Roxanne asked.

"That's right."

"That's a great monkey you have there, Cody," Roxanne said, then she smiled at Kim. "So. Where did you move from?"

"New Jersey," she said, then added, "but I like it here much better. Have you lived here long?" She wanted to get the conversation off herself and New Jersey as quickly as possible.

"We've lived here ten years," Roxanne said. "My husband teaches at the Naval Academy. What does your husband do?"

"I'm recently divorced." Kim felt suddenly embarrassed by her single parent status. It was doubtful she'd run across many other divorced mothers who had children Cody's age. Maybe she should have made Kim Stratton a recent widow. More sympathetic. Too late to change the story now, though.

"Oh, that must be hard, having to raise Cody on your own," Roxanne said. Then she brightened. "Listen, I try to bring the boys here about this time every day. Maybe you could come at the same time, and the kids could play together."

"Sounds good. At least until I start working."

Jack suddenly leapt off one of the plastic tubes and ran toward the swing set. He crashed right into the swing in which his brother was sitting, and Brandon burst into tears.

"Jack, stop that!" Roxanne grabbed her older son by the arm. "What did I tell you about playing rough?" She looked up at Kim. "Someone is a little resentful of someone else these days," she said.

Kim nodded, but her eyes were riveted on the plastic gun in Jack's hand. It was small, but looked real. Real enough to make her want to duck.

"Now you go sit over there until we're ready to leave." Roxanne pointed to the picnic table near the path.

Jack lifted his hand and pointed the gun at his mother. "Pow!" he said, and Kim caught her breath.

Roxanne gave a grunt of annoyance. "Could you watch Brandon for just a sec?" she asked.

Kim nodded, and Roxanne latched onto her older son's shoulder. She marched him over to the picnic table, where she sat down, held on to his arms, and spoke to him quietly.

Brandon began to whimper, and Kim gave his swing a few gentle pushes. Roxanne was back in less than a minute and she took over pushing Brandon, a wry smile on her lips.

"Is this your only child?" she asked, nodding toward Cody.

"Yes."

"Let me give you a word of advice. Stop while you're ahead."

Kim laughed as she lifted Cody out of the swing. "I'll remember that," she said. "I think we'd better get going."

"Already?" Roxanne looked disappointed. "Well, I hope to see you here again."

"I'm sure you will." She settled Cody back into his stroller, bade Roxanne good-bye, and walked up the path to the street. She doubted very much that she would return to the park at this time of day. She wouldn't have Cody playing with kids who used toy guns. That was one absolute nonnegotiable. No more guns in her life again, ever.

There was a piece of mail waiting for her at the house.

Ellen had propped it up against the vase of silk flowers on the table in the foyer, and Kim nearly walked past it before she noticed her name on the cream-colored envelope. *Kimberly Stratton.*

She shifted Cody to her other hip, then stared at the envelope for a moment before picking it up. Mail for her? Here?

It was a squarish envelope with a typewritten label. Mystified, she carried it upstairs to her apartment. She put Cody down for his nap, then sat on the sofa to open the envelope. Inside was a formal looking invitation.

*You are cordially invited*
*to a showing of Adam Soria's work*
*at the Cherise Gallery*
*October 3, 7:00 P.M.*

The mural painter. How on earth? She studied the card, then peered inside the envelope as if she might find a clue as to why she'd received the invitation. Maybe someone had gone through an Annapolis directory—a very *recent* directory—and sent invitations to everyone within the town limits. Or maybe Ellen had something to do with it. That had to be it. Ellen probably knew someone at the gallery and asked them to invite the friendless new kid on the block to the showing.

She set the invitation aside and pulled her sketchbook from the magazine rack by the sofa. Sitting in a chair by the window, she began working on the sketch she'd started the day before of the house across the street. She'd gotten a couple of books from the library on drawing, and the techniques she'd learned in high school were coming back to her. Too bad she had stayed away from art for so long. She had to keep reminding herself that there was no one she had to answer to for her drawing these days. There was no one around to tell her she had no talent, no one who could take this sketchbook away from her. She was finding it hard to concentrate, though. The invitation kept creeping back into her mind.

As soon as Cody awakened from his nap, she carried him downstairs and loaded him back into his stroller. "We're taking another walk, kiddo," she said.

She headed in the direction of the Cherise Gallery. After fifteen minutes of walking, she found it on a narrow, cobblestone side street. A simple wooden sign hung from the front of a brick facade: Cherise Gallery.

Kim peered in the front window. The walls of the gallery appeared to be covered with Adam Soria's work, the paintings on a smaller scale than the murals, of course, but still possessing that distinctive play of light and dark, that half-real, half-surreal quality that had enticed her on the street.

A handwritten sign taped to the door read "back in twenty minutes." She wondered how long ago that twenty minutes had started, but it didn't matter. She wouldn't hang around here and let herself be that conspicuous. She had already made up her mind, though, that she was going to the show the following night.

Ellen was coming out the front door of the house, the mesh bag she used for groceries hanging over her shoulder, when Kim and Cody arrived home.

"Hi, Kim. Hi Cody," Ellen said. "Guess what? You two are going to have a new neighbor."

"We are?" At the bottom of the porch steps, Kim lifted Cody out of the stroller.

"I just took her deposit a few minutes ago. She seems very nice."

Oh. The other apartment. Kim masked her disappointment. "Really," she said.

"Her name is Lucy O'Connor," Ellen continued. "She's sixty-ish, I'd say. Divorced, so that makes three of us, huh? She's a writer and works at home. She's been published in lots of magazines and newspapers, and she didn't have a problem with there being a baby next door. She says she writes articles for parenting magazines, so babies are right up her alley."

Kim forced a smile. "Sounds perfect." She collapsed the stroller and started up the porch steps. "When is she moving in?"

"Tomorrow night." Ellen reached out to take the stroller from Kim's hands and set it next to the front door. "Some friends are helping her. You can meet her then."

"Oh, I'm going out tomorrow night. To an art show." She waited for Ellen to say, "Oh, so you got the invitation! I asked them to send you one," but Ellen didn't even seem to hear her.

"Well, you can meet her when you come home then," she said as she started down the stairs. "I'm going to the store. Do you need anything?"

"No thanks."

At the bottom of the stairs, Ellen turned to study her quizzically for a moment. "You know, I might be able to find a babysitter if you want to get out without Cody sometime. It must be hard for you, not knowing anyone."

"No, thanks," Kim said again. "It's really not a problem." She didn't plan on being separated from her son any time soon. Yes, he made it more difficult for her to be able to move through town—through her *life*—incognito, but that was the risk she had to take. She wondered, though, if it would be completely inappropriate to show up at an art show with a baby in tow.

It was quite dark by seven o'clock the following evening, and she decided to drive to the gallery instead of walk. There was no parking on the tiny street, but she found a space a block away.

Even from that distance, she could hear the noise from the gallery as soon as she got out of her car. Laughter bounced off the buildings on the opposite side of the street, and she could see light spilling onto the cobblestones from the gallery window and the open front door. She decided against trying to maneuver the stroller through a crowd of people and carried Cody in her arms instead.

She began walking toward the commotion. A few people were outside the gallery itself; a man and woman stood laughing on the narrow stone steps. This was probably a bad idea, Kim thought, but already she was close enough to the building that people had noticed her, and she would have felt silly turning around and walking back to the car.

"Excuse me." She stepped between the couple on the steps and walked through the open front door.

The bright lights and press of people nearly took her breath away, and she stood still for a moment, trying to get her bearings. She was definitely the only person carrying a child, and she was not as formally dressed as most people. Her fifty-cent garage sale skirt, the only skirt in her nearly empty closet, had seemed appropriate before she left the apartment, but now she felt dowdy. Some of the women in the gallery looked as if they belonged in a nightclub.

A few people, plastic cups of wine in their hands, glanced at her as they conversed with one another, and she was glad she'd remembered to tuck the invitation into her purse in case anyone asked her what she thought she was doing there.

A tall black woman, her hair braided and beaded, suddenly emerged from the throng, shaking hands, touching shoulders, talking quickly and loudly. She looked as though she was in charge.

"Excuse me." Kim tightened her hold on Cody and took a step toward the woman. "Is it all right if I bring my son in? I'll hold him."

"You will *not* hold him." The woman laughed. "Because I'm gonna hold him." She snatched the baby, monkey and all, from her arms so quickly that Kim felt a second of panic before realizing that the woman meant no harm.

"I'm Cherise, honey," the woman said. "And you're . . . ?"

"Kim."

Cherise waved at someone leaving the gallery. "Take care of that woman, now, Kenny!" She returned her attention to the little boy in her arms. Cody was fascinated by her long dangling beaded earrings, and Kim feared he might tug on one of them any second.

"And what's your name?"

"Cody," Kim answered. "Don't pull her earring, Cody." She reached out to brush Cody's hand away.

The woman didn't seem to share her concern.

"Cody," she repeated. "He's just like my sister's little boy. Well, not the same color, but he's the same age. Just about a year, right?"

"Close to it," Kim said.

"And just as handsome as my nephew. Well, almost, aren't you?" She suddenly grabbed the arm of a woman who was walking past her. "You get yourself another glass of wine, honey," she said to the woman. "You're going to need it with the night you've got ahead of you."

Kim found herself smiling. There was something comforting in the gallery owner's electric chatter and her easy, unpretentious hospitality. She wanted to ask Cherise how she'd come by her invitation, but decided against it.

"I'm relatively new here," she said instead. Her words sounded slow and sluggish next to Cherise's. "I've been admiring Adam Soria's murals all over town."

"Oh, yes, aren't they something? He's a genius, that man. Of course, all the paintings in the gallery tonight are his old work." She waved her bangle-studded wrist toward one of the walls of paintings. "I was just about to have a showing of these pieces when the accident happened. I put it off, of course, and it's taken Adam till now to feel ready to do it. He worries me to death. Do you realize he hasn't done a single new piece in the six months since it happened?"

Kim shook her head.

"We have to get that man working again, don't you think?" Cherise asked.

"Absolutely," Kim agreed, as though she shared some ability to make that happen. She had no idea what the gallery owner was talking about, and she wasn't about to ask. She reached for her son. "Let me take him off your hands."

"He does get heavy, doesn't he?" Cherise handed the baby over to her. "You must have some muscles, girlfriend. Hey!" She suddenly grabbed Kim's shoulders and turned her to face the far wall. "Come on," she said. "There's Adam. Have you met him?"

Kim shook her head and hung back slightly, but Cherise nudged her forward.

"Come on, girl. You need to meet the artist himself."

She saw him from the back first. He was average height, average weight, with short, salt and pepper hair. His arm hung loosely around the shoulders of a dark-haired woman. They were talking with another couple, and Kim cringed at the thought of interrupting them, but Cherise seemed to have no such reservations. Kim was relieved when the other couple slipped away just as she and Cherise were approaching.

"Adam!" Cherise said. "I want to introduce you to a couple of admirers."

He turned to face them. Unlike everyone else in the gallery, Adam Soria had not dressed for the occasion. He wore jeans and a gray knit cardigan over a pale blue shirt. He sported a very short beard and mustache, which were graying like his hair, although he looked to be only in his mid-thirties. He had warm, brown eyes, but they were hooded by a frown, and there was a tiredness in his smile, as though he had to force it. He dropped his arm from the woman's shoulders to shake Kim's hand.

"I'm Kim," she said.

"And this is Cody," Cherise added.

"What a doll!" The woman's large, dark eyes lit up at the sight of Cody. She looked young, probably no more than twenty-five. "I'm Jessie," she said to Kim. "Adam's sister. May I?" She reached out her arms to Cody, who did the same in response. It was frightening how easily he went to strangers.

"Oh, I'm in love!" Jessie settled the little boy into her arms. She took the monkey from Cody's hand and made the ragged stuffed animal dance on Adam's shoulder, eliciting a giggle from the little boy, and a slightly more animated smile from the artist.

"Kim's been admiring your murals, sugar," Cherise said to Adam. "She's just moved here from—whoops!" She looked toward the front door as a new stream of people filed into the gallery. "Gotta run."

Kim smiled apologetically at Adam as Cherise rushed off. "I didn't mean to interrupt your conversation with—"

"You didn't," he said.

"I think I've seen you walking Cody in a stroller, right?" Jessie said, placing the monkey back in Cody's hand.

Nothing like being noticeable. "Right. This is a wonderful town for walking. That's how I stumbled across the murals. They're beautiful."

"Thank you," Adam said.

"I always wanted to paint." That sounded stupid, but she wasn't sure what else to say. Nor was she sure what to do with her arms. She was so accustomed to having Cody in them that without him they seemed overlarge and in the way. She folded them across her chest. "I was going to be an art major in college, but had to drop out."

"Where did you move from?" Jessie asked.

"New Jersey."

"What brought you to Annapolis?"

"Oh, I have some family nearby. In Bowie. And it's pretty here. I like being near the water."

"Are you working around here?" Jessie asked.

What was with the first degree? "I'm just starting my own business. Word processing out of my house. I don't want to work away from home while Cody's so young."

"Really?" Jessie asked. "Do you use a word processor or a computer, or—"

"*Jessie.*" Adam laughed. "Give her a chance to catch her breath between questions, all right?" He looked at Kim. "My sister's the curious type."

"Sorry." Jessie smiled. She pointed toward one corner of the gallery. "Can I take Cody over to see the ice sculpture?"

Kim looked in the direction she was pointing, and for the first time noticed the huge ice statue of a dolphin on the table in the corner. "Sure," she said bravely. He would only be a few yards away from her.

She watched as Jessie carried Cody through the press of people, then directed her attention to the painting in front of her. It was another jungle scene, similar to the mural she liked best. "Acrylics?" she said. It had to be for him to get those vibrant, opaque colors that marked his work.

"Uh huh," he said.

She wanted to tell him how much she'd enjoyed his murals and hunted for words she could use that wouldn't make her sound completely ignorant. "There's a strength in your paintings," she said. "They're . . . hard to ignore. You can't look at them without feeling something, some emotion, even in these smaller sizes. It's the colors, and I don't know . . ." She cocked her head to study the exotic white bird nestled in the green of the jungle. "It's your style. You really have a style all your own."

"Thanks," he said. "It's probably because I paint what I dream."

She looked over to see Cody reach out to touch the dolphin's icy nose. He pulled his hand away with a surprised giggle.

"You paint what you dream?" she repeated.

"Yeah. Or at least I used to. I used to get up every morning and sketch my dreams. You know, the way some people keep a dream journal? Then I'd pick my favorites and paint them." He reported this without enthusiasm, as though he'd said it many times before.

"No wonder they're so unique. You're not painting what everyone else sees. Just what you see."

"Hmm." He actually seemed to perk up at that, as though he liked her analysis. Then he followed her eyes to the dolphin. Jessie had started talking with someone, a woman who was making the monkey's hand touch Cody's nose over and over again.

"He's all right." Adam touched Kim's arm lightly, kindly. "Jessie's oozing with maternal instincts."

"Adam!" A woman in a red sequined dress approached them.

"Hi." Adam bussed the woman's cheek.

"These are wonderful, Adam," she said. "You shouldn't have kept them locked away for so long."

Kim felt intrusive. "I'd better go get Cody," she said to Adam, but he caught her elbow in his hand and held it firmly.

"Don't go," he said. It was a plea of some sort, and there was such unmistakable sincerity in his voice that she didn't budge. To the woman, he said, "I'm glad you're enjoying them."

"When do we get to see something new?" the woman asked.

"One of these days." That forced smile again.

"Don't make it too long, please." The woman winked at him and slipped back into the crowd.

Adam turned to her. "I would have introduced you, but I can't remember her name," he said.

"Oh. No problem."

"So, which is your favorite of the murals?" he asked.

"Actually, the jungle scene on Duke of Gloucester Street."

"The dream was even better," he said. "I don't think I ever quite captured the feeling of it."

"What about the mural you're working on. The one on the bank? When will it be finished?"

He shook his head. "Probably never." He rubbed his short beard with his hand. "I stopped working on it about six months ago. My dreams turned to shit around then." He looked at her apologetically. "Sorry."

She wasn't sure what to say. There'd been an accident, Cherise had said. What had happened?

"What sort of painting do *you* do?" He turned the focus to her.

"None." She smiled at him. "My dreams turned to shit about thirteen years ago."

He laughed at that, then quickly sobered. "Thirteen years, huh? Now that's discouraging."

Kim looked over at the ice dolphin, but she couldn't spot Jessie and Cody. She stood up on her toes, her heart kicking into high gear, then she turned in a quick circle. Nowhere. "Excuse me," she said to Adam. "I—"

"Over there." Adam pointed toward the back of the room. Jessie was sitting on a countertop, talking with a man standing near her. Cody was on her lap.

"Oh," Kim said, relieved. "I should go free your sister."

"A little separation anxiety?" Adam asked. "I can appreciate that. It was nice talking to you, Kim. Hope you get back to painting one of these days."

"You too," she said. "And I'm very glad I had a chance to meet you." She reached out to shake his hand, but a man stepped in front of her and pulled Adam into an embrace, and she slipped away to get her son.

She was relieved to get Cody back in her arms again, but he was getting antsy, and she decided she would have to come back some other day to see the rest of Adam Soria's paintings. Outside, she started walking toward her car, the chatter and laughter from the gallery following her all the way down the block. The only person who did not seem boisterously happy in that gallery had been the artist himself.

By the time she got home, Cody was asleep in his car seat. There were lights burning in the other upstairs apartment, and a blue sedan she had never seen before was parked at the curb.

She walked up the stairs with Cody in tow and listened for a moment before opening her apartment door. There were no sounds coming from inside the other apartment, but the air in the landing felt different somehow, heavy with the presence of the new tenant, yet another stranger to whom she would have to explain her existence.

*S*he took Cody to the park around eleven the following morning, hoping to miss Roxanne and her pistol-packing son. Sure enough, she and Cody had the playground to themselves. She pushed him on the swing for awhile, then walked with him over to the city dock, where they sat on a bench by the water and shared the bagged lunch she'd brought along.

She was walking home, pushing the stroller past a row of shops, when Adam Soria suddenly stepped out of the small pharmacy on the corner.

"Hey," he said, his smile of recognition slow. "Hello, again."

"Hi." She stopped walking and shaded her eyes to look at him. "That was fun last night."

He made a sound in his throat as if he were not quite certain he agreed with her, and he looked as if he were about to say something else when Jessie walked out of the pharmacy and came to stand next to him.

"Hello." Jessie smiled and stooped down to greet Cody. "Hello again, little guy. Did you like that dolphin last night? Pretty nifty, huh?"

"Mamama." Cody giggled and held his monkey out to Jessie.

"He doesn't offer his monkey to just anyone," Kim said.

Jessie looked up at her. "Out on one of your walks?"

"Yes. I'll get them in while I can. I hope I'll get some work soon, and then I won't have time to walk."

"Word processing, right?" Jessie stood up.

"Right. You have a good memory."

Cody let out a long yawn.

"You tired, Cody?" Jessie asked him. "Did your mom keep you up too late last night?"

"I think I did," Kim said honestly. "Plus, we've had a long morning and it's past nap time. We'd better get home."

"All right," Jessie said. She waved at Cody, raising her voice an octave, "Bye, bye, Cody. Bye bye."

"Nice seeing you again," Adam said. He and Jessie turned and began walking up the street, while Kim hung back to zip Cody's jacket. When she started walking again, she noticed that Jessie and Adam had stopped. They were talking, glancing over their shoulders at her. Suddenly, Adam left his sister's side to walk back to her.

"Since you're new in town," he said, "would you and Cody like to join us for dinner tonight?"

Surprised, she couldn't answer right away. The two of them perplexed her. They seemed to be free spirits who could spend the day flitting around town. Well, she was a fine one to talk. But Adam and Jessie were obviously well-established in Annapolis. They possessed a gallery full of friends. Why were they being so nice to her? She wanted to say yes, her hunger for company at war with her better judgment. What had happened to her plan to keep to herself?

"No," she said. "I—"

"Come on," Adam coaxed. "What else do you have to do tonight?"

She smiled, thinking of her little apartment and the entertainment it offered: the computer, the TV, and her sketchbook. "Not much," she admitted.

"All right, then." He gave her the name and address of a restaurant and she agreed to meet them there at seven-thirty.

She watched them walk away from her. Jessie looked back and waved as they turned the corner, and Kim returned the gesture. "We've got friends, Cody," she said to her son. "Don't quite know how it happened, but we've got them."

She had finished dressing Cody to go out that night when a

knock came at her apartment door. The sound was so unfamiliar that she jumped. She put Cody into the small playpen in the middle of the living room and opened the door to find an attractive, gray-haired woman on the landing. She was dressed in a denim jumper, and she looked as though she might be a well-preserved sixty or so, half working woman, half cookie-baking grandmother.

"Hello," the woman boomed in a voice that held no timidity. She stuck out her hand. "I'm your new neighbor. Lucy O'Connor. "

Kim shook her hand. "Kim Stratton," she said.

Lucy peered around Kim into the room. "Oh, there's the little one Ellen told me about." She marched into the apartment and over to the playpen. "Look at you!" she said to the little boy. Then to Kim, "May I take him out?"

Kim nodded. Lucy lifted Cody out of the playpen and got down on the floor with him. She took one of his toy trucks out of the playpen and began scooting it across the floor.

"Duk, duk!" Cody squealed. He was entranced with Lucy, as he was with everyone, and Kim watched the scene with a brand new seed of paranoia growing in her head. If Jim were really smart, he could do no better than to hire a grandmotherly private investigator to move in next door to her.

"He reminds me of my little grandson," Lucy said. "Who I haven't seen in months, unfortunately."

Cody pulled himself up by her shoulder and dropped his little body onto her lap. "Oh, is he ever lovable! And he has your eyes, doesn't he?" She looked up at Kim.

"Yes, I guess so."

"Such an unusual, pretty light blue." She ran the truck up Cody's leg, speaking to Kim without looking up. "Ellen told me you're newly divorced. Must be terrible with such a little one."

Kim nodded. "It's hard, but I think we're better off without him than we were with him," she said.

"Oh, one of *those* sorts. He helps out with child support, I hope."

Kim hesitated. What was the best answer? She couldn't think through all the ramifications quickly enough. She'd told Ellen she received child support. "A little," she said.

"It's never enough, is it? Does he live nearby? Does Cody get to see his papa ever?"

Kim was anxious for a change of topic. "Not too often." She made a show of looking at her watch. "I hate to tear him away from you, Lucy, but we have to meet some people for dinner."

"How lovely for you." With some effort, Lucy was back on her feet again. She returned Cody to the playpen. "Actually," she said, dusting off the back of her jumper, "I came over to see if you might have an extension cord I could borrow."

"Oh, I'm sorry, I don't. I just moved in myself—not quite two weeks ago—and I haven't had the need for one. Maybe Ellen?"

"Maybe." Lucy walked toward the door. "I'll check with her. She's something, isn't she? She probably has a scented extension cord that chants when you plug it in."

Kim had to laugh. "I wouldn't be surprised." She followed the older woman to the door.

"Ellen said you work at home?" Lucy asked.

"I plan to. I'm hoping to take in word processing jobs."

"Well, that will be wonderful. I work at home too, so maybe we can take a coffee break together every once in a while."

"Sure," Kim said, but she didn't know about that. Lucy seemed a bit too intrusive. Overbearing.

"And if you ever need someone to watch Cody, you just let me know, okay?"

Kim nodded with a smile, but once she'd closed her door on her new neighbor, she shook her head. "Don't hold your breath," she said.

The restaurant was a small, Italian eatery, and Kim was relieved to discover the relaxed atmosphere. She'd been worried about taking Cody into someplace fancier. He was usually well behaved, but in case this turned out to be one of his rare cranky evenings, she didn't want to embarrass her new friends.

She spotted Adam and Jessie, already sitting across from one another at a table near the middle of the restaurant. They were involved in an animated, perhaps even angry, discussion. Adam had his back to the door, but Jessie spotted her and waved, a smile instantly replacing the frown on her face.

Kim collapsed Cody's stroller and left it by the coat rack, then walked toward the table. She sat down next to Jessie, and the waitress brought a high chair to the end of the table so Kim would have easy access to her son.

"Did you walk here?" Adam asked.

"Yes. I do own a car, in case you're wondering, but I don't live that far."

"There's no place to park around here, anyway," Adam said. "Where do you live?"

"On Maryland Street. I'm renting one of the upstairs apartments in a big house near the Naval Academy."

"I bet I know the house," Jessie said. "There's been a for rent sign out front of it for a few weeks. Isn't the woman who owns it a massage therapist?"

"Right. Ellen King."

"Is that who Cherise goes to?" Adam asked his sister.

"Yes."

"Ah." Kim smiled. "That's got to be the connection, then. I didn't understand why I got an invitation to your show last night. I mean, I don't know anyone in Annapolis except Ellen. But if Ellen knows Cherise, then I bet she asked Cherise to invite me."

"That's probably it," Jessie said.

Kim unwrapped a breadstick and handed it to Cody. "Cherise seems really nice."

"She's a character," Adam said. "One of those people who never met a stranger. She has an eye for art, though, and she's really been my champion. Always after me to get back to painting again."

"Do you think you ever will?" she ventured.

He shrugged. "All depends on my dreams. I've never been able to have much control over them."

"They'll come back, Adam," Jessie said reassuringly.

He looked directly at Kim. "What happened six months ago was that my wife and two children were killed in a car accident."

"Oh, no." She was stunned he would reveal something that personal so quickly, so openly, and she felt a painful rush of sympathy for him. She had been through some tragedies in her life, but nothing she'd endured could compare to that sort of loss. "I'm terribly sorry," she said. "I can't even imagine . . . " Her voice trailed off. She did not know what else to say.

Jessie reached across the table and squeezed her brother's hand. "Don't talk about it, Adam," she said. "Not here."

"I wasn't planning on it."

"I'm so sorry." Kim felt guilty for bringing up something that was not her business.

"I just wanted to tell you what happened so you'd understand why I was monopolizing you last night," Adam said. "I wanted to apologize. I didn't give you a chance to meet anyone else."

"It certainly didn't bother me at all." She'd spent a good part of the evening talking with the star of the show and he was apologizing to her?

"I used you," he said. "There were so many people there who know my background. They know about the accident and that I'm not working any more. I really had no desire to talk to them and answer their questions and listen to them try to persuade me to get back to work. I welcomed the opportunity to talk to someone who didn't know a thing about me."

So that was it. "Glad I could serve some purpose," she said with a smile. She guessed that this dinner out was meant as some sort of payback.

"You did," Jessie said, and there were tears in her eyes. "We were both dreading last night. We've discovered that we can't talk too easily about what happened when we're in a public place. We tend to fall apart a lot."

"Of course you do," Kim said.

"About the same time as the accident," Jessie continued, "I split up with the man I'd been living with for five years. And I was going to school, but all of a sudden, I couldn't concentrate. So I dropped out. Just for a year I hope. I was working on my master's degree in engineering."

"Wow," Kim said, impressed.

"So Adam and I are both trying to put the pieces back together."

Kim felt overwhelmed by their openness, and frightened by her desire to be open in return. "Well, it's great that you have each other," she said.

The waitress appeared at their table and took their orders. Kim ordered pasta to share with Cody.

"So let's switch the topic to *you*," Jessie said when the waitress walked away. "Tell us your life story."

Kim laughed, and she hoped that neither of them picked up the nervousness in the sound. "I don't want to put you to sleep," she said. She'd been on the run less than three weeks, and already she was longing to spill her guts to the first people who'd befriended her. She was used to relationships based on honesty. She felt guilty about offering them anything less than that.

"Well," she began, "I was born and raised in Los Angeles." Nice, big, anonymous city. She had been born in Boulder. Never lived anyplace else, either. "I loved art, growing up. All through school, art was the only class I could get decent grades in. I was planning to major in art when I started college, but then I met my husband and I dropped out to put him through school." No harm in being honest about that part, she thought. Nobody was going to be looking for her based on the fact that she had once hoped to major in art. Jim probably wouldn't think to mention that fact in his description of her.

"Ouch," Jessie said.

"Worse than ouch," Kim said. "Once he was done with college, he decided he wanted to go to medical school." She'd make him a doctor, the arrogant, egocentric sort. "So I kept working to put him through medical school."

"What kind of work were you doing?" Adam asked.

She'd told Ellen she'd worked in a bank, but she wouldn't make that mistake again. "Receptionist," she said. "For some nondescript business in L.A."

"So what happened after he got out of medical school?" Jessie asked.

"He met someone better educated than me."

Adam sat back in his seat and laughed. "Oh, man. I bet you wanted to kill him."

"I'd considered it." She smiled. "But I was pregnant at the time and didn't want to give birth in prison."

"You were pregnant and he went out on you?" Jessie asked. "What a prick."

"Yeah." She grinned. She liked this. They were definitely on her side. She had to be careful where she took her tale in terms of truth and lies, though. Already she'd forgotten to add in the part about living in New Jersey.

"So what happened?" Jessie asked. "Did he ask for a divorce?"

"No, I did." It was a lie, of course, but it made her feel powerful just to say it. "He was weepy and remorseful and everything, but I was so angry. He'd cost me all those years when I could have been getting an education myself. Plus, I knew he was still seeing Babette, and I—"

"Babette?" Jessie laughed. "That was her name?"

"That's the name I gave her." Peggy was no Babette, but it didn't matter. Kim was on a roll. "Anyhow, I knew I could never trust him again. I didn't even *like* him anymore."

"Who could blame you?" Adam said. "He doesn't sound particularly likable."

"And Babette," Jessie added. "I would have hired a hit man, I think."

"I did, in my dreams a few times."

"What about the baby?" Jessie asked. "What about Cody? Didn't your husband—what was his name?"

She had not thought of a name for him. "Ted," she christened him. "And no, he wasn't very interested in Cody." She wanted to tell them the truth. She wanted to tell them what a creep Ted had turned out to be. What a traitor. But she couldn't. "He didn't care, and I really didn't want him around my son."

"He pays child support, I hope," Adam said.

"No. If I took child support from him, I'd have to let him visit. And I don't want that." She would have to change the stories she'd told Lucy and Ellen.

"Well, it must help that he lives out on the west coast," Jessie said.

"Well, actually we were living in New Jersey at the time we split up."

"Really?" Adam asked. "Where in New Jersey did you live?"

"Sort of between Trenton and Princeton," she answered vaguely.

"Dana—that was my wife—was from Passaic."

"Oh." She nodded, hoping she shouldn't be making more of a connection than she seemed to be.

The waitress delivered their salads, and Kim cut a wedge of tomato on her bread plate and set it in front of Cody.

Adam shook his head as he started on his salad. "Some people take marriage for granted, you know? They don't appreciate what they have."

"Right," she said. "I know."

"So you're all on your own with Cody, huh?" Jessie asked. "That must be hard."

"It is," she agreed. "That's why I hope I get some word processing jobs soon."

Adam looked at his sister. "We can probably help out with that, huh, Jess?"

Jessie nodded. "Sure. Betty's always complaining she has too much typing to do, and maybe Noel's worn out his latest typist by now."

"How about those offices in the Spire Building?" Adam asked his sister. "You know, Les and those guys?"

"Good idea. I'll give Les a call and see what he thinks."

"I sent brochures to a lot of the businesses around town," Kim said.

"Great," Adam said. "And Jess and I will put in a good word for you. Get you some work."

She felt her eyes burning. Her nose was probably turning red. "That's really nice of you." She was embarrassed by her reaction to their warmth.

They walked her home after dinner, telling her it was not too far out of their way.

"Do you live together?" she asked, hoping that was not too personal a question.

"Just about," Adam said.

"I've been renting the house next to his for the last five years," Jessie explained. Jessie was pushing Cody's stroller, and the little boy was nearly asleep by the time they reached Ellen's house. The talk was light and easy, and Kim could not believe the level of comfort she felt with the two of them. She was *too* comfortable. It would be easy to slip up and reveal something she should never reveal.

And that was why, when they reached her house, she said good night without inviting them in.

*I*t's quarter to one, Linc." Grace warned. She pushed her shopping cart closer to the organic gala apples and pulled one of them out of the bin to sniff.

"Uh huh." He picked up a few oranges, slipped them into a plastic bag, and dropped them in his cart. He knew what time it was, but he wasn't anxious to do what he had to do that afternoon, and he didn't feel like rushing. He liked taking his time when he shopped at Alfalfa's. He and Susanna usually shopped here together, Tyler in the cart. They'd buy lots of good-for-you food, which was easy to do at this particular grocery store, but then they'd blow their good intentions in the bakery department.

Grace was not nearly as much fun. She disdained the bakery— "All that sugar!"—and she kept harping about the time. He had a one-thirty appointment on the other side of Boulder, and he would have to drop her off at her house first.

"You know, maybe giving Tyler's birthday present away is a stupid idea," he said as he bagged a head of lettuce.

Grace merely gave him a tolerant smile. He'd been saying the same thing all morning.

Tyler's birthday wasn't until the following week, but the rocking horse had been standing in the corner of Linc's guest room for over two months, waiting to take someone for a ride. Now it was in the back seat of his car, covered by a blanket. The horse was beautiful, carved out of maple and sporting a white yarn mane and tail. He'd had one very similar to it when he was a child, and since the day Tyler was born, he'd imagined getting one for him. Now it looked as though he would never have the chance to give it to him, and his anger at Susanna for disappearing without letting him say good-bye to either her or Tyler was mounting.

"Maybe I should wait until next week, *after* Tyler's birthday, just in case they're back by then."

Grace put her arm around his waist and gave him a squeeze that meant *I love you, but when are you going to face reality?*

He sighed and looked toward the dairy section. "Can't get any dairy stuff, since I'm not going straight home."

"Right, so why don't you get in line and I'll pick up my milk and yogurt and meet you there?"

"All right." He walked toward the front of the store, but took a detour at the bakery to pick up a couple of big chocolate chip cookies. Grace would never have to know.

All the checkout lines were long. He pushed his cart to the shortest he could find and looked at his watch. It was already ten after one.

He'd called the hospital the day before to see if they might know of a child who'd enjoy the rocking horse. The social worker at the hospital told him about a little boy, a cancer patient, who was about to celebrate his second birthday. He was an outpatient, coming to the hospital regularly for chemotherapy treatments. He lived with his mother, who was single and on welfare, and the social worker was certain he would receive little, if anything, for his birthday. "And he's a little doll," she added.

But the clincher came when Linc asked the boy's name.

"Tyler Jones," the social worker replied, and Linc knew then that the little boy was meant to have the rocking horse.

Still, what if Tyler was home by next week?

Grace suddenly appeared behind him in the line. "Even if Tyler's home by his birthday," she said, reading his mind, "you'll still be doing a wonderful thing for this other little kid."

"I know," he said. He turned in the line to face his friend. "I threw in something to acknowledge Tyler's birthday when I recorded the show on Wednesday. Just in case Susanna's still listening." How would he ever know? Would he go on for the rest of his life, playing a song for her here and there, never knowing if she heard him or not?

No one was telling him what was going on. It was clear they didn't trust him. He'd called Jim a few times, trying to glean some information from him, but Jim was evasive and Linc knew they'd decided not to let him in on anything. It was only from listening to the news and reading the paper that he knew the FBI was now involved in the case. And if the FBI was involved, they must have evidence that Susanna had crossed state lines. He was torn. He didn't want her found, for her sake. He did want her found for his own. He'd considered trying to find her himself, but gave up quickly on that idea. If the FBI couldn't find her, he doubted he had much of a chance. Besides, what was the point? It was clear that she had deliberately cut him off with the rest of her past.

He found himself paying careful attention to his mail and his faxes, in case she risked writing to him. He doubted she would, though. She was serious about this. She had obviously planned it for a while. Susanna had come to grips with leaving him even though he seemed unable to accept it himself.

He dropped Grace off at the house she shared with Valerie, then followed the directions the social worker had given him to Tyler Jones's neighborhood. He was running late, but at least he had not completely copped out.

At one forty-five, he pulled into the parking lot of what had to be the sorriest apartment complex in the sorriest neighborhood in Boulder. The apartment buildings were nothing more than depressing brick rectangles dotted with small windows, some of them broken, some boarded up with plywood. Children played on the sparse lawn or ran on the sidewalks.

Linc checked the address. He got out of the car, opened the rear door and removed the blanket covering the horse. He folded the blanket and set it on the seat, then lifted the wooden horse into his arms. He felt some guilt as he carried it past the other children. They looked at the horse with curiosity and longing, their eyes wide, and Linc knew it was only serendipity that little Tyler Jones would be the lucky recipient.

He had to climb two flights of stairs with the horse and was winded by the time he reached number 301. There was a hand-made cutout of a grinning pumpkin on the peeling brown paint of the door, and it made him smile.

A young woman answered his knock. She was wearing jeans and a red sweater. Her blond hair was damp.

"I'm Linc Sebastian," he said. "Did the social worker from the hospital tell you I'd be coming?"

"Yes." The woman stepped aside to let him in. "I'm Sandy, Tyler's mother. I couldn't believe it when Lonnie—the social worker—called. This is so nice of you."

He set the horse down on the living room floor. "Well, I was really pleased she could suggest someone who might like a brand new rocking horse."

"Oh, it's *beautiful*," the woman said. "Tyler's going to be crazy about it. I'll go and get him." She started to leave the room, then suddenly stopped and turned around. "Can I get you something to drink first?" she asked.

"No thanks."

"Okay. I'll be right back."

She disappeared down a short hallway, and Linc stood in the center of the tiny living room. Tyler's mother had obviously tried to brighten the place with colorful pillows on the sofa and scarves draped over the lampshades, but the room was dark and dismal despite her efforts. He wondered if Susanna and Tyler were living like this.

The woman was gone a few minutes, and when she returned she was carrying a little boy with mocha-colored skin, huge dark eyes, and no hair. He looked like a frail little famine survivor. Linc had to work to mask his shock.

"This is Tyler," the woman said.

The little boy stared blankly at Linc, but then he suddenly spotted the horse and his face instantly came to life. He struggled to get down from his mother's arms. She set him on the floor, and he ran to the horse with a yelp of delight.

"Would you like to ride him, Tyler?" Linc asked. It felt good to say the name Tyler out loud again.

Tyler looked at him with his big dark eyes and nodded. Linc lifted him up and set him carefully in the saddle. He knelt down to hold the little boy steady as the horse rocked back and forth.

"Does he talk?" he asked the mother.

She shook her head. "He was starting to, but when he got sick and had to go to the hospital so much, he just stopped."

Linc smiled at the pure joy in the toddler's face. He'd buy a hundred of these horses if that's all it took to put such pleasure on a sick child's face. Tyler giggled, and Linc could feel the sound in the delicate network of ribs and spine beneath his hand where it rested on the little boy's back.

"How is he doing?" Linc asked past the lump in his throat.

"He's almost done with the chemo," his mother said. "Then we wait and see. But I think he's doing real good, myself."

"What do you think, Ty?" Linc asked. "How do you like this horse?"

Tyler didn't look at him, but he leaned over and pressed his cheek against the horse's yarn mane in an obvious gesture of affection. Linc was touched.

"Do you have kids?" Sandy asked.

"No. But—" Linc sat back on his heels, one hand still on Tyler's back. He wasn't certain why, but he knew he was going to tell her. "Actually, I bought this horse for my girlfriend's son, whose name is also Tyler."

"Really?" Sandy frowned. "Then why—"

"She lost custody of Tyler to her ex-husband and his wife, and she didn't want to give him up, so she took off with him."

"Took off? You mean you don't know where she is?"

"That's right. And right now, I'm pretty angry with her about it."

"No, don't be," Sandy said quickly. She sat down on the arm of the old, moth-eaten sofa and leaned toward him. "I would have done exactly the same thing if I was in her shoes. If anybody tried to take my Tyler from me—" She shook her head. "Well, I'd be outta here so fast your head would spin."

"Without saying good-bye to people who love you?"

"And if she'd said good-bye to you, what would you have done?"

"Tried to stop her from going," he admitted.

"Right." She smiled. "You can't hold it against her for picking her son over you. It doesn't mean she doesn't care about you. It's just something that happens with mothers. She carried him. She gave birth to him. I bet you she would give up her own life in a heartbeat for that boy, wouldn't she?"

He nodded. He'd even heard Susanna say as much.

"So, even though she's probably lonely without you, she's got her boy with her. Believe me, right now that's all she's thinking about." Sandy had tears in her eyes, but she blinked hard, then suddenly changed the topic. "I'm never going to get him off that thing, you know," she said, smiling at her son.

"It makes me happy to see how much he likes it." Linc stood up, one hand ready to latch onto Tyler's shoulder, but the little boy seemed to be balancing well without his help. "I sure hope he gets better quickly," he said.

"Mmm." Sandy looked at her son. "Me too."

Linc glanced at his watch without really noticing the time. "Well, I guess I should go now." He walked slowly toward the door, one eye still on Tyler.

Sandy followed him. "Thanks so much, Mr. Sebastian," she said as she opened the door for him.

Linc leaned over to lightly buss her cheek. "You're welcome," he said. "And I appreciated your words of wisdom. I think I needed to hear them."

He walked down the dark stairway and out into the sunshine. The children eyed him as he passed, probably wondering which apartment now possessed the beautiful horse he'd been carrying earlier. They had no way of knowing that he'd taken away far more from that apartment than anything he'd left behind.

im sat with Cody on the floor of the porch, helping him play with his garage sale blocks, taking them apart, putting them back together again. The weather was clear and warm, the sky a perfect blue that reminded her of Colorado, and classical music poured through Ellen's open window.

In two days it would be Cody's—Tyler's—birthday, but she wouldn't dare celebrate on that day. She'd decided that Cody Stratton's birthday would be nearly a week later. She had not thought through the ramifications of changing Tyler into Cody, not the way she'd considered her own change in identity. What would she do when she needed to produce a birth certificate for her son? As far as the world knew, Cody Stratton had never been born.

The front door opened behind her, and Lucy stepped onto the porch, a mug in her hand. She was wearing dark palazzo pants, a white sweater, and a necklace made of huge green beads.

"What a beautiful day!" She sat down on the glider and took a sip from her mug. "I love this street. It's so pretty and quiet. And you can *feel* the presence of the water even if you can't really see it."

"I love it, too," Kim said. The street was not pretty, exactly, but it was interesting with its old homes and red brick sidewalks.

"It feels so good to be settled in, finally," Lucy said.

Kim was mildly curious about her neighbor, but hesitant to ask questions, lest she receive questions in return. But she had to say *something*.

"Ellen said you're a writer?" she prompted.

"Yes," Lucy said. "I write magazine articles, mostly. Mainly on parenting issues. I'm dabbling in the health world right now, though. Alternative health care, that sort of thing. I was tickled to discover that Ellen is a massage therapist. I think I'm going to do a big article on massage. I can take a couple of different angles with it—you know, the sensual, splashy approach for *Cosmo*, the therapeutic benefits for *Prevention*. I try to get a few different articles out of every piece of research."

"It sounds like fun," Kim said sincerely. She envied Lucy's enthusiasm for her work.

Cody crawled over to Lucy and pulled himself up by hanging on to her knees.

"Hi sweetheart," she greeted the little boy. Then to Kim, "Does he walk yet?"

"Almost."

"Oh, yes." Lucy watched him balance next to her legs. "He's almost there, isn't he?" She lifted Cody onto her lap and let him play with her necklace. "This is one easy baby you have," she said.

"Yes. I'm very lucky."

"Don't you just hate it when people say a baby's a 'good baby?'" Lucy smoothed Cody's fly-away blond hair. "I hate hearing that word 'good' applied to little children, as though they could be anything but. A 'bad' baby isn't being bad. He just has something that's bothering him, poor thing. I hate that."

"People do it all the time, though." Kim remembered the nurses at the hospital referring to Cody as a "good baby" because he didn't cry when they poked him with needles. She'd wanted him to scream his outrage at the world.

"That would probably be a good topic for one of your articles," she suggested. She was liking Lucy a bit more this morning.

"Oh, I've written that one a thousand times."

Kim watched Lucy bend over to pick up a couple of Cody's blocks. She held them out to the little boy, weaning him away from her necklace.

"Do you have children of your own?" Kim asked.

"Five. And eight grandchildren."

"Wow. Do they all live around here?"

"Well, I raised all my kids here in Annapolis, but only a couple of them still live here. Two are in California. One's in Florida."

"Do you happen to know of a good pediatrician close by?" she asked. It was nearly time for Cody to have his inoculations and a checkup. He'd also need to have an echocardiogram sometime in the next few months, but she'd deal with that later.

"Oh, sure," Lucy said. "I used to take my kids to Dr. Sweeney over in West Annapolis. His son's taken over his practice, and he's supposed to be just as good."

"Thanks." She stared out at the street, committing the doctor's name to memory and wondering how she would be able to give him the information in the medical records. It was essential that he know Cody's medical history, yet every sheet in those records had the name Tyler Miller printed on it, not to mention the names of the doctors who had treated him and the names of the hospitals where he'd been a patient. She had a sudden disconcerting thought. Could doctors around the country have been alerted to look for a year-old male child who'd had surgery for coarctation of the aorta?

"That's right," Lucy said to Cody. "That's the red block, and it fits into the blue one. Just like that."

The radio in Ellen's living room switched from music to the news, and Kim heard the newscaster announce that there were still no leads in that bombing at the house she'd walked past the previous week.

"Did you hear about that woman who was killed by a bomb at her house?" Kim asked Lucy.

"*Yes*, I did," Lucy said. Cody was squirming to get down, and she set him on his feet in front of her. He started walking, holding on to the glider, then dropped to the floor and crawled over to his blocks. "They said it was an express mail package. Only it didn't actually come through the mail, I guess. Someone just left it on her porch and rang the bell."

"That's what I heard, too."

"Probably an ex-husband," Lucy said with a smirk. "You and I'd better watch what mail we open."

"Do you know anything about her?" Kim asked. "Was she married? Did she have kids?"

"No, I haven't heard a thing, though I did hear the police say they had no suspect and no motive." Lucy drained her mug and set it on the floor next to the glider. "You know, Kim, I've been toying with the idea of writing an article about single mothers with small children," she said. "Seeing you with Cody here is inspiring me. Maybe you'd let me interview you?"

Kim was still imagining the horror of being blown apart, maybe leaving a little child behind, but she was able to catch the danger in Lucy's suggestion nevertheless.

"Oh, I don't think I'd make a very good . . . " Her voice drifted off as she noticed a man walking on the sidewalk a short distance away. He was looking in their direction, and she followed him anxiously with her eyes until she realized he was Adam Soria. He waved and turned onto the sidewalk leading up to the house.

"Good morning!" he called out.

"Hi, Adam." She smiled, waving back.

He stopped at the bottom of the porch steps, holding a white bag in the air. "Would you ladies care to join me for some bagels and cream cheese?" He still looked tired, but his smile this morning was genuine.

"Lucy, this is Adam Soria," she said. "He's the artist who paints the murals around town. Have you noticed them?"

"Oh, of course!" Lucy said. "My, you're very talented."

Adam bowed slightly. "Thank you." He turned to Kim. "And besides breakfast, I've brought you some work."

"Work?"

"Yeah. You know, that activity people perform to earn money?"

"*Really?*"

"Really." He reached into his pocket and pulled out a scrap of paper. "Kitty Russo. She's a secretary in an engineering firm in the Spire Building. She's a friend of ours, and I spoke with her yesterday and she said to have you call her. The woman who usually does a lot of their typing has a new baby and is taking a break, so Kitty was happy to hear about you."

She reached out to take the scrap of paper from his hand, trying to hide her disbelief. "Fantastic," she said. "Thank you so much."

"So how about it?" he asked again. "Bagels, anyone?"

"I'd love one," Kim said.

"No thanks," Lucy said. "Sunday might be a day of rest for some people, but not for me." She picked up her coffee cup from the floor and got to her feet.

Kim leaned over to put Cody's blocks back in their canvas sack.

"It was nice meeting you, Adam, " Lucy said as she opened the door and headed into the house. "You two have a good breakfast."

"Thanks," Kim said. She looked at Adam. "Why don't you come up to my apartment? I'll make some coffee."

"Great idea."

Cody wanted to walk up the stairs holding on to her hands, and the going was slow, but Kim was buoyant. She had work! What a stroke of luck it had been meeting Adam and Jessie.

She let Adam into the apartment, glad she'd spent the day before fixing it up a bit. She had picked up a couple of paintings at a garage sale. Nothing special, but they gave the living room some color and warmth. The computer and printer still took up half the table in the dining corner of her living room, though. When she made some money, she would buy a desk.

Kim started the coffee while Adam took the bagels out of the bag and set them on a plate. He spotted one of her brochures on the kitchen counter and picked it up.

"Hey, this is nice!" he said. "Did you design it?"

"Yes."

"Very nice work." He opened it and read the information inside. "Do you do mostly graphics?"

She laughed. "I don't 'do' mostly anything," she said. "I taught myself how to use a graphics program because I had to come up with something for the brochure. And I sketch a little. That's about it."

"Really? Let me see your sketches," he said.

She wrinkled her nose. "Do I have to?"

He smiled. "Uh huh."

She walked across the living room and pulled the sketchbook from the magazine rack, knowing she wanted his appraisal of her drawings despite her hesitation. She'd been drawing every day, but she felt as if she were working in a vacuum. It wasn't like high school, where she'd received constant feedback. She had no idea if she was any good or not.

She handed the sketchbook to Adam and leaned against the cabinets, arms folded across her chest.

He set the book on the counter and went through it, page by page.

"Not bad," he said when he reached the fifth page and her first drawing of the house across the street. He turned the page and saw her sketch of the sofa with its downy cushions. "You seem to be improving on every page," he said.

"I got some books out of the library. I'd forgotten a lot. I haven't really done any drawing since high school, so I'm afraid I'm stuck at that level."

"Hmm. No, you don't seem stuck at all." He turned the page to one of her numerous sketches of Cody. "Wow," he said, and she couldn't help but beam. "People are your forte."

"You think so?" She remembered hearing the same words from one of her teachers in high school, although that praise had been overshadowed by her father's rage when he found one of her books on figure drawing.

"Absolutely." Adam leafed through the book until he found another sketch of Cody. "I can't believe you didn't keep up with this. You're very talented."

"Thank you. I planned to, but . . . I sort of lost steam when my father died." She wondered if that made any sense to him at all.

"When was that?"

"When I was seventeen," she lied, but only by a year.

"You must have been very close to him, huh?"

It took all her strength to force herself to nod.

"How did he die?"

She thought quickly. "Cirrhosis of the liver." Almost certainly her father would have killed himself with his drinking if Linc hadn't beaten him to it with a gun.

Adam raised his eyebrows. "Alcohol?" he asked.

She nodded.

"That stuff ruins a lot of lives," he said bitterly.

"Well, it was more than my father dying, really. My husband wasn't very supportive."

"Oh, that's right. The doctor, huh? I remember you said you put him through school?"

She had almost forgotten that she'd made Jim into a doctor. A doctor named Ted. She really had to get her story straight. "Right," she said.

"I hate that." Adam closed the sketchbook. "I hate hearing about a creative person who's been forced to put their creativity aside. I feel personally cheated of whatever they might have produced that I could enjoy, whether it's a book or a play or a painting. It's a crime."

She nodded. She felt cheated herself.

"You know, it's never too late to get back to it," Adam said. "This sketchbook is a great start."

"Well, I'm just dabbling, actually."

"You're free of your husband now. Don't let him hold you back even when he's not with you. Why don't you let me give you a lesson or two? I'm not painting myself. I might as well help someone else do it."

"Maybe," she said hesitantly. She was afraid of committing to anything anymore without thinking through every possible consequence.

She put Cody down for his nap, then poured them each a cup of coffee and cut the bagels. "Shall we take these down to the porch?" she asked. "I can leave the window open so I can hear Cody."

"Good idea." He took one of the mugs from her and led the way down the stairs, where the scent of vanilla now filled the air.

They settled down on the porch, Kim on the glider, Adam in the rocker. He told her more about Kitty Russo, the woman who needed her typing help. He told her about the Spire Building and the variety of businesses it housed. She was certain she'd sent some of her brochures to that building.

"It was very nice of you to tell Kitty about me."

"Glad I could help both of you out. I wish—"

She held up a hand to stop him, cocking her head to listen. Had she heard a noise from upstairs?

Silence. The only sound was the soft music from Ellen's radio. "Sorry," she said. "Didn't mean to interrupt you."

"You're hypervigilant," Adam said.

"What does that mean?"

"It means that you're always on the lookout, as if you're expecting something terrible to happen. You startle easily. I noticed it the first night I met you at the gallery, and the other night at dinner."

She looked down at her cup so he couldn't read her eyes. "I think you're imagining things."

"Maybe," he admitted. "I've been hypervigilant myself, since the accident. It's not that I actually *expect* someone to leap out of the shadows at me, but I wouldn't be surprised if they did. I don't trust the world much anymore. I don't trust it to be the same tomorrow as it is today. Things can change so quickly." He stared out at the street.

She nodded slowly as she broke off a piece of the bagel and slipped it in her mouth. A dark curtain was falling over him, and she wasn't certain whether she should try to lift it or simply let it do its worst and be done with it. She didn't want him to confide in her, though. She didn't want him to bare his soul to her when she couldn't reciprocate. She would make a mockery of his honesty.

But he wanted to talk. "It was Molly's tenth birthday," he said. "We'd had a little party. Just Dana and Molly and Liam—my son, who was five—and Jessie and Noel, her boyfriend. After the party, we all planned to go to a bike store to pick out a bike for Molly. There were too many of us to fit in one car, so Dana took Liam and Molly, and Jessie, Noel, and I followed in my car. We were driving down Route Fifty, and we came to an intersection. Dana's car was in front of me. She pulled into the intersection on a green light, but a guy from the other direction ran the red at full speed. He was drunk."

"Oh, my God. You saw the whole thing?"

He nodded. "He bulldozed into Dana's car and smashed it up against the side of a truck. The three of them were killed instantly. I know that for a fact, since I was there and saw them." He looked down into his cup, and she wondered what horrors he saw reflected there. "I doubt they even had a chance to realize what was happening. I hope not, anyway."

"What happened to the other driver?" she asked. "The one who hit them?"

Adam snorted. "Essentially nothing. Not in the accident, and not in court. He got off with a slap on the wrist."

"That's not fair."

"An understatement. I would like to personally lay him down in the street and run my car back and forth over him until he . . . " He looked up at her, his cheeks red. "Sorry," he said.

"Don't be. I don't blame you a bit. No one would. As a matter of fact, I'd hold him down for you while you ran over him."

Adam smiled. "So now I start over. Not doing a bang-up job of it, either."

"It's too soon to do a bang-up job. I think you're supposed to let yourself grieve for a while."

"Let myself? My self isn't giving me any choice in the matter."

She wished she could tell him the extent to which *she* was starting over. She'd lost Linc. Lost her friends in Boulder. And she'd nearly lost Cody, first to heart disease, then to Jim and Peggy. It was not the same thing, of course, and she had to admit that losing Linc and her friends had been her own doing. Still, she felt a bond with Adam. She wanted to share back. *Be careful*, she told herself.

"When Cody was born," she said softly, "he had a heart condition. They thought he would die. They had to transport him to a hospital with a pediatric cardiac surgeon who saved Cody's life." She would be forever grateful to Ron Myerson for the care he took with her son. Somehow, she'd managed to separate her feelings about Ron from her feelings about his sister. "But for those few days when he was so sick," she continued, "I was in terrible shape. I imagined his death over and over again." She felt suddenly embarrassed that she'd tried to make a comparison between her experience and his. "I know it's not the same as what you've gone through. I can only imagine what it's been like for you."

"Cody seems so healthy," Adam said. "I'm surprised to hear there was anything seriously wrong with him."

"He was very lucky. Me too. The one thing I don't think I could survive is losing him. He seems so vulnerable to me. If I'm hypervigilant, that's why. I'm always afraid something might happen to him. I hate loving someone that much. It seems . . . unhealthy. I would do anything for him. I would give away government secrets."

"Do you have any?"

"Any what?

"Government secrets?"

She laughed. "No."

"You'd better not get any, then." He finished his coffee and set the cup on the floor of the porch next to his empty plate. "I know what you mean, though. I'd about gotten over feeling afraid for the kids all the time. I'd gotten complacent. Liam broke his arm, and he bounced right back. Molly fell and cut her cheek, and it healed in a few days. I began to take their resiliency for granted. Then suddenly *wham*, they're gone."

Kim winced.

Adam stretched his arms out in front of him and let out a sigh, obviously bringing the conversation to a close. "Well," he said, standing up, "I didn't mean to get into all of *that.*"

She stood too. "I'm so glad you stopped over. And thanks for the bagels. Not to mention the job."

"You're very welcome." He started down the stairs. "Jessie says hi, by the way. She's excited because Victoria's pregnant."

"Victoria?"

"Her cat. Jess is so thrilled, you'd think she's pregnant herself."

She remembered Jessie's affection toward Cody. "She seems like she's cut out to be a mother."

Adam opened his mouth as though he were about to say something, but then he changed his mind.

"What happened with her boyfriend?" Kim asked. "Noel, is it?"

"Nice guy, but he drinks too much," Adam said.

"Oh." Kim nodded. "Say no more."

Adam waved and turned to leave, and Kim carried their plates and mugs upstairs, anxious to return to her sketchbook.

She put Cody to bed at quarter to eight that night, turned on the radio on the shelf behind her bed, and crawled under the covers to wait.

Linc was her one source of pain, and she'd made a decision this week. She would not allow herself to think of him except on Sunday nights from eight to ten. Otherwise, those thoughts would take over her life. She had to remind herself that she had her son; that was the most important thing. And she had a few friends.

Even Lucy was not so bad. Having Lucy next door would be a bit like having a mother to turn to for advice. She certainly had never had that when she was growing up, although Linc's mother had filled that role for a long time. She'd actually lived with Geri after her own mother kicked her out of the house. Geri had gotten her a job waitressing at the coffee shop where she worked, and on weekends the two of them would visit Linc in prison. Linc and Geri became her family. She'd grieved when Geri died. Now Linc was dead to her, too.

Immediately after Simon and Garfunkel sang "Song for the Asking," Linc played a recording of Pete Seeger singing "Froggie Went a-Courtin'," and Kim knew that was his birthday present to Cody. Or rather, to Tyler. Linc sang that song to him often. She thought of waking Cody up to hear it, but what could she say to him? "Listen, Cody, Linc's playing one of your favorite songs!" She never mentioned Linc to Cody anymore. It could only confuse him. So she gave up on that idea, got comfortable under the covers, and figured she would be the first person in the universe to listen to "Froggie Went a-Courtin'" with tears in her eyes.

She waited to hear if Linc would say anything after "Froggie" ended, but he moved right on to another Seeger song, and her mind began to drift.

Linc had moved in with his mother when he got out of prison, and Kim—Susanna—had been overjoyed by his long-awaited freedom. She'd always blamed herself for his incarceration. If it weren't for her, he never would have been at her house that night her father went crazy. He would not even have known where her father kept his gun.

Susanna had married Jim the summer before Linc's release from prison, and she'd wanted Linc and Jim to get to know one another. She had visions of the three of them doing things together. Linc would need friends, she told Jim. He'd need family. But Jim was not only cool to the idea, he was dead set against it.

"I don't want an ex-con as my best buddy," he told her. "I'm going for a law degree. I need to keep clean."

There was no way she could cut off her own long-standing friendship with her former neighbor, though, and she asked Jim if he would mind her seeing Linc every once in awhile. She could visit him at Geri's, she suggested, or go out to dinner with him some night when Jim had class. Jim forbade it, flat out, and she was too afraid of fighting with him to try to negotiate a compromise. So she saw Linc on the sly. She nurtured that old friendship. She encouraged Linc when he was looking for a job in radio, listened to the trials and tribulations of his relationships with other women, and called him when she was troubled about something and Jim was not around to listen. It had been a mistake, though, trying to keep that relationship a secret from Jim, and when Jim finally realized she was seeing Linc, he assumed there was more between them than friendship. "Your father was right!" he'd yelled at her one night, after spotting them together in a restaurant. "You've probably been fucking him since you were fifteen!"

She'd tried to reassure him that her relationship with Linc was as pure and platonic as that of a brother and sister. Linc even called Jim to talk to him about it, but Jim could not be reasoned with. She knew later that reason was not what Jim was after. He was looking for an excuse to leave their marriage.

The beginning of the end came when she attended a bank conference in Denver. She checked into the hotel on a Friday evening, locked herself in her room, and pulled out a home pregnancy test she'd bought earlier that day. Her period was ten days late, and she was hopeful and excited. She'd said nothing to Jim about it, in case she was wrong, but she was not surprised when the test bore out her suspicions.

She thought of calling Jim, but decided against it. She wanted to celebrate with him by her side, not alone in a hotel room an hour from home. Besides, if it hadn't been for the conference, this weekend would have been their first together in their new house. She could zip home, spend the night with her husband, and return to Denver before the meetings began in the morning. Within a few minutes of making that decision, she was on the road back to Boulder.

There was a strange car in their driveway when she pulled up to the new house in Wonderland. She figured Jim was showing the house to one of his friends and hoped she'd be able to get him alone long enough to tell him her news.

When she walked in the front door, the living room lights were dim, and soft music played on the stereo. She called out Jim's name, but there was no response, and she started up the stairs to their bedroom.

When she opened the bedroom door, she was greeted with gasps of surprise and a flurry of sheets being drawn up, covering flesh. Susanna stared at her husband and the woman in her bed, unable to speak. They seemed equally frozen, Peggy watching her from beneath her tousled dark hair, Jim open-mouthed in shock.

She was finally able to step out of the room and close the door. Walking numbly down the stairs, she wondered how she had failed him. She had not been good enough for him. Not pretty enough or smart enough. The image of that beautiful woman in bed with Jim would never leave her mind.

She had to escape, from the scene upstairs as well as from the pain in her heart. She drove to Linc's house, where he held her and let her cry, let her curse. What he wouldn't let her do was blame or belittle herself.

"Jim's done enough of that," Linc said. "You don't need to do it to yourself."

Jim came over the following day—he'd had no problem figuring out where she'd gone. He explained that he wanted to end their marriage, that he was sorry, he hadn't wanted her to find out that way. He'd buy her out of the house, he said, but it would take him a few years to pay her off. He went on and on about financial details while she pretended to listen.

When he finally paused for breath, she told him about the pregnancy, and he reacted with anger. She'd stopped the pill too soon, he said. Yes, he'd said they could start a family when he was done with law school, but he hadn't meant right away. She would have to have an abortion.

He began badgering her about it, calling her several times a day at Linc's to try to persuade her, and she slipped deeper and deeper into a pit of despair. She couldn't go to work, couldn't even get out of bed in the morning. Permanent escape began to sound like a wonderful idea, but when she confided that thought to Linc, he called Valerie, who arranged to have her locked up in a psychiatric ward. She was bitter about that for a few days, but as she began to feel better, she became grateful for their intervention.

While in the hospital, she decided she could not have an abortion. She had no family. Her father was dead, her mother was as good as dead, and she no longer had a husband. She wanted her child above all else, and it was concern for her baby that finally got her well. She would have to be strong and healthy to take care of a child on her own.

Linc told her that if Jim wouldn't be there for her, he would be, and he meant it. He called Jim and told him to stop harassing her about an abortion. He went to her doctor's appointments with her. He was there for her first sonogram, and he never missed any of the childbirth classes. The woman he'd been dating broke up with him because of his "obsession" with Susanna and the baby, but he didn't seem to care.

He was with her every minute of her labor, and he was there during those frantic moments in the delivery room when it became obvious that something was terribly wrong. But it was when she saw Linc weeping over her baby's tiny, gray body that, in her mind, he became Tyler's father. Jim was nothing to her after that. Less than nothing. As though they shared her feelings, everyone at the hospital treated Linc as if he were indeed Tyler's father. The nurses. The social worker. After all, Jim was nowhere to be found.

"He was anxious to be there," Peggy had said on the witness stand, "but he stayed away out of consideration for Susanna. He knew what a difficult time that was for her and didn't want to make things harder for her."

Tyler was four months old when she and Linc became lovers. She'd been sleeping in his guest room for over a year by then, and one night he simply came into her room, woke her up, took her by the hand, and walked her back to his own bedroom. And there he made love to her, and it felt so rational, so simply *right*, that she wondered why they had put it off for so long. The commitment between them had been forged a long, long time ago, and they both knew it.

"Pete Seeger created this next song when he set a biblical passage to music." Linc's slow, soft radio voice floated from the radio behind Kim's head, "It's sung here by the Byrds."

There was a lump in Kim's throat as the music started for

"Turn, Turn, Turn." Linc's voice had sounded so close. She could shut her eyes and pretend he was lying next to her on the bed. Eyes closed, she reached out and touched the other pillow, imagining that she was stroking Linc's cheek with her fingers, touching his lips. She rolled away from the pillow with a sense of defeat. How could she go on this way, living for Sunday nights, when she could lie in the darkness, listening to Linc's voice, imagining she was with him? And all the while she would know that the morning would reveal the truth: her lover would be gone, leaving in his place only the impersonal hum of a stranger's voice on the radio.

What do you want on your sub?" Peggy asked her brother. She was talking to Ron from the phone in her Legal Aid office.

"The works," Ron said. "Except hold the raw onions. I still have some patients to see today."

"All right. I'll be over in a little while." She hung up the phone and picked up the one remaining chart on her desk before walking down the hall toward the waiting room. She would see her last client for the day, Bonnie Higgins, the woman whose husband wanted a divorce, then grab a couple of subs and drive to Ron's office to have lunch with him. There were a few things she wanted to talk to her brother about.

Bonnie stood up as soon as she saw Peggy at the door of the waiting room. Once again, she looked as though she'd been doing more than her share of crying.

"Everything's changed," she said as she followed Peggy back to her office.

"For better or worse?" Peggy asked, although the answer was obvious.

"A thousand times worse." Bonnie sat down in front of Peggy's desk and pulled a tissue from her purse. "I found out he's been having an affair," she said, blowing her nose.

"Oh, I'm sorry," Peggy said, although she was not surprised.

"It's been going on for years." Bonnie still looked stunned by the news. "It's his *secretary*. He's not even original. I've talked to that woman on the phone a million times a week. She's one of those . . . trashy looking women, you know what I mean? Tight clothes, too much makeup. I never thought he'd be interested in someone like that."

"Do you have evidence?" Peggy started making notes on a legal pad. "How did you find out?"

"She called me and told me all about it. She asked me to please let him go. 'Don't make it so hard on him,' she said. Is that enough evidence for you?"

"Has he denied it?"

"No. He told me everything. He's feeling guilty."

"Okay." Peggy leaned forward. "This changes your case, but only slightly. It gives us something to use against him if he gives us a hard time, and we'd better get to work immediately on a property settlement. We need to take advantage of his guilt."

She spent another forty-five minutes with Bonnie, then left the Legal Aid office and headed for the sub shop.

Ron was waiting for her in his sunny office when she arrived.

"Hi, sis." He kissed her cheek and sat down behind his desk.

She took a seat herself and handed him his sub and a can of root beer.

"How are you doing?" Ron popped the top on his root beer and took a sip.

"All right," she said. She unwrapped her sandwich slowly. "This whole thing with Tyler is dragging on way too long, though."

"How long's it been now?" Ron asked. "Three weeks?"

"Three and a half. And babies change so quickly." She peered uninterestedly inside her turkey sub. She really wasn't hungry. "I worry that Tyler won't look like his picture very much longer. His birthday was two days ago, you know. He's a year old now."

Tyler's birthday had been a sad day for her, made even sadder by the fact that Jim did not remember the date until she reminded him of it at dinner. Even then, Jim had looked perplexed. "His birthday is October eighth?" he'd asked. "I guess I never knew that."

"A year already, huh?" Ron said. "Doesn't seem that long ago that I did his surgery."

"I was thinking," Peggy said. "We should probably send some

information about Tyler to general practitioners around the country, in addition to the cardiologists. You said yourself that he wouldn't need to be seen regularly by a cardiologist now. But Susanna will have to take him to a doctor at some point."

Ron had already helped Bill Anderson put together a medical report on Tyler, which they'd sent to hospitals and pediatric cardiologists around the country. But that no longer seemed like enough to Peggy.

Ron sighed. "I'm not going to write another report, Peggy. You can use the one I already wrote, if you think it's so important."

She played with a piece of lettuce hanging out of her sandwich, disturbed by his tone of voice. "I wasn't suggesting a new report." She could hear the hesitancy in her voice. "But . . . I guess I don't understand you, Ron. Why wouldn't you want to do everything possible to find Tyler?"

"Peggy." He swallowed a bite of his sandwich, then set it down on the wrapper. "I can't continue to support you in this. Not to the extent you want, anyway. When I listen to you talk about all this supposed danger Tyler is in with his mother, I just . . . I can't be party to that sort of hysteria."

*"Hysteria?"* She was incredulous.

"Yes. I can't listen to you talk about this situation and keep my thoughts to myself any longer. If you want to tell me what's going on with Tyler, you're going to have to hear what I think."

"Are you saying you think Tyler is better off with Susanna than he would be with us?"

"If 'better off' means having anything money can buy and the attention of two parents, then of course he's better off with you and Jim. But if it means being loved and well-cared for, then I see no difference which parent he's with."

"The court—"

"I don't care what the court said. Susanna didn't lose custody because she was an unfit mother. She lost because she lacked the resources to fight you and Jim."

"Oh, Ron, that's simply not so." She slammed her root beer on his desk with such force that it bubbled out of the top of the can. "Money had very little to do with it. There were many other things that came into play, and you know it. What about Linc Sebastian?

Susanna was probably going to end up married to him. Do you like the idea of Tyler living with someone like that?"

"Linc served his time. He paid for what he did. And I think he genuinely cared about Tyler. When I was called into the hospital for Tyler's emergency surgery, it was Linc who was there. Not you. Not Jim."

Peggy bristled. "We weren't there because we knew it would make things more complicated if we—"

"Peggy," Ron interrupted her, "listen to me. Jim became interested in Tyler when *you* became interested in Tyler. If you can't accept—"

"You've never liked Jim," she interrupted him. "You've always hated lawyers."

Ron laughed. "You're a lawyer and I love you."

"I don't feel very loved at the moment." She felt the pout forming on her face and wanted to kick herself. She was a competent woman, a competent lawyer, at home and at work. When she was with Ron, though, she became the little sister she'd always been with him.

"I have nothing against Jim," Ron said. "You're missing my point. I think you're a wonderful person. So is Jim. So is Susanna. So is Linc Sebastian, as far as I know. There's no right or wrong here. There's just a lot of pain."

"What do you mean, no right or wrong? Susanna broke the *law*, Ron. She kidnapped a baby and is probably hiding out under an alias somewhere. She's a criminal."

"You and Jim *made* her into a criminal when you pressed criminal charges. You turned a loving, very frightened mother into a felon, for Christ's sake."

"We *had* to make her a felon," Peggy argued. "The only way we could get the authorities to take the case seriously is if *we* took it seriously."

Ron leaned across the desk toward her. "How would you have felt in Susanna's position? You get pregnant, then discover your husband is sleeping with another woman."

Peggy winced. Ron was the one person to whom she'd confessed that miserable incident in Jim's bedroom. "I never should have told you," she said.

"So you find your husband with another woman," Ron continued, "and then you have to give up your new home to her. Not only that, but—surprise!—the other woman wants your baby, too."

"That's not fair. You're making me sound like a villain."

"No one's a villain. But just because you were not lucky enough to be able to have a baby yourself doesn't mean you're entitled to someone else's."

Peggy sat back in her seat, wounded. She could think of nothing else to say. She stared at her brother in silence for a moment, then rewrapped her sandwich, picked up her purse, and started for the door. He made no move to stop her.

One hand on the doorknob, she turned around to look at him. "I thought I'd only lost my stepson," she said, her throat tight, "but I see now that I've lost my brother, too."

"You haven't lost me." Ron did not look the least bit upset by this exchange. "All I'm saying is that I can't, in good conscience, join you in bashing Susanna any longer."

Jim was late getting home that night, so it wasn't until they were in bed together that she finally had the chance to tell him about her conversation with Ron. He listened, then put his arm around her.

"Don't blame him," he said. "He doesn't really know Susanna. He's just trying to be fair."

"He said just because I can't have a baby of my own doesn't mean I'm entitled to Susanna's." Ron's words still cut through her. She hadn't known her brother could be so cruel.

"But you *are* entitled to mine." Jim gave her shoulders a squeeze. "And so am I. We'll get him back, Peg, don't worry. Detective Rausch called me today to say they finally got a court order to disclose Susanna's credit card records. I guess she only has a Visa, and apparently, she hasn't used it yet. But we'll be able to trace her if she does."

"That's good," she said, but she was thinking that if Susanna hadn't used her card by now, she would never use it. Susanna was smarter than Jim gave her credit for.

Jim raised himself up on one elbow. "You're so beautiful," he said. He leaned down to kiss her. "All I want is for you to be happy." He kissed her again, with some heat this time, and she nearly started to cry. The last thing she felt like doing was making love. But she'd put him off for too long.

She returned the kiss, determined to meet his passion with her own. It was going to be difficult, though, because when she closed her eyes, all she could see was the disappointment and disdain in her brother's face.

*I* love this early autumn smell." Ellen sat down in one of the rockers, a cup of tea in her hand, and took a deep breath. She smiled at Kim and Lucy. "It's one of those comforting smells from childhood, you know?"

Kim did not know. The smell of an eastern fall was not familiar to her, but Lucy seemed to understand.

"Oh, yes," Lucy said. "It's just like where I grew up in Pennsylvania."

"I guess you didn't have this sort of smell as a kid in L.A., huh Kim?" Ellen asked.

"No." Kim leaned over to fix the cuff on Cody's jeans. "It's the smell of smog that comforts me."

They laughed, and Kim chuckled herself, pleased with the sense of ease she was beginning to feel with her two neighbors as she settled into Kim Stratton's life. As she *created* Kim Stratton's life. She'd learned to deal with Lucy's many questions by saying whatever popped into her head, and Lucy did not seem put off by the inconsistencies in her answers. As a matter of fact, she did not even seem to notice them. People accepted whatever you told them, Kim was discovering, as long as they had no reason to doubt your story. With each passing day, she was becoming more and more Kim Stratton. Susanna Miller was beginning to feel like some long-deceased relative she'd never taken the time to grieve over.

144

She and Cody had drifted into a routine, one that lulled her into a soft, easy complacency and let her hope her new world might hold promise and not pain. Her early mornings were spent over coffee on the porch with Lucy. Ellen usually had clients in the morning—those vibrant, clear-eyed early risers who needed their massage fix before going off to work—so it was rare for her to be able to join them. This morning, though, Ellen's first client had canceled, and since Kim had proclaimed this to be Cody's birthday, Ellen had joined in the modest celebration. The four of them ate doughnuts, and Cody unwrapped a pull toy—a wooden basset hound—from Lucy and a mobile of stars and planets from Ellen.

After coffee on the porch, Kim would usually take Cody for a walk through town and then to the park, where she could push him on the swing. She loved to see the healthy glow from the fall air on his cheeks and smell the outdoors on his skin and in his hair. And now she *tried* to be at the park the same time as Roxanne and her boys. There seemed to be no danger in making friends with Roxanne, and she'd decided Jack was not such a terrible kid. Cody was enamored with him and his brother, Brandon. Cody needed to be around other children, Kim thought, and fortunately, the gun had not reappeared.

Cody was crawling around on the porch floor, drooling mightily, one hand pushing the basset hound.

"Push him over here, Cody," she said. She didn't like him to get too close to the stairs.

He crawled in her direction, looking dapper in his new blue sweater with the sailboats on the pockets. She'd bought it for him this past weekend on one of her garage sale outings. Fifty cents, and it was adorable. Even if she woke up wealthy some morning, she would not go back to store-bought clothes.

She'd had a fairly substantial amount of work this week. Kitty Russo had kept her busy, and she'd even received a paycheck when she turned in the last of the typing on Friday. Kitty had nothing for her this week, she'd told her, but next week she would need her again. It was a good start.

Cody pulled himself up to his feet, one hand on the glider, and Kim showed him how he could walk by holding onto the glider with one hand and pulling the wooden dog with the other. She studied her son. In a few hours, she was taking him to the pediatrician Lucy had recommended, and she was not looking forward to it. She'd tackled Cody's medical records over the weekend. There was a two-inch thick stack of them. She went through them carefully, pulling out the information that looked important and typing it into a fresh document. On the sheets with the most recent blood work, she whited out the name of the lab as well as Tyler's name and typed Cody Stratton over it, along with the fictionalized name of a lab in Trenton, New Jersey. She took her re-created work to a nearby copy shop and made two copies. Then she stayed up half the night wondering whether or not doctors would be on the lookout for a year-old boy with a telltale scar on his chest. She was two thousand miles from Boulder, she reminded herself. No one knew her here.

This paranoia had to end. She'd watched *America's Most Wanted* on television the week before, holding her breath, waiting to see her own face and Cody's on the TV screen. She'd had a dream sometime that night that Lucy and Ellen saw them on a similar program and had the police breaking down her door by morning.

"I've got *another* cancellation this afternoon," Ellen said. She was holding Cody's mobile in the air, watching the floating planets as they caught the sunlight. "I hate having two cancellations in one day. It throws me off." She set the mobile down carefully on the porch floor. "Maybe I'll call Cherise Johnson and see if she wants to come in. She's got a flexible schedule."

Kim looked up at the mention of Cherise's name. "I keep forgetting to thank you for asking Cherise to invite me to her gallery when I first got here," she said.

Ellen looked puzzled. "Well, you're very welcome, but I don't know what you're talking about."

"You probably don't remember," Kim said. "Cherise had a showing of Adam Soria's paintings at her gallery, and she sent me an invitation. I didn't know a soul in town at the time, so I assumed you must have mentioned me to her and that's why she invited me."

"Hmm." Ellen leaned her head against the back of the rocker and looked at the ceiling. "I might have mentioned to her that someone moved in upstairs, but I don't think I went into more detail than that. I'm glad she asked you, anyhow."

"Me too." Kim helped Cody untangle the basset hound's string. "That's where I met Adam and Jessie."

"Ah, yes. Adam," Lucy said, as if she'd been waiting for precisely that opening in the conversation. "So tell us, Kim. Is he your boyfriend?"

Kim looked at her in surprise. "Adam?" she asked, as if the question were ridiculous—which it was. "He's just a friend." He *was* a friend, as was Jessie, and that was more than she'd expected to find for herself.

"And Jessie," Lucy said. "She's just his sister, isn't she?"

"Yes," Kim said. "And they're *both* my friends."

Adam and Jessie had stopped by yesterday afternoon and coerced her into going to the movies with them, a decision which had been a mistake, since Cody was teething and she'd spent much of the movie comforting him in the lobby. She'd seen them one other time this week as well, meeting them at the little Italian restaurant again for dinner.

"Well," Lucy said. "Let's find me a friend that handsome."

She hadn't thought of Adam as handsome. She hadn't evaluated his looks, one way or the other.

"And one for me, too, while we're at it," Ellen piped in. "Actually, mine doesn't have to be all that handsome. Just spiritually evolved. And a Scorpio, of course. He has to be a Scorpio."

Lucy laughed. "Of *course.*"

"What sign is your Adam?" Ellen asked.

"He's *not* my Adam." Kim laughed. "And I have no idea what his sign is."

"Well, what's yours?" Ellen persisted.

"Pisces," she said, and then realized with a jolt that Kim Stratton was no such thing. "I mean," she stammered. "God, I forget. What's August sixteenth again?"

"Leo."

"Oh, right. I always get those two mixed up."

Ellen looked at her as if she couldn't believe anyone could be so nonchalant about her astrological sign. "You cannot possibly be a Leo," she said. "You are about as un-Leolike as anyone I've ever met."

"Ah, you just don't know the real me," she tried to joke. What were Leos supposed to be like?

"I think you had it right the first time," Ellen said. "At the very least, your moon must be in Pisces."

"Maybe." She shrugged, wondering if there might be something to this astrology nonsense after all.

Through the open upstairs window, she could hear her telephone ringing. Setting down her mug, she quickly reached for Cody.

"I'll watch Cody," Lucy said. "You go ahead or you'll never get there in time."

She hesitated another moment before going into the house and taking the stairs two at a time. She hoped Kitty Russo had found more work for her, but it was an unfamiliar male voice on the line.

"This is Noel Wagner," the man said. "I'm a friend of Jessie Soria's."

Kim remembered the name. Jessie's old boyfriend. "Yes?" she asked.

"Jessie told me you type."

"Yes, I do."

"Well, do you feel like typing the great American novel?"

"I beg your pardon?"

He laughed. The sound was throaty, as if he were a smoker. "I've been working on a book," he said. "But I write in longhand. Never did master the typewriter. Do you think you could type it for me?"

"I'd be happy to. I charge two dollars a page, double spaced."

"Sounds good to me," he said. "I'm in no rush for it. I'll drop by a couple hundred pages to start you off."

"I don't mind picking them up, if you live close by. I have to go out today anyway." The sooner she could get started on his book, the better.

"Well, that'd be great," he said. "I've been living in an apartment above Kelly's Music Shop ever since Jessie kicked me out. Do you know where that is?"

"Yes." She could picture the little music store on East Street. "Is sometime between three and four all right?" She could stop by on the way back from the doctor's.

"I'll be here," Noel said.

She was grinning as she hung up the phone. She immediately picked up the receiver again and dialed Jessie's number.

"Thank you," she said, when Jessie answered.

"For what?"

"For giving Noel my name. He just called, and I'm going to be doing some typing for him."

"Great," Jessie said. "He's a good writer. All the best alcoholics make good writers." There was an edge of bitterness to her voice. "But I bet he told you his handwriting is legible."

"He didn't say."

"Well, it's not, trust me. He's been through a couple of typists already. Their optometrists ordered them to give him up as a client."

Kim laughed. "Listen," she said impulsively. "I'd like you and Adam to come over to dinner tonight. As a thank you for all you guys have done for me. And besides, it's Cody's first birthday."

"Is it really?" Jessie asked. "Well, we'll definitely have to come then. I'll check with Adam and get back to you."

The doctor's office was packed. Dr. Sweeney apparently shared space with a number of other doctors, and seeing the crowd in the waiting room helped Kim relax. There were two other mothers with toddler-aged boys there. Cody would be one patient among many. He would not stand out from the crowd.

There was a short, broad plastic table in the middle of the room covered with toys and books, and Cody was squirming to get out of her lap and join the other children playing with them. The receptionist had given her forms to fill out, so she reluctantly let Cody go, wondering what incredible array of germs those toys were harboring.

After a long wait, a young nurse ushered them into an examining room. She instructed Kim to take off Cody's shirt and pants, then left them alone. A few minutes later, the doctor walked into the room and shook her hand.

"I'm Dr. Sweeney," he said. "And this is," he checked the chart, "Cody?"

"He's here for a checkup and inoculations. Here's what he's

had." She handed him the sheet bearing the record of Cody's inoc-ulations, but she could see that the doctor was already fascinated by the scar on Cody's rib cage.

"What's this?" He ran one finger lightly over the smooth skin and Cody giggled.

Kim licked her lips. They were very dry. "He was born with coarctation of the aorta," she said, "which was corrected by surgery. I brought those records with me, too, in case you wanted to see them."

"Yes, I'd like to." Dr. Sweeney sat down in the only chair in the room and began leafing through the records, while Kim rubbed Cody's bare back. It was chilly in the room.

Midway through the records, deep lines began to form across the doctor's forehead, and Kim read all sorts of things into that frown. Her muscles tightened. She was ready to bolt for the door. She vowed to herself that if she and Cody made it through this appointment without being caught, she would come up with a plan of escape from Annapolis that she could put into place at a moment's notice.

"Who was the surgeon?" Dr. Sweeney turned one of the pages over, as though the back of the paper might reveal a name.

"Dr. Farnhager." The fabricated name popped out of her mouth. It was so silly, she almost laughed.

"Never heard of him," he said.

"He's in L.A." She hoped that would explain the unfamiliar name.

"I used to practice in L.A.," the doctor said.

Kim's heart threw an extra beat against her ribs.

"What hospital was he affiliated with?" Dr. Sweeney asked. "I don't remember his name."

"I'm not sure how long he's been practicing there." She strug-gled to convey an air of indifference in her voice. "But he has an excellent reputation. We were lucky to get him."

*L.A.* If anyone ever requested a time line of where she'd been living when, she'd be in deep trouble.

She had not answered the question about the hospital where Dr. Farnhager practiced, but Dr. Sweeney seemed finished with his interrogation. At least for the moment.

He examined Cody. His manner was very quiet, and she squirmed in the silence. She shouldn't have written her correct address on the forms she'd filled out in the waiting room. The police would probably be waiting for her by the time she got home.

Cody barely let out a whimper when the doctor gave him his shots. It saddened her that her son was so accustomed to pain and discomfort that he seemed to accept it as his lot in life.

"You can go ahead and get him dressed," Dr. Sweeney said. "He seems hale and hearty. I'll give you the name of a cardiologist who can do the echocardiogram on him, but I don't think you need to rush."

"Thanks," she said as he left the room. She dressed Cody quickly, paid for the appointment with a hastily written check, and breathed a sigh of relief when she and Cody were back in her car.

That doctor had been entirely too uncommunicative, she thought as she drove toward town. She had no idea if he'd been merely thinking about a tennis game he had scheduled for that afternoon or if he was plotting a call to the police about her. "I don't know what her story is," he might say to them, "but it's obvious that the records she brought me had been falsified." Or worse, he might be staring right this minute at a picture of her and Cody that had somehow made its way to his office on the front of a flyer or the back of a milk carton.

She needed an escape plan, she thought again. She would buy a fat, black felt-tipped marker to keep in her glove compartment, which she could use to alter the license plate on her car. And she should keep a good amount of cash with her in the apartment rather than having it all at the bank. That way, if she had to leave in a hurry, she wouldn't lose everything. What would she take with her? That would depend entirely on how much time she had. Under the best of circumstances, she could take the computer and printer with her, but she would have to carry them out to her car under the cover of darkness. At the very least, she would take the portable playpen and the stroller. She wondered if she should keep her duffel bag packed and ready to go.

She found the music shop, and a car was pulling away from the curb in front of the store just in time for her to grab the parking place. She got Cody out of the back seat and walked around the side of the small building, hunting for a way to get to the upstairs apartment.

The only stairs were in the rear of the building, and they had the look of an old metal fire escape. She balanced Cody on her hip for the climb.

Noel greeted her at the door, looking every bit the hard-drinking novelist. His shirttail was half in, half out, and his brown hair was uncombed and falling across his forehead. He wore a distracted-looking smile. She could smell the subtle scent of alcohol and the stronger scent of tobacco as she walked past him into the room.

They were in a small living room with chipped and worn furniture and a carpet so old she could not determine its color. The sound of a flute wafted up through the floorboards from the shop below.

"You must have music here all day long," she said.

"Yes, I do." He motioned her to take a seat on the ancient sofa. "And unfortunately I can't control it. They give lessons. I look forward to the flute, though, actually. Every Monday at three. But the beginning violin lessons . . . " He shuddered. "Well, I have earplugs."

She laughed as she sat down on the sofa. Cody immediately tried to get out of her lap, but she held onto him firmly. Who knew what was lurking in the pile of that raunchy carpet?

Noel sat down at a desk in the corner and began stacking sheets of yellow paper into a pile. From where she sat, Kim could see into the next room, a bedroom, and she was staring directly at a computer.

"You have a computer," she said, surprised.

He glanced at her. "What? Oh, yeah, I do, but I only use it for e-mail and the net. I never mastered typing. Do all my writing longhand." He smiled at her. "Pathetic, huh?"

She bounced Cody on her knee. "Well, I hate to be selfish," she said, "but I'm frankly glad you never learned to type."

Noel returned his attention to the stack of papers, and Kim spotted a picture of him and Jessie on the desk. They were caught in a grinning embrace. Jessie looked so happy that, for a moment,

Kim did not recognize her. She guessed it had been awhile since Jessie had grinned with such abandon.

Noel noticed her looking at the picture. "Jessie doesn't call me often anymore," he said. "Only when she wants something. And it seems she wants to help you out."

"She and Adam have been very kind to me."

"Yeah, they're good people," Noel said. "Screwed up by the accident, though. They sort of went off the deep end. I wish they'd get on with their lives. Both of them."

"Well, it hasn't been all that long," she said.

"Long enough. I don't think they're good for each other." He looked at her appraisingly. "I'm glad to see that Jessie's made a friend who has nothing to do with what happened. Maybe she's finally moving on."

He loved Jessie, still. That was apparent.

"Here we are." Noel carried the thick pile of paper over to the coffee table, where he tried to fit it into a cardboard box, without success. The edges of the paper jutted out here and there, dozens of pointed yellow corners, but he seemed to think the fit was adequate. The papers were covered with a disheartening chicken scratch.

"I'll carry this down for you," Noel said. "Your hands are full."

"How soon do you need it back?" she asked as she followed him to the door.

"No rush," he said. "I'm working on the second part of the book. That will take me a good month, at least. Then I'll be ready to go back and edit what you type. Okay?"

"Fine," she said, then added, "although I'd like to be paid each Friday for whatever I've finished that week. Would that be all right?"

"Not a problem."

They climbed down the metal staircase and walked around the building to her car. Kim buckled Cody into his car seat, then took the box from Noel and put it on the passenger seat.

"Call me if you have trouble reading any of it." He grinned.

"I will," she said, and as she drove away from Noel's odd little apartment, she thought she'd probably be calling him a great deal over the next few days.

She made one more stop—to pick up chicken and an ice cream cake for Cody's birthday dinner—then drove home. There were no police waiting for her in front of her apartment, and she felt silly for having been so worried. The doctor's visit was behind her, Cody was taken care of, and she had a bundle of work to do with a paycheck promised at the end of the week. She was glad she'd invited Jessie and Adam over to celebrate with her.

Jessie was carrying a wrapped gift, and Adam, a bottle of sparkling cider, when they arrived. "To toast the employed one," Adam said, holding the bottle in the air. "Told you we'd find you work." He surprised her by kissing her cheek as he walked into her apartment, as though they were old friends, and she was warmed by the gesture.

Jessie seemed more interested in Cody. "How's the birthday boy?" she asked, picking him up from the playpen in the middle of the room.

"I'm not sure what I would have done if I hadn't met up with you two," Kim said. "I haven't heard anything back on all the brochures I sent out."

"Those things take time," Adam said. "People file them away until they need them. You'll get some calls."

"Noel can keep you going for a long time," Jessie said, bouncing Cody on her hip. "He's prolific. Lives for his writing."

Kim heard the bitterness again. "He seems to miss you," she said.

Jessie shrugged. "He could have me or the booze. Couldn't have us both."

Kim nodded. Fair enough.

"What word processing program do you use?" Jessie walked over to her computer, now perched on the coffee table. Kim had moved it to clear the dining room table for her dinner guests.

"WordPerfect," she said.

Jessie bent over to lightly touch the keys with her fingertips. "What else do you keep on it? Do you have any games? Myst or anything? I love computer games."

"No, sorry," Kim said. She'd removed the games the day after setting up the computer. "I'm afraid I'd never get any work done if I had games on it."

"You're more disciplined than I am." Jessie gave Cody a big kiss on the cheek and lowered him carefully into the playpen again. "Will you bring Cody over to my house when Victoria has her kittens?" she asked. "Wouldn't he be fascinated by them?"

"We'll see." Kim tried to smile. It was true that Cody would probably love the kittens, but she would rather not see them herself. A litter of kittens was a reminder of things she'd rather forget.

Jessie walked into the kitchen. "What can we do to help?" she asked.

She put Jessie to work with the lettuce and the salad bowl, and Adam with the potatoes and the peeler, while she cut up the chicken. The chicken was an extravagance. She usually ate pasta or rice and beans. But tonight was special.

The three of them chatted as they worked together, and she felt lighthearted. She was actually having fun. She'd nearly forgotten about the possibility of the police showing up at her door. It seemed like a good sign that it had been four hours since the doctor's appointment and there had been no repercussions.

Adam spotted the sketchbook next to the computer on the coffee table. "May I show Jessie your sketches?" he asked.

She nodded. Adam brought the book into the kitchen, set it on the counter, and started leafing through the pages with Jessie peering over his shoulder.

"They're really good, Kim." Jessie sounded surprised.

"You've added a few new ones," Adam said.

"Yes." She would have to buy another book soon.

"When are you going to let me give you a lesson?" he asked. "Come on. You'd be doing me a favor."

How could she turn him down when he worded it that way? "All right," she agreed. "Whenever you say."

"Good." He closed the book. "You'll come to my studio, which is in my house. But till then, why don't you try to use your dreams? Keep your sketchbook under your bed and as soon as you wake up in the morning—before you even get out of bed—start sketching what you've dreamed."

"I don't remember my dreams." It was a lie, but her dreams were every bit as negative and frightening as his. Better to pretend she had no memory of them.

"You will," he said. "Just give it a try."

Dinner was ready quickly and the four of them sat down at the table, Cody next to Kim in his high chair.

"To Cody." Jessie raised her glass of sparkling cider in the air. "On his very first birthday."

Adam raised his glass as well. "And to Kim," he said. "The only one of us who's working these days."

Kim took a sip from her glass, glad they'd brought cider instead of wine. She couldn't recall telling them that she didn't drink. Maybe they didn't either.

"Do you two drink alcohol?" she asked.

"Not anymore," Adam said. "I stopped drinking after the accident, when I saw exactly what havoc it could wreak on the unsuspecting. I have sort of a knee-jerk reaction to it now."

"And that's the reason I split up with Noel," Jessie said. "I'd never given it much thought before, but after the accident, I couldn't handle seeing him drink every day."

Kim remembered the scent of alcohol in Noel's apartment that afternoon. It had, frankly, reminded her of home and her childhood.

"My parents were alcoholics," she confided. Turning to Adam, she said, "I mentioned about my father being a drinker, but it was actually both my parents. They were sloppy drunks. Mean drunks. They turned me off to alcohol. I can't stand it."

"We were made for each other," Adam said, and there was something in his eyes that told her he was beginning to feel that was the truth. She dodged his gaze, a well of conflict springing up inside her. She liked Adam, but she could not imagine loving him. He was not Linc. Even if she never saw Linc again, she wasn't ready to give up the *idea* of loving him.

Yet there was such warmth in Adam's eyes. Such tenderness. Jessie saw it too. Kim noticed her studying her brother's face, and she did not seem to like what she saw.

When dinner was finished, Jessie stood up abruptly and carried her empty plate to the sink. "I think we should go soon, Adam," she said. "I don't want to be out too late tonight."

He looked at Jessie in surprise. "It's early," he said.

"You have to have dessert," Kim said.

"And Cody has to open his presents," Adam added.

Jessie stood in the center of the kitchen floor, looking momentarily helpless. She let out a sigh. "All right," she said. "Sorry. I felt worn out all of a sudden."

Kim saw the worried look on Adam's face as Jessie cleared away his plate. She rose to get the gifts, suddenly feeling the need to hurry the festivities along.

Even though he'd never had a birthday before, Cody seemed to know what was expected of him. He happily tore the wrapping off his presents. Kim gave him a couple of toys she'd found at one of the garage sales, while Jessie and Adam's gift was a beautifully illustrated book about animals.

Kim cleared the unwrapped gifts away from the table so they wouldn't get soiled, then brought out the dessert—the ice cream cake, a candle burning in the center of the icing. The three of them sang "Happy Birthday" as the cake was placed in front of Cody, and with a little help, he blew out the flame.

"Ice cream cake." Jessie said as Kim cut the first piece. "Molly's favorite. Remember Adam?"

Adam nodded, and as if Jessie had popped a pin in him, he deflated. The smile he'd been wearing most of the evening was gone, the ease in his face replaced by a wanness. "We had it at her birthday party the night of her accident," he said.

"Oh." Kim drew back from the cake. "I wish I'd known. I guess this was a bad choice."

Adam touched her hand, moving it toward the cake again. "Don't worry about it," he said. "It looks great."

The mood of the evening, though, had lost its charm. Jessie didn't eat any of the cake. She took it on her plate, but Kim knew it would not be touched, and she was not surprised when Jessie once again pleaded fatigue immediately after Adam had finished his piece.

"You can stay if you like, Adam," Jessie said. "But I'm going home."

Adam looked clearly torn for a minute, and so was Kim. Adam had grown more attractive to her in the last hour, yet she was not at all certain what she wanted from him. She was too needy for her own good, she thought, unable to separate desire from loneliness.

Jessie brushed a hand over Cody's head as she passed his high chair on the way to the door. She was serious about going, and going *now*. She seemed almost panicky in her need to get out of Kim's apartment. She waited at the door, one hand on the knob, for Adam's decision.

"I'll come with you, Jess," he said, looking apologetically at Kim. He stood up and carried the dessert plates into the kitchen.

Kim had lifted Cody into her arms, and she walked with him to the door.

"Thanks for coming," she said. "And Cody thanks both of you for the wonderful book."

"It was a great dinner." Adam said. "I'll call you and we can set up a time to—"

"Adam?" There was a plea in Jessie's voice as though she might disintegrate if she had to stand there one more second.

"All right, Jess." He put his arm around his sister, then said over his shoulder to Kim, "I'll call you."

"All right," Kim said. "Good night, both of you."

She watched them walk onto the landing, Adam holding tight to his sister's shoulders, and when they turned to start down the stairs, Kim did not miss the unmistakable relief in Jessie's eyes.

"I think we need music," Adam said as he walked toward the stereo in the corner of his studio. "Loosening-up music."

Kim stared at the empty canvas on the easel in front of her. Although this was the third night she'd painted in Adam's studio, it would be her first time painting on canvas, and she felt paralyzed. After watching Adam stretch the canvas, staple it into place, and prime it, she was afraid to touch her brush to it for fear of making a mistake.

"You *can't* make a mistake," Adam said, as slightly jazzy, slightly soulful piano music filled the air. She recognized the musician. Keith Jarrett. Linc had many of his recordings.

Adam took her hand, moved it to the palette, and dipped her brush into a blob of pale blue. Before she could protest, he'd swept her arm across the canvas, leaving a long blue streak. She gasped, then laughed.

"Now you don't have to worry about wrecking a pristine canvas," he said. "So have at it."

She stared at the blue streak, wondering what to do with it, trying to free her mind from any constraints. The first night she'd painted in Adam's studio, she'd felt awkward and embarrassed. She'd found herself holding back, afraid to show him her best for fear of hearing him pronounce it poor. Adam seemed to see through her, though, and he encouraged her to stretch, to challenge herself, and soon she was doing her best and better. "You're a quick study," he told her. But while she drew and painted, Adam only dabbled like a man who suddenly found himself in a glorious studio, surrounded by a wealth of art supplies, with no memory of how to use them.

The color and angle of the blue streak looked suddenly familiar to her. It reminded her of the sky above the house across the street from her apartment, the house she'd been drawing in her sketchbook. She began to paint the house from memory, trying not to be intimidated by Adam's frequent glances in her direction.

She might not have been falling in love with Adam himself, but she *was* falling in love with his house and his studio. Adam lived in a small, two-story white house, the mirror image of Jessie's rental house next door. Inside, the house was decorated in the same strong, opaque shades that marked his paintings. The carpet was a pale gray, the sofa navy blue, the chairs a white-and-navy stripe. Dotting the walls and covering table tops and bookshelves were photographs and paintings of the family he'd lost. Dana had been attractive and slender, with angular lines to her body. Sharp shoulders, long arms, and a pretty, engaging smile that was hard to imagine stilled forever. Her hair was a deep red, framing her face in soft waves.

A painting of Molly and Liam hung above the fireplace. Kim would have recognized it immediately as an Adam Soria painting, with its vivid green background and the white clothes of the children. Molly was dark haired like Adam, Liam a redhead like his mother. The first time she saw the painting with its stark colors— the green, white, black, and red—she was struck only by its beauty. It was only after she'd studied it for a while that she wondered how Adam could tolerate having it there in his home, that exquisite reminder of what he had lost. She felt dishonest and intrusive, being witness to the things Adam held dearest. He did not think to hide anything from her, while she hid everything from him.

The studio was in what had once been an attic but was now a spacious and well-lit room. It still had the odd wall angles and pitched ceiling of an attic, but every surface was painted white and the effect was bright and inviting. A sink and counter space lined one of the walls, and two deep, soft, red leather love seats were tucked into alcoves on either side of the room. The easels stood near one corner.

Cody slept in Liam's old bed while she painted, a chair propped up against the edge of the bed so he wouldn't roll out. She'd felt uncomfortable when Adam first suggested that Cody use his son's bed. The room was still a little boy's room, filled with pastel colors and stuffed animals and a lamp shaped like a dump truck. She worried that it would pain Adam to have another child in that room, but it seemed instead to please him.

As a matter of fact, Adam seemed happy in general these past few days. There was laughter in his studio. More than once, though, she'd felt his eyes on her instead of on her work, and she knew she would soon have to sort out her own feelings about him. All she knew now was that she needed his company. She wondered how she'd ever thought she could survive living in isolation.

From downstairs, there was the sound of a door slamming shut.

"Sounds like Jessie's here," Adam said.

They heard footsteps on the stairs and after a moment, Jessie appeared in the doorway to the studio. She looked tired.

"Hi," she said, her voice flat.

"Hi," Kim answered. "How are you?"

"You look wiped out," Adam said. "What's up?"

Jessie shrugged away the question. "Nothing's up," she said. "I brought some pizza home with me if anybody wants some."

Adam looked at Kim. "Hungry?"

She nodded. "Pizza sounds good."

"Do you want a Coke, Kim?" Jessie asked as she started back down the stairs.

"That'd be great," Kim called after her.

Adam carried her brush and his own over to the sink, while she covered the paint palette with plastic wrap.

Jessie had come over every night she'd been there, and Kim began to see her as their chaperone. Any potential for intimacy between Adam and herself seemed cut short with Jessie's arrival, and Kim wondered if that was their plan. Maybe Adam had asked Jessie to arrive at a given time to prevent him from . . . what? It was clear that, tonight at least, Jessie looked as though she'd rather be home in bed.

Jessie had set plates and the pizza on the coffee table in the living room and poured them each a glass of Coke. Kim sat on the floor, her back against the sofa. Jessie sat next to her and Adam sat in a chair at one end of the coffee table. The television was on, the news a white noise in the background.

"Are you okay tonight, Jess?" Adam asked his sister.

"Sleepy." Jessie swallowed a bite of pizza, her eyes on the television. Then she looked at Kim. "So, how are you doing with Noel's opus?" she asked.

Jessie seemed very curious about Noel's work, questioning her about it nearly every time she saw her, and Kim knew that neither member of that couple had truly put their relationship to rest yet.

"Just fine," Kim said noncommittally. Noel's book was a coming-of-age story about an adolescent boy growing up in a working-class neighborhood in Baltimore. It was mildly interesting, but she hoped he planned to do some major revisions before trying to sell it.

Suddenly, Adam leaned toward the TV. "That's right near here," he said. He picked up the remote from the coffee table and turned up the sound.

A young female reporter stood in front of a blackened building, an office front. There'd been an explosion in the building that afternoon, she said. An attorney was killed, along with a receptionist and her two small children who happened to be in the office with her at the time.

"What caused it?" Kim asked.

"It was a bomb," Jessie said. "I heard about it on the car radio when I went to get the pizza."

"Wasn't there another bombing around here recently?" Adam asked.

"Yes," Kim said. "I walked past the house where it happened. A woman was killed when she opened an express mail package someone left on her porch."

"Do they know—" Adam stopped mid-sentence and squinted at the image of the building on the television. "It's that law firm down on Duke of Gloucester Street, isn't it?" He leaned toward the TV again, as if to make out the details of the destroyed facade. "Sellers, Sellers, and Wittaker? Isn't that it?"

The name was familiar. She must have walked past the office at some time and noticed the sign. Or maybe she'd sent them one of her brochures.

"I've heard of them somewhere," she said.

"You've probably walked right by the building," Jessie said, "although their sign is really tiny."

That wasn't it, Kim thought. She'd heard the name of the business somewhere. Maybe someone had mentioned the law firm to her. It didn't matter. Her attention was drawn to the image on the screen, a picture of the young receptionist and her husband as they cuddled their two small children.

"That's so unfair," she said. She wanted to go upstairs and hug Cody close to her.

Adam abruptly reached for the remote and hit the off button. "Can't watch it," he said. His face was white, his jaw set, and the old pain she'd seen in his eyes when she'd first met him had returned.

"I'm sorry," she said. "It must be a terrible reminder."

"Are you okay, Adam?" Jessie asked. Her own eyes were red.

"Well, I'm in better shape tonight than that guy in the picture," he said.

"Why the hell did she have her kids with her in an office building?" Jessie asked.

"Maybe she'd just picked them up from day care," Kim suggested, "or maybe someone dropped them off. Do they have any idea who's behind it? Was it another express mail package, by any chance?"

"Yeah, it was," Jessie said. "That's what I heard on the car radio."

Adam shoved the pizza box away from him as if he couldn't bear the smell any longer. "I think I've gotta turn in," he said, standing up. "Sorry, Kim. I'm falling rapidly into my 'life sucks' mood." He tried unsuccessfully to smile.

"I understand," she said. She started to get to her feet, but he held her down with a hand on her shoulder.

"No need for you to run off. You and Jessie can stay here and visit. I just need to . . . " He didn't finish his sentence. Instead, he merely shrugged and turned toward the stairs.

Impulsively, Kim got to her feet and put her arms around him. He returned the gesture in a restrained hug, and Kim was keenly aware of Jessie's presence in the room. Maybe it was Jessie's comforting he needed right now? She let go of him and saw that Jessie's concerned brown eyes were indeed glued to her brother's face. She should leave. This was a family pain she'd stumbled into.

"I really want to go," she said, and this time neither of them objected. They didn't say a word to her as she walked up the stairs to Liam's old room. While she was getting Cody out of bed, she heard the door to Adam's room close, then heard it open again as Jessie softly followed her brother inside.

Kim's eyes lit on the photograph of Liam on the night table, and before she knew what had hit her, she was crying. She couldn't have said if it was Adam and Jessie's loss she was crying over or the tragedy she'd just witnessed on TV, but she hugged her sleeping son to her chest and let the tears flow.

Downstairs, Adam's house was quiet and dark, and she closed the front door quietly behind her as she left. Cody slept all the way home, and Kim climbed the stairs to her own dark apartment with her son a heavy, dead-to-the-world weight in her arms.

She lowered him into his crib, then got into her own bed. There was something discomforting gnawing at the edge of her mind. She couldn't quite get a grasp on it, not until she had lain there, staring at the ceiling, for more than half an hour. Then it hit her.

She got out of bed and rummaged in her lingerie drawer until she found the disc containing the file the previous owner had left on her computer. She turned on the computer, inserted the disk and called up the information on it. That odd list filled the screen again, and there it was: *Sellers, Sellers, and Wittaker, 5588 Duke of Gloucester Street, Annapolis, every damn day of the year. Use October 17, 2 P.M.,(so all will be there).*

October 17. Today's date. And when had the bomb gone off? Hadn't the reporter said two o'clock, or was her imagination simply flying out of control?

Her hands were shaking as she looked at the previous name on the list. *Katherine Nabors, 448 Labrador Lane, Annapolis, 47, 2 children, 2 adults, September 27, 8:30 A.M., home.*

Labrador Lane. She was certain that was the name of the street where the previous bombing had occurred, but she did not know the name of the woman who had been the victim of that explosion. It couldn't be this Katherine Nabors. It simply couldn't be. It was unimaginable that the list in her computer could have anything to do with the carnage that was striking Annapolis.

There were eight other people and businesses on the list. Kim printed the file in its entirety, set it on her desk, and tried to put it out of her mind so she could fall asleep. It wasn't so much those names that haunted her as she drifted off, though, as the white-jawed pain in Adam's face.

She skipped coffee on the porch the following morning, telling Lucy she had to start her work early. That was the truth. She needed to get a good start on her typing for the day, because as soon as the library opened, she planned to be there.

She intentionally drove past the office of Sellers, Sellers, and Wittaker on her way to the library. It took her in the wrong direction, but she needed to see the destruction for herself. The front of the office building was blackened, and police tape was stretched around the perimeter. Several people stood on the sidewalk, gawking at the wreckage.

In the library, she found a picture book to keep Cody occupied while she sorted through back issues of the local newspaper until she found the edition for September 28. The article she dreaded finding leaped out at her from the front page: WOMAN KILLED IN EXPLOSION. There was a picture of the house on Labrador Lane, with its sagging front porch and pretty garden, and beneath it the caption: *Katherine Nabors, 47, was killed by a bomb left in a package outside her front door.*

The room began to spin, and Kim closed her eyes. By some bizarre twist of fate, she had a hit list on her hands. But why these people? Why a housewife and a law firm? And what was the meaning of the *2 children, 2 adults,* the *every damn day of the year?* Who were the other people on the list? How could she warn them? What on earth was she going to do?

She could hardly go to the police with the list. There would be far too many questions and far too much explaining to do, and that would put a quick end to her low profile. But she couldn't simply ignore the information, either.

The next name on the list was that of a man. *Ryan Geary, 770 Pioneer Way, Annapolis, 51, elderly couple, November 13, 9 P.M.*

November 13. She had nearly a month to figure out what to do. Maybe she could write anonymously to the local newspaper. Would the authorities have some way of tracing a letter? The television images of that young mother and her two small children filled her head. If only she'd made the connection before. If only she'd recognized that address on Labrador Lane as having been on the list in her computer, maybe she could have somehow prevented that tragedy. It was frightening to think that the previous owner of her computer might be a calculating murderer, and she was suddenly relieved that Computer Wizard had not cared enough to inform him that she had stumbled across his files.

She checked out a few books for Cody and then drove to the city dock to eat a take-out lunch on her favorite bench above the water. Usually an hour by the water calmed her, but this afternoon nothing could ease her anxiety. She gave up trying to eat, throwing away most of the fish and chips she'd bought, then began pushing the stroller aimlessly around town. She was not anxious to go home to her computer.

She took Cody to the park on her way home, so it was nearly five by the time she finally turned onto her street. She'd lost a day of work and would have to call Adam to tell him she wouldn't be over that night for her lesson because she had to catch up on her typing. But Adam was already there, sitting on the top porch step, and she was immediately flooded with the desire to tell him about the computer and the list of names. She wanted to tell him everything, and knew she could tell him nothing.

"Hi," she called as she pushed Cody up the walk.

"Hi." Adam didn't get up from his seat on the stairs. "I've been waiting for you."

"We took a long walk." She stopped the stroller at the bottom of the stairs and lifted Cody out of it.

"Let me take that for you." Adam reached for the stroller and collapsed it with the quick action of a man who had raised two children through the stroller stage. Then he looked her squarely in the eye. "I'm sorry about last night," he said.

"Don't apologize. I know that news report upset you."

"Well," he said, "you're very understanding."

She knew instantly that something was different about Adam. There was a new tenderness in his smile, and he did not seem to want to take his eyes from her face. He rested his hand on her back as she passed him to go into the house, and she knew as surely as if he'd told her, that he was falling in love with her. She didn't know whether to be flattered or afraid.

Once they were in her apartment, she heated Cody's dinner and settled the little boy in his high chair. "I was going to call you," she said to Adam. "I have to work tonight, so I was going to cancel our lesson."

"I was going to cancel our lesson too." Adam sat down at the minuscule kitchen table. "I was going to cancel because I wanted to see you tonight, but not over a canvas and paints. And not with Jessie around."

She winced at his openness, his willingness to be vulnerable, when she was allowing herself to be anything but. She sat next to Cody and slipped a spoonful of carrots into the baby's mouth before responding.

"Adam," she said finally, deciding to be as frank as she was able, "I think I'd better tell you that I'm in love with someone."

He raised his eyebrows in surprise. "Ah," he said, as if that explained everything.

"I mean ... " She fed Cody another spoonful. "It's confusing. Hard to explain. I doubt very much that I'll ever see him again. I left him behind when I moved here, and our relationship is over. But he's still ... in my heart. You need to know that."

"You mean ... Are you talking about your ex-husband?"

"No. Someone else."

"What was the problem? Was he married?"

"No. Nothing like that. We both just knew it wasn't meant to be." Her chest tightened with the lie.

"Well, I'm glad you told me." Adam picked up a napkin from the table and wiped a carrot spill from the edge of Cody's high chair tray. "And it's all right. I don't think my feelings are very trustworthy these days, anyhow. All I know is that I think about you a lot. And when I do, I feel very ... happy." He smiled. "It's been a long time since I've felt happy, so I'd like to enjoy it for awhile, if you don't mind. Jessie says it's too soon for me to . . . really care about anyone. She says I can't trust what I'm feeling for you."

"I think she's right," Kim said. "I don't think either of us is ready to get involved right now."

Adam crumpled the napkin in his hand. "It's just that . . . I keep thinking about the way you reacted to the news of that bombing last night," he said. "It hurt you to the core, I could tell. You're a very kind-hearted person."

She studied Cody's plate, an unshakable guilt weighing her down, as if she herself had been responsible for the explosion.

"Well, listen," Adam said with a sigh. "How about I make you dinner?"

"I don't have a thing in the house," she said.

"Oh, I bet I can find something. You go ahead and get Cody ready for bed and I'll whip something up."

It was obvious he had no intention of leaving, and Kim gave up on the idea of getting any work done that night. It was a relief, actually, to have an excuse to avoid the computer. With its unsavory past life, the computer suddenly felt like a tainted presence in her home.

She gave Cody a bath and read him one of the library books before putting him to bed. By the time she returned to the kitchen, Adam had created a dinner of black beans, rice, frozen green beans, and chopped tomatoes. He'd arranged a plateful for each of them, and the stark contrast of colors made the food look like one of his paintings.

After dinner, Adam tuned her radio to a station that played one slow, sensuous song after another. She danced with him, well aware of his gentle attempt at seduction. She could feel his need to hold and be held, and she gave into it, realizing after a time that it was her need as well. She was hungry for closeness, and when he tipped her head back to kiss her, she responded in spite of herself.

"I want to stay over," Adam said into her hair.

Her head was on his shoulder and she closed her eyes with the effort of choosing her answer. She wanted him to stay. He felt so warm beneath her arms. So solid. Linc had spoiled her. She could not do without intimacy for very long. She wanted to accept it now, even in this less perfect form, but she was afraid of hurting Adam in the process.

"I'd like you to stay," she said, "but—"

"I know. You've been honest about the other guy. I'm not asking you to feel something for me that you don't."

They danced a while longer and then moved easily to her bedroom, where Cody was sleeping soundly in his crib. They undressed each other as they stood by the side of the bed, and Kim was surprised by her level of comfort. She trusted Adam. His kisses were tender and sweet, his touch on her skin warm and exciting. It was she who drew back the covers on the bed and pulled him down next to her, and his hunger for her was matched by her own for him as they began to make love. It wasn't until he was inside her that she thought of Linc. Once the image of Linc's face was in front of her, she couldn't rid herself of it. Adam's gentle, skillful movements were lost on her, and by the time he had finished and was lying quietly next to her, she was in tears.

She was glad it was too dark for him to see the misery in her face. She wanted to speak, to say something kind and loving, but she knew her voice would fail her if she tried.

Adam put his arm around her and gave her a hug. "Are you all right?" he asked.

"Fine." She pressed her fist to her mouth to hold in her crying. She wanted Linc to be the man lying next to her. She'd wanted Linc to be her lover for the rest of her life.

"You made me feel wonderful," Adam said. "You completely cleared my head of anything negative."

"I'm glad." She quietly wiped her eyes with the sheet, then raised her head to kiss him before snuggling close to him for the night. She would try to clear her own head as well.

Adam was already awake when she opened her eyes in the morning, and he was watching her.

"Where's your sketchbook?" he asked. "You need to sketch your dreams."

She groaned. "I told you, I don't remember my dreams."

"Before you go to sleep at night, you should tell yourself that you *will* remember them." He stroked her hair back from her fore-head, and she felt affection in his touch.

"All right," she said. "I'll try it tonight."

She looked over at the crib where Cody was still sound asleep, a splash of sunlight shimmering on his blanket. Then she looked at Adam and felt a smile form, unsolicited, on her lips. To her sur-prise, she was not at all unhappy to wake up with him beside her.

They ate breakfast—toast and orange juice—at her small kitchen table.

"Jessie's going to be upset," Adam said as he poured himself a second glass of juice.

Kim knew he was alluding to the fact that he'd spent the night at her apartment. "Do you have to answer to Jessie for every-thing?" she asked, as she untied Cody's bib from around his neck.

"She worries about me, that's all. And she's had good reason to. I need to convince her that I'm okay and I know what I'm doing." Adam reached across the table for her hand. "Thanks again for your honesty last night," he said. "For telling me about . . . you know, the other guy."

She smiled, but said nothing. She deserved no praise for her honesty.

"Well." He let go of her hand and stood up. "I'd better let you do the work you were supposed to do last night."

She walked him to the door, and as she kissed him good-bye, she tried not to regret anything she'd done the night before.

Except for one short walk to the park with Cody, Kim spent the entire day at the computer. Every once in awhile, the television images of the bombing swept into her mind, and panic rose in her chest at the thought of what she knew about that catastrophe. She'd brush the thoughts away, telling herself she had time to fig-ure out what to do with the information. Still, those images kept barreling their way into consciousness each time she let down her guard.

She put Cody to bed around seven that evening and was sitting once again at the computer when she heard the slamming of a car door. She looked out the window to see a police car parked at the curb and a male police officer on the walk leading up to the house.

She jumped up from her seat and switched out the overhead light before returning to the window to see the man disappear beneath her onto the porch. She thought she could feel the vibrations of his steps on the floor of the porch, but she did not hear him ring the bell to be let in. She tiptoed over to her door and pressed her ear against the wood.

The front door creaked open, and she heard the man's heavy footsteps on the stairs. She checked the lock on her door, then moved quietly to the sofa and sat down, her heart pounding in her ears.

She would hold very still. Pretend she was not here. How did he know? The doctor? A private investigator? Had someone been watching her every move?

The knock came, and although she'd been expecting it, she jumped. It was a soft knock, muffled, and only when he knocked again did Kim realize the officer was knocking on Lucy's door, not her own. Holding her breath, she walked quietly to her door again and pressed her ear against it. She heard Lucy open her door and a mumbled exchange of greetings. Lucy's door shut again. She had let him in.

Kim lowered herself to the floor. What was going on? Had Lucy figured out who she was? Had she turned her in? Would it be a matter of minutes before the officer left Lucy's apartment and knocked on Kim's door, for real this time?

She'd taken two thousand dollars out of her bank account the day before and stuffed it under her mattress so she'd be ready to leave at a moment's notice. Was this the moment? Did she have the time to pack up a few things and leave quietly before the police officer knocked on her door? It would not take them long to find her though. People knew her car, and she'd forgotten to buy a marker she could use to change her license plate number.

Paralysis set in as she tried to think through her limited options, and she jerked back to attention when she heard Lucy's door open again. She waited stiffly for the knock on her own door, but instead, the man's footsteps thudded on the stairs once again. She listened as he opened and closed the front door. A moment later, his car engine coughed to life.

She leaned back against the door, breathing hard. What the hell was that about? Was he getting some backup? Or might he have been seeing Lucy about something totally, blessedly, unrelated to Kim Stratton?

Thirty minutes passed before she could make herself get up. She turned off the computer. There was no way she could work any more tonight.

Moving mechanically, she packed her duffel bag and filled a couple of garbage bags with other things she didn't want to leave behind. She would wait until the middle of the night to carry her computer out to the car. The thought of leaving was suddenly appealing. She'd gotten herself in too deep here in Annapolis. She knew terrible, incriminating information she did not want to know. She'd gotten involved with a man she seemed destined to hurt. It would be so easy to simply pile up her car with her belongings and drive away. She could leave before sunrise.

In her bedroom, she leaned over the side of the crib to look at her sleeping son. He'd adjusted so beautifully to the move from Boulder to Annapolis, and he seemed to love his little world: the apartment, the park, the wonderful long walks around a town filled with charm. How could she uproot him again so soon?

She stroked her hand over Cody's hair, breathing in his scent. She'd wanted more for her child than she'd ever had for herself, and she was well on her way to giving him less.

*"You always run away from your problems,"* Linc had told her, more than once. *"You're always looking for an easy way out."*

She hadn't wanted Kim to be that way. She turned the garbage bags upside down on the bed and shook out their contents. Susanna Miller had been the escape artist; Kim Stratton would have to be stronger than that.

*K*im awakened to the sound of Cody crying. It was dark in her bedroom, and for a moment she couldn't remember where she was, or even *who* she was. She guessed she was at Linc's house, until she reached over to the other side of the bed and felt the empty space next to her.

She could hear the dripping of the leaky faucet in her bathroom and began to get her bearings. Leaning toward the window, she raised the shade. The sky was black above the roof line of the darkened houses across the street, and the clock on her radio read 5:14. Far too early for Cody to be awake. In an instant she was out of bed, maternal alarm bells clanging in her head.

She felt the heat of Cody's fever beneath her hands even before she'd lifted him out of the crib, and her heartbeat accelerated. Fever terrified her. Ever since Cody's surgery, after which he'd had to be monitored carefully for symptoms of infection, fever had become an enemy, the harbinger of dire news.

She carried Cody to her own bed and turned on the night table lamp. The baby rolled away from the intrusion of light, irritably rubbing the side of his head and neck with his fist. An ear infection? That was probably all it was. She took his temperature—103 degrees—then gave him some water and rocked him in her arms, waiting for eight o'clock to roll around. It was Sunday morning. She didn't dare call Dr. Sweeney before eight.

Cody was quiet as he lay in her arms, but he wore a small

frown she had never seen on his face before. She pressed her lips to his warm forehead, thankful she had not tried to flee in the middle of the night. She'd be stuck on the road with a sick baby. Right now, she could not even remember the reason for her urge to run.

It came to her slowly. She recalled the police officer's visit to Lucy the night before as if she'd dreamt it. If only she had. Soon, though, the memory was sharp and clear. She recalled with a shiver every footfall on the stairs, the knock on Lucy's door. What had Lucy said to him in the privacy of her apartment?

She called Dr. Sweeney at eight o'clock, and the answering service told her he was out of town for the weekend and was being covered by another doctor. This other doctor called her back at eight-thirty. He must have picked up the worry in her voice when she told him about Cody's heart problem, because he suggested she take him to the nearest emergency room to be checked out. Obviously, the doctor himself had no intention of working that day.

Kim hung up and returned Cody to his crib, then pulled her checkbook from her purse to study the sad reality of her account balance. She had to admit that a lack of health insurance was one problem she had not thought through before leaving Boulder. Insurance was one of those things you tended to take for granted when you were living a normal life.

She was certain there was not enough money in her checking account to cover whatever the emergency room might cost, so she dipped into her beneath-the-mattress fund. She took two hundred dollars, hoping it would be no more than that. Kitty Russo was supposed to have more work for her this week, and she was counting on it.

She had Cody dressed and was heading for the door when Adam called.

"Cody's sick," she said. "I have to take him to the emergency room, since it's Sunday and his doctor's not in."

"I'll go with you," Adam offered.

"That's not necessary," she said, although she was hoping he'd insist. She wanted him there.

"I know it's not necessary," he said. "But I'd like to go."

"All right," she said. "We'll wait for you on the porch."

He arrived within minutes. They took her car to the hospital, since it had the car seat, and she described Cody's symptoms to him on the drive.

"Ear infection, definitely," Adam said. "Liam used to get them all the time. You'll need antibiotics. And drops."

"I wish you could prescribe as well as diagnose," she said. "It would save me a bundle."

"Won't your insurance cover it?"

"I don't have any," she admitted.

He looked at her sharply.

"That's crazy, Kim. You've got to have insurance for him, not to mention for yourself. What about through Cody's father?"

"I don't want anything to do with his father."

"But for Cody's sake. He needs to be covered."

Her eyes stung. She knew he was right, and if she'd turned Cody over to Peggy and Jim, there would be no worry over insurance, over money, over medical care. At a stoplight, she turned to look at her miserable baby, his face red from crying, and pressed her palm against his warm cheek.

She felt Adam's hand on her shoulder.

"I'm sorry," he said. "It's none of my business."

"No, you're right. I've got to find a way to get insurance for him." Her voice was thick, and she brushed the back of her hand across her eyes.

Adam squeezed her shoulder. "Is it the money that's got you upset, or are you worried about Cody's heart?"

"Both," she said, although the real answer was neither. Right now, she was simply weighed down by guilt. She could not protect her son the way she wanted to. The way a good mother would. Certainly not the way Peggy would.

"I get my insurance through an organization for self-employed people," Adam said. "I'll give you the information, and you can apply."

She knew all about those applications. They would want detailed medical information, doctor's names. Things she couldn't tell them. But she nodded as though Adam had come up with a way to solve her problem.

They waited in the emergency room for nearly two hours. Half the children in Annapolis seemed to have taken ill that morning, and she held Cody protectively on her lap.

Adam entertained Cody with the stuffed monkey, while Kim nursed her guilt and her fear. Here was yet another doctor she would have to inform about Cody's heart surgery. And wasn't it more likely that a doctor in a hospital would have been alerted to be on the lookout for a baby with his heart condition? She thought of the police officer again, thumping up the stairs to her apartment the night before, and the thought of escape tempted her again. Maybe she should leave Annapolis once she had medication for Cody. But then what? Where would she go? She'd heard of parents who ran off with their children and then moved from place to place, staying one small step ahead of being caught. She didn't think she could live that way, although she would if she had to.

Across the room from her sat a blond woman and her two lethargic-looking toddlers, and Kim was suddenly reminded of the receptionist at Sellers, Sellers, and Wittaker and her ill-fated children. Maybe there was no way she could have predicted that explosion, but she *could* predict the next one, most likely with perfect accuracy. Even if she ran away from her new life in Annapolis, she would not be able to run away from what she knew.

"Hey." Adam looked at her with sudden concern and she knew her various worries must be showing in her face. He put his arm around her shoulder to give her a hug, and she let herself lean against him.

"It'll be all right," Adam said. "It's only an ear infection."

The doctor was a young woman who seemed intrigued, but not alarmed, by the scar on Cody's chest and the explanation behind it. "What a lucky little boy," she said simply, and proceeded to check his ears and throat and listen to his lungs, only to verify Adam's diagnosis of an ear infection and prescribe antibiotics and ear drops.

Adam winked at Kim, as if to say, I told you so, and she smiled at him in relief.

Back in the reception area, she counted out one hundred and twenty dollars, adamantly refusing the fifty Adam tried to press into her hand.

Adam offered to drive home so she could sit in the back with Cody. She was quiet in the car, and she felt herself stiffen as they turned onto her street. She half expected to see the police car, or maybe two or three, waiting for her out front. But only Adam's car was parked at the curb.

Adam pulled her car behind his and looked at his watch. "Two o'clock," he said. "Let me make you guys lunch."

She bit her lip, uncertain how to respond. It was Sunday. In six hours she would be able to hear Linc on the radio, and all she really wanted to do between now and then was take care of her son and wait. She would have liked to have Adam wait with her. She would have liked to have him lie in her bed with her, holding her, while Cody slept—but only until eight, when she'd want him gone. That was hardly fair.

She shook her head. "I'm so tired," she said. "Cody had me up before the sun this morning. I'd really like to spend the rest of the day sleeping and puttering."

For a minute she thought he was going to suggest sleeping and puttering with her, but he seemed to think better of it, and she was relieved.

"All right." He looked worried. "Promise you'll call if you need anything?"

She nodded. "Thank you so much, Adam."

They got out of the car and Adam handed her the keys.

"I'll bring that insurance information over tomorrow," he said, as she lifted Cody into her arms.

"Okay." She kissed him on the cheek. "I'll see you then."

Except for one, too-brief nap, Cody was fussy much of the afternoon, and she was glad she'd elected to be alone with him. She divided her time between cuddling him, touching up the pale roots of her hair, and talking to Ellen about the leaky faucet in the bathroom. When the apartment was perfectly quiet, the dripping sounded like a sledgehammer.

She'd just gotten Cody to bed that evening when she heard Simon and Garfunkel's "Song for the Asking" on the radio. She turned off her bedroom light and got under the covers to listen.

"Welcome to Songs for the Asking," Linc said. "Tonight we'll be listening to Van Morrison, the old and the new."

As usual, his voice brought tears to her eyes.

*I miss you, Linc.*

She listened to the music, willing the songs to go quickly so she could hear his voice in between them. She could picture him sitting in his studio this past Wednesday, taping this particular show. She saw him shuffling the CDs, leaning back in his chair, drinking coffee from the mug she'd given him for his last birthday.

There was a knock on her door as Linc began playing "Moondance." She jumped from the bed, startled, and looked out the window, expecting to see the police car again. But except for her own car and Lucy's, the street was empty.

"Kim?" She heard Lucy's voice through the front door. "It's Lucy, honey."

She walked into the living room and opened the door, blinking against the sudden intrusion of light from the hallway. In its glow, her neighbor no longer looked like the benevolent, grandmotherly woman who shared coffee with her on the porch in the mornings.

"Why are you sitting here in the dark?" Lucy asked.

"Oh." Kim looked behind her at her unlit living room, as if she was as surprised by the darkness as Lucy was. "I was in the bedroom. Cody's had an earache today and I—"

"Oh, that poor little guy. How's he doing now?"

"Fine. I have some medicine for him." She should probably invite Lucy in, but she wanted to spend the evening with Linc, not the neighbor she no longer trusted.

"That's good," Lucy said, then added, "Listen dear, I'm having a heck of a time with that oven." She pointed behind her toward her own apartment. "It's the first time I've tried to bake in it, and I can't even get it turned on. Is yours the same? Have you figured it out?"

Ellen had shown her how to use the temperamental oven weeks earlier. You had to hold the on/off dial in with one hand the same time you set the temperature with the other. She knew she had no choice but to give Lucy a hands-on demonstration.

"I'll show you." She stepped into the hall, leaving her door open so she could listen for Cody.

She walked ahead of Lucy into the older woman's apartment, fighting the fantasy of being surrounded by police once she stepped over the threshold.

Lucy's apartment was smaller than hers, but filled with a similar collection of second-hand furniture supplied by Ellen. The dining room table had been taken over by a computer, much as Kim's had been, but there were stacks of papers and magazines and books piled over any blank space on the table, as well as on the chairs and kitchen counters. The walls were entirely bare, and the general feeling in the apartment was stark and temporary.

Except for the refrigerator. Photographs nearly covered the surface of the freezer door. Babies. Children. Young adults. Kim thought she should ask Lucy about them, but that would have to wait. She could still vaguely hear Linc talking on the radio in her own apartment, although from this distance, she couldn't possibly make out his words.

She bent over to show Lucy how to work the finicky oven. She spoke little, afraid that her voice would be husky and her recent tears evident. Only when she stood up straight did she notice that Lucy's own eyes were red. Circles of pink stood out on her cheeks and throat.

"Are you all right?" Kim asked.

"Oh." Lucy waved her hand through the air and took in a long, jerky breath. "I just had a conversation with one of my sons on the phone."

"What's wrong?"

"I haven't seen any of my children in six months," Lucy said. She picked up the cookie tray that rested on the counter only to put it down again. "Not to mention my grandchildren. That's why I dote on your little boy so."

Kim had no idea why that police officer had paid his visit to Lucy, but she suddenly felt certain that Lucy had no malicious intentions toward her. "Why don't you see them?" she asked.

"Because I walked out of my marriage. After thirty years. If I'd had any self-respect, I would have left long before then, but I toughed it out as long as I could. My kids should have applauded me. But, no. I've wrecked their lives, they say." Lucy's lower lip trembled.

"Oh, I'm so sorry." Kim touched her arm. "I bet they'll see the light in time, though." She knew she should ask more questions. Why Lucy had left, what had been so awful about that marriage.

Lucy was inviting it. She wanted to talk. Probably she'd known full well how to get that oven working. But the clock on the oven read 9:47 and Kim could hear the soft hum of Linc's voice from across the hall. She had to get back to him. She would let Lucy talk on the porch the following morning. She'd listen for hours if need be.

"I have to get back, Lucy," she said. "I'm sorry, but I don't want to leave Cody alone. Can we visit on the porch in the morning?"

"Yes, please. I'd like that." Lucy brightened at the thought. "I'll bring the coffee."

She stepped into the dark living room again and closed her apartment door behind her. There was an instant of silence from the radio, and then Leonard Cohen's voice filled the air. *Suzanne takes you down . . .*

The end of the show. She wondered what she'd missed. Had he said anything, played anything he would have wanted her to hear?

When Linc's show was over, she sat on the sofa for a long time, writing a letter to him in her head. The letter was filled with innuendo, with esoteric meaning only he would understand. It made her laugh out loud, and somewhere around the third or fourth paragraph, she knew she was going to actually write the letter. On paper. And mail it. No, fax it, from some other town. He received hundreds of faxed requests for music, his songs for the asking. Anyone sifting through his mail to see if she were in contact with him would never be able to separate her requests from the others. She would have to make sure of that. But *Linc* would be able to. If he were paying the least little bit of attention to his mail, he would know.

She sat down at the computer and began to type.

*Dear Linc Sebastian,*

She looked out the window toward the dark river.

*I'm writing from my place near the river*, she began, a cryptic allusion to a line from the song "Suzanne."

*I would appreciate it if you would play the following for me.*

She listed several songs he would recognize as her favorites. Then she signed the letter, *S.T.U. Downe*, in reference to the first line from "Suzanne."

*Read carefully, Linc*, she thought to herself.

She slept well that night, content that in a few hours her words would find their way into Linc's hands.

In the morning, she met Lucy on the porch for coffee, as promised. Lucy cuddled Cody on her lap as they talked. Cody had recovered remarkably overnight, but he was still subdued enough to want to cuddle rather than play.

Kim listened guiltily as Lucy divulged the miserable workings of a long-failed marriage. Everyone was confiding in her, and she gave them dishonesty in return.

What she really wished Lucy would talk about was the visit from the policeman the other night. When Lucy finally seemed to run out of words, Kim mustered up her courage.

"I saw a police officer here a few nights ago," she said. "I was worried something was wrong."

Lucy instantly colored. "Oh, I'd just ... I'd heard a noise. I've always been one of those jumpy people, you know. Imagining things. I'm not used to living alone. So ... I'm sorry if he disturbed you. I felt ridiculous after I called him. It was nothing, of course."

Lucy was talking far too fast, and Kim could not shake the feeling that she was lying. But the older woman seemed so uncomfortable that Kim felt sorry for her.

"I've done that, too," she said. "Once when my husband was out of town, I could have sworn someone was breaking in the back door and I called the cops." It was a lie, but Lucy looked relieved by Kim's empathy.

After her visit with Lucy, she loaded Cody in the car and headed east, the letter in her purse. It took her an hour to reach Rockville, which seemed like a big, reassuringly anonymous place. She drove around until she found a large, busy office supply store, and it was from there that she faxed the letter to Linc, marching right up to the counter as though she faxed things every day.

And then she drove the hour back to Annapolis, her hands perspiring on the steering wheel, hoping she had not made a mistake.

*W*hew!" Peggy looked at Nancy across the ruins of the Currys' family room.

Nancy put her hands on her hips. "Glad that's over," she said.

Peggy sank into the chair closest to the front door and grinned at her friend. "So that's what life is like with kids in the house." She'd spent the afternoon helping Nancy with a birthday party for her twelve-year-old daughter, Renee. They'd taken twenty wild and giggly preadolescent girls bowling, watched a movie with them in the family room, sat through the boisterous opening of gifts, and eaten pizza and cake. Even with the last of the girls out of the house, Peggy's ears still rang from the din.

She surveyed the damage in the room. Dirty paper plates and plastic cups littered every table, and wrapping paper was ankle deep on the floor. "Let's get this mess cleaned up," she said as she started to get out of her chair, but Nancy motioned her to stay seated.

"Nah," Nancy said. "Let's just visit for a while. You've done your duty. Gary and I can clean up later."

Peggy gratefully remained in her chair. She felt as though she'd spent the afternoon in a foreign country, trying to speak the language and master the currency, and she was truly exhausted. But it had been fun.

"Renee's adorable," she said.

Nancy chuckled. "I don't know how I'm going to make it

through the teen years with her. She's already got boys on the brain, in case you didn't notice."

"I noticed." She smiled, then cocked her head at Nancy. "Do you think girls are easier to raise than boys?" she asked.

"No way."

"Well, I hope I get the chance to find out." It had been five weeks since she'd last seen Tyler, and she was losing her optimism. "Just think," she said. "I'll be pushing fifty when Tyler's a teenager. Not that it will matter if we don't get him back."

"You will," Nancy said. "You've got to. It was meant to be."

"Nothing's worked so far," Peggy said with a sigh. She picked up a pink ribbon from the floor near her foot and laid it flat across her lap. "All the legal channels seem to be failing us."

"Have you thought about a psychic?"

Peggy laughed.

"I'm serious," Nancy said. "I've never been to one myself, but some of my friends swear by them. You could take a piece of Tyler's clothing with you, or a toy he loves, and she might be able to tell you where he is."

Peggy was surprised not so much by the suggestion as by her reaction to it. It actually seemed worth considering. She wished Tyler had left his monkey behind. Talk about a toy he loved.

"I can just hear Jim's reaction to *that* idea," she said.

Nancy looked suddenly pensive. "You know ..." Her voice drifted off and she leaned her head against the back of the chair and stared at the ceiling.

"Know what?" Peggy asked.

"Oh, I'm just confused about something."

"About what?" She ran her fingers over the smooth ribbon in her lap.

Nancy kept her eyes on the ceiling. "Well, I feel awkward talking to you about it, but—"

"*Nancy.* What?"

Nancy looked at her. "I was talking to my sister the other day. Remember? She worked with Susanna?"

"Yes."

"Well, her take on the whole situation is so different from yours."

Peggy's defenses immediately sprang to life. "How do you mean?" she asked.

"Julie said that everyone *liked* Susanna at the bank. They thought she was really nice and a very good mother."

"They're her friends," Peggy said. "Of course they'd think that."

"She *did* say that Susanna was pretty unassertive, though. A very passive sort of person. Certainly not the type to take the law into her own hands. She said no one at the bank could believe she'd leave like that, but they all . . . well, they all seem to think she did the right thing. Julie said that when their supervisor first told them Susanna had taken off, there was this stunned silence, and then everyone started cheering."

"They cheered?" Peggy was incredulous.

Nancy nodded.

Peggy shifted uncomfortably in her seat. "That's crazy, but then, they've only heard Susanna's side of things."

"Well . . ." Nancy shrugged.

Peggy could tell that Nancy had more to say. "What else?" she asked.

"Well, it's Julie's opinion that Jim held himself above everyone at the bank. He'd never come to any of the bank parties or picnics or anything."

Peggy shook her head. "He was probably too busy. Law school was incredibly demanding, and his job is even worse."

Nancy nodded as though that explained everything, and Peggy said nothing to alter her thinking, but she knew in her heart there was some truth in Julie's assessment. Jim *did* tend to see himself as superior to many people. It annoyed her sometimes, especially when he'd tell her she was wasting her skills working with the "sort of clients" she saw at Legal Aid. Right now, though, she felt a need to defend him.

"He can seem a little haughty sometimes," she admitted, "but I think it's because he worked so hard to get where he is." She smiled at Nancy. "You still haven't met him," she said. "I don't want your feelings about him tainted by other people before you've gotten to know him yourself."

"Oh, I know," Nancy said quickly. "And don't worry, I'll keep an open mind. To be honest, I felt uncomfortable talking to Julie about the whole situation, as though I were betraying you. And according to Julie, Susanna thought Jim was pretty great herself, at least until they broke up. She was really in love with him, I guess." Nancy leaned over to pick up a piece of crumpled wrapping paper. "Everybody at the bank, though, is under the impression that you were having an affair with Jim while he was still married to Susanna," she said. "I told Julie that was off the wall. It really got my back up. I hate people to think of you as a home wrecker."

Peggy had not thought about Susanna's world of coworkers at the bank. It hadn't occurred to her that they talked about her, that they saw her as the enemy. Even worse than imagining those conversations was the realization that they were not entirely "off the wall" in their thinking.

She tied the pink ribbon into a knot, then glanced across the room at Nancy. "I *was* seeing Jim for a while before he officially ended things with Susanna," she said quietly. "But Jim's marriage was really over by then."

She spotted headlights in the driveway and knew Gary had returned from taking some of Renee's friends home. She cursed his timing.

"Oh, Peg." Nancy grimaced, disappointment in her face. "I wanted it to be a rumor. Something Susanna was making up."

Gary suddenly walked in the front door. He shook his head at the mess, a smile on his bearded face. "I was hoping you two would have this place cleaned up by now," he said. He sat down, oblivious to the tension that had worked its way into the room in the last few minutes. "Remember we have to sign that form for Renee to take to school tomorrow," he said to Nancy.

Nancy nodded, but her eyes were still on Peggy. She was probably wondering what it would be like to discover your husband was seeing another woman, Peggy thought. How much did she know? Had she heard about Susanna walking in on her and Jim? Nancy was probably viewing things from Susanna's perspective for the first time, and now, with Gary in the room, there was little Peggy could say to change the direction of her thinking.

"Well, if you're sure I can't help, Nance, I'll leave you two to clean-up duty." Peggy got up from the chair. She walked to the closet near the front door for her coat, a pocket of shame burning in her chest.

"You were a hit with the kids, Peg," Gary said as he leaned over to pick up a few pieces of wrapping paper. "They were all talking about becoming lawyers when I drove them home."

Peggy was flattered in spite of herself, but she groaned. "I'm glad you have a few years to talk them out of it." She slipped into her coat.

Nancy stood up to walk her to the door. "Thanks for helping out," she said. "I don't think I couldn't have gotten through today without you."

Peggy looked at her friend, wishing Gary were not in the room. She felt a desperate need to clear the air. "Seriously," she said as she opened the door. "Let's get together sometime soon. The four of us."

Nancy touched her arm in what Peggy hoped was a gesture of understanding. "We'd love to," she said.

Peggy walked out to her car, which was parked at the curb. She was remembering the last time she'd mentioned going out with Nancy and Gary to Jim. The first thing Jim had asked her is what sort of work the Currys did, and he had not seemed impressed that they were both teachers. "We wouldn't have much in common with them," he'd said. She wondered now if he'd been referring to interests or income.

She took a long, circuitous route home despite her tiredness. She needed time to think, time to cleanse herself of all disconcerting thoughts about Jim—and about herself—before she returned to Wonderland.

Forty-two faxes had arrived during the night.

Linc carried them from his studio to the breakfast room. He opened the shades, wincing against the Boulder sunshine, then sat down with a cup of coffee and his first cigarette of the day. He only had an hour before he had to leave for the university, but he figured he could get through most of the requests.

He began reading the faxes, chuckling over some of them, jotting requests on a notepad. There were a few excellent suggestions for songs he hadn't played in quite a while, and a woman from Cleveland wanted him to do a profile of Donovan. Good idea. He made a note, then flipped to the next fax.

*I'm writing from my place near the river.*

Did he know this person? Seemed like an odd way to start. He glanced down at the name. *S.T.U. Downe.* Weird. He read on.

*I would appreciate it if you would play some of my favorite songs on your next show: "Desperado," "Circle Around the Sun," "Fire and Rain," and "Suzanne."*

He looked out the window. Lit another cigarette. Then he turned to the fax again with a fresh eye.

Susanna. It had to be.

*I'm writing from my place near the river . . . S.T.U. Downe.* He laughed out loud, shoving the other faxes aside to read this one through once more. Susanna was alive and well, and still in possession of her sense of humor.

The return line at the top of the fax listed a phone number with a 301 area code. He picked up the cordless phone from the table and dialed the operator.

"Could you tell me what state has the area code 301?" he asked.

"Maryland," the operator said.

"And how about the 598 exchange?"

He heard the operator searching for the answer. "Rockville," she said finally.

He hung up the phone and stared at the fax. Rockville. He'd been there once. It was near Washington, D.C. Not too far from the Potomac River. Was that the river Susanna was referring too? He doubted it. She wouldn't put as much effort as she had into disappearing and then fax him from the very town in which she was living. But at least he now knew what part of the world she was in.

He was grinning like a fool as he drove to the university to teach his graduate class in American Folk Music. He felt energetic during the class itself, although he was planning next Sunday's *Songs for the Asking* in his mind as he taught. His students picked up his good mood, if not his lack of concentration, and the classroom was filled with jokes and laughter. It felt like the old days, the before-Susanna-disappeared days, and he realized as he laughed along with his students that he'd been a pretty gloomy presence in the classroom this past month or so.

His students were probably wondering what had happened to alter his mood so dramatically, he thought. His personal life had always been fodder for their speculation. It was unavoidable; he was a public figure. People were intrigued by the fact that he'd spent time in prison, as well as by his radio persona. Susanna's much-publicized disappearance only added to their interest. Like everyone else in Boulder, Linc's students knew he'd been involved with her, and they also knew she'd taken her son and split town. None of his students had said anything to him about it, though. He wondered if they felt sorry for him, or if, perhaps, they thought he knew more than he did. A few of his female students—more than the usual number—were taking advantage of the situation, coming on to him, hanging around him after class. One of them even called him a couple of nights ago, ostensibly to discuss an assignment. Word was out: Linc Sebastian was available. Now he needed to get word out that Linc Sebastian wasn't interested.

He drove directly home after his class and spent the rest of the afternoon in his library, carefully selecting music for the show he would tape the following afternoon. He was not going to play the songs Susanna had requested, at least not at the beginning of the show. Instead, he was going to send her a message. He would have to reach far outside the type of music he usually played, and he would probably take some flak for it, both from listeners as well as from the powers that be, but he didn't care. He could get away with it once.

He deliberated for hours over what he would say to her, poring over tapes and CDs and his own scribbled notes. He wished he could tell her what was going on in Boulder. He wanted to let her know how aggressively Jim and Peggy were looking for her. And he wanted to chastise her for risking the fax. Yet, he was extremely glad she did.

The phone rang as he was finishing dinner that night.

"All right," Grace said, by way of greeting. "I've found the perfect woman for you."

"Pass," he said.

"Well, I've warned her you're a bit burned at the moment, but that doesn't mean the two of you can't at least have a cup of coffee together. See how you hit it off." She hesitated at his silence. "Can I tell you about her?" she asked.

"I'd rather hear about your last root canal, Gracie. Honest."

"You could at least go out with all three of us," Grace said. "Fran—that's her name—and Val and me. Would that make it easier for you? Safety in numbers?" She didn't give him a chance to respond. "How about tomorrow night."

"Gee, I'd love to, but that's the night I scrub the grout in my bathroom."

There was a moment of loaded silence from Grace's end of the line. "You win," she said finally. "I give up. Aren't you relieved?"

"Uh huh."

Grace launched into a description of the party she and Valerie had attended the night before. Linc half listened. He wanted to tell her about Susanna's fax, but knew he couldn't. The fax was something he would have to keep entirely and forever to himself.

After getting off the phone, he took Sam for a long walk up and down the hilly, winding streets around his house and then went to bed early. He knew he wouldn't be able to fall asleep, but sleep was not was he was after. He wanted uninterrupted time to think about Susanna.

In a way, this past month had reminded him of his four years in prison. He'd thought of Susanna constantly then, yet she'd been out of his reach, as she was now. For those few months before his incarceration, Linc's feelings about Susanna had undergone a dramatic shift. He'd stopped thinking of her as the needy, gawky little girl next door. Instead, she had quite suddenly become a talented, beautiful young woman in his eyes.

He was working as a gofer in a radio station, but his band still met in his garage on weekends, with Susanna their artist in residence. Susanna had wanted more though, and she finally asked Linc if he would pose alone for her. "Fully clothed," she'd assured him, and he'd laughed, the alternative being unimaginable. He'd agreed, and he'd sit for hours in her bedroom—when her parents were out—while she'd sketch him. They did a lot of talking, their conversations on a deeper level than ever before.

"Why don't you go out with anyone?" he asked her from his perch on the edge of her bed. Only recently had he realized she was old enough, interesting enough, for someone to want to take her out.

"I *do* go out," she said, her hand working rapidly above her sketchbook. "But I do it on the sly. Do you think I'd want to bring some guy home to meet my parents?"

He was instantly, painfully, jealous. "Who?" he asked. "Who are you going out with?"

"You don't know them," she said.

"Well, have you . . . you know, had sex with anyone?" He couldn't stomach the thought of her being that intimate with someone, especially some guy he didn't even know.

Her head darted up. "None of your business," she said.

He felt himself color. "I'm just asking to make sure you know about protection. You know, birth control." He knew she wouldn't get that sort of information from her parents, and he told himself he was only interested in her safety. But in reality, he simply had to know.

"I'm not doing it, nosy," she said, returning her attention to her sketch, but only for a moment. "And what about you?" She looked at him from beneath her pale bangs.

"Well, of course. I'm twenty-two, for Christ's sake." He'd first had sex at her age, but he wasn't about to tell her that.

"Who with?" Her eyes were riveted once again on her sketch-book, but her hand was barely moving.

"That's personal."

"Rosie?" she asked. "Tammi?"

"Yes."

"*Both* of them?"

"Yes, but they don't know about each other, so keep your trap shut."

She was quiet for a minute. "Well, I think Nigel's kind of inter-ested in me," she said finally. Nigel was the new bass player in Linc's band, and he was indeed interested.

"I don't like the idea of you with him," he said.

"Why not?"

"Because he's too . . . stuck on himself. And besides," he took in a deep breath, knowing he was about to change everything between himself and his neighbor, "I'd be jealous."

Her hand froze above the sketchbook. She looked at him, but there was no surprise in her face, no expression at all. He felt embarrassed, but then she said, "I feel jealous when I see you with Rosie or Tammi or any of those girls." Her voice was quiet. "I've been jealous of your girlfriends my entire life."

He was surprised and touched by her admission, and he let out a stunned laugh. "Well, whaddya know?" he said, thinking to him-self: *She's sixteen. She's been like a little sister to you. She's a virgin. And her parents are insane.*

Those thoughts held him back from doing anything he might come to regret—at least for a while—and it wasn't long after that conversation in her bedroom that he went to prison for the mur-der of her father. Once incarcerated, he was cut off from his friends in the band, and he never gave Rosie and Tammi another thought. Susanna was the only girl on his mind, and certainly the only girl who came to see him. He wished later that, sometime during those visits, he had let her know how much he needed her.

Wanted her. How much he wished she would wait for him to get out. She would have waited, had she known. He was certain of that. And so he had only himself to blame when she fell in love with Jim.

He never would have wished for her marriage to end. He would have done anything to protect her from the heartbreak she'd endured with her husband. Yet once she was free of her marriage and he could finally let her know his feelings, it was as though fate had given them the chance to start fresh. This time, he would not let that chance slip away from him. He refused to be locked up again, whether behind bars and barbed wire or in a prison of his own making.

And that was why he was lying awake, anxious for morning to come so he could get up and begin taping Sunday's show.

$\mathcal{S}$he arrived for her lesson at seven, but Adam simply turned her and Cody around at the door.

"We're going over to Jessie's for a few minutes," he said. "Victoria had her kittens today, and I promised we'd come over to look at them. I think she has it in her mind to pawn a couple of them off on you."

"Uh uh." Kim shook her head. Her life would not accommodate a pet right now. Nor was a pet allowed in her lease with Ellen. Besides, she'd sworn off cats a long time ago. At least, *Susanna* had sworn off cats.

They walked out Adam's front door to the sidewalk. It was only a few steps to Jessie's house, but they moved slowly, Cody toddling along with them as he held Kim's hand.

Adam didn't knock on Jessie's door, but simply walked into her house as though it were his own. It was nearly identical to his house, at least in terms of architecture. The floor plan was simply the reverse of his, the kitchen to the right of the living room instead of the left, the stairs off the east side of the hall instead of the west. But where Adam's home was decorated in the stark, bold colors that mirrored his paintings, Jessie's was a soft mix of prints and textures. It offered a warmer, cozier atmosphere than Adam's house, but Kim liked the different styles equally. It made her sadly aware of the nonexistent decorating scheme in her own apartment.

"We're here, Jess," Adam called from the living room.

"In the bedroom," Jessie called back.

They followed the sound of her voice upstairs. Jessie was lying flat on her stomach across her bed, peering over the edge at something on the floor. She looked up at the three of them.

"Come see," she said.

They walked around the side of the bed. Jessie's fat, tiger-striped cat and her squirming mass of kittens lay in a pillow-lined basket on the floor. The sight was jarring to Kim, and she had to force her smile.

"They're adorable," she said, kneeling low. She didn't want Cody to pick up her discomfort. She set him on the floor next to her, but held him back with one hand hooked in the straps of his overalls. "Look, Cody," she said. "See the kitties?"

Cody was clearly enamored. He squealed in delight, reaching out to touch the tiny balls of fluff.

"Gentle, Cody," Kim said, guiding his hand. "That's it. Gentle."

"I think he needs a kitten all his own, don't you?" Jessie asked. She reached down from the bed to stroke her hand over Cody's head.

Kim smiled at her. She hadn't seen Jessie since before she and Adam had slept together, and she didn't feel entirely comfortable in her presence. Did Jessie know? What had Adam told her?

"We're not allowed to have pets in my apartment, unfortunately," she said.

"Oh." Jessie screwed up her nose. "Nuts."

"How many are there?" Kim asked, trying to count.

"Five."

There had been six kittens born in her bedroom closet many years ago. Six beautiful kittens, three of them multicolored, three of them orange.

"How old should they be before you can give them away?" Adam asked. He was sitting on the edge of Jessie's bed.

"About eight weeks," Jessie said.

"And then you'll get Victoria spayed, right?" Adam sounded hopeful.

Jessie made a face at him. "You're such a scrooge."

"I just think there are enough kittens in the world," he said.

"It's not that I don't like them. As a matter of fact, I was thinking of taking one of them."

"Really?" Jessie brightened. "Oh, Adam, that's great. How about two? They could keep each other company."

"Don't push your luck." He stood up and touched Kim lightly on her shoulder. "Ready for your lesson?" he asked.

Kim got to her feet and lifted Cody into her arms, ignoring his wailed protests over being torn from the kittens.

"Coming over tonight?" Adam asked his sister.

"No, I'm going to stay here with my babies." Jessie didn't look up from her prone position on the bed.

"Okay. See you tomorrow, then." He slipped his arm around Kim, and they walked out of the room.

Back in Adam's house, Kim settled Cody into Liam's bed. She sang "Froggie Went a-Courtin'" to him, trying to sing away the ugly memories making their way into her head. She thought she had succeeded until she went upstairs to the studio, where Adam was squeezing paint onto the palette. She knew she wouldn't be able to paint. Not tonight.

"Adam?" She stood in the middle of the floor, hands locked together in front of her. "Could we skip tonight?"

He raised his eyebrows in surprise.

"Did you ever have one of those days when you know you won't be able to concentrate on what you're painting?" she asked.

He laughed. "I've been wondering if I'll ever again have one of those days when I *can* concentrate on what I'm painting," he said. "No problem." He put a sheet of plastic wrap over the palette, then sat down on the red leather loveseat. "Come here and talk to me."

She joined him on the loveseat, and he put his arm around her.

"What's got you down?" he asked.

She'd thought it was seeing the kittens that had disturbed her, but she suddenly realized that was only one of many things weighing on her. She'd been watching the news and reading the paper, hoping that the police would find the person who planted the bombs and save her from having to do something about the information in her possession. The list of names haunted her. She had the unwanted power of being able to predict who was going to die. One more week, she'd told herself. If the police had not found the killer by then, she would have no choice but to find some way to help them out.

"What is it?" Adam asked again. "You seemed upset over at Jessie's."

"Did I?" She thought she'd done a good job of covering her distress.

"You were trying to hide it, but I could tell."

She was surprised he was so perceptive. "You're right," she said. "I was upset. Seeing the kittens reminded me of when my own cat had kittens. It's a terrible story, though." She looked at him, as if waiting for permission to continue.

"When was this?" he asked. "What happened?"

"I was about nine years old, and I found a stray cat wandering around outside my house one morning. I'd always wanted a pet, but my father wouldn't let me have one. I brought the cat into my house and gave it some milk, but when my father came home that night and saw it, he blew up. He said I had to get rid of it. The only problem was, I was already in love with it. So I hid it in my room."

"You were a rebel." Adam chuckled.

"No, I wasn't," she corrected him quickly. "I'd had the rebel beaten out of me by then."

"Beaten out of you?"

She waved away the question. "Anyway, she was a great cat. She'd come and go through my bedroom window. I didn't name her. I think I was afraid to. Deep down I knew I'd better not get too attached to her. One day, I came home from school to discover that she'd had a litter of kittens in my bedroom closet. I panicked. I ran next door—I always ran next door when I couldn't figure out what to do."

"Who was next door?"

"Friends. An older boy and his mother, Geri. They were always very nice to me. Geri was wildly allergic to cats, though, so she couldn't take them in, but she said she'd help me find homes for them. She wanted to call my mother and try to reason with her so I wouldn't get in too much trouble, but I talked her out of it. That never worked with my mother. I told Geri I'd just keep the kittens hidden until she could find a home for them." That, of course, had not worked either.

"One night, I came home from school and they were gone. My closet was empty. No one said a word to me about it and I couldn't really ask 'where are my cats?' when I had never acknowledged they'd been there to begin with." Kim rubbed her hands together in her lap. "So, after this long, horribly quiet dinner that night, my father said, 'What did I tell you about that cat?' and I said that Geri was going to find homes for the kittens and I was only keeping them until then, and he said I'd disobeyed him and that he'd gotten rid of both the cat and the kittens."

"How did he get rid of them?" Adam sounded as though he only half wanted to know.

"I thought he'd taken them to the pound, and my mind was working really fast. I figured I could call Geri and we could go to the pound and rescue them before they were put to sleep. And then my father said, 'Don't you want to know where I took them?' And I said, 'To the pound?' and he laughed. 'Why make the taxpayers pay to get rid of those cats when I could do it just as easy?' he said."

She could still see her father's red-nosed smirk across the dinner table from her. "I was starting to feel sick. I said, 'You killed them?'" She looked at Adam. "I saw him kill a squirrel once, with a gun. I figured maybe that's what he'd done to the cats."

"And was it?"

She shook her head. "He told me he didn't actually *kill* them. He said he just buried them in the back yard. Buried them alive." Her voice tightened as she spoke. Twenty years had passed, yet she could still tear up when she thought of those kittens.

Adam sucked in his breath. He tightened his arm around her shoulders.

"All I could picture was those tiny kittens," she continued, "my beautiful, nameless cats, underground, scared and trying to breathe, trying to claw their way out, not being able to figure out which way was up. I started to run out of the house, but my father grabbed me and hit me and told me to go to my room for the rest of the night. After he and my mother were asleep, I snuck out, but it was too dark for me to find where he'd been digging. I knew it was too late by then, anyhow. I went next door and told Geri and . . . her son what had happened. I was sick—throwing up sick—and Geri kept me there overnight." Kim remembered feeling, for the first time in her life, truly mothered. Geri held her and stroked her hair while she cried, and Linc flew around the house with the sort of rage only a fifteen-year-old boy could muster.

"In the morning, Geri called the police. They came to my house and my father laughed when they asked him about the kittens. He said he'd given them away to a coworker of his, that he'd just told me he'd buried them to punish me. The police searched my yard and couldn't find any sign of digging, and I was so relieved." She leaned her head back against Adam's arm and looked at the ceiling. "A few years later, though, Geri's son told me that he'd found the grave in *his* yard. My father had buried the kittens next door. Li . . . Geri's son found the grave just a few days after it all happened, but he didn't want me to know about it."

She had been fifteen when Linc finally told her. Fifteen and already so filled with hatred toward her father that the news of the kittens only served to crystallize that loathing into something hard and permanent inside her.

"Your father beat you?" Adam asked quietly.

"When he was drunk, yes. Which was most of the time."

"What about your mother?" Adam asked. "Did she stick up for you?"

"No, he'd hit her, too. She was afraid of him, so she'd usually take his side against me. I think she drank to escape the misery of living with him." Kim wondered if it might be a mistake to tell Adam so much of the truth.

"Where's your mother now?"

"I don't know where she is, nor do I care. We've been estranged ever since my father's death when I was sixteen."

"I thought you said he died when you were seventeen."

She shrugged. "Sixteen, seventeen. I don't really remember."

Adam pressed his lips against her temple. "Stay here tonight, Kim," he said. "Stay with me."

She had not intended to spend the night with him, but now she wanted to. She couldn't deprive herself of the comfort of his arms around her tonight. It would only be the second time they'd slept together, and her memory of the first time, when visions of Linc had clouded her head, was still keen. She would have to keep Linc

from creeping into her mind tonight, although that would be difficult. Over and over again, she'd imagined him reading the fax
she'd sent. He would either know it was from her or he'd overlook
it in the stack of requests. By now, he had done one or the other,
and there was nothing she could do to change that outcome.

"Can we watch the late news if I stay over tonight?" she asked
Adam.

"The news?" He looked surprised. "We can do anything you
like."

"I'm curious about the bombings," she explained. "I keep
watching to see if they've gotten any clues. They haven't mentioned anything about it in days. It's like they're not even trying to
solve the mystery."

"Oh, I'm sure they are. The cops often know more than they say
publicly, in case the bomber or whoever's following the news.
They're probably setting a trap for him right now."

She hoped he was right. They watched the news from Adam's
bed, and the only allusion to the bombing was the mention of a
memorial service for the secretary's children. Seeing pictures of
those children reinforced her gloom, and she was glad she'd
agreed to stay the night.

Very early the following morning, she opened her eyes to see
Adam propped up against his pillow, drawing in a sketchbook. She
didn't stir, didn't want to disturb him, and she feigned sleep when
he finally got out of bed and walked into the bathroom. Curious,
she leafed through his sketchbook where he'd left it on his side of
the bed. The book was about one-third full, and she recoiled from
the first several pictures. They were filled with ghastly images of
hollow-eyed people, wolves with their teeth bared, jagged lines,
and tongues of fire. His dreams had indeed "turned to shit," she
thought. The last few pictures, though, were entirely different.
Trees, flowers, dolphins, ships, a woman fishing from a dock, a
small town viewed from the air.

Adam walked back into the room as she was studying one of
the sketches. She looked at him. "I hope you don't mind," she said,
nodding toward the book. "I couldn't resist."

He shrugged as he pulled on a T-shirt. "You let me look at
yours," he said. "Fair is fair."

"The beginning of the sketchbook, though." She shook her head in sympathy. "What terrible nightmares you were having."

Adam smiled and walked over to the bed. "Ah, yes. But you, my sweet thing," he leaned over to kiss her, "have completely changed my dreams."

Kim was working on Noel's book later that morning when someone knocked on her apartment door. She'd heard no footsteps on the stairs, and she jumped, a small well of panic rising in her chest. Ever since seeing the police car in front of the house, she had not been able to react calmly to the phone ringing or to an unseen visitor at the door.

"Who is it?" she called out.

"Jessie."

Relieved, she got up and opened the door. Jessie stood on the landing, shivering in a light sweater. "Your landlady let me in downstairs," she said. "Hope that was okay."

"Of course. Come in."

"I didn't want to interrupt your work." Jessie walked into the living room. "But I was nearby and wondered if you might be taking a lunch break soon."

Kim looked at her watch, and only then realized how hungry she was. "Sure."

"Great." Jessie smiled, but it was a guarded smile. "We could walk down to the deli, or—"

"Let's eat here," Kim said, heading toward the kitchen. "Cody just got up from his nap and he's hungry. I've got tuna salad. Peanut butter and jelly. Grilled cheese. Or," she picked up a can from the kitchen counter with a wry smile, "mini-ravioli. Cody's favorite."

Cody crawled across the floor and lifted himself to a standing position by hanging onto Jessie's pant leg.

"Tuna sounds good." Jessie said as she picked up the little boy. She pressed her lips tenderly to his cheek, and Kim was touched by the gesture.

"Have a seat." She opened the can of ravioli first, emptying the slithery pasta into a bowl and putting it in the microwave before getting the can of tuna from the cupboard. "How are the kittens this morning?" she asked.

"Oh, they're beautiful. You liked those kitties, didn't you, Cody?" Jessie sat down at the table. "I really like having some other living beings around. I don't think I live alone very well."

Kim dumped the can of tuna into a bowl. "You know," she said warily, "this isn't any of my business, Jessie, but I got the feeling when I met Noel that he misses you a lot. He still has pictures of you around his apartment."

Jessie smoothed Cody's hair off his forehead. "I know he does. I miss him too, but he wouldn't acknowledge that he had a problem and . . . " She shrugged.

"I understand," she said quickly. The last thing she wanted to do was talk someone into a relationship with a drinker. She finished making the tuna salad and put it on the table, along with a few slices of bread and a couple of plates. Then she took the ravioli out of the microwave and lifted Cody from Jessie's lap to his high chair.

"Anyhow," Jessie said, "I didn't come here to talk about Noel."

"Ah." Kim sat down next to Cody. "You have an agenda."

Jessie nodded, but she couldn't seem to meet Kim's eyes. She took a slice of bread on her plate and spooned tuna salad onto it. "I like you, Kim," she said. "And if Adam were ready to get involved with someone, I'd be really happy it was you." She carefully placed a second slice of bread on top of the tuna. "But he's *not* ready," she continued. "It's too soon. He lost his entire family. He hasn't had time to get over it yet, and I'm afraid he's jumping into something with you just so he can stop feeling the pain." She looked at Kim. "I understand him wanting to do that. I'd like to find an escape from the pain myself. But I know I need to feel it for awhile. And he does too." She looked down at her sandwich as though she didn't know what to do with it now that she'd made it. "I'm afraid he's going to get hurt," she said.

Kim fed Cody a piece of ravioli. "I've been honest with him, Jessie," she said. "I've told him that *I'm* not ready for a relationship either. Right now, we're just a comfort for each other."

Jessie began to cry. The tears were sudden, catching Kim by surprise, and she reached across the table to touch Jessie's arm.

"I'm sorry." Jessie wiped her eyes with her napkin. "I know I'm being selfish. Up until you came along, Adam and I were both wallowing in grief. It was awful, but at least we were doing it together. Now he's happier because you're around, and I'm still wallowing, all by myself. And I think it's *right* to still be wallowing. It hasn't been that long."

"You must have been very close to Dana and the children."

"Molly and Liam were everything to me." Jessie stood up and pulled a tissue from the box on the kitchen counter. "I don't think I'm the marrying type. I may never have children. Molly and Liam felt like the closest I might ever get to having kids of my own."

"There'll be other guys for you," Kim said. "There'll be children." She knew her argument was weak, even offensive. Molly and Liam were no more replaceable than Tyler Miller would have been had she lost him to Jim.

Jessie wrinkled her nose as she returned to her seat. "I don't think so. I couldn't go through this again. This . . . losing everybody."

Kim leaned toward her. "Things will get better, Jessie," she said. "It takes time. But you're a strong person." She recalled hearing those words from her therapist during her hospitalization. She hadn't believed them then, and she doubted Jessie believed them now.

"It would have helped if the guy who killed them had to pay for what he did." Jessie tore at the tissue in her hands. Her face was red, and there was anger in her eyes. "This way there's no justice. No resolution."

"I know," Kim said. "I think Adam feels the same way."

"He *used* to feel that way," Jessie said bitterly. "At least until you came along. Now, everything's just peachy."

"No, everything's not peachy," Kim argued. "It's just that Adam's learning to—"

"Look." Jessie seemed suddenly angry. "Quit trying to fix my brother, okay? He needs to get better at his own pace."

Kim was surprised by the hostility in her voice. "I'm not trying to—"

"Right. I know." Jessie held up her hands to stop Kim's words. "I know you're not *intentionally* doing anything to help or harm, but it's happening, anyway." She stood up and took a step away from the table.

"Aren't you going to eat?" Kim asked.

"I'm sorry." Jessie looked at the untouched sandwich. "Maybe you could save it for your dinner." She started for the door, and Kim felt distressed by the sudden turn their conversation had taken. Jessie was jealous all right, but not of the attention Adam was paying to Kim. She was jealous of her brother's ability to get on with his life. Jessie was stuck, and she was determined to keep Adam stuck with her.

Kim made sure Cody was strapped into his high chair, then followed Jessie to the door. "I know this has been an awful year for both of you," she said, when she'd caught up to her, "but it's not fair for you to try to hold Adam back this way."

"Don't tell me what's fair." Jessie's voice had lost it's volume, but not its anger. "Nothing, absolutely nothing, about life is fair. Maybe you haven't figured that out yet, Kim. You have this great little boy and a comfortable life. You don't know how quickly all of that can change."

Kim opened her mouth to argue that point, but wisely closed it again. "Maybe not," she said quietly. "Maybe I don't."

Shutting the door after Jessie left, she leaned against it, eyes closed and her knees shaking from the confrontation.

She knew more than Jessie could ever guess about life's unfairness.

$\mathcal{I}$’ve started working on the article," Lucy said from the glider on the porch.

"Which article?" Kim set down her mug of coffee to zip her jacket. It was chilly this morning.

"The one you've inspired me to write. You know, on young single mothers."

"Oh. How's it coming along?"

"Well, I need to interview some mothers, and I'd like to start with you, if you're willing."

Kim picked up her mug again and sat back in the rocking chair, her eyes on Cody. He was standing up on the rocker nearest her, and she was ready to grab him if he lost his balance. "I don't know, Lucy," she said.

"It would be fun," Lucy said. "I'd have a photographer come out and take pictures of you and Cody and—"

"Oh, no." Kim shook her head. "No, thanks. I just want to live a nice quiet, anonymous life." She wondered if this could be a trap of some sort. Maybe the police told Lucy to see how she'd react to the idea of having her picture in a widely circulated magazine.

"Well, believe me," Lucy chuckled. "People won't recognize you on the street on the strength of one of my articles. I wish I had that sort of readership, dear, but I don't."

Kim finished her coffee. "Maybe the interview part," she said, "but no pictures. Okay?"

"All right." Lucy gave in. "Though I hope you'll change your mind. Maybe we could do it next week. I should have the article outlined by then."

"Can you change my name in the article?" Kim asked. "A lot of writers do that, don't they?"

"If you like." Lucy looked thoughtful for a moment. "I guess I understand how you feel," she said, "and you're probably right about not putting in a picture. You're a young single woman and you don't want some strange person to come looking for you and Cody. I think you're right."

"Good. Thanks." She stood up and moved Cody from the rocker to the floor of the porch. "Are you about ready for a walk, kiddo?" she asked him.

"By the way," Lucy said as Kim was putting Cody in the stroller. "I worry about you when you don't come home at night."

Kim looked at her in surprise. "Oh." She smiled. She hadn't thought about what the neighbors might think. "Sorry, Mom."

"Well, how do I know you're not lying in a gutter somewhere with your throat slit?" Lucy sounded defensive.

Kim leaned over to zip up Cody's jacket. "Thanks for worrying about me, but I'm all right."

"Well, you're old enough that I don't need to give you advice, I suppose," Lucy said. "Maybe that can be another part of my article." She gazed into space. "You know, how to balance single motherhood with your love life."

Kim laughed. "You'll have to find someone else to interview for that part of the article," she said. She turned the stroller toward the street just as Ellen poked her head out the front door.

"My client isn't here *yet?*" Ellen sounded exasperated.

"Haven't seen anyone," Lucy said.

"Ellen?" Kim asked. "Will someone be able to fix that faucet in my apartment soon?" She'd taken to stuffing pieces of tissue in her ears at night to block the sound.

"Soon," Ellen said. "The plumber I use is really backed up." She looked down the street and shook her head. "Guess I have a free hour." With a shrug, she disappeared inside again.

"You need to be more assertive," Lucy said once Ellen had shut the door. "You've been after her about that leak for days. You should give her hell."

"I'm not much of a hell-giver," Kim said. Besides, she needed to stay on Ellen's good side. "We'll see you later," she said.

"Bye, dear," Lucy waved. "Have fun."

Kim started walking toward the park. The conversation with Lucy had left her half amused, half unnerved. It was nice to know she had a neighbor who wanted to watch out for her safety, but she didn't want anyone to know her every move. It was best to keep Lucy in the dark about her comings and goings. That way, if she ever did leave for real, it would take Lucy a few days to realize she was actually gone.

The leaves seemed to have deepened to richer golds and reds overnight, and she felt as though she and Cody were moving through a tunnel of color as they approached the playground. The stroller made a crackling sound as she pushed it through the layer of fallen leaves.

Roxanne was there with her two boys. Jack stood at the top of the slide, yelling at some imaginary playmate; Roxanne pushed Brandon on the swing. Kim joined them, pushing Cody, chatting with her new friend about the weather and raking leaves and Halloween costumes.

"Jack insists on being a monster this year," Roxanne said. "Not that he needs a costume for that." She laughed. "But anyhow, he apparently has this specific monster in mind, with this green head and warts all over its neck. Yuck! The store had to order the costume in his size. Do you believe it? Special ordering a Halloween costume for a four year old. I must be out of my mind. So it's supposed to arrive sometime this week, and it better get here by Halloween or someone's going to be upset."

"I'm sure it will be worth the wait," Kim said, although she couldn't imagine spending that sort of money on a costume for a child. Apparently, Roxanne did not do her shopping at garage sales.

"I told my husband he'll have to be the one to open the package when it arrives, though," Roxanne continued. "After those bombings, I'm nervous about opening anything that gets delivered to the house."

"Well, those bombs didn't actually come through the mail, so I think you'll be safe," Kim said. She wished she could tell Roxanne that she had nothing to fear. She could practically guarantee that Roxanne could safely open any package that came to her door. It was Ryan Geary who had to be careful, and it was beginning to look as though it was up to Kim to make sure he never got that package.

She left the park after half an hour and started walking toward town and the bank. She'd gotten a check from Noel the day before and she couldn't cash it soon enough.

As she neared the bank building, she noticed something different about the unfinished mural painted on its outside brick wall. At first she thought it was the clean, bright October sunshine that gave the painting its new look, but then she saw that the enchanting little snow-covered village depicted in the mural had been given a few new buildings, and children now skated on a frozen pond, surrounded by pine trees laced with snow.

Best of all, though, the artist himself was there. Kim stopped in the middle of the sidewalk, a smile spreading across her face.

Adam stood on a ladder at the far side of the mural, a huge paintbrush in his hand as he worked a white cloud into the vivid blue sky above the village.

"*Hooray*," she said under her breath. There was a bench on the sidewalk a few feet from where she stood, and she quietly took a seat, then leaned over to whisper to Cody. "Adam's painting, Cody," she said. "See the pretty church? See the children on the pond?"

She sat there at least five minutes before one of Cody's squeals caused Adam to turn around and spot them. He smiled, waving the hand with the paintbrush in it, and climbed down the ladder to walk toward her.

"How long have you been sitting here?" he asked.

"Just long enough to feel overjoyed. How wonderful to see you working."

Adam looked over his shoulder at the mural, then sat down next to her. "Great weather for this," he said. "My favorite time to paint. And the dreams were there this morning. They've been there for a few days. Guess all I needed was a couple of rolls in the hay." He grinned at her.

With a jolt, she realized that was the sort of thing Linc would say. Adam and Linc shared an irreverence she found appealing.

"Glad I could help," she said. She lifted Cody out of the stroller and let him climb on the bench.

"My dream last night was about you, actually," he said. "I think that means I should paint you."

She groaned. "Try to find some other meaning in it, okay?" Everyone wanted to immortalize her today.

An elderly woman walked by and let out a gasp of pleasure when she saw the mural. Then she noticed Adam sitting on the bench.

"I've been praying every day to see you back at that wall again, Mr. Soria," she said.

"Thanks." Adam waved at her. "I can use all the prayers I can get." Once the woman had passed, he returned his attention to Kim. "Want to go to a movie with Jessie and me tonight?"

She wondered if Jessie would want to go out with them, given the conversation she and Kim had had the day before.

"I don't think I'd better." She nodded toward Cody. "Remember how noisy he was the last time we tried it?"

"Look," Adam said. "I've got a list of baby-sitters a yard long. We used them for Molly and Liam, so they're tried and true. Let me call one of them for you. They can watch Cody at my house or yours or wherever—"

"No." She wrapped her arm lightly around her son. He was standing on the bench next to her, bouncing up and down, grinning at the traffic as it passed by on the street.

Adam frowned. "It would be good for you to have some nonmaternal time, Kim. Good for both of you."

She couldn't quite shake the feeling that leaving Cody with someone else for a few hours made her a bad mother. But Adam was right. She didn't want Cody to grow up afraid of being separated from her. Even the best mothers left their kids with sitters from time to time.

"All right," she agreed. "But I'll want to talk to the baby-sitter myself, okay?"

"Sure. That's great."

She needed to talk to him about Jessie, but now was not a good time. He was too happy. She didn't want to bring him down.

Adam glanced at his mural. "You going to watch for a while?" he asked.

"If that's okay with you."

"Be my guest."

She watched him work with a mixture of envy and admiration. There was something about the vast canvas that appealed to her, that made her arm ache with longing to sweep paint across that wide brick wall. Other people joined her on the bench, all of them smiling and fascinated by the work of art taking shape in front of them.

She thought back to her conversation with Jessie. Adam was ready to move on, no matter what Jessie thought. His being back at work had to be a good sign; his relationship with Kim could only be helping. Why should he suffer any longer than he had to just to keep his sister company in her misery?

Kim left Cody with a baby-sitter that night while she and Adam and Jessie went to the movies. The sitter, a seventeen-year-old girl who brought a stack of textbooks with her to Adam's house, seemed competent enough, and Adam assured Kim that the girl had taken care of Liam and Molly for several years before the accident.

There were actually periods of time during the evening when Kim didn't think about Cody at all, but she declined Jessie's suggestion to get something to eat after the movie, and Adam supported her need to get home.

"It's mama's first night out." Adam hugged Kim's shoulders as they left the theater. "She needs to make it short."

Jessie didn't argue. Although she was quieter than usual, she did not seem to harbor any ill feelings toward Kim, and she even attempted to comfort her on the drive home with stories of the sitter's trustworthiness.

Kim felt ridiculous for her anxiety once they arrived at Adam's house. The sitter reported that Cody had slept through the entire evening. Kim checked on him, and found him still sound asleep, peacefully curled up with his monkey in Liam's bed.

Jessie went over to her own house to "check on the kittens," she said, but she returned shortly, and although she was cheerful and agreeable, she seemed determined to foil any attempts at intimacy between her brother and Kim for that night. Kim finally went home around eleven.

The following night, though, Adam escaped from his chaperone and stayed at Kim's apartment. They spent the evening playing board games and watching a movie on TV. They spent Sunday together as well, Adam showing her sights around Annapolis she hadn't yet taken the time to explore. As Sunday night approached, though, and Adam gave no indication of going home, Kim finally had to tell him she needed some time alone.

"You needed to be alone last Sunday night, too," Adam said. It did not sound like a complaint, but she thought she detected some hurt behind the words.

"I just like to have some time for myself once in awhile," she said.

"I bet I know how you spend your Sunday nights," Adam said. "You probably pamper yourself, right? You take a long bath with exotic oils in the water. You sip herbal tea and lather cream on your skin."

"How did you know?" she asked, and he didn't press her further. She could hardly tell him that she spent Sunday nights lying in bed, the radio playing on the shelf behind her head, with her mind—and her heart—two thousand miles away from Annapolis. She was having an affair with a voice on the radio.

She lay in her bed that night as she waited for the start of Linc's show, trying to form an image of his face in her mind. She wished she'd saved a picture of him. Even when he'd been in prison, she'd had pictures of him to hold on to and visits with him every month. Now, her memory of his face was beginning to blur.

"Song for the Asking" came on the radio, and she closed her eyes to wait for Linc's voice. But before he even bothered to greet his listeners, he played the Everly Brothers' "Wake Up Little Susie," and she sat up straight in the bed.

"I'm awake, Linc," she said, as she tuned in the station more clearly. She was impatient as she waited out the rest of the song. She knew without a doubt that he was playing it for her. He never played the Everly Brothers on his show.

"Good evening, everyone," Linc said, in his slow, easy radio voice.

She could immediately see him again in her mind's eye. His blue eyes, his high cheekbones and shaggy blond hair.

"Got a lot of requests this week, from all over the country," Linc said. "Requests from Leslie Potters . . . and James Abbott . . . and S.T.U. Downe."

Kim grinned to herself. He rarely read the names of his requesters. He was letting her know. Not only had he received her fax, he was saying, he had understood it, and he knew she was listening right now. Although she knew he'd taped this show four days earlier, she felt more connected to him than she had since before leaving Boulder.

"Some songs for Ms. Downe," he said, and he opened with "Philadelphia" by Bruce Springsteen. She hadn't requested "Philadelphia," and he didn't ordinarily play Springsteen. He had to be trying to communicate something to her.

She grabbed her sketch pad from under the bed and wrote down the song title and a few of the lines which seemed as though they might have some sort of meaning. Did he think that's where she was? Philadelphia?

Next he played Simon and Garfunkel's "At the Zoo." Frowning, she wrote it down.

Then "The Lion Sleeps Tonight," and she thought she was beginning to understand. Was there a zoo in Philadelphia? When he played "Saturday Night's All Right for Fighting," she laughed out loud. Did he mean next Saturday? And how would she know what time? The lion sleeps tonight. Was the zoo open at night?

But then he played "Five O'Clock World," by the Vogues.

"Yes!" She laughed.

Linc finally spoke again. "Those were all for Ms. Downe," he said. "And now we'll move on to Leslie Potters's selections."

Kim continued to listen, to write down every song, every odd turn of phrase, but it was apparent that Linc was simply covering his tracks, not wanting anyone to be able to put two and two together. The music Leslie Potters and his other listeners had requested were a melange of songs more typical of *Songs for the Asking*. Old Joan Baez and Tim Hardin and Tom Paxton. Linc's listeners had to be wondering why S.T.U. Downe had ever tuned in to the Linc Sebastian show in the first place.

She looked down at her pad again. Unless she was reading him completely wrong, Linc was asking her to meet him the following Saturday, at five o'clock, at the lion enclosure at the Philadelphia zoo. She had one single tiny fear that it might be a setup of some sort. Perhaps he was being coerced. Maybe they'd bargained with him. If they thought he was aiding and abetting her, could they threaten him with jail time again if he didn't cooperate to help them find her? Or maybe Linc himself was convinced that she'd done a terrible, criminal, insane thing and he would have the cops waiting there for her, at the lion enclosure. Or worse, the men in the white coats. He'd had her locked up once before. But he would never betray her. If there were anyone in the world she could still trust, it was Linc. What she didn't trust completely was her own judgment. She knew that the thought of seeing him was sapping her reason, but she didn't care.

Tomorrow she would buy a map of Philadelphia.

*P*eggy hated Sundays. She hated weekends, actually, because she couldn't talk to the man who was working on Tyler's case at the National Agency for Missing Children. She couldn't talk to the police, or to Bill Anderson, either; that is, she wasn't supposed to. She did call Bill yesterday, though, to ask him if he'd checked Susanna's health insurance records again and if he'd thought of looking up her old friends from high school. Jim had Susanna's yearbook from her junior year, she told him. She'd been reading the things people had written to her, personal notes that made Susanna sound quiet and sweet natured. Maybe she'd kept in touch with some of those old friends.

Bill didn't appreciate being bothered on a Saturday, and he let her know it. She backed down with an apology. The last thing she wanted to do was alienate any of the people who were supposed to be helping them find Tyler, but she was disgusted with herself for her weakness. She was changing, and the change was not for the better. Her entire life, she'd been strong and capable, someone who took action, who righted wrongs. Now she'd been reduced to a timid, ineffectual woman who was expected to wait around for others to solve her problems. And it was taking those others entirely too long. No one cared as much as she and Jim did about getting Tyler home. She worried that she was not putting enough of her own effort, her own brain cells, into finding him.

Jim took her to an afternoon movie in an attempt to "get her mind off things." She still did not understand how her husband could simply block the situation with Tyler from his thoughts with such ease. He turned everything over to the authorities, put his trust in them, and then concentrated on his day-to-day workload. Peggy, on the other hand, was fairly useless on the two days a week she was spending at Legal Aid. She wondered if she could still call herself a good lawyer.

When they got home from the movie, the plot of which she could not have recounted for any amount of money, she made dinner while Jim did some work he'd brought home with him. She left him parked in front of his computer while she boiled water for rice and turned on the radio. In five minutes, Linc's show would be on.

She was sautéing chicken breasts when she decided there was something strange about Linc's show tonight. True, she'd only been listening faithfully to the program since Tyler's disappearance, but she'd never before heard Linc name the people from whom he'd received requests. And he usually had a theme to his program, some featured musician or a certain type of music. Tonight's music was a mishmash, some of it rock and roll instead of the old and mellow folk-type songs he usually played. And he played "Wake Up Little Susie." And a little later, "Fire and Rain," with the line "Suzanne, the plans they made put an end to you," and that's when she turned off the burner under the chicken and ran upstairs to Jim's study.

He was hunched over his computer and didn't look up at her as she rushed into the room.

"Dinner ready?" he asked.

"Turn on Linc's show," she said, reaching for the power switch on his radio. "He's doing something weird. He's up to something."

"What do you mean?" Jim sat back from his desk as Peggy tuned his radio to the show. Linc was playing a song by Peter, Paul, and Mary.

"He's been playing songs with the name 'Susan' in them," she said. "And he's playing a different type of music than he usually plays. And he's naming the people who made requests."

Jim seemed unimpressed. "This sounds exactly like the sort of song I'd expect to hear on his show."

"Well, this one, yes. But before. He was playing . . . " Her mind went blank. "I don't know, but believe me, I've been listening to him ever since Susanna took Tyler, and this show is different." She sank into the armchair in the corner of the study. "Really, Jim, he's up to something."

Jim hit the save button on his computer. "What can he possibly be up to?"

She leaned toward him. "I think he's in touch with her some-how. He's communicating with her."

"Hon." With a sigh, Jim rolled his chair over to hers and took her hands in his. "I think you're reading too much into it," he said. "You're making yourself nuts with this stuff. If it will make you feel better, tomorrow we can call Bill Anderson, and he can try talking to Linc again."

Tears of frustration burned her eyes. "He'll just deny he knows anything, as usual."

Jim leaned forward to kiss her. "You know what we need?" he asked. "I think we need a vacation. Where would you like to go? This thing with Tyler has become our total focus."

"Of *course* it's our total focus," she said. "A member of our fam-ily is missing. How are we supposed to think about anything else?"

Jim nodded. "But worrying about it all the time is hurting us," he said. "I think we need a break."

Peggy pulled away from him and sat back stiffly in the chair. "Then take a vacation by yourself," she said angrily. "I'll let you know when I find your son."

Jim's jaw dropped open in surprise, and she immediately regretted her words. She leaned forward to hug him. "I'm sorry," she said. "But I can't think about a vacation until we have some-thing to celebrate. All right?"

He nodded and touched her cheek. "All right," he said. "It's just that . . . sometimes I feel as though my son isn't the only person who's missing. My wife is gone too."

She winced. "Oh, Jim. Forgive me. I know I haven't been very . . . attentive to you lately." She had become not only a negligent lawyer and a helpless mother, but a lousy wife as well. "Dinner's almost ready. You want to come down?"

"Sure." He rolled back to his computer. "I'll be down in a sec."

She was quiet during dinner, but if Jim suspected that Linc and his show were still on her mind, he didn't mention it. He talked about the case he was working on. It was high stakes, he said, and she tried to insert appropriate comments into the conversation. But she was thinking about what she would do after dinner, and she knew she couldn't tell Jim her plan. He would try to dissuade her, and she did not want to be dissuaded.

She waited until after the dishes were done and Jim had parked himself in front of the computer once again before walking upstairs to their bedroom and dialing Linc's number. She sat down on the edge of the bed, waiting. The phone rang for a long time, and she had already planned her speech for his answering machine when he picked up.

"Linc Sebastian."

"Linc, this is Peggy Miller."

A second of hesitation. "Hello, Peggy," he said.

"Could you please tell me the meaning of your show tonight?" she asked.

Linc laughed. "The *meaning* of my show? That's for each listener to decide for him or herself. A personal sort of thing, don't you think?"

He was insufferable.

"Are you in contact with her? With Susanna?"

"Only in my dreams."

"What does that mean?"

"That means no, Peggy. I'm not in contact with Susanna. I've told you and your people that a hundred times."

"Then why were you playing all those Susanna songs tonight?"

"Pardon? Susanna songs?"

"God, you make me so angry! 'Suzanne.' 'Wake Up Little Susie.' Those songs."

"Did I? It wasn't intentional, Peggy. I admit she's on my mind a lot. I was probably driven to play them by my subconscious or something."

Peggy felt her lower lip begin to tremble, but she was determined not to cry. She wouldn't give him that satisfaction. "Linc, I want my baby back," she said. "Jim's and mine. I want him safe and sound, here with us. I doubt very much she'll use Jim's health insurance any more, so that means she has no coverage for Tyler. And very little money. How can she possibly be getting him decent care?"

"I'm sorry, Peggy. I know you sincerely care about Tyler, but he is not, no matter what the courts say, your baby."

She gritted her teeth. He had a way of throwing you off track. She was certain he knew more than he was telling her. "Would you meet me for lunch sometime next week?" she asked.

"No, I won't. What's the point? So we can grouse at each other some more? Make each other feel miserable and end up with indigestion? Bad idea."

"Please, Linc. If you'd rather not talk over lunch, we could meet at your house. Or mine. Or neutral territory. You name it. But please. I know you care about Tyler. Let's be on the same team for once."

She heard him sigh. "All right," he finally agreed. "Thursday?"

"Is that the soonest you can do it?"

"God, woman, you do not give up, do you? Thursday, take it or leave it."

"Thursday's fine. Where?"

"Russian Cafe. Do you know where that is?"

"Yes. What time?"

"Noon."

"I'll be there."

She hung up the phone, but remained on the bed another few minutes, still reeling from the conversation. Finally, she opened the bedroom door. She could hear a few beeps from Jim's computer. He would be working for the rest of the evening and probably through much of the night, and she felt a wave of loneliness wash over her. She wished she could call her brother, but she hadn't spoken to Ron since their falling out in his office, and she no longer felt as though she could turn to him with her problems. Nor did she want to call any of her friends. They would be busy with their families on a Sunday night, and besides, they had to be tired of hearing her lamentations about Tyler. What had she talked to her friends about before? She couldn't remember.

She listened for another minute to Jim's methodical tapping on the keyboard of his computer, then walked downstairs to lose herself in her book on one year olds.

$\mathcal{K}$im was feeding Cody that Wednesday night when Lucy stopped by.

"Just wanted to give you a few of my magazine clippings." Lucy set a red folder on the kitchen counter. "I thought reading them might make you feel a bit more comfortable about being featured in one of my articles."

"Thanks." Kim slipped the last spoonful of peas into Cody's mouth, then looked at her neighbor. "By the way, I wanted to let you know that I'm going away for the weekend."

It had taken her two days to come to a firm decision. Two days to weigh the possibly dire consequences of going to Philadelphia against her need to see Linc. In the end there was no contest. She had to go.

"Oh, really?" Lucy said. "Where are you going?"

"New York." She untied Cody's bib and wiped his face with it, avoiding Lucy's eyes. "To visit some friends."

"Are you taking the train up?"

"No. I'm driving."

"Driving in New York! Ugh. Are you sure you want to do that?"

Kim gave her a reassuring smile. "I've done it lots of times," she said. She had never even stepped foot in New York.

"You know," Lucy said, "I'd be happy to watch Cody for you. Then you wouldn't have to cart him around with you. I'd love having his company for a few days."

Kim tried not to react with overt horror to the suggestion. "Oh, that's sweet of you, Lucy." She wet a hand towel and washed Cody's hands. "My New York friends haven't seen him for several months, though, and they'd be furious if I didn't bring him along."

"Okay." Lucy gave up. "And when you come back we can do that interview."

"Sure." She glanced at the clock on the stove top. She was supposed to be at Adam's in a few minutes. Lifting Cody out of his high chair, she smiled at her neighbor. "I'm going out now, Mom," she said. "I have a painting lesson with Adam. And I may be gone overnight, so don't worry about me, all right?"

"That's a pretty long painting lesson." Lucy shook her head as she walked toward the door. Then she laughed. "Don't mind me, dear. I'm just jealous, that's all."

Kim gave Cody a quick bath and dressed him in his pajamas for the ride to Adam's. Once in the car, though, she took a detour to West Annapolis. She wanted to drive past the home of Ryan Geary, the next victim on the list. She felt the need to see where he lived. It was the only way she could make herself believe that the man and his home were real, not some fictitious name and address on her computer.

The neighborhood was very different from her own. The houses were large, with spacious, tree-filled yards, and they were set quite a distance back from the street. The Geary house had the distinction of being separated from its neighbors by a small patch of woods on either side. The house was real, all right. It was big enough to hold any number of people, all of whom were in danger.

Kim finally had a plan, of sorts. She would wait until November 6, exactly one week before the bombing was to occur at the Gearys' house. If she'd heard nothing encouraging on the news about the capture of the killer by then, she would have to act. She would send the information on the list to the police, along with a brief letter of explanation, but she'd drive to a town at least a few hours away to mail it. Then she'd sit back and hope that the police would hunt for the killer instead of the messenger.

She'd considered sending the information from Philadelphia, but didn't want to take the risk of doing so until she had no other choice. She was hoping against hope that the police would close their net on the bomber before she had to intervene. There hadn't been any mention of the bombings in the paper in nearly a week, and she was beginning to wonder if the police even had a net to close.

She stopped at a Chinese restaurant a few blocks from Adam's house and picked up some lo mein. Once at Adam's, she tucked Cody into Liam's bed while Adam and Jessie set the kitchen table. Adam was in a good mood—cheerful, hungry, and excited about a dream he'd had the night before.

"My colors are back," he said as he dug into the lo mein. "Everything's vivid again."

"The bank mural looks wonderful," Kim said. "It's almost finished, isn't it?"

"Finished it today, actually," Adam said. "Now I'm starting to think about something new. The Waterfront Museum has been after me to paint a mural on one of the walls of its entryway for years. So I've been telling myself before I go to sleep at night to focus my dreams on the museum. I've already gotten a few ideas."

"That works?" Kim asked skeptically.

"It takes some practice, but it definitely works. At least it does for me now that my mind's freed up a bit."

Jessie looked up from her plate where she'd been running her fork idly through the noodles. "Do you think you should start another painting right away?" she asked. "Maybe you should take a break first."

"I'm on a roll, Jess." He squeezed his sister's hand reassuringly. "Everything's under control."

Kim and Adam talked about his dream from the night before, while Jessie continued toying with her food. She helped them do the dishes after they were finished, then excused herself.

"A friend of mine's coming over to see the kittens," she said. "She has two kids. I'm hoping she'll want a couple of pets for them."

Upstairs in the studio, Kim worked on her painting of the house across the street from her apartment, while Adam experimented with colors, hunting for the shades in his dream.

"Does Jessie seem depressed to you?" Kim asked as she worked.

THE ESCAPE ARTIST      221

"Seem?" Adam didn't take his eyes from his canvas. "No, she doesn't seem depressed. She *is* depressed. So was I until recently."

"Well, maybe she needs some . . . you know . . . professional help."

"She saw a psychiatrist for a while. We both did. We were both on antidepressants. Jessie still gets into a funk now and then, but believe me, she's much better than she was. And I am much, *much* better." He sidestepped toward her and planted a kiss of gratitude on her neck, then returned to his own canvas. "Listen." He changed the subject. "I was wondering if you might like to go with me to Washington on Saturday? There's an exhibit at the National Gallery I'd like to see."

She bit her lip. She would have to tell him about Philadelphia sooner than she'd wanted to. "Oh, Adam, I'm sorry," she said, "but I have plans for the weekend." The words came out in a rush, and she wondered if he heard the guilt behind them. "Actually, I have to go out of town."

"You do? Where are you going?"

She studied the tip of her brush, thinking. If anyone came looking for her, asking questions about her, it would be better if Adam didn't know where she was. But she couldn't lie to him any more than she had to.

"Philadelphia," she said. "I'm visiting a friend there." She hoped he and Lucy never compared notes.

"Oh." Adam began playing with the paints again, and she almost thought the topic was finished. But it was not. He glanced over at her. "Is this friend, by any chance, the man who's 'still in your heart?'"

She had not expected the question, and she hesitated long enough to let him know he was right. She knew that he would believe no other answer.

"There's a possibility that he'll be there," she said. It was, after all, only a possibility.

Adam nodded without speaking and returned to his work, and Kim wasn't certain if the tension she felt between them was real or imagined. They painted quietly for another twenty minutes or so before Adam set down his brush and left the room. She heard his footsteps on the stairs and figured he was going to get something to drink, but when he didn't return after a quarter of an hour, she knew something was wrong. He was more upset over her plans for the weekend than he'd let on.

Her first thought was to leave. She could get Cody out of Liam's bed and let herself out quietly. No confrontation, no conflict.

*Grow up*, she told herself. Escape would have been Susanna's way out. Kim was supposed to be a different sort of person.

With an apprehensive sigh, she covered her palette, then walked downstairs to the first floor.

He was sitting in the living room by the window, barely visible in the dark, and she knew her announcement had troubled him deeply. She walked into the room and sat down in the chair nearest his.

"I'm sorry if my plans upset you," she said.

He drew in a long breath. "Well," he said, "I guess you and I made it pretty clear right from the start that we weren't viewing our relationship as something serious. At least we said that. I'm not sure I meant it, though. I realize that now. I don't like the idea of you seeing him."

She nodded. "I don't blame you. I'd feel the same way." She wasn't certain that was the truth, but what else could she say? "And I'm not certain that I *will* see him. But I have to, if I can. We left too many things unfinished."

"So this is some sort of . . . closure then?"

She sighed and sat back in the chair. "Adam, I don't know what it is," she said. "I can't make promises to you. Or to him. If you need more of me than what you've got . . . well, I don't know what to say. I can't give it. Not right now." The fear of pushing him away with her words took hold, and she felt her body tense. She needed him at least as much as he needed her. Yet she wouldn't lie to keep him.

"So," Adam said, "my choice is to either end my relationship with you or accept the fact that you'll be sleeping with someone else this weekend and I'd better get used to the idea, huh?"

His words brought tears to her eyes. She remembered how it felt to care about someone when you knew they were sleeping with someone else. She stood up and walked behind his chair. Bending low, she put her arms around his neck, kissed the top of his head.

"I don't even know if I'll be seeing him, much less anything else," she said. "I'm sorry, Adam. I'm trying to be honest. I've tried since the start."

He squeezed her hand where it rested on his chest. "I know. I wish you'd be deceitful and bitchy, instead. It would make things much easier." He slipped out of the circle of her arms and stood up. "Back to work, all right?"

She nodded uncertainly, but with relief nevertheless. The conversation was over. Yet she knew neither of them had said all that needed to be said.

She followed him up the stairs to the studio, and they continued to work together for another hour or so. The tension was gone, or so she thought, and she felt the usual camaraderie between them, but when it came time to decide if she should stay over or not, he didn't suggest it and she didn't ask.

Peggy was getting antsy. She waited in the tiny Russian Cafe, nursing an iced tea. She should have guessed Linc would be late. Probably he'd forgotten. Or maybe he'd never intended to keep this date with her to begin with. She was about to give up on him when she spotted him at the front door. Leaning back in her seat, she tried to relax.

"Sorry I'm late," he said as he sat down across from her.

"I'm just relieved you're here," she said. "We really need to talk."

"I don't think we have a damn thing to talk about, frankly," he said. He looked as though he'd aged in the past few weeks. There was a tired look to his eyes, and his lips were pressed into a tight, tense line. The small gold loop in his left ear was ridiculous.

She pushed a menu toward him. "Let's order first, okay?" she said.

Linc ordered the goulash and she did the same, although she was not in the least hungry. She could take the leftovers home to Jim.

"Look, Linc," she said after the waitress left their table. "You don't have to admit to me that you know where Susanna and Tyler are. I feel quite certain you do, but my purpose here isn't to grill you about that. My purpose is to get you to see that Tyler's welfare is in danger as long as he's with her."

"I don't agree."

She rolled her eyes. "Look, just the fact that she took off with him doesn't show the best judgment, does it?"

"It shows her desperation. It shows how frightened she was about losing her child. Sort of like how frightened you are."

He leaned toward her. His blue eyes were so intense that she had to force herself to hold his gaze. She opened her mouth to speak, but he cut her off.

"You know how you feel?" he asked. "Well, trust me, she felt ten times worse about losing him. She gave birth to him. She carried him around in her body for nine months."

"There are plenty of birth mothers who carry their babies for nine months and still don't care a whit about them."

"That isn't true of Susanna, and I think you know it."

"No, I really don't know it. It's not that I think Susanna is a terrible person, but I do think she's misguided. And to be honest, I think you've done some of the misguiding." She immediately regretted her words. She didn't want to put him on the defensive.

"Susanna's perfectly capable of guiding herself, mis- or otherwise."

"Linc, listen to me, please. She needs help. By disregarding that fact, by pretending she's a perfectly sane, untroubled person, she'll never get the help she needs."

"Gee, I didn't realize you were so concerned about her needs."

She tried not to react to his sarcasm. Instead, she looked down at her hands. "Do we have to be enemies, you and I?" she asked quietly. "Is there any way we can work together on this?"

"I don't see how. You think she's a terrible mother and I think she's a terrific mother, and never the twain shall meet."

"Terrific mothers don't cut their child off from all the people who love him, and from good medical care. Her running away only proves how unstable she still is. She's . . . infantile." Jim had used that word to describe her. "She's poorly educated. A high school dropout. A very dependent person who probably can't take care of—"

"Oh, I know what you mean," Linc said. "It's terrible how those dependent women are always running off to raise their children on their own."

She wanted to tell him to go to hell, but bit her tongue instead.

"They probably let her out of the psychiatric hospital too soon," she said. "I'm not blaming her for her breakdown. It makes sense that someone like Susanna, who was so totally dependent on her husband, would—"

"Peggy, just shut up, all right?" Linc interrupted her, shaking his head. "I'm going to tell it to you like I see it, and you're not going to like it, and that's fine. But I am going to tell you anyway." He waited while their bowls of goulash were set in front of them, then began again. "You have bought into Jim's propaganda," he said. "Yes, it's true that Susanna was a high school dropout. Her father was dead, she had no support whatsoever from her mother, who was an alcoholic, and she couldn't continue to live at home. So yes, she dropped out. She lived with my mother then. Did you know that?"

"Yes. Jim mentioned it."

"And she worked as a waitress to make money, and she studied like the devil to get her GED. And go to—"

"I know you're trying to defend her, but you're digging her grave even deeper," Peggy said. "Her father was dead because her boyfriend—*you*, in case you've forgotten—murdered him. You left that part out. And I know that both her parents were alcoholics, and I'm supposed to want Tyler to be with a woman who was raised in that sort of environment?"

Linc closed his eyes, and he looked as though he were trying to draw patience from somewhere deep inside himself. "I wasn't her boyfriend," he said, leaning across the table and looking at her squarely. "I was her neighbor, period. She can't help what her parents were, and she doesn't even drink. And being raised the way she was only made her want to be a better mother for Tyler." He lowered his voice. "And yes, I killed her father. I killed him to stop him from hurting his wife and his daughter. And although I am anti-gun and anti–taking the law into one's own hands, I've never been able to muster up regret for what I did. He was a terrible, cruel, and abusive husband and father and human being."

She was fascinated by his candor. "Did he abuse her sexually?" She had wondered about that. "Maybe that's why she's so . . . disturbed."

"No, nothing like that. Verbal and physical abuse are quite

degrading enough, though. And frankly, it's amazed me how *undis-*
turbed Susanna is, given the environment she was raised in."

This was going nowhere. "Look," she said. "It's ridiculous to
argue about all of this, about who's sane and who's insane, and
who should have Tyler, because that's already been decided. What
we have to figure out now is—"

"I'm not done," Linc said. He swallowed a spoonful of goulash
while she waited. "So," he said, "Susanna got her GED and went to
college. But she dropped out, not because of a lack of ambition,
but because Jim asked her to support him as he finished school
himself. He never told it to you that way, I bet. Maybe you'd like to
ask yourself exactly who was dependent on whom, huh? Susanna
was planning to go back to school, but then Jim wanted to go to
law school, so they still needed her income. Her turn would come
later, he told her. And so she waited. She worked in that bank,
which she hated, because it was steady money. And when Jim
finally started working, she applied to go back to school." He took
a swallow of water. "She loves art, and she's very talented. Did Jim
ever tell you that?"

"You make Jim sound like some chauvinistic despot," Peggy
said. "If Susanna was so unhappy, why didn't she just tell him,
'Sorry, Jim, it's my turn now.'"

"Good question," Linc said. "And the answer is simple. Because
she loved him and she trusted him, that's why. She believed him
when he said her turn would come later."

"Well, I'm sure he—"

"I'm not done." He shot her a withering look, and she closed
her mouth. "Finally," Linc continued, "they could afford a house.
Susanna spent weeks looking and found a terrific house in
Wonderland. She was so excited about it. Couldn't wait to decorate
it herself. And then to make things even better, she discovered she
was pregnant."

"But things were not good between her and Jim at that point.
She must have known—"

"Known what? Jim wasn't telling her anything about being
unhappy. As a matter of fact, she thought that things were going to
be great. He had a super job, she'd finally be able to go back to
school, a baby was coming. Life looked like it was going to be per-

fect. Until that day she came home early from her business trip and discovered that Jim wasn't the loving, faithful husband he'd pretended to be. That Jim was fucking some lawyer."

"Keep your voice—"

"And *that* was who he planned to live in Wonderland with. He'd let Susanna find the house, let her fantasize, while all the time he was setting his trap for you."

Peggy looked down at her untouched lunch, her insides churning. "I guess this was a mistake, trying to get together with you. You're impossible." She reached for her purse. She would put a twenty on the table, leave her bowl of goulash, and get out of there. But as soon as Linc realized her intent, he grabbed her wrist.

"Look, you asked me here," he said. "You listen to me. Then you can leave and not believe a word I say, but you're going to hear me out. I know you think Jim wants Tyler just as much as you do. But guess what? Susanna wasn't making it up when she said Jim wanted Tyler aborted."

"I don't believe that for an instant. Not an instant."

"Believe it. Susanna called me the night after they fought about it. She was in tears. He'd gotten her the names of doctors and offered to pay for it. He even suggested a few low-tech ways she might take care of the problem herself."

"Why am I listening to this? If Jim had ever wanted Tyler aborted, which I don't believe, it was only because he thought he might be yours."

Linc stared at her, wide-eyed. "Oh, Jesus," he said. "That's rich."

"He did. He even asked me how I would feel if it should ever come out that Tyler was yours and not his."

"Well that's one thing you don't have to worry about, Peggy. Tyler is not mine. Susanna and I never—not ever—had sex until quite a while after Tyler was born. Not when we were next door neighbors. Not when she was married to Jim."

He sounded so sincere that she almost believed him. "Whether you and Susanna were lovers or not is a separate issue," she said. "The fact is that Jim loves Tyler, and he—"

"Maybe he does, maybe he doesn't." Linc shrugged. "I can't speak for how Jim feels now, but I'm telling you, Peggy, he didn't want shit to do with that baby until he realized you wanted a child and couldn't have one. Then all of a sudden it was 'Are you taking care of yourself, Susanna? Taking your vitamins?'"

"That's an ugly accusation."

He laughed. "You bet it is." He took in a breath and cocked his head at her. "I think you're a catch, Peggy. Not for me, I hasten to add, and I know that doesn't upset you. But you're one in a million for someone like Jim. He knows that, and I believe he'd stand on his head in the middle of traffic if that's what he had to do to hold onto you. Making his ex-wife look like an unfit mother is nothing."

"Forgive me, Linc, but I'm having trouble believing the word of a convicted murderer over that of my husband."

He smiled at her. His teeth were very white, and for the first time she could detect what some women saw in this man.

"You know, Peggy, I don't dislike you." His voice had suddenly softened. "Actually, I admire you. You work for Legal Aid when you could be making a ton of money privately. I respect that. And I know your heart's in the right place. I know you love Tyler, and I know you're genuinely worried about him."

A lump rose in her throat. "Do you know if he's okay?" she asked. "You don't have to tell me where he is, but can you just tell me he's all right?"

He shook his head. "I don't know how to say this any more clearly. I don't know where he is. Susanna left me as much in the dark as she left you. She did that on purpose, I'm sure. She didn't want me put in the position of having to cover for her. So I don't know where they are. But I can just about guarantee you that Tyler's safe and happy. Her whole point in leaving here was to be able to take care of him. I won't help you find her."

It was unbearable, the kindness in his voice. She did not want tenderness from him. She did not want to see him in a sympathetic or credible or amiable light. She wanted to slough off all he had told her, discard it and return to her former disregard for him.

"That show you did the other night?" she asked.

He nodded. "You're right. I did play a couple of Suzanne and Suzie songs. I miss her. I hope she's someplace where she can hear my show and know I'm thinking of her."

She looked down at her lunch again, then at his. His bowl was nearly as full as her own. "We didn't do too well with the goulash," she said.

"We weren't here to eat."

She nodded. It was, perhaps, the first thing they'd agreed on. With some fear in her heart, she thought it might not be the last.

She felt sick the rest of the day and although she'd never planned to tell Jim about her lunch with Linc, she knew too much had been said and too much needed clearing up for her to keep it to herself. She managed to wait until they had finished dinner and were sitting in the living room reading the paper. *Trying* to read the paper, at least. She couldn't concentrate.

"I had lunch with Linc today," she said finally.

"You did?" Jim looked up from the sports section. "Why?"

"I thought he knew something. I was still thinking about that weird show he did on Sunday, and I needed to pick his brain."

"What there is of it to pick." Jim set the paper down on his knees. "I wish you'd told me your were going to do that. I already had one wife seeing Linc Sebastian behind my back."

"This was hardly the same thing," she said. "Anyway, it was something I wanted to do on my own." She realized that Jim had not asked if she'd learned anything about Tyler. That would have been the first question out of her mouth.

"He said some things I really need to check out with you," she said. "I know he's a lunatic, but—"

"What sort of things?"

"Well, he denies that he and Susanna were ever lovers prior to Tyler's birth."

"Did you expect him to admit it?"

"He said that you truly did want Tyler aborted. That you gave Susanna the names of physicians and offered to pay for it."

Jim sighed. "Well, I might have said something about it right in the beginning. I didn't want her to go through all that when I knew we weren't going to be together."

She was taken aback. "But you denied that you'd ever suggested abortion to her."

"I never actually *suggested* it. We were just weighing the options. We never discussed it seriously."

"And you gave her a list of doctors?"

"I don't know where Sebastian got that from. It didn't go that far. Susanna didn't want an abortion, and that was her choice."

"Linc said that Susanna thought your marriage was fine at the time she . . . found out about us."

Jim scoffed. "If she thought our marriage was fine, then she had her head in the sand."

"But you told me it was over then."

"It was, as far as I was concerned."

"But you'd never told her that? That you were feeling that way and—"

"What is this third degree? I swear, Linc Sebastian can twist a woman's head around until it's upside down. I can't believe you let him get to you like this. And I'm really ticked off that you'd see him behind my back."

"It wasn't behind your back."

"I already lost one wife to him. I'd just as soon not lose another."

For a startled moment, she wondered if this was how Susanna had felt, defending an innocent relationship with Linc to a jealous husband.

"You haven't asked me if he said anything about knowing where Tyler is," she said.

"I haven't had a chance. You're badgering me with all these other questions about irrelevant issues. Things I thought we resolved long ago."

"Well, he said he doesn't know where he is."

"What a surprise."

"I think I believe him."

Jim shook his head, a look of utter disbelief on his face. "So what does that mean? You and Linc are buddies now?"

"Of course not. I'm just saying that he might be telling the truth about not knowing anything. We probably shouldn't waste any-more time barking up that particular tree."

Jim sighed. "Whatever you say."

"Sometimes I still feel as though it's far more important to me than it is to you to get Tyler back."

"Are you kidding? I can't wait to get him back. Maybe then you'll feel like making love again."

"*Jim.*"

"Sorry." He folded the paper and put it on the end table, then stood up and walked over to her. He bent low to kiss her forehead. "I'm sorry. Really. No sex makes for a short fuse."

She hesitated for a moment before reaching up to put her arms around his neck. She couldn't blame him. She did have a one-track mind these days. If she didn't keep her marriage healthy, Tyler wouldn't have a mother and father to come home to.

"Let's go upstairs," she said. "I promise, no more talk about Linc, or Tyler, or anything except you and me."

It was 4:45 when Kim and Cody reached the lion enclosure
at the Philadelphia zoo. A busload of elementary school children
were laughing and screaming in the area in front of the enclosure,
and Kim had to push Cody's stroller up to the fence so he'd be able
to see the lions. He was enthralled with the maned male and the
muscular female, while Kim barely noticed them. She was hunting
for Linc in the sea of children.

Two frazzled-looking women were trying to maintain some sort
of order with their charges, but other than the two of them and
Kim, there was no one over four feet tall in front of the enclosure.
For the first time, she seriously entertained the possibility that she
had misunderstood Linc's message. Maybe it had not been a message at all. Maybe he'd simply played a few songs he thought she'd
like.

From out of nowhere, a police officer appeared in the crowd and
began talking to one of the two chaperones. Kim turned so that her
back was to him. She realized too late that she should have stayed
off to the side and let Linc be the first to arrive at the enclosure.

After a few minutes, she glanced at the chaperones again. The
police officer was still chatting with one of the women. He was
pointing into the enclosure as if he were explaining something to
her, and he and the woman were both laughing. Kim looked more
closely at his uniform. He was not a cop after all. Just a security
guard, and she shook her head at her paranoia.

It was nearly five when she felt someone's arms wrap around her from behind. She started for a second, then let herself sink back against that familiar embrace. She recognized the feel of him and turned her head to breathe in his scent.

He kissed her cheek. "I've missed you," he said.

She turned to face him, wrapping her arms around his neck. She tried to speak, to tell him that she'd missed him too, but the words wouldn't come, and she pressed her head against his shoulder instead.

"I almost didn't recognize you." He touched her hair. "You look very different. It's kinda cute." He kissed her tenderly, then let go of her to bend down to Cody.

"Hey, Ty," he said. He lifted the little boy out of the stroller and stood up. "I think you've put on about ten pounds, fella." He kissed Cody's cheek.

"His name isn't Tyler any longer," she said.

Linc's eyes widened. He looked so beautiful that she had to reach out and touch his arm.

"What is it?" he asked.

"Cody."

Linc grinned. "Well, if you had to change it, I'm glad that's what you changed it to. And he's still got his monkey, huh? Grace and Val would be pleased." He turned toward her. "And how about you?" he asked. "Who has Susanna become?"

"I don't think I should tell you," she said. "I think the less you know, the better off you'll be."

He studied her face a moment, then nodded. "All right," he said. "Besides, you'll always be Susanna to me."

She glanced around them. The security guard was no longer in sight, and the children were moving on to the next exhibit. She felt exposed without their noise and activity forming a shield around her. "Is there a chance anyone could have followed you here?" she asked.

He shook his head. "No one knew I was going anywhere, except Grace, and I told her I was going to Denver overnight. I took a circuitous route to get here. I've been all over the damn country this morning. It was kind of fun."

"It gets old quickly," she said.

His smile disappeared, and he shifted Cody to his other arm. The little boy wrapped his own arms around Linc's neck and rested his head on his shoulder, in total comfort. "Just tell me this," Linc said. "Are you on the run? I mean, moving from place to place? I can't stand to think of you doing that."

"I'm not. I've settled down somewhere. I hope it's a place I can stay. People think I'm someone else. I have work. Except for missing you, I'm okay."

Linc looked away from her, and she knew he did not quite share her joy over her having a new life that didn't include him.

"There's a hotel near here," he said. "I thought we could get a room."

"Good." She was tired from the drive, and she wanted to be someplace where she could curl up with him in safety. She was weary of having to look over her shoulder.

They drove in her car to the hotel. It was a Holiday Inn, anonymous and utilitarian.

"Let me sign for the room," she said as they walked into the lobby. "My name is less recognizable than yours."

"Make it a good room," Linc said. "I've got the cash to give you for it."

She wouldn't argue. She filled out the registration form, wincing just slightly when the clerk referred to her as Ms. Stratton. Linc's eyebrows shot up, but he said nothing.

The seventh floor room was spacious, with huge windows and a view of the city, and she carried Cody's tippy cup and the can of formula into the bathroom, while Linc flopped down on the bed.

"I have no interest in going out to eat, do you?" he called to her.

"None whatsoever." She walked out of the bathroom, shaking the bottle. Linc was propped up against the headboard with a couple of pillows, and Kim's strongest interest was to lie in bed with him and hold him all night long. And all day tomorrow, if he were willing.

"Let's just do room service." Linc reached for the bottle in her hand. Cody crawled across the bed and snuggled up next to him to drink his formula. Linc smoothed his hand over Cody's head. The two of them looked so content and comfortable together that Kim felt guilty about keeping them apart.

"I have something in my backpack for him," Linc said. "It's for his birthday. I'll give it to him when he's finished with his bottle."

She started to tell him she'd given Cody a different birthday, but thought better of it.

"I actually had a more impressive gift for him," Linc said, "but I gave it away, since I didn't know if I'd ever get to see him again."

"Oh, Linc." She sat on the edge of the bed, her hand resting on his knee. "This must be awful for you. I'm so sorry for everything I've put you through."

"Let's not talk about it. Not tonight." He picked up the room service menu from the night table and handed it to her. "Are you hungry?"

"Famished." She'd stopped on the road for lunch. Cody'd eaten a torn-in-pieces peanut butter and jelly sandwich, but she hadn't been able to touch her grilled cheese.

They ordered their dinner, and Cody opened the gift Linc had brought with him while they waited for the food to be delivered. The wrapped package contained a large plastic activity box, with built-in doors that opened, drawers that pulled out, and a half dozen other working parts guaranteed to keep small hands occupied for a long time. Kim laughed when she saw it.

"Smart man," she said. "That ought to keep him busy."

Their food came, and she and Linc sat on the bed as they ate fried chicken and baked potatoes. They kept their conversation light.

"Did I miss any of the clues you sent me in your show?" Kim asked. She ticked off the song titles she could remember.

"Nope. Sounds like you got them all." Linc spooned another dollop of sour cream on his potato. "You wouldn't believe the complaints I got about that show. My listeners thought I'd gone off my rocker."

"Well, even if you lost one or two, I hope it was worth it."

He touched her knee. "Absolutely," he said.

When they finished dinner, she took Cody into the bathroom and gave him a quick bath, then held his hands to walk him back into the main room where his pajamas were waiting.

"Hey, Cody." Linc moved to the edge of the bed and reached his arms toward the two of them. "Come here, fella." He motioned for

Kim to let go of Cody's hands. She did so, gently, and Cody took one wobbly step toward Linc, then another.

Linc leaned low. "Come on, Cody, you can do it!"

Kim watched as her naked son toddled over to the man who was, in all ways but one, his father. Linc grabbed him just as he was about to fall and lifted him high in the air. "What a champ!" he said. Cody giggled from his lofty position. "He did it!" Linc lowered the little boy and nuzzled his neck, and Kim swallowed hard. She knew how Cody's skin would feel under Linc's lips, and how he would smell, fresh from his bath.

"Yes, fans, Cody . . . Miller?" Linc looked at Kim quizzically and she shrugged. "Cody whoever the heck he is has broken the record in the free form upright toddle. A bit shaky at the start, and that little wobble at the finish line will cost him with the judges, but what style this kid has."

Cody didn't need to understand what Linc was saying. Linc's rapid-fire delivery made him laugh anyway. Kim leaned against the wall and watched them with a smile.

"Toddlers around the world are watching, Cody," Linc said. "What do you have to say to them?" He held an imaginary microphone in front of Cody's face, but the little boy was wiped out from his fit of giggles. He simply collapsed against Linc's chest, thumb in his mouth, the other hand clutching Linc's blue shirt, and Linc suddenly sobered. Closing his eyes, he wrapped his hands around Cody's body and pressed his lips to the top of the baby's head.

A lump ached in Kim's throat. She'd never seen Linc cry, but she had a feeling he might do so now. When he looked up at her, she said quietly, "That was his first time."

"Really?" he asked.

She nodded, then without a word stepped back into the bathroom. She didn't know if Linc was close to tears, but she definitely was, and she didn't want to cry in front of him.

When she came out of the bathroom, she found Cody already in his pajamas and in the crib. The room was dark, except for one light near the door. Linc sat on the bed, his back against the headboard, and she felt his eyes following her as she walked across the room.

Kim tucked Cody's monkey next to him under the covers and

rubbed his back. Then she closed the drapes and moved to the bed, sitting down cross legged in front of Linc. Taking his hands in her own, she looked deeply into his eyes, his face. There was still enough light in the room for her to see him clearly, and she was determined to commit every one of his features to her memory.

Linc sighed. "Where do we begin?" he asked.

"Tell me how Grace and Valerie are doing." It seemed a safe topic to start with.

"They're slightly annoyed with you," he said. "I mean, they understand your motivation, and they sympathize with you, but you really have shaken up everybody's lives, you know."

She couldn't tell if he was speaking from anger or not.

"And what else? What else is going on in Boulder? Are they still looking for me?"

"Oh, yes." He nodded. "They'll be looking for you until they find you. *If* they find you." He squeezed her hands. "Jim and Peggy have hired a private investigator. Plus they have the National Center for Missing and Exploited Children working on it. I think Peggy talks to them a few times a week. She really has it in her head that you're not a fit mother. She thinks Tyler"—he smiled— "Cody's going to wither under your care."

"That makes me angry."

"Don't blame her. That's what she's gotten from Jim. She's heard all the negative press on you. And she sincerely cares about Ty . . . Cody."

"I know that." She suddenly had a clear picture in her mind of Peggy, the way she looked as they were all leaving the courtroom. Pretty, white-skinned, dark-haired, and smiling with the knowledge that she was about to gain a son. "How close do you think they are to figuring out where I am?" she asked.

"I don't know. They don't keep me informed. I *do* know that the FBI's gotten involved, though."

"The FBI!" Somehow that made her feel hopeless.

"They've questioned me *ad nauseam* and I guess I have to thank you for not telling me anything, although, I swear, Suze, I thought I was going to go out of my head at first. I was so angry with you."

"I'm sorry. I didn't know how else to—"

"And you were right. If you'd let me in on it, I would have tried to stop you and I would have had a harder time talking to the cops. This way I didn't have to lie."

She undid the buttons on his shirt sleeves and slipped her fingers up his forearms. "Do you think they're going to find me?" she asked.

"I don't know. I've been impressed with the means they have. You should know that they've alerted doctors around the country to be on the lookout for a child with Cody's condition."

"I was afraid of that. But we've been to a doctor and even to the emergency room once, and—"

"The emergency room? Why?"

His arms were warm beneath her hands. "Cody had an ear infection, but it was on a weekend. I had no choice. No one said a word to us, though. No one seemed the least bit suspicious." Of course she'd had Adam with her. Adam's presence had made her look less like a woman on the run with her child.

"That's good," Linc said. "Did you use your insurance, though? They can probably trace you that way."

"No. I knew that would be a bad move."

"So . . . how did you pay the doctor?"

"With some of the money I brought with me."

"Let me send you more. You must be running low."

"No, Linc. I have to make it on my own. Besides, it would be dangerous for you to send anything to me. I don't want you to know where I am."

He grimaced, and she felt the muscles of his arms tighten beneath her hands.

"I don't like this," he said.

"I know. Neither do I."

Linc sighed. "The National Center Peggy's working with sends out these postcards with pictures of missing children on them. They can send them to just about every household in the country, and I've heard they're really effective."

"Have they sent one out with Cody's picture on it?" She'd seen one of the cards only the week before in a stack of Ellen's mail. There were two pictures on the card, two sisters who had been abducted by a parent. There was a number to call if you'd seen them. The card had frightened her for a few hours, but then she'd convinced herself that there were far too many cases of missing children for hers to attract such attention.

"Not that I know of," Linc said. "Peggy keeps badgering them to, though. Peggy's a real squeaky wheel. And they get tons of responses from those cards."

"You sound as though you think it's only a matter of time till I'm found."

Linc was very quiet. He looked down at his splayed shirt sleeves and her hands where they rested on his arms. "Please consider coming home with me," he said.

"And give Cody up?" She felt a wave of anger. "No."

"It's true he'd go to Jim and Peggy, but hopefully you'd be able to see him. I'll do whatever I can to help you. I'll hire the best lawyer I can find to keep you out of jail." He turned his palms up and leaned back to draw her hands into his. "And the truth is, Suze," he said slowly, carefully, "in some ways, Cody would probably be better off with Jim and Peggy. He'd have a stable home. He'd have better medical care than—"

"I'm doing fine with him, thank you." She pulled her hands away from his and folded her arms across her chest.

"You can't run away from your problems for the rest of your life," Linc said.

"Have you forgotten what happened the last time you said those words to me?" He lowered his eyes and she knew that he understood exactly what she was talking about.

"That was half your life ago," he said quietly. "This is totally different." He leaned back against the headboard. "I know I'm being selfish," he said. "My motivation's simple: I want you home with me again. Grace keeps talking about fixing me up with other women. I'm not interested. I want my buddy back."

She forgave him for suggesting she might not be doing a good job with Cody. She knew he didn't mean it. "I want you back too," she said, "but I'm not willing to give up my son, not even for you."

"All right." Linc shook his head as if clearing it of the conversation. "Let's not talk about it anymore tonight. We don't have that much time together. I don't want it to spend it arguing with you."

"Me neither."

"Come here, then." He reached his hand toward her as he stretched out on the bed, and she lay down next to him.

She rested her hand lightly on his side, and for a moment, neither of them said a word.

"I'm afraid to kiss you or touch you," she said finally.

"Why is that?" He was on his side, facing her, stroking her cheek.

"Because I'm afraid if I do, I won't be able to leave you again. Deprive myself of you again."

"That's what I'm counting on."

She drew away from him. "Don't," she said.

"Don't what?"

"Count on that."

"All right. I'm sorry." He leaned forward to kiss her. His lips were so warm, so familiar. She drew out the kiss, making it last. She wanted this entire night to last. She would not let herself think about tomorrow, or the day after that.

Linc sat up. He straddled her, then leaned forward to kiss her again and she felt her hunger for him mounting. It had been too long. She reached for his belt buckle, but he gently moved her hands to the bed and began undoing the buttons on her shirt.

She rested her hands on his denim-covered thighs, her eyes closed, as he slipped her shirt off her shoulders. He unfastened her bra and lowered his head to her breasts, and when he slipped his legs between hers, she felt the heat of his erection pressing against her through their jeans. She arched her back as he caressed her breasts with his lips, as he drew her nipple into his mouth. A moan escaped her own lips, and she had to fight the urge to rip his clothes from his back.

*Slow down,* she told herself.

The memory of tonight might have to last her an eternity. Linc seemed to feel the same way, because he lingered over every inch of her body, touching her softly with his hands and his mouth, and it was a long time before she finally gained permission to undress him, and longer still until he was inside her. Even then, his movements were slow and measured, as they'd always been. He knew how to bring her to the brink and hold her there until she begged him for release.

She succeeded in blocking thoughts of the future from her mind until that instant, when all the longing she'd felt for him this past month and a half exploded inside her. Despite the exquisite pleasure of that moment, she found herself sobbing as the sensations faded.

"Don't think," he said, holding her tightly. "Don't think about anything."

But she could not put an end to her heaving sobs. She held on to him, her fingers clutching his skin, and he rolled onto his side and pulled her into his arms, kissing her eyes, her cheeks, as he waited for her tears to stop. For a while, it seemed as though they never would.

She must have tired herself out, though, because when next she opened her eyes, the room felt different, and she knew there'd been a shift in time. She must have fallen asleep.

"Are you awake?" Linc asked.

"Yes. How long was I out?"

"Half an hour or so. You okay?"

"Yes." She rolled onto her back and looked at the dimly lit ceiling, trying to sort reality from her dreams.

"I took your photo albums from your apartment," Linc said. "I didn't want Jim to have them."

"Thank you." She'd thought about those albums, about how carelessly they would have been treated in Jim's hands.

"I loved seeing the few remaining sketches you did of my old band," Linc said. "Haven't seen them in a while."

She remembered the summer nights she'd spent in his garage, sitting on the lumpy old sofa, sketching the band while Linc and his friends played music and joked with one another. She'd treasured the warmth and security she felt in his house, and she'd hated going home, never knowing if her father would be a mean drunk or a weepy drunk that night.

"Your house was my oasis," she said.

"I know."

Unbidden, the memory of the night her father was killed slipped into her head. Linc was quiet, and she wondered if his thoughts were on that grisly night as well.

"Sometimes I think about what happened that night," she said, "and I realize I've told the story the way you said it happened for so long that I've almost come to believe it's the truth." It wasn't that far from the truth, anyway. Just a little twisting, a little distortion of the facts. She had even managed to pass a lie detector test corroborating Linc's account of her father's death.

"Well, it's all behind us."

"I just regret that you had to do time."

"Shh. Water under the bridge."

She pulled closer to him. She didn't want to fall asleep again and waste this time with him, but she was sinking down. Dreamlike images floated in and out of her head, and she comforted herself with the fact that, at least for tonight, she would be sleeping with the man she loved.

*L*inc woke up to find her still asleep. She looked very young, like the delicate little girl he'd loved as a sister before he'd loved her as anything else. The reddish-brown hair didn't fit her, and he wondered how anyone could look at her and not realize she had made herself into someone different. He brushed the hair back from her forehead, searching for the pale roots, but she had taken care not to let them show. Leaning forward, he pressed his lips to her hairline. She did not wake up, and he liked to think that she was sleeping happily and securely in his company, just as Cody was sleeping soundly in his crib.

He got out of bed, used the bathroom, then opened the drapes and looked out at a still quiet, still dark Philadelphia.

She'd brought up the night her father was killed, opening a whole world of memories for him. And they all began with him posing for her in her bedroom.

"Fully clothed," she'd assured him. Right, Susanna. That had lasted about a week. Then she'd upped the ante. She'd gotten those books on figure drawing from the library, and she wanted to draw "more of him," she said. Would he please take off his clothes?

"You wouldn't have to be totally nude," she assured him. "You could leave on your . . . you know." She glanced at his crotch, giving him an instant erection.

He posed as she wanted him to, although he knew he was asking for trouble. He could still picture her bedroom clearly. It was quite small, a bed in one corner, a desk against the wall next to it. She'd lock the bedroom door with the big key that hung from the doorknob, then he'd sit or lie on the bed, while she'd sit in the desk chair, her feet propped up on the bed, the sketchbook on her lap. Carefully taped to the walls were her dozens of sketches of his band. Some were of the instruments, some of the guys themselves. Most of the drawings were in black and white, but some were in colored pencil. She was very proud of all of them. He didn't blame her. They were excellent, and she was about to enter them in a statewide competition, along with the work in one of several sketch books resting on her desk. She'd already won the local competition with what she called "The Garage Band Series." Winning the state would guarantee her scholarships for college. It was almost all she talked about.

She wore a serious look on her face as she sketched him, and he felt guilty for the prurient thoughts running through his twenty-two-year-old male mind. But sitting there would have been intolerably boring if it were not for those fantasies; they kept him returning to her bedroom time and time again.

One evening, she set down her sketch pad with a sigh and stepped over to the bed. Linc was sitting up, his back against the wall. Susanna sat down and leaned forward, slipping the tips of her fingers under the waistband of his boxers, tugging them gently. He grabbed her hands in surprise.

"Don't freak out," she said. "I just want to draw all of you. Let me, please?"

He was uncertain how to react. "Not a good idea," he said.

She looked disappointed. "I'm so frustrated," she said. "I mean, when have you ever seen figure drawings of people wearing boxer shorts?"

She had a point. He stood up and dropped his shorts before he had a chance to change his mind. If she wondered why his penis didn't look like those flaccid organs in her figure drawing book, she didn't say.

She returned to her seat and started drawing again, a small crease of concentration between her eyebrows, and he wondered how any living, breathing man could tolerate being scrutinized that way without going out of his mind.

She had not been drawing long when she looked up from her pad. There was a small smile on her lips, and she seemed to be struggling to keep it in check.

"I think I want you to make love to me," she said, and he knew her serious artist routine was not all it was cracked up to be. He could see his own longing mirrored in the pale blue of her eyes.

But he shook his head. "You're too young," he said. "I could get arrested for statutory rape."

She set the sketch pad on her desk and moved over to the bed. She kept her eyes on his as she pulled her T-shirt over her head, and without a moment's hesitation, she unfastened her bra. Her breasts were small, high, and pink nippled, and her long hair brushed over them, caught on them, hid them and exposed them and drove him crazy as she leaned toward him.

He remembered the conversation he'd had with her a few short weeks earlier about birth control. All those paternal-type warnings he'd issued. And now he was going to make love to her without any protection at all. There was no way he could stop himself. Her lips were on his; she lifted his hands to her breasts. He'd never before thought of her as aggressive, yet there was no other word to describe her behavior. He guessed she'd seen the uncertainty in his eyes and wasn't about to let it get in her way.

She was a virgin. She had not been lying about that. She was so tight and small around his fingers that he couldn't imagine how he would get inside her. He could tell that it hurt her when he tried, but still she drew him in.

"I love you," she said, and he offered the words back to her without hesitation, and with all his heart.

Linc rested his hands on Cody's crib as he stared out the window. Dawn light was beginning to filter into the room, and he turned to look at Susanna, still asleep beneath the multicolored bedspread. He would not remind her of that long ago night. He knew she still held the memory inside her, and yet they never spoke of it, never even acknowledged that it had happened. When he told Peggy that he and Susanna hadn't been lovers until after Tyler was born, he nearly believed it. He and Susanna had turned their backs on that memory because of what happened afterward. They could not recall one incident without the other.

They were so lost in each other that night that they didn't hear Susanna's father come home. Not until he began pounding on her bedroom door did they realize he was there. He and Susanna flew out of the bed and began pulling on their clothes.

Susanna was reaching for one of her shoes when she suddenly froze.

"Oh my God," she said. She was staring at the keyhole and she quickly leaped out of its range. "He saw us!" she whispered, and Linc felt as though he had rocks where his stomach should have been.

"Open this damn door!" her father snarled.

White-faced, Susanna began trying to open the window, but it was stubborn and she could only lift it two or three inches.

"What are you doing?" Linc asked her.

"We've got to get out of here," she said. "He'll kill us."

For a moment, he thought she was right. Escape seemed like the only solution. But he knew better. Maybe they could escape for a few hours or a day, but eventually they would have to face Susanna's father and his wrath.

Linc grabbed her hands. "You can't always run away from your problems, Susanna," he said. He had to speak loudly so she could hear him over the racket her father was making at the door. "You'll only be putting off the inevitable. We have to face him. I'll tell him it was my fault, that I coerced you. You're only sixteen. I should have known better."

She looked unconvinced. There was terror in her eyes. She looked like a trapped animal, frightened for her life.

"I won't let him hurt you," he promised.

He stepped away from her and put his head close to the door. "I'm opening the door, Mr. Wood," he said. "Stop pounding."

There was sudden silence from the other side of the door, giving Linc a false sense of safety. He reached for the key and slipped it into the lock, thinking about what he would say when he was face to face with Paul Wood. He could hardly deny what had occurred. But he didn't have a chance to speak before Susanna's father burst into the room. He grabbed his daughter by the hair, and yanked her back and forth like a rag doll, cursing at her, spitting his foul, whiskey breath into the air. Susanna screamed with pain.

"Who brought you up to be a whore?" her father boomed at her. "Who raised you to be a slut?"

"Leave her alone!" Linc lunged at him, and Susanna's father let go of her to take a punch at him. Paul Wood was very drunk though, and his fists were easy to dodge.

"You fucking son of a bitch!" Susanna's father managed to land a punch on Linc's shoulder. "How long you been screwing my daughter? I'm going to break your skull!" He raised his fist to strike again, but then suddenly spotted the open sketchbook on Susanna's desk. "What the hell's this?"

Susanna tried to grab the sketchbook, but her father was too fast for her.

"Is this the kind of drawing you've been doing?" He pulled out the top sketch of Linc and tore it in half. But there were plenty more below that one, and he started shredding them in a fury. "Sixteen years old and a whore already." He poked one finger in the air toward Linc. "You're going to jail, boy," he said. "And your girlfriend there's going to reform school, if I decide to let her live."

Linc spotted the other sketch books on Susanna's desk. Her Garage Band series was in them, and he didn't know whether to try to grab them or not. Maybe it would be better not to draw attention to them. Just then, he heard footsteps in the hall.

"What the hell's going on in here?" Susanna's mother appeared at the door to the bedroom. She was every bit as drunk as her husband, if not more so. "Paul! What are you doing to her pictures?" She reached for the sketchbook in his hands. "You shouldn't—"

Paul Wood knocked his wife off her feet with one sweep of his arm and she landed like an old, limp washrag against the radiator. Her eyes were closed, her head on the floor, and Linc was not at all certain she was still alive. Nor did he care.

He pulled Susanna behind him, trying to get her out of harm's way. She was trembling with fear, but when her father reached for one of the band pictures on the wall, she darted out from Linc's protection.

"Please, Daddy, please not those!"

Her father yanked her away from the wall with another jerk of her hair. In an instant the picture was down and torn, and he was on to the next.

"They're for her competition!" Linc grabbed the much bigger man by the shoulder, but although he was drunk and his aim was lousy, Paul Wood was strong as an ox and numbed by booze. He seemed to feel no pain.

Susanna frantically tried to pull the other drawings from the wall in an effort to save them, but her father tore them from her arms and held them in front of her eyes as he shredded them. Helpless tears ran down Susanna's cheeks. She looked as if she were watching her children drown. She clawed at her father's hands, but nothing could stop the big man's destruction. When he'd finished with the drawings on the wall, he reached for her other sketch books, and that's when Susanna ducked beneath his arm and ran out of the room.

Linc was glad to see her go. He almost called after her, "Run! You were right. Just run!" But he was too busy dodging her father's wild punches to say a word.

In a few seconds, though, Susanna was back. She stood in the doorway to her bedroom, red-faced.

"Dad!" she called out. "Get away from Linc or I'll shoot!"

Only then did Linc see the gun she had in her hands. She held it out in front of her, and it bounced and shivered in her trembling grasp.

Paul Wood looked surprised for only a second before lunging at his daughter.

"Gimme that!" He plowed into her, catching her in the rib cage with his shoulder, and the gun flew from her hands across the room. In an instant, Linc had grabbed it. Before he had a moment to think, he aimed it at her father's back and pulled the trigger.

The next few minutes seemed to happen in slow motion. Paul Wood flung his arms out to his sides. His blood sprayed across his daughter's white T-shirt, and as he started to fall toward her, Susanna took one small, calculated step to the side to let him land hard on the floor, face first.

Susanna stared at Linc across the broad expanse of her father's body. Blood was pooling on the floor around her bare feet, and with his stomach churning, Linc realized the bullet must have pierced the man's heart. He felt his own blood drain from his face, and he sat down on the edge of Susanna's bed, the gun lying flat on his palms.

He looked at Susanna, and when he spoke, he was surprised by the calmness in his voice. "It happened like this," he said. "Your father came home drunk. He started beating you and your mother up, for no good reason. I knew where he kept his gun . . . in his night table, right?" He remembered her telling him about the time she saw her father kill the squirrel.

Susanna nodded.

"I got the gun. He threw your mother down and then went for you, and that's when I killed him. I killed him to stop him from hurting you and your mother."

"Yes," Susanna agreed. "That's what happened." She glanced at the shreds of paper at Linc's bare feet. There was no expression whatsoever on her face. "What about the drawings?" she asked.

Linc got slowly to his feet and moved around the room, picking up the scraps of paper. He opened the bottom drawer of her desk and put the paper into one of the file folders. There would be no evidence of his nudity; there was no witness to their lovemaking. He and Susanna were neighbors. Friends. Nothing more.

His knees shook, and he sat down on the bed again. "Why was I over here?" he asked her.

She looked at the ceiling. "Maybe you wanted to tell me something," she said.

"Right. I stopped over to let you know that the band would be practicing tomorrow if you wanted to work on your sketches. That's when your father showed up."

She let out a small cry and pressed her fist to her mouth. "All my work," she said.

He could only imagine the depth of that loss. He had never worked as hard on anything as she had on her drawings. He wanted to go to her, hold her, but numbness had settled over him like a sickness. It was only later that he would feel the irony of that moment. Her father lay dead at her feet, her mother lay unconscious on the other side of the room, and the loss she felt was limited to her drawings.

"We need to call the police," he said.

She nodded, her face once again expressionless. She turned, her feet leaving bloody footprints behind her as she walked down the hall toward the kitchen. And he did not move from his seat on the bed until the police came to take him away.

A pale sun cast its soft glow on the buildings of Philadelphia, and Linc suddenly became aware of the chill in the air. He turned and went back to the bed. Susanna's body radiated warmth under the covers, and he lay close to her.

Susanna. He'd thought he'd be able to bring her back with him. Persuade her, somehow. But he could see that wasn't going to happen. She was settled, she'd said. She was doing okay. He wanted that for her. Wanted her to be happy, to be safe. He was selfish to want her to be happy only with him. Today she would leave him, again. And maybe this morning would be the last morning he'd be able to look at her, feel her close to him. Or maybe he would be able to see her again sometime, and then perhaps *that* would be the last time. Or the time after that.

He rolled onto his back, wide awake and filled with frustration. He couldn't live this way. If she was getting settled in her life without him, he would have to get settled in his. He had never thought that he loved her more than she loved him, but right now he wondered. At least until she opened her eyes and gave him a startled smile at finding him next to her. She pulled him closer then, and began to cry.

"Can we stay here longer?" she asked. "Do you have to go back today? Can we stay a few more nights? Please?"

"I have to go back," he said, putting his arm around her shoulders. He feared being gone too long. They'd suspect he was with her, maybe try to look for him. Much as he wanted her back, he would not lead them to her.

Cody began talking to himself, that little soliloquy that could go on for minutes or half an hour. It made Linc smile to hear it again. It felt good to smile after the torturous thoughts of the last half hour.

"Can I ask you about something?" Susanna wiped the back of her hand across her eyes. "Your advice?"

"Of course."

"Well, something weird happened." She smoothed her hand over his chest. Her voice was still thick. "I bought a computer," she said. "I bought it from a store, but it had been used by someone before me, so I got a really good price on it. When I got it home, I discovered that the person who owned it before me had left a file on it. I called the store to tell them, but they didn't seem to care. So I made a copy of the information in the file and then erased it from the hard drive. And forgot about it. Then a few weeks later, I heard about a bombing at a law firm in . . . the town where I'm living. I recognized the name as being in the file. I looked at the file again. It was a list of" —she lifted the blankets and started to get up—"here, I'll show you."

He watched her walk across the room to the table. Her body looked a little like a stranger's from the back. She was thinner, and the long pale hair was missing. But when she turned around, the shape of her breasts, the curve of her waist, was completely familiar, and he lifted the blankets to hurry her back to bed.

She slipped in next to him, shivering, and he rubbed her bare skin. She'd brought two folded sheets of paper back to the bed with her, and she held them above the blankets so he could see them.

"Oh!" She suddenly lowered the papers face down again. "You'd see the name of my town."

"Let me see," he said. Unwise though it may be, he desperately wanted to know where she was living.

She hesitated only a moment longer before raising the papers again. "See?" she said. "It's a hit list. This woman was killed in an explosion. And this law firm was bombed too. Both of them on these exact dates."

Annapolis. All the addresses were in Annapolis. But she had lost him. "Wait a minute," he said. "You're saying this is a list of people that the previous owner of the computer somehow knew would die?"

She nodded. "Not just die. Be killed. This first woman opened an express mail package left on her porch and it had a bomb in it. Then someone at the law firm opened an express mail package, and it too had a bomb in it."

Cody's babbling was getting louder, working its way toward his angry, I-want-to-get-up sounds.

"That's insane," Linc said. "It's probably some sort of coinci—"

"It's not, Linc. The packages weren't mailed; someone simply left them there for the victims to open. How can it be a coincidence that on these dates and at these times, two separate bombings occurred, killing the people on this list? Well actually, at Sellers, Sellers, and Wittaker, an attorney and a receptionist and her two children were killed. I don't know if they were meant to be the targets, but—"

"What does this 'two children, two adults' mean?"

"I have no idea. But anyway, I'm stuck. As you can see, the next date is November thirteenth, and I can't just sit by and let this guy get blown up. I've been trying to figure out what I should do. I think my best bet is to send a letter anonymously to the police, but it scares me. If I explain how I got the information, then could they trace me through the computer store? Or—"

"This sounds way too dangerous," Linc interrupted her. "I think you need to forget it. Wash your hands of it. Pretend you never saw this list."

"But I *have* seen it."

He ran a hand through his hair. She was right. He'd never be able to turn his back on something like this. He couldn't ask her to do so, either.

"Is there any way the person who had the computer before you could know you have it? I mean, could you be in danger?"

"I don't think so. The salesperson at the store didn't even write down my name when I called back. And the person who had the computer before me probably thought they'd erased the file. Why else would they have turned it in with something so incriminating on it?"

"I don't know, but this is bad news." He didn't like the dilemma she was in. "Maybe you could send the information to the police without any explanation . . . or better yet, *I'll* send it. Leave it with me. I'll mail it from Boulder to the police in Annapolis."

"No, that's out." She gave her head a violent shake. "You're always rescuing me, you know that? Susanna was a weak and needy person. I'm trying to be stronger, now."

It was odd to hear her talk about herself in the third person. "I don't think of you as weak and needy," he said.

"And besides, if you sent the information to the police and they somehow traced it to you, how would you explain it? With your record, they'd never believe anything you said and you'd be back in prison again."

He wasn't certain if her reasoning was on target, but the thought of prison was enough to make him back down.

"All right," he said, "but let's do it this way. You leave this copy of the list with me, and if you can't figure out a safe way to get the information to the authorities, let me know. Fax me again, and sign it S.T.U. Downe. And then I'll take care of it."

She pursed her lips and looked up at the ceiling. "Okay. But promise me you won't do anything with it unless I ask you to?"

"Promise."

Cody started to cry.

"Let me get him a bottle," Susanna said.

He watched her get out of bed, slip on her robe, and disappear into the bathroom with Cody's bottle and the can of formula. He looked at the list of names and addresses again. Annapolis. He suddenly wished he didn't know where she lived. It made it harder somehow, imagining her with a new life in a new place. He'd been to Annapolis once as a child. He remembered it vaguely as a picturesque little town.

Susanna walked back into the room and leaned over the side of the crib to give Cody his bottle.

"Tell me about your life in Annapolis," he said.

"No." She dropped her robe and climbed under the covers again. "It makes me nervous that you know I'm there."

"Well, come on. Now that I know you *are* there, I might as well know the rest of it. What kind of place are you living in? What are you doing for work? Have you made any friends or do you keep to yourself?"

It was a moment before she answered. "I live in a house that's divided into a downstairs, where my landlady lives—she's a massage therapist—and two apartments upstairs," she said. "I rent one, and another woman, a writer, rents the other. My landlady and the writer are both very nice." She shivered, and he put his arm around her.

"I expected to keep to myself," she continued, "and that might have been the best plan, especially if those postcards show up with my picture on them. But I've made some friends in spite of myself. And I'm self-employed. Doing word processing. I've gotten a few jobs through my friends and I designed brochures and sent them to a bunch of businesses."

"Wow." He had to admit he was surprised at how well she was doing. She had truly created another life for herself, and that thought did not entirely please him. She'd left him behind a bit too easily.

"And—you'll love this—I'm taking painting lessons from an artist who paints murals around town."

"Really? I'm proud of you," he said, but he could hardly bear the sudden jealousy burning in his chest. Exactly how complete was this new life of hers?

"Is there a man there?" he asked.

She hesitated, and he thought his question had been unclear. He was about to reword it when she answered him.

"The artist," she said. "Yes."

He hugged her tightly. "Shit, shit, shit."

"Please don't be angry or upset or ... I'm sorry, Linc." She rolled toward him and smoothed her hand over his cheek. "I didn't know if I'd ever see you again. I know you and I can have nothing more, at least nothing permanent. And I'm not in love with Adam, not that way, but he is a good friend and we—"

"I'm not angry." He closed his eyes and couldn't speak for a minute, and he felt her rest her head on his chest as she waited out his silence. She knew him well enough to do that, he thought. Knew him better than any other woman ever could. And now she was happily keeping company with an artist in Annapolis, in her brand new life.

"I'm amazed you even took the time to come here to see me," he said.

She sat up, eyes blazing, and he knew he deserved her anger. But instead of chastising him, she began to cry again.

"Linc, I *love* you," she said. "I listen to your damned show every Sunday night, no matter what else there is to do. I live for it, okay? Is that what you need to hear? It's the truth. I cry when I hear your voice. I miss you. It probably was dangerous for me to meet you here, but I did. I had to see you. I'll meet you anywhere I can, anytime. I want to be with you. But I can't be with you and have Cody too." She touched his arm. "I understand how you feel, Linc. I'd feel terrible, too, if I thought you were sleeping with someone else."

He winced. She was already sleeping with the guy. Shit.

"And besides, I've told the artist about you."

He raised his eyebrows.

"Not who you are specifically or why I had to leave you, but I've told him that you exist. That you're still very important to me. I've told him that so he understands why I can't get serious with him right now. And I think the same is true for him. His whole family was wiped out by a drunk driver. Wife and two kids. It was only seven months ago. So we're two lonely, miserable people. Please don't be upset. Please—"

"All right." He raised his hand to stop her. He didn't want to hear any more. She had already humanized the bastard. It was easier to think of him as some faceless, nameless guy with no past and no future.

She lay down next to him again, her arm across his chest. "I don't want to end our time together on this note."

Neither did he. He kissed her, but knew the kiss would go nowhere. He could not possibly make love to her again. Not now. He could hold her, though. Hold her and tell her he loved her. Tell her he admired her for being able to start over.

When he returned to Boulder, he would have to find a way to start over himself.

$\mathcal{S}$o, I'll fax you every once in a while and sign it S.T.U. Downe," Kim said on the drive to the Philadelphia airport, "and maybe we can work out some sort of code for you to use to send messages to me in your show."

"Maybe," Linc said. He was quiet this afternoon. Kim could not get a smile from him. She didn't feel much like smiling herself. In a few minutes she would drop him off at the airport, and then what?

"Do you think we could meet like this every so often?" she ventured.

Linc let out a sigh. "I don't know, Suze." He reached over to take her hand from the steering wheel and hold it on his thigh. "The way I feel right now . . . I wonder if we've only made things harder on ourselves by getting together."

His words hurt her. "It was worth it to me," she said softly.

He raised her hand to his lips. "I'm not saying it wasn't great spending time with you. But I guess I had a fantasy that you'd come back with me. My hopes were high, and seeing you only makes the fall that much steeper. Besides, you have a new life and a new—"

"There's no comparison." She was starting to feel panicky. "The only thing that's better about my 'new life' is that I have Cody securely with me."

"But the reality is that you *do* have a new life, for better or worse. If you ever want it to be normal, if you ever want to have a relationship with another man, the artist or whomever, how are you going to see me? Think you can find some guy who'll understand that you want to spend a weekend with an old lover every once in a while?"

She wished she had not told him about Adam. He was right, of course. She could not have a serious relationship with another man and continue to see Linc on the side. But she had no plans for that sort of relationship.

"And frankly, Suze, if I should meet someone *I* want to get serious with, I'm not going to be able to, in good conscience, leave her alone while I go have a tryst with you."

The road blurred in front of her eyes. "You're really angry with me," she said.

He didn't answer for a moment. "I'm angry at the whole situation," he said.

She pulled into the turnoff for the airport, and neither of them said anything as she approached the terminal. He'd told her he didn't think she should come in with him on the off chance that someone might recognize him. Unlikely, but it had happened before.

There were other cars jockeying for a position next to the curb and it was a minute before she managed to find a space herself.

Linc turned to her. "Don't get out," he said. He leaned over and pulled her into his arms, kissing her. "I love you," he said.

"I love you, too."

She watched as he got out of the car. He opened the rear door to get his suitcase, and leaned over to plant a kiss on Cody's cheek.

"I'll miss you, Cody." He looked over the seat at Kim. "He's a beautiful kid," he said, but before she could respond, he backed out of the car and shut the door behind him.

Her heart tightened in her chest as she watched him walk into the terminal, and she remained parked in the drop-off zone until a uniformed officer told her she had to "keep moving."

In a few minutes, she was on the road to Annapolis. While Cody was awake, she chatted to him and sang songs and tried to make him laugh. But during those few times he fell asleep, she allowed herself to cry. Linc was right. They should not see each other again. The parting was simply too painful.

She reached Annapolis after nightfall, and the house was dark when she pulled up out front. Ellen's car wasn't in the driveway nor was Lucy's at the curb.

There was an almost wintry nip in the air as she unbuckled Cody from his car seat. The little boy was tired, and she carried him and her suitcase up the walk to the house.

She couldn't manage both Cody and the luggage on the stairs, so she left the suitcase on the front porch. She'd get Cody into bed first. His head was lolling against her shoulder and he would be out before he hit the pillow.

At the top of the stairs, she started to put her key in the lock, but stopped short when she saw that the door was not completely closed. She stared at it for a minute, trying to remember. She distinctly recalled closing the door and locking it behind her when she left on Saturday. She remembered the feel of the key in her hand as it turned in the lock. Maybe that memory was from some other time she'd locked it? No. She definitely had left this door locked.

She hugged Cody tighter, trying to still her trembling. Had the private investigator finally caught up to her? The FBI?

She touched the door lightly with her fingertips, and it creaked open a few inches more. She peered inside. Her apartment was dark except for a pale glow on the wall of the dining area, probably from the streetlight outside. There was no way she could make herself walk into the living room. Instead, she grabbed the railing and ran down the stairs as fast as she was able to with Cody in tow.

She half expected to see the PI's car pull up in front of the house, but except for her own car, the street was still empty. She forgot about her suitcase on the porch. Instead she quickly loaded Cody into the car and drove two blocks to the nearest pay phone. She dialed Adam's number.

"Adam, it's Kim," she said when he answered.

"You're back."

"Yes. But I went to my apartment and I think someone might have broken into it. The door's unlocked and I'm afraid to go in by myself. I'm calling from a pay phone."

"Did you call the police?"

She should have guessed that would be his first question. "No, I—"

"I'll be right over. I'll call the police from here and have them meet us there."

"No!" She panicked, leaning toward the phone. "I mean, please don't. Please just come over yourself."

He hesitated. "All right. I'll be there in a few minutes. Don't go in by yourself."

She hung up in relief, trying to ignore the little wave of guilt she felt over turning to Adam for help when she'd spent the night before with Linc.

She was pulling up in front of the house again when she suddenly remembered the leaky faucet, and she felt like a fool. Of course. The plumber had probably gone in to fix the leak and neglected to shut the door tightly when he let himself out.

She had convinced herself of that explanation by the time Adam arrived. She was sitting on the front steps with Cody, shivering in the cold, and although Cody was dressed warmly enough, he was fussy, annoyed at being carted around when he belonged sound asleep in his crib.

"Hi." Adam stood at the bottom of the porch steps and looked up at the darkened windows of her apartment.

"I think I know what happened," she said. "I forgot that I'd asked Ellen to fix the faucet in my bathroom. The plumber probably did his work and then forgot to lock the door."

"Well, let me take a look." Adam started up the porch steps.

She stood up. "I'll come with you."

"No. You and Cody stay down here while I make sure the coast's clear."

She walked into the house with him and waited at the bottom of the stairs while he went up to her apartment. After a minute, he leaned his head out the door. "All clear," he said.

She walked up the stairs, her exhausted son in her arms. Adam had turned on the lights in the apartment, and Kim carried Cody into the bedroom and laid him in his crib. She would get him into his pajamas later. She turned on the heat and began to look around the apartment. "Nothing's out of place," she said. "I bet it was the plumber. Although . . ." She cocked her head to listen. The drip of the faucet was as loud as it had been when she left. She rolled her eyes. "I don't believe it," she said.

"Did you leave your computer on?" Adam was standing in front of the computer, and she walked over to join him. The screen saver was on, and she realized that had been the source of the pale light she'd seen reflected on the wall.

"No." She stared woodenly at the screen. "No, I'm certain I didn't."

The floppy discs were out of their storage case and scattered across the table top. "And I didn't leave these out either."

"Why would anyone care about your floppy disks?" Adam asked.

"Just a minute." She walked into her bedroom and opened the lingerie drawer. The disk containing the hit list was still there, under her bras. *You could be in danger,* Linc had said.

"What's that?" Adam asked when she returned with the disk.

Her hands were shaking. "I have to tell you something," she said. She sat down in front of the computer, then looked up at Adam. "When I bought this computer, it was very inexpensive because someone had owned it before me." For the second time in two days she repeated the story of how she'd come to own the computer and described the information she'd found on it.

Adam sat down on the sofa, the color draining from his face as he listened to her. When she had finished, he stood up and paced toward the kitchen, then back to the sofa again, running a hand over his beard.

"You mean that bombing we saw on TV," he said, "that law firm . . . that's on the disk?"

"And that woman, too." She slipped the disk into the drive and the list of names appeared on the screen. Adam stood behind her. "This first woman was killed in an explosion on this exact date." She pointed to the information on the screen. "And here's Sellers, Sellers, and Wittaker. And as you can see, there's a man scheduled for the thirteenth of November."

"Good God." Adam looked even more shaken by the information than she had been. "Jesus, Mary, and Joseph, Kim. How long have you known this?" There was a reprimand in his voice. "Why haven't you called the police?"

She stared straight ahead at the screen, unsure how to answer him. She felt his hands on her shoulders.

"Kim?" His voice was gentler now.

She turned to look up at him. His face was puzzled but kind, and lined with worry. She bit her lip, then took his hand.

"Can I trust you?" she asked.

"What do you think?"

"I want to tell you, but I . . . " She knew she was going to tell him everything. She was exhausted from keeping it in. "Can we sit on the couch?" she asked.

He nodded, and they walked over to the sofa and sat down. She faced him, gripping his right hand with both of hers.

"Please, please, don't tell anyone what I'm going to tell you. Not even Jessie. Promise me?"

"I promise."

"I can't call the police about this because . . . I have to avoid the police."

He looked puzzled. "Have you committed a crime?"

"Some people would say I have. You see, my ex-husband and his wife were given custody of Cody. I was going to be allowed to see him once a week. That's all. So I left with him before I had to turn him over to them."

"But why on earth would you lose custody? You're such a good mother to him."

His words made her smile, but only for a second. "Because they're rich and have good jobs—they're both attorneys—and live in a great house," she said. "I should know. I picked it out thinking my husband and I would be living there."

"Did your husband have an affair with this woman?"

She liked the way he said "this woman," as if the words tasted sour in his mouth. "Yes."

"I didn't think their having more money than you would be enough for them to win custody."

"Probably in and of itself, it wouldn't be. But the woman's brother was the doctor who performed heart surgery on Cody. So that added to their argument about being able to take better care of Cody than I could." She couldn't tell him about her involvement with Linc and his conviction for the murder of her father. It was far too complicated, and she didn't want Adam to think the court had made the right decision.

Adam's face had not yet regained its color. "I'm stunned," he said. "I thought I knew you and now I—"

"I know," she interrupted him. "I'm sorry."

"Is Kim Stratton your real name?"

She shook her head.

"You poor thing," he said. "You must wake up in the morning and not know who you are."

"That was true, at first. But now I do feel like Kim Stratton."

"Are they looking for you?"

"Yes, absolutely. Some sort of organization that hunts for missing children is looking for me. Plus the police. Plus the FBI. And a private investigator."

"Holy shit, Kim. How do you know all that?"

She hesitated. "Because of the friend I saw this weekend," she said. "He told me."

"Oh." Adam's lips tightened. "The man in your heart."

She nodded.

"I don't like him much."

She smiled. "He's not crazy about you either."

"You told him about me?"

"I'm honest to a fault." She nodded toward the computer. "So anyhow, I realize I do have to get this information to the police, but I want to do it without them being able to trace it to me. I thought I could print out a fresh copy of it and send it to them from—"

"Give me the disk," Adam offered quickly. "I'll find a way to get it to them."

"No, I really have a need to do this myself," she said.

"Kim, that's ridiculous. Why take the chance when you don't have to? I'll figure out a way to get it to them without implicating you."

She gnawed at her lower lip again. Maybe he was right. "How would you do it, though?" she asked.

"I'm not sure, but I'll think of something."

"All right." She stood up and popped the disk out of the computer, then handed it to him with an undeniable sense of relief. "But they need to know right away," she said. "The next bombing is only a little more than a week away."

"It'll be in their hands tomorrow. I promise."

She looked around the room. It was still cold in the apartment, and she shivered. "Creepy, imagining someone being in here." She sat down next to him again. "I feel violated."

He nodded. "Come home with me. You and Cody." He reached out to tenderly touch her cheek.

She couldn't look him in the eye. A few hours ago, Linc had touched her the same way.

"Just temporarily," Adam said. "You'll be safe there. And I'd love having you around."

She could not stay with Adam tonight, not after spending the previous night with Linc. She was about to answer him when she heard Lucy's unmistakable footsteps on the stairs and the sound of her neighbor's apartment door opening and closing

"Thanks," she said. "But I'll be all right. Lucy's home."

"Are you going to tell her what happened?"

She shook her head. "No. I don't need someone else asking me why I didn't call the police."

"Good. The fewer people who know, the better."

She could hardly believe how easy it had been, telling him everything. "Thanks for being so accepting, Adam," she said. "And for not getting upset."

He looked pensive for a moment, then asked her, "All those things you've told me about your life, though," he said. "Were they true? That stuff about your parents being alcoholic?"

"Yes. That was the truth."

"And the kittens?"

"The truth."

"So the guy you saw in Philly. He was someone you left behind when you ran away with Cody?"

"Yes."

"But you're in touch with him. Isn't that risky?"

"I'm not really in touch with him."

"But you must be if you knew to meet him."

She groaned with a smile. "This is hard to explain," she said. "He's a ... public figure. He was able to get a message to me through a radio show."

"Ah," Adam said, as though that made perfect sense. "Do you see him often?"

"This was the first time since I left. And it might be the last. It's too dangerous to see him."

"But you wish you could."

"Adam . . ." She felt herself being backed into a corner. "He and I have been close friends since we were kids. I still miss him very much. I may very well never see him again, but even so, I still care about him. That's why I can't give our relationship, yours and mine, one hundred percent of myself. I'm not ready yet."

He nodded with a rueful smile. "I think you might be too honest for your own good," he said. "Makes you too vulnerable."

"The last thing I feel these days is honest."

Adam stood up. "Well, look. You have a safe night tonight, and I'll come over tomorrow and put a deadbolt on this door for you, okay?"

She nodded. "I'd appreciate it."

He leaned forward for a light kiss, and she gave it willingly and without guilt. She'd been as honest with him about Linc as she was able to be.

She changed her sleeping son into his pajamas after Adam left, then walked across the hall to Lucy's door.

It was a minute before Lucy answered her knock. She was dressed in a beige terry-cloth robe, and the glow of her own computer burned on the table in her dining area.

"*Hi* there," Lucy said. "Welcome back. Did you have a good little getaway?"

"Great. How's everything here?" She was curious to know if Lucy had heard anything during the break-in, but didn't dare ask her outright.

"It's been quiet. I'm working on an article, but would you like to come in for a minute? I could use a break."

"No," she said. "I'm tired. I just wanted to say hi."

"Well, good night, then, dear. See you in the morning."

Kim lay awake in bed for an hour before finally getting up and pushing an end table in front of her apartment door. Even then, she couldn't sleep. It already felt like days since she'd been with

Linc. She'd had far too short a time with him. It was like getting a taste of something rich and sweet and wonderful, and then being told she could never taste it again. She wished they had come up with some system of communicating, but maybe Linc was right. It would only make things harder for both of them.

Adam arrived in the morning with his bag of bagels and a deadbolt lock. She was working on Noel's novel, but put it aside when Adam told her he had good news.

"It's taken care of," he said.

"What is?" she asked, then thought she understood. "You mean, the police have the disk? Already?"

He nodded.

"How did you do it?"

He set the bag of bagels on the kitchen counter and began to explain. "I felt like I was in a movie," he said. "A thriller. First, I copied the information to another disk, so there'd be no fingerprints on it. Then I typed a note, explaining the significance of the information, and I put the disk and the note in an envelope marked 'urgent.' Then I drove around last night until I found a police car—it was parked at the all-night doughnut shop, of course." He smiled. "I put the envelope on the windshield. It was dark and I'm positive no one saw me. I parked a half a block away and watched as the cop came out of the shop and found the envelope. I saw him open it. It's in their hands now."

She threw her arms around him. "Oh, thank you," she said. "I'm so relieved."

She made coffee to go with the bagels, but she didn't really have time to visit with him. "I'm behind in my work," she said.

"That's all right. Will I make too much noise for you if I install the deadbolt now?"

"I don't think so."

She poured him a second cup of coffee to sip as he worked on the door, then returned to her seat in front of the computer. She began typing the next chapter in Noel's book, but was unable to concentrate. She wished now that she hadn't left that list of names with Linc. What if he tried to get it to the police himself? She hadn't really thought about the whole issue of fingerprints. Linc's would be easily traceable.

She closed the file containing Noel's book and opened a new document.

*Dear Mr. Sebastian,* she typed,

*Thanks for playing my favorites for me, but you don't have to worry about that other list I sent you. The artist has taken care of it. Still, I do hope you'll play something special for me from time to time.*

*S.T.U. Downe*

*L*inc was reading a paper written by one of his students when the fax arrived. He studied the brief message, his eyes instantly drawn to the middle two lines—*you don't have to worry about that other list I sent you. The artist has taken care of it.*

He knew he should be pleased and relieved, but he was not. The artist was taking care of entirely too much, it seemed.

He had not been able to shake this heavy, dejected feeling since leaving Philadelphia the day before. Maybe it had been a mistake to see her. He wanted to be glad that she and Cody were well, that she was making friends and had so efficiently begun her life again. It had taken him by surprise, though. He thought she needed him more than she apparently did. So what did he want? Did he want her to be miserable, to have no one?

Let her go, he told himself. Let her and Cody go.

He remembered what she'd told him about the artist's family: they'd been killed by a drunk driver, wiped out in an instant. He should pretend that's what had happened to her. Then he could grieve, assign her and Cody to a warmly remembered part of his past, and move on. He would send her no messages in this week's show. He would not even play "Suzanne" for her. What was the point?

The list of names and addresses and dates she'd given him was tacked on the bulletin board above his desk. He removed it from the board and carried it into the kitchen, where he poured himself a bowl of cereal and a cup of coffee. Then he sat down to eat, both the list and Susanna's fax lying on the table in front of him. Very bizarre, that list. Halfway through his breakfast, he reached for the phone and dialed Grace's number at the university library.

"Have a minute?" he asked when he'd gotten her on the line.

"For you," she answered.

"I have a situation I want to discuss with you," he said. "If I had a list of people who all had something terrible happen to them, and I suspected that they all had something terrible happen to them because they all had something in common, how could I find out what that something is?"

Grace was silent, and he knew he had not explained himself well.

"Could you run that by me again?" she asked.

He laughed. "Okay. Let's say you knew of a bunch of people who had been killed. Murdered. On the surface, they seem to have nothing in common, but you suspect that there must be something that unites them. Some reason they've been singled out for murder. Assuming they did have something in common, how would you find out what it is?"

"Linc, what have you gotten yourself mixed up with now?"

"This is hypothetical, Grace."

"Oh, right. If you say so. Hold on. I've got to take another call."

He used her absence from the line to light up a cigarette. In a moment, she was back.

"Okay, so you think something unites these people. Do you have addresses for them? Do they all live in the same neighborhood, or work in the same office, or go to the same university?"

He felt instantly overwhelmed. It could be any of those things and there was no way he could possibly know the answer to those questions. "I have no idea," he said.

"Well, you know what I would do? I would start by looking at the news coverage of their murders to see if you can tie them together that way. Or you could check the newspaper abstracts using the names of the victims to see if there might be any other articles on them that could tell you something about them."

"How do I . . . how does one check the newspaper abstracts?"

"In the library, Linc. Remember that big building with all the books?"

"But what if the people live far away?"

"You'd want to check the local papers in the area where they live."

"Could I check local papers from here?"

"Depends on what we mean by local. What city are you talking about?"

"Annapolis, Maryland." He blew a stream of smoke away from the phone, hoping Grace couldn't hear him.

"Hmm," Grace said, "they might have too small a paper to be indexed. And no, you couldn't check from here. You'd have to . . . look, I know a reference librarian who works at the Naval Academy in Annapolis. I met him at a conference. If you call him and use my name, he'd probably help you with it, as long as he's got the time. Hypothetically, of course."

"Thanks, Grace."

She left the line for a few minutes, and when she returned, she gave him the name and number of the librarian.

"Linc, just promise me you're not doing something stupid."

"Promise," he said. Then with a sigh, "By the way, I'd be willing to go out with your friend. Not as a date. But maybe dinner with you and Valerie." He cringed in anticipation of her elated response.

"All *right*," she said. "Maybe we could do it this weekend."

"No rush," Linc said.

When he got off the phone he called the librarian in Annapolis, hoping that no one scrutinizing his phone records would think a call to the library at the Naval Academy was suspicious. The librarian sounded dour and uncooperative until Linc mentioned Grace's name. Then he perked up and was unabashedly friendly. Linc gave him the name of the woman who had been killed. He considered giving him the name of the law firm, but was worried the librarian might recognize it. Surely in a town that small the killings would have been big news, and he didn't want the librarian to assume the connection was the bombings themselves. Instead, he gave him the names of a few other individuals on the list, along with the dates written next to their names.

"Do those dates refer to this year?" the librarian asked.

"I assume so." Linc looked at the list. "Well, actually, I don't know."

"And how soon do you need the information?"

"Whenever you can get to it," he said. "I'm curious, that's all."

"I'll see what I can do."

Linc hung up the phone and crushed out his cigarette. Sam sauntered into the room and rested his heavy dark head on Linc's knee, and Linc scratched the dog behind his ears. He thought he detected a disapproving look in Sam's big eyes.

"I know, I know," Linc said. "I'm done with Susanna, okay? I'm just curious about that list, that's all."

His words did nothing to alter the look in Sam's eyes, and with a sigh, Linc pushed back his chair and lit up another cigarette.

On her way to Adam's house, Kim stopped at Noel's to drop off one hundred pages and pick up another chunk of his manuscript—and a check. His apartment was smoky and chilly, but Noel himself was in a good mood.

"This looks really super," he said as he leafed through the typed pages. "Helps me delude myself into thinking I'm writing a real book."

"Oh, I think you are," Kim answered. Noel's protagonist was growing on her. "I really got into the part where they were hiding in the museum all night." She reached down and scooped Cody into her arms. Now that the little boy had mastered walking, he was constantly on the go, and Noel's apartment was not particularly child-safe.

"Did you?" Noel beamed, and his open need for approval made her like him more than she already did. "I wanted to add some accurate details about the museum, but I left my book on the Smithsonian at Jessie's house. It describes the Natural History Museum, floor by floor." Noel shook a cigarette from the pack on his desk. "Actually, I was wondering if you might be able to pick it up for me. I called Jess about it but she said she'd rather I didn't stop by myself."

"Sure," Kim said. "I'll ask her for it."

Noel lit the cigarette, then picked up a check from his desk and handed it to her, his expression pensive. "Have you seen

272

Jessie lately?" he asked. "She sounded so down on the phone."

"Well, I think she goes into a funk every once in a while. She's still very sad about the accident . . . and about you, I think."

"I suppose she told you why we split up?"

Kim wondered if she should have kept her mouth shut. "She said she wasn't comfortable with your drinking." Cody struggled to get out of her arms, and she tightened her grip on him.

Noel made a sound of disgust. "She's making a problem out of nothing," he said. "She and Adam went on this no-alcohol kick after the accident. Like that's going to bring Dana and the kids back, right?"

Kim shrugged uncomfortably. She had nothing against Noel, but she could only admire Jessie for her decision.

Cody intensified his wriggling and pouting, and she felt as if she were trying to hold on to a bag of jumping beans. "He's getting restless," she said, as she took a couple of steps toward the door. "I'll try to get that book for you tonight."

"That'd be grand." Noel carried the next installment of his manuscript down the metal stairs for her and said good-bye to her at her car.

She was anxious to get to Adam's house. For the first time, she'd had a dream she could use. She'd gotten out of bed that morning and sketched quickly and quietly, listening to Cody as he babbled to himself in his crib.

Turning off Noel's street she came to a stop sign. She stepped on the brake, but her car gave no sign of slowing down. Panicked, she pressed harder, finally coming to an uncertain stop in the middle of the intersection. From the corner of her eye, she spotted a black station wagon speeding toward her from the right. She pressed on the gas pedal with all her strength, pulling out of the intersection just in time to avoid a collision, but not the horn-blaring wrath of the other driver.

Her heart racing, she carefully turned the car around and headed home, driving very slowly. Her brakes felt spongy and soft as she pulled to a stop in front of the house, and she swiveled in her seat to look at her son. "Are you all right, Cody?" she asked. She felt shaky and sick, but Cody smiled at her, unaware that he should be anything other than all right.

Her arms trembled as she carried him up the sidewalk to the house. There was no doubt in her mind that if she had stopped in that intersection one second later, she and Cody would be dead. If Cody had been with Jim and Peggy, however, riding around in their perfectly tuned BMW instead of in her second-hand bargain, he would never have been in danger.

And if she and Cody had been killed, how would Linc ever find out? That thought was so distressing that she had to blink back tears as she climbed the stairs to her apartment. It hurt every time she remembered that quiet, solemn ride with Linc to the airport, when she'd been longing to work out some way of communicating with him, while he'd been thinking of how untenable their relationship had become. Would he say anything to her through his choice of music on Sunday night? If he didn't, she knew she would have to accept his decision to move on without her. She could hardly blame him.

She called Adam and told him she couldn't come over because of the problem with her car, and she was pleased when he offered to pick her up. He was at her door within minutes.

"Is there some place I can take it where they won't rip me off?" she asked on the drive to his house.

"Yeah," Adam said. "You can let me fix it."

"No, I couldn't."

"Yes, ma'am. I've always done the work on my car. Jessie's too. If you can wait till the weekend, I can work on it then."

"Really, Adam? That would be wonderful." She would have to find some way to repay him. "I really appreciate you picking me up. I had a dream last night."

He grinned at her. "I told you it would happen."

"It took place in a park," she said. "I think it was the park where I take Cody to play, but it had all these rays of sunlight coming through the trees. And there was this group of children playing in a circle on the ground." The dream was still vivid in her mind. "I don't know if I can paint the children, though."

"Save them for last," Adam said, as he turned into his driveway. "Although I have complete faith in your ability, *especially* when it comes to painting people."

They ate Adam's homemade minestrone soup for dinner, then

Kim put Cody to bed and joined Adam in his studio. He was well into his painting—a tree-lined road leading to a lake dotted with sailboats—and she was inspired by his creation to get to work on her own. The minutes ticked by unnoticed as she transferred her dream of the night before from her mind to the canvas.

"The dream artists," Adam said after a while, as he glanced over at her work. "You are getting damn good."

"Thanks." Kim took a step back to look at her canvas, and for the first time, she thought she truly deserved his compliment.

"You know why you suddenly had a great dream, don't you?" Adam asked now, as he worked on one of the sailboats.

"Why?"

"Because you feel freer, now that you've told me everything. You have nothing to hide anymore, at least not from me."

"Maybe," she said. It did help that Adam knew the truth about her. Adam seemed to have taken the news in and then tucked it away, where it could do her no harm. She knew it tied her to him, though, and every once in awhile that thought frightened her. She must never make an enemy of Adam. If at some point their relationship came to an end, she would have to be certain it did not end badly.

There was another reason she felt freer the past few days: the information from the computer was finally in the hands of the police. She had seen nothing about the police's receipt of the list in the papers or on the news, however, and hoped they were keeping it quiet in order to catch the bomber before he could harm the next victim.

She would not have said she felt totally free, though. Anyone who, despite the presence of a deadbolt, slept with an end table in front of her door, who looked over her shoulder several times a day, wondering if the man keeping pace with her across the street might be the private investigator, or worse, the previous owner of her computer, and who kept her duffel bag still packed and ready to go at a moment's notice, could not claim to be free.

Adam walked over to the cupboard to get a rag. On the way back to his canvas, he stopped behind her, putting his arms around her waist.

"I think you have to stay here tonight," he said. "I refuse to drive you home."

She leaned back against him. She had not slept with him since her return to Annapolis. She'd been holding tight to her memory of Saturday night with Linc.

"Maybe," she said, remembering that Linc had held her this way at the zoo in Philadelphia. She brushed the thought quickly from her mind.

"I love the idea of waking up with you, now that you're dreaming," Adam nuzzled her ear. "Both our heads will be packed with dreams, and we'll grab our sketchbooks in the morning and fill page after page after page."

"All right," she said with a smile. "But can you take me home early in the morning? Noel gave me another chunk of his novel this afternoon." She suddenly remembered the book Noel had asked her to pick up. "Is Jessie coming over tonight?" she asked. "Noel wanted me to get a book he left at her house." She realized she had not seen Jessie all week.

Adam let go of her with a sigh and walked back to his own canvas. "I doubt it," he said. "She's been under the weather. I took her some of the minestrone. I don't think she's been out in days. Just hangs around her house, watching her kittens grow."

"Does she have a cold or something?"

"No. I think she's just depressed."

Kim put her brush in the jar of water in the sink. "I'm going over to say hi to her and pick up Noel's book." She stopped at the top of the stairs and looked at Adam. "I worry that she's mad at me because you and I are . . . together."

"She doesn't blame you." Adam didn't turn around from his canvas. "She blames me."

Kim started down the stairs. "Will you listen for Cody while I'm gone?" she called behind her.

"I'll listen for Cody and warm up the bed."

There were lights burning in the house next door, but Kim still had to knock several times before Jessie answered the door.

"Hi." Jessie smiled at her, but her face was gray. She was wearing a pale blue chenille robe and her feet were bare.

"Hi, Jess," Kim said. "Can I come in for a minute?"

"Sure." Jessie let her in, and Kim walked into the living room. There was an almost imperceptible aroma of cat box in the air, but given the fact that Jessie owned a full grown cat and five kittens, it did not seem too bad.

"How are the kittens doing?"

"Good." Jessie sat on the arm of her sofa. "And how's my brother doing?"

It felt like a trick question. "He's fine," she said, although Adam seemed far better than fine. She didn't want to rub Jessie's nose in the fact that her brother was doing better than she was.

She noticed a box of pictures on the coffee table in front of the sofa. A few of the photographs were spread haphazardly on the table top, and Kim could see that one of them was a five-by-seven of Molly and Liam. She wouldn't be surprised if *all* of the pictures in the box were of the children, and she wondered if Jessie had been tormenting herself with them all week. She pulled her eyes back to Jessie's face.

"Noel asked me to pick up a book he left over here. Is that okay with you?"

Jessie pointed toward the floor to ceiling bookshelf next to the fireplace. "His are on the third and fourth shelves down."

Kim walked over to the shelves and, after a moment's search, found the book on the Smithsonian that Noel had requested. She pulled it from the shelf, then looked at Jessie, still gray-faced and perched on the arm of the couch.

"I haven't seen you in days," Kim said.

Jessie shrugged. "I have major PMS," she said. "Not fit to be around."

"Are you angry with me?"

Jessie looked surprised. "Why would I be?"

"Because of Adam. You thought he should still be grieving, and instead he—"

"No," Jessie interrupted her. "I'm not mad. Just grumpy as hell."

"Well, I hope you feel better soon." Kim felt like hugging her, but something held her back. She hated leaving Jessie alone with that box of pictures. "Why don't you come over for awhile? We could watch a movie or—"

"No, thanks, Kim. My bed is calling."

Kim was reluctant to let her off that easily, but she didn't know what else she could say.

"Well, if you change your mind, come on over," she said.

She checked on Cody once she was back in Adam's house, then climbed into his bed, with its dark sheets and light feather comforter. Adam was in the bathroom, and she could hear him singing, although she couldn't make out the tune. She tucked her sketchbook beneath the bed, lay down, and closed her eyes.

Like magic, an idea came to her for the painting she was working on. She sat up, retrieved the sketchbook, and grabbed her pencil from the top of the night table.

She'd barely gotten a few lines on the paper before the point of her pencil snapped off.

Optimistically, she pulled open the night table drawer in search of another pencil, but the drawer was completely empty. Leaning across the bed, she opened the drawer to Adam's night table, then drew back with a yelp. Poking out from beneath a few sheets of paper and a couple of receipts was the unmistakable steely gray nose of a gun. Kim stared at it, instantly transported back to her parents' bedroom and her father's night table.

She closed the drawer gingerly with her fingertips as Adam came into the room. He leaned over to kiss her, then stood back with a frown. "What's wrong?" he asked.

"I opened your night table drawer to look for a pencil and saw a gun," she said.

He looked briefly surprised. "Oh, jeez, I forgot it was there," he said. "Let me get rid of it right now."

He opened the drawer and lifted out the gun, handling it with entirely too much ease. Kim cowered in the bed as he carried it to the closet. She watched him slip it onto the end of one of the overhead shelves.

"There," he said. "Now it's out of our way. I'm sorry."

She was still shaken. She wished the gun were out of the house entirely. Better yet, she wished Adam didn't own it.

"Is it loaded?" she asked.

"No. At least, not anymore."

She shuddered. "I hate guns. Why do you have it?"

279 the escape artist

He let out a long sigh. "Do I have to say?"

"If you want me to sleep easy tonight, yes."

He lay down and took her with him, his arm around her shoulders. "I bought it shortly after the accident, because, frankly . . . I was considering killing myself."

She put her arm across his chest. "Oh," she said. "I'm very glad you didn't."

"Yes, so am I. I didn't do it because of Jessie. That was the only reason. Jessie was so despondent. I knew I couldn't do that to her. She knows I own the gun, but she doesn't know I'd ever considered using it on myself, and I'd appreciate it if you never told her."

"I won't."

"So now we know each other's secrets, huh?" he said.

"Mine's a little heavier than yours."

"Well." He raised himself up on his elbow and ran his hand gently over her cheek. "Your secret is safe with me."

They spent the weekend together, dragging Jessie out for dinner on Saturday night and taking Cody to the park and for a couple of long walks, but most of their time was spent immersed in their painting. So much so, that the brakes on her car did not get repaired. Adam promised to work on them first thing Monday morning, and Kim went home late Sunday afternoon, looking forward to spending the evening with Linc—or at least, with Linc's voice. Five minutes into his show, though, someone knocked on her door.

She jumped out of bed and ran to the window. No police car. She walked quietly to the door.

"Who's there?" she asked.

"It's me." It was Adam's voice, and she pulled the door open to find him standing on the landing, a toolbox in one hand, a huge, boxy flashlight in the other.

"Oh, good," he said, "I was hoping to catch you before you started your pampering session."

Linc's voice was no more than a murmur in the air behind her. She could not make out a word he was saying.

"Did I wake you up?" Adam looked at her curiously.

"Oh, no. Sorry. Come in." She let him in, knowing there was no alternative short of rudeness.

"I should have called first, but I thought I'd take a chance. Cherise wants me to go to D.C. with her tomorrow, so I was hoping I could work on your car tonight."

"In the dark?"

"Well, I'll need you to hold the light for me."

A dozen thoughts ran through her head. What excuse could she give him? She thought of asking him if he could wait until Tuesday, but that would leave her without a car the following day. Plus, it was hardly fair of her to dictate when he should work on the car, since he was doing it for free. She could bring the radio outside with them, but Adam would probably realize that Linc Sebastian was the man she'd met in Philadelphia. She should never have told Adam that her old lover had gotten a message to her through a radio show.

"Kim? Are you sure you're awake?" Adam was smiling at her, and she shook her head as if clearing away the cobwebs.

"Yes," she said. "I'm fine. Let me get my jacket and make sure Cody's asleep, and I'll meet you down there, okay?"

"Okay. Bring a roll of paper towels, will you?"

Cody was sleeping like an angel, and Linc was in the middle of a set of Donovan songs. She felt like crying as she put on her jacket and started down the stairs, leaving the radio playing softly behind her.

Adam needed her for more than holding the light. He had her sit in the car, pumping the brakes until her leg ached. She stared at the car radio, wishing she could turn it on. A few times she went back to the apartment to "check on Cody," but if Linc was talking to her, through his own words or through the music, she was not getting the message.

"There," Adam said as he finally crawled out from under the car. "That should do it. Let's take it around the block once and see how they feel."

"I can tell they feel tight now," she said from behind the steering wheel, her foot on the brake. "We don't need to drive it." There was still a half hour left of *Songs for the Asking*.

"Yes, we do. Just to make sure. I'll stay here and listen for Cody, and you take it around the block. Then you can have your bath."

He grinned at her as if he'd discerned her secret. "I know that's what you're dying to do."

She looked at him apologetically. "I really appreciate this, Adam," she said. "I'm sorry if I haven't seemed like I do."

He waved her off, and she drove down the street, knowing it would be quicker to drive around the block than to argue about it. The brakes were fine, and she was soon back at the curb in front of her apartment.

Adam was waiting for her on the porch steps. He gave her a little wave, and, even from the road, she could see the car grime on his hands.

*He's a good man*, she thought. He must have been a terrific husband and father. And he could be a significant part of her life, if she could only let go of her addiction to that voice on the radio.

"They're perfect," she said as she approached the porch steps, and she leaned forward to kiss him. "Thank you so much. Do you want to come in for a little while?" She had to offer. She couldn't simply send him on his way.

"No." He walked down the steps and stood next to her. "No, I know you're anxious to have some time to yourself." He gave her a hug. "How late can I call you tomorrow night? I'm not sure what time we'll get back from D.C."

"Eleven?"

"Okay. I'll talk to you then."

Upstairs, she flopped down on her bed and listened as Linc wrapped up his show. She'd expected at least to be able to hear him play "Suzanne," but he closed with yet another Donovan song. She listened carefully to the words, hunting for some personal meaning in them but coming away with none, and by the time she turned off the radio, she was in tears.

"Thank you so much, Kim," Lucy switched off the tape recorder lying on Kim's coffee table. "Your candor is going to make this a good article."

The interview had been relatively painless. From her seat on the sofa, Kim had slipped into her "I'm Kim Stratton" mode and answered Lucy's questions with ease. She wondered, though, if candor and honesty were truly the same thing.

"Just promise me that you'll give us interesting names," she said.

"I've already come up with names for you." Lucy flipped open a notebook. "I always try to pick names my readers can relate to. I'm going to call you Laura, and Cody, Tyler."

"What?" Kim felt the color drain from her face.

"Laura's a common name, and the name Tyler is very popular right now. A lot of women will be able to see their own little boy in him."

Kim's hands clutched the edge of the seat cushion. She knew she'd better choose her words carefully. "Do you think you could pick another name for Cody?" she asked. "A friend of mine had a Tyler and he was a horrible little kid." She expected to have to explain herself further, but Lucy seemed unperturbed.

"How about Matthew, then? Matthew's always a good name."

"I like Matthew," Kim said. The phone rang, and she rose to answer it. "Thanks for indulging me," she said over her shoulder as she walked into the kitchen.

"Hello?" she said into the phone.

"Ms. Stratton?"

The formal-sounding, unfamiliar voice put her on guard. "Yes?

"This is Barb Kotter from Kotter Enterprises?"

The company name was vaguely familiar, but she could not place it.

"We received your brochure regarding word processing," the woman continued.

"Oh, yes," she said.

"Well, we're in a bit of a bind," the woman said. "We have an urgent job and the person who usually does our word processing for us is ill. Is there a chance you could come over for a quick interview? I know it's nearly five, and this is terribly late notice, but—"

"Yes. I can do that." She glanced at Cody. He was sitting on the living room floor, playing with the activity box Linc had given him. She wanted to ask if she could bring her baby along, but thought better of it. She had a feeling people didn't bring their children to interviews at Kotter Enterprises.

"Oh, that would be wonderful," the woman said. "I can only be here another hour, though. Can you make it before then?"

"Yes." She wrote down the address and got off the phone, wondering if she had time to change into a skirt and put on some makeup. "I have a job interview," she said to Lucy. "Right now. They're in a bind."

Lucy stood up from the sofa. "Let me watch Cody for you," she offered.

Kim looked down at her son. He was opening and closing the little red door on the activity box, oblivious to her dilemma. She chewed her lip.

Lucy let out an exasperated sound. "I'll have to remember to include how overprotective some single mothers can be when I write the article," she said. "Come on, Kim. Cody and I will be fine."

"You're sure you don't mind? I shouldn't be long."

"You run and get dressed." Lucy prodded her on the shoulder. "Hurry up, now."

\* \* \*

Kotter Enterprises was located on the third story of an office building near the water. The building was clean and modern, but it seemed deserted, and Kim found herself glancing over her shoulder as she made her way to Barb Kotter's office. She was thoroughly glad she'd left Cody at home. Given the formality of the setting, she doubted a baby would be seen as a cute accompaniment to a job interview.

Barb Kotter probably wouldn't have cared, though. Desperation showed in the woman's face. She asked Kim a few perfunctory questions, looked greatly relieved, and handed her a pile of work to be returned in two days. Kim would have to put everything else on hold, but she knew she could get the work done. And then she'd have a new client, as well as a good reference.

She saw the police car the second she turned on to her street. It was parked in front of Ellen's house, and she pulled close to the curb several houses away, her heart in her throat. From where she sat, there did not appear to be anyone sitting in the car. There were lights on all through the house, in Ellen's first story as well as in her apartment and Lucy's. "Cody and I will be fine," Lucy had promised. Had she called the cops the second Kim was out the door?

She had to get to her son. She parked behind the police car and ran up the front walk and onto the porch. Racing up the stairs, she reached the landing as the police officer was emerging from Lucy's apartment. Lucy stood behind him, Cody in her arms.

"Here's mommy now," the policeman said.

Kim was trembling as she reached past him for Cody. Lucy relinquished her hold on the little boy without protest.

"How did the interview go?" Lucy asked.

"Is something wrong?" Kim looked from Lucy to the policeman and back again.

The policeman laughed. "Wherever I go, people think there's something wrong."

"Not a thing, honey. This is Frank Ragland. Frank, this is Kim Stratton."

Frank touched Cody's cheek lightly. "You have a good-looking boy there," he said.

She couldn't answer. She was so nervous, her teeth were chattering, and she wrapped her arms more tightly around her son.

"I'll be in touch, Lucy," Frank said as he headed down the stairs.

Lucy smiled after him, then turned to Kim. "You get in here and tell me all about your interview. It must have been terrible. You're white as a sheet. Do you want a cup of tea?"

Kim followed her into the apartment. Her legs were about to give out, and she sank into a chair. "I just . . . when I saw the police car in front of the house, I thought that something might have happened to Cody."

Lucy set a pot of water on the stove and shook her head. "You are the most overanxious mother I've ever seen," she said. "That little boy's going to grow up afraid of his own shadow if you don't start to relax about him."

"But . . . then what's going on? Why were the police here? Did you hear another noise?"

Lucy sat down with a great sigh. "No. No noise," she said. "And it's a little embarrassing for me to talk about. I'd appreciate it if you could keep it to yourself. Okay?"

Kim nodded. Cody squirmed out of her lap, and she reluctantly let him go.

"Frank and I are . . . involved."

"Oh." Kim sat back. She had not expected that.

"He's the reason I left my marriage, as well as the reason my children no longer want anything to do with me. I had a terrible marriage, from day one, as I told you. A loveless, dishonest sort of existence. But I stuck it out, because . . . well in my generation, that's what you were supposed to do. Life was not a bowl of cherries and you just accepted it. And I did, for thirty-six years, until I met Frank. Suddenly a man treated me like I was a human being. I'd forgotten what it felt like to be taken seriously by someone on a personal level. Professionally, I was taken seriously all the time. But this was different. I realized then that I'd been a doormat, both for my husband and my kids. They walked all over me. Frank gave me the strength to do something about it. So I left." She pursed her lips. "It was not a popular decision. Now I've been cut off from everybody."

"Maybe that's temporary," Kim suggested. "They'll come

around in time. Your kids are bound to realize you did the right thing."

"I doubt it. But it's my fault, actually. I did everything for them. They were spoiled. They still expect everything to be done for them, even though they're all old enough to know better. They expect me to sacrifice my happiness for theirs. So this is the price I pay for happiness."

"I'm sorry." Kim watched Cody as he explored the bowl of blocks in the middle of Lucy's living room floor. She wondered if happiness always had to come with a price tag.

"Frank makes it worthwhile, though." Lucy's eyes lit up. "He's good looking, don't you think? Did you see how blue his eyes are?"

Kim hadn't noticed, but she nodded all the same. She felt a little giddy. The cops didn't have a clue who she was. Her paranoia had been entirely unfounded. And so, as Lucy went on and on about her boyfriend and his blue eyes, she listened in numb relief.

# 33

*S*ome mornings, I wake up and think it's all a bad dream." Bonnie Higgins wiped her eyes with a ragged tissue.

Peggy reached across the desk to hand her another. Her concentration was even worse than usual today. Bill Anderson had called prior to her appointment with Bonnie to tell her that *Missing Persons* was moving its parental kidnapping show up by several months. "This Wednesday night, to be exact," Bill had said. He'd gone on to explain the reason for the show's change in schedule, but she hadn't listened. She didn't care. All she knew was that, in a few days, Tyler and Susanna's pictures would be splashed across the country. Someone was bound to recognize them. She wasn't certain why that realization didn't give her more of a thrill than it did.

"I mean, how do you explain it?" Bonnie asked. "First everything seems fine. Then all of a sudden, he wants out. Then I find out he's been seeing his . . . skanky secretary. And now he says he wants the kids. My life's falling apart."

Peggy forced her attention back to her client, who had not stopped crying since entering the office thirty minutes earlier. Her husband was now fighting actively for their two children, Bonnie had said, and he'd even threatened to steal them, although he denied saying as much to his own attorney, whom Peggy had promptly called.

Peggy had felt close to tears herself a few times during her appointment with Bonnie, despite the encouraging news from Bill. The threatened kidnapping hit a little too close to home, and there was no way she would let what had happened to her happen to one of her clients. She leaned toward Bonnie. "Your husband is not getting the children, legally or otherwise," she said firmly.

"But he—"

"Has he done anything that might indicate he's planning to take off? Has he quit his job, for example? Closed out a bank account? Sold a car?"

"Not that I know of."

"Good." Of course, they'd had no indication at all that Susanna was about to run, either. "You need to do a few things," Peggy said. "Your kids are . . . " She looked down at her notes.

"Four and five," Bonnie said.

"Do they know how to use the telephone?"

"Yes."

"Teach them how to make a collect call, and tell them they can call you that way any time they want to."

"*I* don't even know how to make a collect call."

"But you're going to learn how and teach them, right?"

"Okay."

"And first chance you get—*today*—you need to contact their day care provider and . . . is the older one in school yet?"

"They're both in preschool."

"Let the preschool know that their father has threatened kidnapping. And we're going to modify your custody order. We'll restrict visitation and say he can't take the children out of Boulder."

She spent another half hour with Bonnie, discussing what they could do to prevent her children from suffering the same fate as Tyler. Peggy loved experiencing that sense of power, that feeling that she could actually do something to prevent Bonnie's husband from taking off with the children. By the time she left Legal Aid after Bonnie's appointment, though, she was drained.

She drove to Ron's office. She had called her brother early that morning, telling him she couldn't bear the silence between them any longer. When he suggested they take a walk together after work, she'd readily agreed.

"He's still with patients," Ron's receptionist told her when Peggy walked into the waiting room. "Have a seat."

She took a seat, leafing idly through a magazine, until Ron emerged from the rear of his office. He was already dressed in his sweats.

"Hi, Sis." He gave her a kiss as she stood up. "It's good to see you."

"You too." She hugged him. She wanted this to be a healing visit, and she was determined to keep the conversation off Tyler. She'd steer clear of anything that might feed into conflict with her brother. She missed him too badly to risk alienating him again.

His office was close to Cuyamaca Park, and they set out in that direction. They talked about Ron's work and his kids, the plans for his vacation, and the movies he'd seen recently. Peggy hadn't heard of any of them. She'd been living in a vacuum for the past couple of months.

"So enough about me," Ron said finally. "How are things going in the search for Tyler?"

She hesitated. "I wasn't going to talk about him," she said. "You made it pretty clear you'd rather not discuss the situation with me."

Ron put his arm around her. "I'm sorry if I made you feel that way," he said. "I don't want you to feel as though you have to censor what you say to me."

"Well, I do have some good news, I think."

"What's that?"

She described Bill Anderson's call. Ron pursed his lips as he listened to her, and she was certain he was trying hard not to respond in a way that might upset her. She appreciated the effort.

"Well," he said, when she had finished, "I just hope that all parties concerned come out of this none the worse for wear."

It was an ambiguous statement, to say the least, but she decided not to press him on what he meant by it.

"So, what's new at Legal Aid?" He changed the topic.

Again, she hesitated. The only Legal Aid case occupying her mind was Bonnie's, and she wasn't certain she could safely discuss that particular case with him.

"Well," she began, "I saw a woman this afternoon whose case

really gets to me. But I don't know if I should talk to you about it, because it reminds me of what we're going through with Tyler."

"I just told you not to censor what you say to me," Ron chastised her.

They were walking uphill, and Peggy spoke between taking gulps of air. "It started out as a simple divorce case," she said. "The woman's husband told her he wanted a divorce. She was distraught, but ready to learn how to protect herself legally. Then she found out her husband had been having an affair with his secretary, so she was hurt and angry. Now he says he's going after the kids, and he's alluded to the fact that, if she puts up a fight, he'll kidnap them, although he's denied he's said it. But I believe her and—"

"Let me get this straight." Ron dug his hands into his pants pockets. "You're relating to this case because the husband might kidnap his kids?"

"Yes."

He shook his head. "You just don't get it, do you, Peg?" he asked. "For a smart woman, you can be pretty dense."

"What are you talking about?" She hated the tone of his voice and braced herself for whatever he might say next.

"This sounds very familiar to me. Her husband had an affair, and now he's threatening to get custody of the children. Your sympathies are with *her,* but your client is to *her* children as Susanna is to Tyler. The betrayed wife about to lose custody of her children to her cheating husband and his new girlfriend."

She was appalled. "There is no comparison. No analogy. This guy's girlfriend is a tramp."

"What makes her a tramp and you not? The fact that you're an attorney and she's a mere secretary?"

"Why do you always have to attack me?" she asked, her voice rising. "I thought you didn't want me to have to censor what I say to you? Do you *enjoy* fighting with me? It's as if you're waiting for a chance to jump down my throat again." She was talking fast, trying to evade the logic in what he was saying. She didn't dare entertain the idea that he might be right.

"I just find it hard to listen to you compare yourself to your betrayed client."

"I wasn't talking about the infidelity part of—" She stopped walking suddenly and shut her eyes, trying to rid herself of the trapped feeling that was closing in on her. When she opened her eyes again, Ron was looking at her closely.

"That's what it's all about, isn't it?" she said to him. "You've been angry with me ever since I told you I'd slept with Jim. I never should have told you. You're never going to let me forget it."

"I was disappointed in you, yes. I've never given you grief about the affair because I didn't want to come off as your judgmental big brother. But when you start comparing what you're going through to what this poor client of yours is experiencing, when you can't even see that she is Susanna and not you, then I can't keep my mouth shut any longer."

"I really believed Jim when he said his marriage to Susanna was over."

"You did it in the woman's *bed*. How would you feel if your client told you she'd come home and found her husband and his girlfriend together in her bed?"

"I'd feel outraged, but that's totally different."

Ron laughed. "How exactly is it different?"

"Because her husband's a self-centered, arrogant bastard."

"Oh. Jim's a nice guy, so that makes it all right."

Peggy was exasperated. "Look, I didn't want to fight with you again. I just wanted—"

"You downplay your part in what happened with you and Jim. You take no responsibility for—"

"I'm ashamed of what I did. Is that what you want to hear me say? I convinced myself it was all right, because Jim said it was. I was upset when Susanna came home early, but I didn't really feel sorry for her, because Jim always said that she . . ." Her voice trailed off. She was sick of this argument, sick of defending herself. She let out her breath and sat down on a large rock close to the sidewalk. "I don't know what I think anymore," she said. "I'm confused." She looked up at her brother. "I had lunch with Linc Sebastian the other day."

"Did you?" Ron rested one foot against the rock, but remained standing.

"Yes, and he said some things that shook me up. I shouldn't listen to him. I don't know why I did. Ordinarily I can shrug off whatever he says, but sometimes he sounds so sincere."

Ron nodded. "I think Linc *is* sincere," he said. "He doesn't care enough about what people think of him to bother lying to them."

Peggy let Ron's words sink in. She knew they were the truth, but she didn't want to hear it. "So now I'm mixed up."

He sat down on another rock opposite her. "About?"

"Everything. There's a part of me that wishes Linc *did* know where Susanna was. I wish he were slipping her money. The fact that she has no insurance for Tyler really distresses me."

"I'm confident she'll get Tyler medical care one way or another."

"But let's say we never find her. Even with the *Missing Persons* show, it's possible that we never will. I'd rather know that she's out there with good insurance and plenty of money for Tyler than for her to have to struggle to take care of him."

Ron's smile was slow to form. "That's the Peggy I know and love," he said, his voice gentle. "Welcome back, Sis. I know that deep down you have Tyler's best interests at heart, but when you start directing your hostility at Susanna, I tend to forget that."

Peggy put her head in her hands. "Being angry at Susanna gives me something to do," she said. "Otherwise I sit around feeling helpless. Jim says we should leave everything up to the 'authorities,' and the authorities say—"

"Forget about what Jim wants and what the authorities want," Ron said. "Take a few steps back from this mess so you can see it clearly. Then follow your own head and heart, all right?"

She stared at him. "I'm not sure that would make any difference," she said.

Ron got to his feet and leaned over to help her up. "I think it will make all the difference in the world," he said.

She thought about Ron's words as she made dinner that night. She couldn't shake her brother's anger at her, nor could she shake her guilt. Ron was right. She hated to admit it, but she was no better than the "skanky secretary" Bonnie's husband was shacking up with. Right now, she didn't like herself very much.

Still, she'd appreciated her brother's counsel. There was something freeing about approaching the problem with a fresh eye, but she knew as she sat down to the table with her husband that she would have to tread softly in presenting her thoughts to him.

Jim had expressed surprisingly little interest when she'd called him to tell him about *Missing Persons*. "I'm amazed they'll have Tyler's case on this soon," was all he'd said, and if she hadn't known better, she would have thought there was disappointment in his voice. He was extremely busy at work, she knew. Even now as he sat at the table, he kept glancing at his watch and jotting notes on a pad resting next to his plate.

"I'll have to go back to the office after dinner," he said.

"I was hoping we could talk a little."

"Can it wait till the weekend?"

"I just have a few questions about Tyler's medical care."

"What about it?"

"Well, is there any way you can keep him on your medical insurance even though you don't know where he is?"

"What do you mean?"

She wasn't sure what she meant. "Let's say the *Missing Persons* show doesn't work out, and we still don't know where Tyler is," she said. "Then I guess what I'm asking is, could Susanna still use your insurance for him without having to let you know where she is?"

"It would be great if she tried," Jim said. "We could probably catch her that way."

"But . . . the most important thing is for Tyler to have good medical care, right? And if Susanna could use your insurance for him, she could get him the best, but she'd have to be assured we wouldn't try to track her down, or—"

"Have you lost your mind?"

"I'm just rethinking some things. I mean, even if we never got Tyler back, wouldn't you want to know that he's getting good care?"

Jim looked at his watch again. "If Susanna wants my insurance for him, then Susanna can damn well bring him home," he said, his face reddening.

She was put off by his anger, but could hardly blame him. She'd suddenly changed her thinking about the whole situation. She couldn't expect him to catch up to her that quickly.

Jim slipped the notepad into his shirt pocket, and it was obvious he was finished with the conversation. "I've got to go," he said. He leaned across the table to kiss her before standing up. "I'm not sure what time I'll make it home," he said as he picked up his briefcase from the counter. "I'll give you a call."

"All right."

She sat at the table for a long time after he left. Finally, she got to her feet and walked into the study. She opened Jim's filing cabinet and pulled out the file on their health insurance. She wasn't certain what she was looking for. A way Susanna could file claims without Jim ever knowing about them, she guessed. The claim forms and information booklet didn't tell her much. She jotted down the company's phone number and was putting the papers back in the file when her fingers caught on a slip of paper.

It was a small sheet of lined paper, and the handwriting on it was unmistakably Jim's.

*S—Here's the list of some Boulder MDs who perform abortions. I'd appreciate it if you'd get it done before your second trimester, since the price goes up after that.*

There followed a list of six doctors, along with their phone numbers and addresses.

Peggy stared at the list. Hadn't Jim said he'd never given Susanna the names of doctors? What else had he lied to her about?

Back in the kitchen, she did the dishes and mopped the floor, trying to keep busy, trying to quiet her thoughts. But it was no use. When she finished cleaning up, she dialed Ron's number.

Ron answered, and she was relieved to know he was home.

"Can I come over?" she asked. "I think I have some decisions to make."

# 34

*L*inc picked up the stack of faxes and sat down in the leather armchair in his studio. He whisked through them quickly, hunting for anything that might be from S.T.U. Downe. Nothing. So what did he expect? He was supposed to be getting on with his life, yet every day he went over his faxes with a fine-tooth comb. He wished now that he'd played "Suzanne" for her during his last show. He pictured her with her ear to the radio, waiting and hoping, only to be hurt by his omission.

The faxes were of the usual "please play this for me" variety, except for several pages that looked like copies of newspaper articles. He found the cover letter accompanying them and saw that it was from the reference librarian in Annapolis.

*Attached are articles from* The Capital, *the Annapolis daily newspaper, relating to the people on the list you gave me. I found the information by checking last year's papers for the dates you gave me on the list. It actually turned out to be quite a simple task, and as you can see, there is one possible connection between these people. I hope this is helpful to you. Give my best to Grace.*

Linc read the first article. Then the second. By the time he'd finished the third, he was certain he understood the connection. And if he were right, Susanna was in grave danger.

Dropping the faxes to the floor, he pulled the phone book from his desk drawer. Within minutes, he had reservations on the next flight to Washington.

The gray dawn light was slipping through Adam's bedroom window when Kim awakened Wednesday morning, and she could hear the patter of rain against the glass. She rolled over to see Adam sitting up against the headboard, leaning into the light from his night table lamp as he sketched on the pad propped against his knees. A dream, no doubt. She smiled sleepily, searching her own head for dreams from the night before, but finding only hazy images and details too thin to grasp.

Obviously, though, Adam was having no such difficulty. He was sketching furiously, and she sat up to peer over his shoulder. He either didn't notice or didn't mind the intrusion. His sketch was of a garden scene—a vegetable garden, with winding vines and huge squash and a dozen or so sunflowers edging one side.

"Interesting," she said.

"I'm going to skip working on the mural today." Adam began sketching a picket fence behind the sunflowers. "I want to get started on this painting."

"It's raining out anyway." She suddenly remembered what day it was. November thirteenth, the next date on the hit list. She still had seen no mention of the bizarre list either in the paper or on the news.

"Today was supposed to be the day for that next guy on the list to be . . . you know," she said.

"Oh, right." Adam stopped sketching briefly. He kissed her

cheek where it rested on his shoulder. "Don't worry about it. I'm sure it's all been taken care of."

"I hope so. You'd think there would have been something on the news, though, wouldn't you?"

"Trust me, Kim. The cops could not possibly ignore the letter I wrote." He started to draw again, and she rolled onto her back and stretched. She could hear Cody babbling contentedly to himself in Liam's room.

"I'd better get up," she said. "I have a ton of work to do today." It wasn't a complaint. She welcomed having her workday spread out in front of her and a paycheck promised at the end of the week. Standing up, she pulled on her robe. "Are we still on for painting together tonight?"

"You bet, although I have to warn you, I might be completely immersed in this by then." He nodded toward his sketch pad. "Sometimes I get so caught up in what I'm working on I don't even notice who's around. That hasn't happened in a long time, but I have a feeling this particular piece is going to—"

"Don't worry," she interrupted him. "Nothing would please me more than to see you lost in your painting."

She got dressed and made breakfast for herself and Cody. Adam was still propped up in his bed by the time she peeked into his room to say good-bye.

"I'll see you tonight," she said.

He barely glanced up from his work. "Okay," he said. "See you later."

She spent the day at her computer, stopping only long enough to take Cody for a walk. It was getting cold out and garage sale season was over. She would have to spend money soon on winter clothes. Thrift stores, maybe.

She returned to Adam's at seven that night, and he greeted her with a quick kiss at the back door. "Hi," he said. "Come see."

She followed him upstairs and into his studio, where the painting he'd been working on all day was well on its way to completion. The sketch he'd made that morning had been transformed into a canvas filled with those intense Soria colors—the yellow of the sunflowers, blue of the sky.

"I love it." She stood back to take it in. "The colors are fabulous."

"I've had a great day," he said. "Don't mind me if I ignore you, all right?"

She didn't mind a bit. She settled Cody in Liam's bed and had just returned to the studio when the doorbell rang.

"Oh, I forgot," Adam looked distracted. "That's probably Cherise. She said she'd stop by to pick up the painting of the sailboats for the gallery." He set down his brush and wiped his hands on a rag.

"I can give it to her," she said. She knew he didn't want to be pulled away from the studio.

"Would you? It's ready to go. It's wrapped and standing by the front door." He looked at her gratefully. "Thanks, Kim."

"You're welcome." She went downstairs and opened the front door.

Cherise stood in the porch light, a wide grin on her face.

"Hey, lady!" She stepped into the room and grabbed Kim by the wrist. "Haven't seen you in a while."

Kim couldn't help but smile at gallery owner's boisterous greeting. "I know," she said. "It's good to see you."

"Where's the man?"

"Upstairs in his studio. Completely engrossed in a new painting."

"Oh, that is music to my ears!" Cherise looked down at the wrapped painting at Kim's side. "I gotta see this one right now, though. Do you mind?"

"Of course not. Come into the kitchen." She led the way. "Want something hot to drink? How about some cocoa?"

"Sounds good to me." Cherise unwrapped the painting on the kitchen counter, while Kim filled mugs with water and hot chocolate mix and put them in the microwave.

"Oh, this is a beauty." Cherise propped the painting against the cabinets. She stood back to look at it, and Kim turned around to see the familiar trees and sailboats.

"That's a Soria, all right," Cherise said. "I'm so glad he's painting again." she cocked her head at Kim. "I have the feeling you're behind that, huh?"

"Oh, I don't know." Kim licked the cold cocoa from her spoon before putting it in the sink. "Maybe enough time's passed, finally."

The microwave beeped and she took out the mugs and handed one of them to Cherise.

"Thanks, hon." Cherise sat down at the table. "And you're painting too, Jessie told me. When are you going to have something for me to hang in my gallery?"

Kim laughed. "I hope you're not holding your breath. I'm no Adam Soria. Besides, I don't have much time to paint. I've gotten a few word processing jobs, finally. They're keeping me busy."

"Well, at least one of the three of you is bringing in some money."

It took Kim a minute to realize who the "three of them" were. Jessie, Adam, and herself. She liked being considered part of a trio.

"Adam has a little bit of the insurance money left," Cherise said, "but Jessie must be living on her good looks." She shook her head. "I'll tell you, the quicker Adam can turn out more paintings like that one"—she pointed to the canvas on the counter—"the quicker he can make himself a living again. People love his work. Tourists come by, asking where they can see paintings done by the mural painter. I show them what I have in the gallery, and they always want to buy one." She took a sip of her cocoa. "I swear, they'd buy a painting right that second, but Adam's so weird about it, you know what I mean? He won't give me permission to make a sale for him. Always wants to know first. He likes to come down and meet the people buying his work. He's crazy, if you ask me. A couple months ago, this elderly couple came in and they wanted to buy that one with the leaves—you know the one I mean?"

Kim nodded. It was one of her favorites.

"But I couldn't reach Adam, couldn't reach him, kept trying, and they finally had to leave. Frustrating! I told him, 'Adam, you need to carry a pager.' Turns out he was over at Computer Wizard, returning a loaner computer or something like that. I asked him, is that as important as selling a painting? I said, if you're going to run around—"

Kim did not hear another word out of Cherise's mouth. Her hand holding the cup of cocoa froze halfway to her mouth. "What did you say?" she asked. "He was returning a loaner computer?"

"You know, a computer the store lends out when you . . . well, I don't know how all that stuff works." She gave an annoyed wave of her hand. "I'm computer illiterate and plan to stay that way. Anyhow, I told Adam he'd better just forget about computers and pick up his paintbrush. But back then, he really didn't care. Now though—" She interrupted herself to lean closer to Kim. "Are you all right, honey? You look a little green."

Kim stood up, her legs shaking. "I'm fine. I just . . . the chocolate's a little too rich for me, I think." She dumped her cocoa into the sink.

"Oh, no." Cherise leaned back in her chair. "That man better not have knocked you up already."

"Cherise!" Kim tried to smile, but she wasn't sure if the effort was successful.

Cherise stood up. "Can I disturb him? I want to see what he's working on."

"Go ahead up," Kim said. "I don't think he'll mind."

Cherise carried her cup up the stairs, and Kim sat down at the table again. She felt truly sick.

*It can't be.*

It had to be a coincidence. Probably hundreds of people borrowed computers from Computer Wizard. But wouldn't Adam have mentioned that he had been one of them when she told him about the history of her own computer? Wouldn't he have nodded knowingly when she'd talked about it being a loaner?

*The invitation.* She nearly groaned out loud. She'd thought Ellen had been behind that unexpected invitation to Adam's show shortly after her arrival, but Ellen had denied knowing anything about it. Had Adam somehow discovered that she'd bought his computer? Had he intentionally befriended her in an attempt to get his file back, or to see if she knew anything? She thought of how attentive he'd been to her at that show, ignoring friends he'd had for years to talk with her.

She stared blindly at the painting on the counter. She had to stay calm. Think this through.

Was it Adam who had ransacked her apartment? Surely he couldn't be responsible for the explosions. For *murder*. She thought of the gun in his night table drawer and a fresh tide of nausea washed over her. Thank God, the police had the disk.

*No*. The police did *not* have the disk. Not if Adam were the killer. He had been so quick to ask her to let him take the information to the police, so quick to suggest that she not send it herself. The pieces of the puzzle fit together with sickening ease. Adam had betrayed her. She thought of how kind he'd been to her, how loving he seemed. He'd even put that deadbolt lock on her door. What a joke!

Her head spun, and she pressed her palms to her temples. It *didn't* fit together. It didn't make sense. Why would Adam want to hurt people? He was a kind-hearted person. She knew about sociopaths—people who could harm others without regret, all the while presenting themselves as caring, even charming, individuals—but she could not force Adam into that category. How could he have sat in his living room and calmly watched the horrific aftermath of that bombing at Sellers, Sellers, and Wittaker if he'd had anything to do with it? With a sinking heart, she remembered that he hadn't. "I can't watch this," he'd said. Then he'd turned the television off.

She walked over to the counter where she'd left her purse and dug out a copy of the list. What were these people to him?

In addition to the names of individuals, there was one other company besides Sellers, Sellers, and Wittaker on the list. Weirs and Taft, targeted for January. It sounded like another law firm. On a whim, she pulled the phonebook from the shelf next to the phone and turned to the yellow pages. She looked under lawyers, and what she saw made her gasp. Two full-page ads, back to back. One for Sellers, Sellers, and Wittaker, the other for Weirs and Taft. In large letters, the Sellers ad proclaimed a specialization in "criminal traffic offenses and DWI." Weirs and Taft promised an "experienced and thorough defense of DWI offenses." They defended drunk drivers. Was that the connection? She checked some of the other names on the hit list to see if they too were attorneys, but none of them appeared to be.

She looked again at the name of the person targeted to be a victim tonight. Ryan Geary. Nine o'clock, it read next to his name. She could picture his house on that big lot in West Annapolis.

She should call the police. Better yet, she should drive to the police station and hand them the list. Maybe she could get away with it. Lucy's friend, Frank, hadn't recognized her or thought her suspicious. Why would anyone else? But there had to be a less risky way for her to keep Ryan Geary safe tonight.

She heard Cherise's footsteps on the stairs and quickly put away the phone book.

"Can't wait till he's done with that one." Cherise set her empty mug in the sink.

"No, neither can I." Kim busied herself wrapping the painting again. Her fingers shook so fiercely she could barely tie the cord around the package.

"And the one you're working on has real promise, girlfriend." Cherise folded her arms across her chest and leaned against the counter. "You get upstairs and finish it."

Kim nodded with a forced smile as she handed Cherise the painting.

"You sure you're okay, honey?" Cherise touched her shoulder. "I swear if you don't look like a woman who just found out she's pregnant. You white women always get that sort of green, paley look around your eyes when you're expecting."

Kim rolled her eyes. "I'm not pregnant, Cherise. I just need a good night's sleep."

"Well then, you better tell Adam to keep his hands to himself tonight, hear?"

Kim tried to laugh as she walked Cherise to the door. She did feel that same sort of buckling-knee sick she'd felt when she was carrying Cody. But this sickness had nothing to do with pregnancy.

She climbed the stairs to the studio, knowing that the man she would see up there was not the same man she had left a half hour ago. He'd suddenly become a monster in her eyes, a monster she'd decided she would stay with every minute that night. She would not let him out of her sight. She would not give him the chance to harm anyone.

"Hi," Adam gave her a distracted smile. He was painting some of the greenery in front of the picket fence.

She looked at the sunflower-filled garden taking shape on the canvas. That painting simply could not be the work of a man about to kill someone. It had been nearly a month since the last bombing. Adam was much happier now than he'd been then. Even if he hadn't given the information on the list to the police, he had probably meant it when he said the bombings were a thing of the past. Whatever demons had driven him to those acts of violence were gone now. They had to be.

She tried to get back to work on her own painting, but the brush trembled in her hand. He did not seem to notice her anxiety or her silence, however; he was too engrossed in what he was doing.

Tomorrow she would have to find a way to contact the police—as well as a way to back out of her relationship with Adam. But how could she? He knew far too much about her.

She was so preoccupied with her own thoughts that it was a while before she realized that Adam was anxious himself. He kept checking his watch and leaning back from his easel to look out the window.

"You seem a little uptight tonight," she ventured finally.

"Do I?" He sounded completely innocent. "I guess I have a lot on my mind. I've been so focused on painting today that I haven't had much time to get anything else done." He looked at his watch again, and she glanced at her own. It was nearly eight-thirty.

"Let's call Jessie and get her over here," Adam suggested suddenly. "I'm in the mood to whip up something to eat. Spaghetti maybe. How does that sound?" He had already set down his brush and was reaching for the phone.

"Sure," she said. She was surprised by the suggestion, but it sounded like a great idea to her. They would get Jessie over here and eat and talk until late, and Ryan Geary would be safe. And *she'd* feel safer with Jessie around. The thought of those nights she'd spent alone with Adam—and his gun—made her shudder.

She continued painting as Adam dialed Jessie's number, but she was watching him from the corner of her eye. With the phone held to his ear, Adam tapped the side of the table with his fingers. He drew in a few deep breaths and blew them out through his mouth. She had never seen that agitation in him before.

Abruptly, Adam hung up the phone. "I just remembered we don't have any tomato sauce," he said. "I'm going to run out and get some."

"*No*." She set down her brush. "I mean, that's silly. We don't need to have spaghetti. We can find something else. Or order a pizza."

But he was already heading down the stairs. She followed him, catching up to him as he took his jacket from the hall closet. His hands shook as he tried to button the jacket, and she had the sickening thought that he had not called Jessie at all. He'd called the Geary residence, wanting to make sure that Ryan was home before making the trip over there.

"I'll go with you." She actually grabbed his arm, but he didn't seem to notice her panic.

"No," he said sharply. "I won't be long." He brushed his lips over her cheek and was gone. A sense of helplessness consumed her as she watched him walk quickly to his car.

She looked at her own watch. Twenty of nine. In her mind, she suddenly saw the television images of those two children killed in the Sellers, Sellers, and Wittaker office. Did Ryan Geary have children?

"You have no choice," she said out loud. She had to call the police. In the kitchen, she once again pulled the list from her purse, and she had the phone in her hand when it startled her by ringing. She stared at the receiver, uncertain what to do, and the answering machine picked up before she could decide. She felt dazed as she watched the outgoing message tape turn on its spool. Then, suddenly, Noel's voice filled the air.

"Hey, Adam," Noel said. "Did you happen to catch that *Missing Persons* show tonight? I'm certain Kim Stratton and her little boy were on it. Her real name's Susanna somebody, and she's from Colorado. You might want to give her a heads up. She's a good lady, not to mention a good typist." Noel laughed. "I need her to stick around. Besides, I'd hate to see her get screwed."

Kim closed her eyes, one hand gripping the counter. She was trapped. They'd shown her picture, told her story, on TV. Who'd seen it? Who'd be the one to turn her in?

No time to waste. She lifted the receiver again, and her fingers felt numb as she dialed. She could do this. She had to. No reason she had to identify herself. She'd make the call, race home, and if the coast looked clear, she could get her money and the duffel bag and her felt-tipped marker before she disappeared, once again.

She could be far away by the time anyone realized Kim Stratton was missing. South. This time she would drive south. She thought about the work in her computer, the paycheck due her on Friday.

*No damn choice,* she told herself.

"Is this an emergency?" the dispatcher asked when she answered the call.

"Yes," Kim said. "I believe someone is planting a bomb to go off at nine o'clock at the residence on . . . " Her hands trembled as she flattened the list on the counter. "Two-oh-seven North Plain Street."

"What is your name?" the dispatcher asked.

"Doesn't matter." She knew that Adam's address was probably flashing on the dispatcher's computer screen as they spoke. She had to get out of there, fast. "Just trust me," Kim said, "the person who's responsible for the explosions that have killed people around Annapolis is about to strike again. At that address." She hung up before the woman could ask her any more questions.

She ran up to Liam's bedroom, where she literally snatched Cody out of the bed and carried him downstairs. He was too sleepy to protest, and he was a warm and heavy weight against her chest and shoulder. She grabbed her jacket and his from the sofa in the living room and raced out to her car.

Her hands shook as she buckled Cody into his car seat, and she'd gotten in behind the wheel when he suddenly began to cry.

"Munka, munka," he said.

The monkey. She bit her lip.

"We have to leave it, sweetheart," she said.

"Munka!"

The thought of leaving that raggedy old stuffed animal behind forever chipped at her heart.

"Wait right here," she said to her son. She ran inside again, ter- rified that the police would pull up in front of Adam's house at any second and catch her there. But she grabbed the monkey and was back in the car in less than a minute.

She drove away from Adam's neighborhood as quickly as she dared, then slowed her speed to the legal limit for the rest of the drive home. The last thing she needed was to be stopped for a ticket.

She tried to plan what she would do when she reached her apartment. Had Lucy or Ellen seen the show? Ellen didn't watch much TV, but Lucy was another story. Could she get in and out of her apartment without either of them noticing her? Thank God she'd thought to keep the bulk of her money at the apartment. Forget taking the computer, though. The felt-tipped marker was the most important thing. The first chance she got, she'd stop to alter her license plate number with it. That thought gave her some comfort, but when she glanced behind her at her son, who was cuddling his monkey, eyes at half mast and thumb in his mouth, she was overwhelmed with the sense of having failed him. She was a terrible mother, uprooting him again. Uprooting both of them. How many times would she have to do that?

She was nearly to her apartment when a unsettling thought crossed her mind. That address she'd given the 911 dispatcher. There was something wrong with it. Hadn't she told her North Plain Street? That wasn't right. She pressed on the brakes so hard that her car skidded to the side of the road, and she yanked the list from her purse with a sense of dread. Switching on the overhead light, she scanned the names. Ryan Geary. Pioneer Way.

*No.* How could she have done that? In her nervousness, she'd given the dispatcher the next address on the list rather than the Geary address.

She looked at her watch. Ten minutes to nine. There was no time to drive to her apartment and call the police from there. She made a left turn at the next corner, wondering if she was thinking straight. This was crazy. She stepped on the gas and headed toward West Annapolis.

Turning into the Geary's neighborhood, she spotted a man walking a dog on the sidewalk. She pulled close to him and rolled down her window.

"Call the police," she said to the man. "Tell them to go to seven-seventy Pioneer Way. It's an emergency. Hurry!"

The man looked at her blankly for a moment, but as she drove away, she could see him in her rearview mirror, running in the opposite direction down the sidewalk.

"Cody, I'm so sorry," she said to her sleeping son as she drove.

"I don't know what's going to happen, but I tried, kiddo. I tried to keep us safe."

She was crying by the time she reached the Geary house. It looked as she remembered it, set apart from its neighbors, small patches of woods on either side of its broad lot. The front porch light was on, along with a few lights in the second story windows. Someone was home. Kim spotted Adam's car parked in front of the wooded lot to the left of the house, but Adam himself was nowhere in sight. Uncertain what to do, she parked her own car behind his.

Then she spotted him. He was crouching in the woods not far from the street. He was looking at the house, and he did not seem to notice her car. What was he waiting for?

She got out of her car and locked it quickly. She hated leaving Cody alone, but had no option. He would be safer in the car than he would be with her.

She ran as quietly as she could toward the woods. She slipped into the trees, nearly tripping over their roots in the darkness and cringing at the rustle of leaves under her feet.

Adam started as she neared him and spun around. "Kim!" His face was lit only by the light coming from the house, but she saw the shock in his eyes. "What the hell are you doing here?"

She stopped a few feet front him. "I know what you're doing, Adam," she said, her voice shaking. She remembered his gun. Did he have it with him? What if he killed her? What would happen to Cody?

"Sh," Adam said. "Get out of here, Kim."

"No, I won't. I can't let you do it. I called the police."

He looked at her, and even in the darkness she could detect anger in his features. "You shouldn't have done that," he said. "I told you I'd take care of it."

"Where is it?" she asked. "Where's the bomb?" Her eyes searched the ground around him for the package.

"You don't know what you're talking about, and I don't have time to explain it to you. You have to get out of here." He turned back to the house, and a terrible thought passed through her mind: maybe he'd already planted the bomb. She peered through the trees, but couldn't see the front porch clearly from where she stood. Maybe some member of the Geary family had taken the package inside and now Adam was merely waiting for the explosion, waiting for whatever satisfaction he could get from hurting Ryan Geary.

"Adam, did you—" Her attention was suddenly drawn to the street, where a taxi swerved to a stop in front of the woods. Kim did a double take when a man emerged from the back seat.

"Linc?" she said softly. Then louder, "Linc! Over here!"

"Shush!" Adam suddenly turned on her, pushing against her shoulders and knocking her down. "Shut up, Kim!"

Linc had started toward the house, but turned at the sound of their voices. Kim raised herself to her elbow and called out to him again, and he ran through the trees and was quickly at her side. He bent low to help her up. "What are you doing here?" he asked her. Then he noticed Adam.

"Get down, you two, and shut up!" Adam demanded.

"Are you Adam?" Linc asked, pulling Kim to her feet. "He's the artist, right?" he asked Kim. "Has he already left the bomb?"

"I don't . . . " She shook her head, unable to believe Linc was truly standing in front of her. "How did you know—"

"I know all the people on the list were convicted of drunk driving, and—"

"Oh." Kim's hand flew to her mouth. "That's it!" she said. "I should have—"

Adam suddenly turned on them both. "Look, neither of you knows what's going on, and you've got to get out of here!" He looked toward the patch of woods on the other side of the house. "There!" he said suddenly. He sprang forward and started to run through the trees toward the house, but Linc was too quick for him. He lunged toward Adam and tackled him to the ground. Adam went down hard, and Kim heard him groan. She saw him roll over, blood on his forehead. Linc crouched next to him, one knee on his chest.

She dropped to the ground by the two men. "We'll hold him here," she said to Linc. "The police are on their way."

"Then get out of here, Susanna," Linc said. "Leave before they come. They don't have to know you were involved in any of this."

Already, she could hear the faint sound of a siren in the distance, and she felt frozen to her spot on the forest floor as she tried to think. Maybe she still had time to escape. But how would Linc ever be able to explain his involvement in this mess?

Looking down at Adam, she couldn't help but feel sympathy for him. Adam touched his hand to his forehead, then stared at the blood on his fingers. He tried to get up, but winced and fell back to the ground even before Linc kneed him again in the chest.

Adam looked at Kim, his eyes narrow with pain. He grabbed her hand. "It's not me, Kim, " he said softly. "It's Jessie. I think she's going around to the rear of the house."

"What's he talking about?" Linc looked at her. "Who's Jessie?"

In a horrified instant, she understood. She looked toward the street, but there was no sign of the police and the siren was still weak and distant. They would never arrive in time.

"Stay with him," she said to Linc.

She ran out of the woods, cutting through the side yard to reach the rear of the house. The small back porch was dark, but the moonlight illuminated a wide, grassy yard interrupted only by a swing set.

She crossed the back yard and stopped short when she came face to face with Jessie, who was emerging from the woods, an express mail package in her arms. She stopped walking when she spotted Kim.

"Jessie," Kim said. "Don't do it."

"This isn't any of your business," Jessie said.

"Please, Jess. Put the box down. Or give it to me." She reached her trembling arms out in front of her. "I understand why you're doing it, but please. Forget the vendetta. It's only hurting you in the long run."

"A vendetta." Jessie looked very calm, and a small smile played at her lips. "Good word," she said. "And I admit that's what it is. Revenge, pure and simple. It feels great." She started walking toward the dark back porch of the house again, but Kim darted in front of her.

"If you leave the package, I'm only going to warn the people who live here not to open it," Kim said. "So why bother?"

"You won't warn anyone," Jessie said calmly. She raised her right hand, and for the first time Kim saw the gun. It looked like the gun from Adam's night table, and it was pointing directly at her. She had the feeling Jessie wouldn't hesitate to use it.

The wail of the siren was closer now, but Jessie did not seem to hear it, and Kim wasn't certain which of them had more to fear from that sound. She raised her own arm slowly to point to the swing set in the back yard. "Did you see the swings, Jessie?" she asked. "Children live here. They could get hurt."

Jessie shook her head. "There's only one person's name on the package. He'll be the only one—"

"What about the children at Sellers, Sellers, and Wittaker? That bomb didn't have their names on it, did it?"

Jessie flinched, and Kim knew she'd hit a nerve. The magnitude of the carnage at the law firm had been an accident.

The barrel of the gun had drifted downward, but now Jessie lifted it again, pointing it at her once more. Kim had to make herself hold her ground. She knew firsthand the damage a gun could do, and she wanted to turn around and run from it.

Her throat was dry, and she swallowed hard. "Liam and Molly were innocent victims," she said. "But so were those children at the law office."

"Please don't talk about them." Jessie hunched up her shoulders as though she could make them reach her ears and block out Kim's voice. The sirens were very close now. Jessie had to be able to hear them.

"And so are the children in this house," Kim said. "They're innocent, too. Just as innocent as Molly and—"

"Stop it!" Jessie said. "I said don't talk about them."

"Are you going to take that risk again?" Kim asked. "Hurting, maybe killing some more little kids?"

Jessie suddenly dropped to her knees, and Kim jumped, fearful that the gun would go off.

"I never meant for those kids to get hurt," Jessie said. She was crying. It was too dark for Kim to see her tears, but she could hear them in Jessie's voice. "Their mother should never have brought them into work with her."

"I know," Kim said. She could hear car doors slamming in front of the house, more sirens. Any minute, it would all be over. Jessie's vendetta, and her own escape. "I know you would never intentionally hurt any children," she continued, and she could hear the tears in her own voice. "And I'm sure you don't want to hurt the children who live here, either."

Jessie was sobbing. The gun shook with the trembling of her body.

"Please put the gun down, Jessie," Kim said.

To her surprise, Jessie obeyed her. She set the gun on the ground next to her, and Kim closed her eyes briefly in relief. She took a step forward, but Jessie immediately raised her hand in the air, palm forward, to stop her.

"Stay back!" she warned.

Kim stopped walking, horrified to see that Jessie had slipped the fingers of her other hand under the lid of the box.

"Jessie, no!" She took another step closer, but Jessie quickly grabbed the gun again, and Kim froze.

"I just wanted Molly back," Jessie said, a catch in her voice. "That's all I wanted." Her fingers still in the box, Jessie quickly lay down on top of it. Before Kim could even think of reacting, the world exploded with a burst of light and noise. She heard herself scream as she fell backwards, and a searing pain cut across her forehead. In an instant, all was black.

The air was filled with smoke and sirens when she opened her eyes again. She tried to get up, but someone was holding her down.

"You're all right." It was Linc's voice, and she leaned back against him.

She was vaguely aware that he was moving her, turning her, and she knew there was something he didn't want her to see. "Linc?" Her voice sounded weak and far away.

"You're all right," he said again. She felt his hands on her shoulders, and she wondered if he was trying to support her or if he was simply holding onto her to keep her from running away again. Maybe they were both the same thing.

She heard voices, so loud they hurt her ears, and wide bands of light cut through the darkness. The earth vibrated as people ran past her. She had the feeling they were running in circles, and she closed her eyes because the sounds and lights were making her dizzy.

*Cody.*

She tried to sit up, but there was no strength left in her body. Letting herself lean back against Linc, she sat still as a statue, waiting for her fate. She knew she would not be running away again.

36

There were more police officers at the hospital than there were doctors and nurses. At least it seemed that way to Kim. Two of the officers, a stern-faced young woman and a man who reminded Kim of her father, were sitting with her and Linc in the small waiting room, but they were not the same two who had been questioning her for the last hour. She had not bothered to lie. The jig was up, and she knew it.

"What time is it?" she asked Linc. He was sitting close to her on the hard, vinyl-upholstered couch, and Cody was on her lap. The three of them formed a tight, inseparable unit. For a little while longer, anyway.

"A couple minutes after midnight." Linc answered without looking at his watch.

Kim had completely lost track of the time. All she knew was that a child protection worker, armed with her own set of questions, was on her way to the hospital, and that unless a miracle occurred, the social worker would take Cody from her. Kim held onto him now as he slept on her lap. The social worker would have to wrench him from her arms.

Kim had come to the hospital by ambulance, Linc had told her, but she had no memory of the trip, nor did she remember the doctor stitching the cut above her eye. She'd been in shock, Linc said. As far as she was concerned, she was still in shock. She couldn't string two coherent thoughts together in her head.

"I still don't get it," she said to Linc. "How did you know where I was?"

Linc explained, for the third or fourth time, how he had learned about the connection between the victims through the librarian at the Naval Academy, how he'd figured out that "the artist," whose family had been killed by a drunk driver, was probably behind the deadly explosions. "So, I knew that Adam would not have taken the information to the police, as he'd told you he would. I had the addresses on the list you'd left with me, and I thought I could try to intercept Adam myself, or at least to provide some warning to the residents in the house."

"And why didn't you just call the police?"

"Why do you think?" he asked. "I was afraid I'd be leading them straight to you."

Another police officer, a dark-haired woman, came to the door of the waiting room.

"We've finished taking Mr. Soria's statement," she said to Kim. "He'd like to talk to you now."

"I'll keep Cody here," Linc said. He reached for him, but Kim held tight.

"No." She pictured the social worker arriving at the hospital while she was in with Adam, marching into the room, snatching Cody from Linc's arms, and spiriting him away to some undisclosed location.

"I won't let anyone take him without talking to you first," Linc said. "You don't need to worry."

Reluctantly, she shifted Cody to Linc's arms, grateful that the little boy had slept through the entire adventure. The thought of him being taken from her while he was still asleep was intolerable to her, though. She couldn't imagine him waking up surrounded by strangers.

She followed the policewoman down the hall to one of the treatment rooms. The room was cold and sterile and made her shiver the second she walked inside. Adam was propped up in a hospital bed, a bandage around his head and a smear of blood on the shoulder of the blue hospital gown. He looked pale and sick, and her heart went out to him. She pulled away from the policewoman to take his hand.

"I'm so sorry about Jessie, Adam," she said, sitting down in the chair next to his bed. "I'm sorry for everything."

Adam squeezed her hand and shut his eyes. "I need to tell you . . . to try to explain things to you," he said slowly. His voice was hoarse, and she had to lean close to hear him. From the corner of her eye, she saw the policewoman sit down in the chair by the door.

"Are you all right?" Kim asked. "Is it just your head?"

"Ribs." Adam opened his eyes, squinting against the light in the room. "Two of them broken. That boyfriend of yours packs a wallop." He tried to smile, but didn't come close to succeeding.

"Adam, I'm—"

"Listen to me," he interrupted her. "I want you to know some things."

"I think I know everything," she said. "I know Jessie was targeting drunk drivers. The people on the list—the 'one adult' or 'elderly couple'—they were the people who were killed in those accidents, right?"

"There's more."

She couldn't imagine what more there could be, but she leaned even closer to the bed. "I'm listening," she said.

Adam closed his eyes again, a deep line in his forehead below the bandage, and it was a few seconds before he seemed able to speak.

"Molly was Jessie's daughter," he said finally.

His words didn't register right away. "Molly was *what*?" she asked.

He looked directly at her. "Jessie got pregnant when she was fifteen. She knew she couldn't raise a child, and our parents were not very supportive. But since Dana and I were already married, we decided to adopt her baby so that Jessie could always be close to her."

"Oh, my God," Kim said. "No wonder Jessie felt such a bond with your children."

"Molly was everything to Jessie," Adam said. "She and I were both nearly insane with fury when that driver got off so easily after the accident. Actually, I guess we *were* insane. Neither of us cared if we lived or died. Then we started thinking about all the other families who had suffered the way we were suffering, all the drunk drivers who were still out there, free to kill again. Jessie joked about taking those drivers out, one by one. At least, I thought she was joking." Adam gingerly touched the bandage wrapped around his head. "I realized after the break-in at your apartment, when you told me about the information on the computer, that Jessie had actually gone through with it. I didn't want to believe it, but I—"

"I still don't understand," she interrupted. "I thought *you* owned the computer before me."

"Uh uh. It was Jessie's. She used a loaner computer while hers was being repaired. One morning, she asked me if I could take it back to Computer Wizard for her and pick up her repaired computer. I said I would do it that night, but then my schedule changed, and I was able to take it that afternoon. I didn't realize there was information on it that Jessie wanted to delete before it was returned. She was furious with me when I told her I'd taken it back." He looked into space for a minute, as if he were remembering that scene. "I never understood why she was so angry—until the day someone broke into your apartment." He returned his gaze to Kim. "When you told me what you'd found on your computer, I knew what had happened. Jessie had called Computer Wizard to see if she could get the computer back to take her file off it, and they told her it had already been sold, but that the person who bought it had called to tell them someone had left a file on the disk. They said you didn't leave your phone number, but the salesman thought it would be okay to give Jessie your address, since you'd seemed concerned about getting the information to its rightful owner."

"So she knew where I lived. Was it Jessie who sent me the invitation to your show, then?"

"Yes. She followed you around for a few days, I guess, and knew that you were interested in the murals."

Kim remembered the feeling of being followed during her early days in Annapolis. She had not been imagining it after all.

"Those kids at the law firm," Adam said. "I can't tell you how upset I was when I realized Jessie was behind that . . . catastrophe. And I wanted to tell you. We were in your apartment and you were telling me all about your life and your running away and I was lying to you through my teeth."

"You said you'd go to the police with the disc and—"

"What I did was go to Jessie's house that night when she was asleep. I checked out her basement. She has a little workroom down there, and it looked like an explosives factory. Then I couldn't deny it to myself anymore. But I couldn't turn her in, Kim. She's . . . she *was* my sister. She was all I had left, and she was obviously sick and needed help. So I talked to her instead of to the police. I told her I knew what she was doing, and she admitted everything. We argued and she cried a lot, but she finally promised me there'd be no more bombings. When I called her last night, though, and got no answer, I was afraid she was on her way to the next house on her list. I was hoping I was wrong. I thought I'd go to that address, and if she did show up, I could head her off." His eyes filled with tears. "But it didn't work out that way."

"Maybe if I hadn't been there, you could have stopped her," Kim said. "But I thought you were the person behind—"

"I know, and I can't blame you for that," Adam said. "Or for any of this, Kim. You're not responsible for what happened last night."

She looked at their hands resting together on the bed. It would be a long time before she could shake her guilt over what had taken place the night before.

"What will happen to you and Cody?" Adam asked.

She kept her eyes on their hands. "Well, Cody will go to my ex-husband and his wife." Her tears started again, and it was a minute before she could continue. "They love him. At least I know Peggy does. She'll take good care of him."

Adam stroked the back of her hand with his thumb. "That's not fair," he said. "You couldn't be a better mother."

She tried to smile. "As for me, I don't know exactly what will happen. I've been told I'm a felon. I suppose they lock felons up. Right now, I don't really care." She shrugged her shoulders. "When I think about my life without Cody, I just . . . I don't see the point."

"Don't talk that way," Adam said quickly. "You sound like Jessie."

Kim tried to wipe her tears away with her fingers, but new ones quickly took their place. "I feel like it's my fault," she said. "If

I hadn't interfered last night . . . if I hadn't tried to stop her, she'd be alive."

"Yes, but someone else wouldn't be," Adam said. "There were five people in that house. You did what you had to do, Kim. You saved at least one life, probably more."

Kim bit her lip. "And Jessie saved mine, you know."

Adam nodded. "Yes. They told me. They said you were so close to the bomb that you would have been badly injured if she hadn't . . . covered it with her body."

Linc poked his head in the door, Cody still in his arms. "The social worker's here, Susanna," he said.

"I'll be right there." She turned back to Adam. "I have to go," she said.

"I'm sorry you had to get mixed up in all of this, Kim," he said. He ran the back of his hand lightly up her arm. "You and Cody mean a lot to me."

"You've meant a lot to us, too."

He smiled at her. "Susanna, huh?"

She nodded.

"So, how is Susanna different from Kim?"

She sighed. "Kim is brave and independent and gutsy. Susanna is weak and needy. But right now, they're both the same person." She glanced at the door leading to the hallway. "Both of them are terrified of walking out that door," she said.

"They've both been the same person all along, Kim," Adam said. "And don't you forget it."

$\mathcal{S}$usanna and Linc arrived at the hotel close to two in the morning, after they'd finished talking with the police at the hospital. Susanna was exhausted and sick to her stomach. She felt as if she'd been riding a roller coaster all night. She'd been nervously waiting to be driven to police headquarters when she was told that charges against her had been dropped.

At first she had not understood. She was standing in the hallway of the emergency room, numbly waiting to be handcuffed or whatever they would have to do to her to take her to the police station, when the policewoman brought her the news.

"You're free," the policewoman said. Susanna stared at her blankly, and the woman continued. "It happens a lot once a child's been located and taken into custody. The custodial parent is really only interested in getting his or her child back."

Susanna never would have figured Jim for one of those parents who would drop charges. Somewhere deep inside her, she knew she should be elated by that news, yet she had no room in her for joy just then.

"And Cody?" she'd whispered.

The social worker who'd questioned her earlier appeared next to the policewoman. "Tyler will be in protective custody overnight," she said. "Colorado's sending a child protection worker out here in the morning, and she'll take Tyler back with her. You can be on the same plane, if you like," she added. "We know you have a good relationship with your son, and it would probably help if you were with him for the flight."

She guessed the authorities were confident she'd be unable to kidnap Cody when she was thirty thousand feet above the ground.

She was sick most of the night. Linc sat up with her in the hotel room, holding her, talking quietly with her, between her miserable bouts in the bathroom. Each time she thought of Cody—he would *always* be Cody to her—alone and confused in some stranger's home, she was overcome by a wrenching pain that felt as if it were turning her inside out.

"Why couldn't he have stayed with me overnight?" she said to Linc. "This is cruel. He doesn't know what's going on. He'll wake up in the morning surrounded by strangers."

Linc did not have to answer for her to know the reason she was not with Cody tonight: they were afraid she'd take off with him again. And the truth was, she might have tried.

In the morning, she visited Adam in the hospital. She brought him a sketchbook and some pencils, but she knew it would be a while before he felt like using them. He was understandably subdued, and she was not much better.

"Jessie said I was using you to hide from my grief," he said. He looked worse than he had the night before. He was paler, and his face was tight with pain. "She was right in a way. It was easier to be with you than to be with people who'd known Dana, who kept reminding me of Dana and the kids." He gave her a half smile. "That doesn't mean I didn't enjoy our time together, Kim. I truly did."

"I'm worried about you," Susanna said. She was wobbly after the long and sleepless night, and she was living for five o'clock when she'd be able to see Cody. "I'd like to stay in touch with you, if that's all right."

"I hope you will," he said.

She rested her hand on his, aware of an emotional distance between them that she knew was her doing. It was not safe for her to get too close to Adam right now. If she were to feel his loss on top of her own, it would be more than she could bear.

"You have a lot of friends here," she said. "People who care about you. I know they remind you of all you've lost, but you need them now. Don't cut yourself off from them, Adam."

He motioned her closer to him. "I want you to remember something," he said hoarsely. "Remember that, even if Cody is living with his father and stepmother, at least he's alive and healthy. You can always have a future with him."

She began weeping then, not for herself and Cody, but for Adam and the emptiness that awaited him once he left the hospital.

"I'll miss you," she said.

Adam gave her a weak smile. "You'll be Boulder, Colorado's dream artist," he said. "Every town should have one."

Cody looked pale and sleepy when Mary Michaels, the social worker, handed him to Susanna as they waited for the plane. Susanna held him close to her, drawing in gulps of air through her mouth as she tried not to cry. Her crying would only upset her son, and he seemed upset enough as it was. His confusing day away from her and in the midst of strangers had been too much even for this resilient little boy. She could tell.

She sat between Linc and the social worker on the plane, Cody in her lap. Cody clutched the arm of her sweater in one hand, the monkey in the other. His sudden lapse into insecurity broke her heart. He even balked at going to Linc, although Linc was finally able to win him over with a song and a tickle or two.

She looked past Mary Michaels at the clouds outside the window, wishing the flight would go on forever. Jim and Peggy would no doubt be meeting their plane in Denver, with outstretched arms and joyful smiles as they greeted their child. Susanna didn't think she could bear to be the one handing Cody over to them. She doubted she could even watch, and she didn't want to hear them call him Tyler. He'd be so confused.

"Excuse me." She interrupted Mary, who was reading a paperback. "I've been calling my son Cody for the past few months. I'm afraid it's going to confuse him if his father and . . . stepmother call him Tyler. Do you think you could tell them . . . or ask them, if they could call him Cody?"

Mary gave her a kind smile. She came across as a nice woman who did not seem to harbor any ill feelings toward her, and

Susanna had the feeling Mary Michaels knew what it was like to love a child. Still, the social worker obviously had a job to do.

"I can understand why that troubles you," Mary said, "but he hasn't been gone all that long. He'll get used to Tyler again in no time."

Linc squeezed Susanna's hand. He knew that Mary's words gave her little comfort.

The plane bounced a few times as it landed on the runway. It lumbered toward the gate, and as soon as it came to a stop, passengers filled the aisle, opening overhead compartments and lining up to leave. Susanna did not even bother to unfasten her seat belt. Neither did Linc, and Mary seemed to know better than to rush them.

Her throat was tight. "Will they be here?" she asked Mary. "Jim and Peggy? Will they meet the plane?"

"I think so," Mary answered.

The four of them were last to deplane. Linc kept his arm locked around Susanna's shoulders as they entered the waiting area. Susanna expected to see Jim and Peggy at the front of the crowd, but the waiting area was filled with strangers.

"I don't see them, do you?" Mary asked.

Susanna searched the crowd. "No," she said.

Cody started crying and she tried to comfort him. Her outward calm could not fool her baby. He knew she was falling apart inside.

Mary led them to the side of the waiting area, then scanned the crowd one more time. "Let me call the office," she said. She took a step away from Susanna and Linc, then seemed to think better of it. She looked directly at Susanna. "If you still want to hold Tyler, you'll have to come with me to the phone booth," she said.

Susanna followed her obediently, although Linc balked for a second before falling into step next to them. Susanna knew he hated being told what to do, but he kept his mouth shut. He probably knew it would do little good to anger the social worker.

Mary was in the phone booth a long time, and Susanna kept one eye on the social worker, the other on the crowd.

"I feel like I'm going to explode," she said to Linc.

Linc turned her around until she was standing in front of him and began rubbing her shoulders. She closed her eyes and tried to relax, but it was impossible. Every few seconds or so, someone was paged over the loudspeaker, and she strained to hear the names, fully expecting her own to be among them.

Mary finally emerged from the phone booth, shaking her head.

"No one seems to know what the plans are," she said. "I've been told to bring Tyler to Child Protective Services. I guess the parents will be meeting him there."

Susanna looked from Linc to the woman and back again. "Do we take a taxi there or will someone pick us up?" she asked.

"I'm afraid it's just me taking him," Mary said, sympathy in her voice. "I'm sorry."

Linc made a sound of disgust. "Seems like things should have been arranged a little better than this," he said. "Now we've got to turn him over to strangers again."

"I'm sorry, Mr. Sebastian," Mary said. "It might not be ideal, but children survive this sort of thing every day, and I'm sure Tyler will be with his custodial parents in no time." She turned to Susanna. "Let me take him now," she said.

The social worker reached for Cody, but Susanna turned away. If Mary wanted to take him from her, she would have to do more than ask.

Linc gently touched Susanna's arm. "Let him go, Sue," he said. "The easier you are about it, the less anxious he'll be."

She knew he was right. She drew in a breath. "Go with Mrs. Michaels, Cody," she said, her voice as bright as she could make it. "That's it. And here's your monkey to take with you."

"What a good, big boy," Mary said. "Would you like to go for a taxi ride with me?" She turned to Susanna. "I know this is hard," she said. "Worse than hard. You're a good mom. I'll be sure they know that."

Susanna nodded woodenly. She watched as Mary walked away from her, but she could no longer see Cody in the social worker's arms. Only the legs of his monkey were visible. They bounced against Mary's side as she walked.

Susanna took a step after them, but Linc caught her shoulder. Without a word, he turned her toward him, and she buried herself in his arms. That old dark cloud dropped over her again, cutting off her words, her breath, and the two of them stood there in silence.

She felt a soft touch on her back.

"Susanna?" It was a woman's voice.

Pulling away from Linc, Susanna came face to face with Peggy. Instinctively, she recoiled.

"You're too late," Linc said to Peggy. "The social worker already took him away. Why weren't you here to pick him up?"

Peggy didn't even acknowledge him. "Susanna," she repeated, and Susanna noticed the red in her eyes. "Please," Peggy said. "Can we sit down?"

She wanted to sit down. Her legs were rubbery as she and Linc followed Peggy to a nearby grouping of seats.

Peggy sat down, her hands folded tightly in her lap. She licked her lips and looked directly into Susanna's eyes. "Jim and I are separating," she said.

Susanna frowned, unable to register the meaning of the word. "Separating?" she repeated.

"It was my decision," Peggy continued. "So much has changed since you left. I've come to realize that Jim and I have very different values."

"And so you're . . . splitting up?" She was still not certain what Peggy was trying to say.

"Yes."

"Is there a chance of reconciling?" Linc asked.

Peggy's eyes glistened, but only for a second. "None," she said.

Susanna shook her head. "But Cody . . . Tyler . . . "

Peggy's lips tightened. "On his own as a single father, Jim is no longer interested in custody," she said.

Susanna glanced at Linc, not certain she'd heard Peggy correctly. "He doesn't want custody of Tyler?"

"No," Peggy said. "That's why he dropped the charges against you. And that's why Tyler's going into foster care instead of home with Jim and me. They need to evaluate the situation to . . . make sure he'd be safe with you before letting you have him back." She leaned forward quickly to cover Susanna's hand with her own. "And I know he is, Susanna. I know he's safe with you. I know you were railroaded. And I was duped. I thought Jim was someone he wasn't."

Susanna opened her mouth but no words came out. This was too fast. Too good. She didn't know if she could trust what was happening.

"I wanted Tyler," Peggy said, "but I didn't want to get him that way."

"How long will this . . . evaluation take?" Linc asked.

"I'm not sure, but his stay in the foster home will be very brief, I promise you that," Peggy said. Her hand was still on top of Susanna's, and it felt suddenly warm and reassuring. "You come to my office in the Legal Aid building first thing in the morning, Susanna, and I'll help you do whatever you have to do to get Tyler back."

Susanna's mind was still fuzzy, but her thinking was sound enough to know that Peggy had paid dearly for the action she was taking.

"Is there a chance Jim might change his mind about custody?" Susanna gave voice to her fear, and Peggy smiled ruefully in return.

"If he does," Peggy said, "I'll represent you for free."

She spent the night at Linc's house. They sat on the sofa, watching the moon and stars over Boulder, and she felt as though she'd come home. She wished she could talk to Cody. She wished there were a way to explain to him that they only had to endure a short period of separation before they'd be together once again. But she and Cody would survive this. In the morning, she would borrow one of Linc's cars to go to Legal Aid and begin the process of getting him back. Ironic though it was, she knew she had an ally in Peggy.

As she fell asleep later that night, she thought of one other thing she wanted to do the following morning. She nearly told Linc about it, but decided it was something she wanted to keep to herself.

She woke up very early, a vivid dream still in her head. She'd dreamed she was looking out Linc's window at Boulder, as she had been the night before, but the town was covered with a pristine blanket of snow.

The dream felt so real. She wanted to wake Linc to tell him

about it, but he looked so peaceful that she thought better of it. He needed his sleep. These past few days had been rough on him as well as on her.

She ate a bowl of cereal alone in Linc's breakfast nook, and only then did she realize that the snow had been more than a dream. Looking out the window, she could see Boulder spread out far below her, clean and sparkling in a layer of white.

After breakfast, she wrote Linc a note to let him know she was on her way to Legal Aid, but he got up just as she was leaving. He came out of the bedroom, shirtless, sleepy-eyed, and beautiful.

"Where are you going?" he asked. "Legal Aid doesn't open till nine."

"I know," she said, "but there's something I want to do on my way."

He looked as if he wanted to know more, but he didn't press her. "All right," he said. "Come home right after your appointment with Peggy, though, okay? I want to hear everything she says."

"I will." She kissed him on her way out the door.

She drove directly to Alfalfa's. She'd missed that store during the past few months and it felt wonderful to stroll up and down the crowded aisles. She bought half a dozen giant chocolate chip cookies for Linc, along with a bouquet of mixed flowers. Then she returned to the car and started driving in the direction of the cemetery.

There were no other cars in the cemetery parking lot, and the snow had already melted from the macadam. She got out of the car and started walking across the frosty grass, remembering the last time she'd been there, back when Cody could only crawl. Back when Cody was *Tyler*, and his future was as uncertain as her own.

A layer of powdery snow still dusted the gravestones, making them all look like one another. She thought it would take her a while to find the stone she was looking for, but to her surprise, she walked straight to it.

Crouching next to the grave, she lay the bouquet of flowers in front of the small stone marker.

"I'm giving you back your name, Kimberly," she said. She dusted the snow from the front of the gravestone. "Thank you for letting me borrow it."

She stayed a moment by the grave, then slowly rose to her feet and began walking toward her car. Halfway to the parking lot, she turned around and saw that Kimberly Stratton's small headstone stood out from the rest, marked by the splash of color from the flowers in front of it. The scene gave her a sense of satisfaction, and she continued walking to her car with a lighter heart.

There was an emptiness in the car without Cody sitting in the back seat, but Susanna felt undeniably optimistic as she drove from the cemetery to Legal Aid. Optimistic, yet determined to be kind to the woman who had wanted to take her son from her. She remembered the pain in Peggy's eyes at the airport the day before. Susanna knew all about that pain, and she would do nothing to add to it. Peggy was no different from her. No better or worse, and she and Peggy were equals when it came to strength and courage. She'd had the guts to try to keep her son. Peggy'd had the guts to lose him.

Susanna turned one corner and then another. She'd had to ask Peggy for directions to her office, yet now she didn't seem to need them. She had the odd sense of knowing exactly where she was going, and as she neared the broad, windowless south side of the Legal Aid building, she thought she knew the reason why. It was the perfect canvas for a mural.

Diane Chamberlain is the award-winning author of seven previous novels, including *Reflection, Brass Ring, Fire and Rain,* and *Keeper of the Light*. She lives in Vienna, Virginia.